Ghost and Horror Stories of Ambrose Bierce

Ghost and Horror Stories of Ambrose Bierce

Selected and introduced by
E. F. Bleiler

Dover Publications, Inc.

New York

This Dover edition, first published in 1964, is a new collection of short stories by Ambrose Bierce, selected from *The Collected Works of Ambrose Bierce,* published by the Neale Publishing Company between 1909 and 1912.

Library of Congress Catalog Card Number 64–13459

Manufactured in the United States of America

Dover Publications, Inc.
180 Varick Street
New York 14, N.Y.

Introduction

I

It was a strange environment into which Ambrose Gwinnett Bierce was born in 1842 in Ohio, an environment that foreshadowed the atmosphere of macabre catastrophe and bitter irony that emerges in many of his later stories.

For one thing, the family situation was mad. Marcus Aurelius Bierce, Ambrose's father, was an ineffectual man dominated jointly by his wife and his religion. Yet he managed to reconcile an enthusiastic hell-fire Calvinism with a love for poetry, including the works of Lord Byron, and he carried through the remarkable whimsical feat of naming all thirteen of his children with the letter "A": Ambrose, Amos, Andrew, Augustus, etc. (The Gwinnett in Ambrose G. Bierce probably entered as a natural association, since the crime story of Ambrose Gwinnett was a common stage play and chapbook in the early nineteenth century.) In later life Marcus Aurelius Bierce came to believe that he had been confidential secretary to a President, and could tell tales of Washington intrigue.

Ambrose's uncle, Lucius Verus Bierce, was something of a minor celebrity. A good stump patriot, he led a filibustering expedition into Canada in 1838 to free the unhappy natives from British oppression. He captured the city of Windsor, but the natives did not rally to him, and Lucius Verus barely escaped with his life. He lived out the remainder of his life in glory as a picnic-shouter and politician, and was mayor of Akron six times.

The same family oddness ran through Bierce's nine older brothers and sisters. (Bierce was tenth; three after him did not survive.) They were apparently organized into small bands that carried on perpetual warfare with one another, and hated each other desperately. One brother rebelled against the stern family religion and ran away to become an actor and a circus strong man. A sister embraced religion more closely, went to Africa as a missionary, and according to local legend was eaten by cannibals.

This all seems grotesque and amusing to us in the twentieth

century, but it seems to have been hell for the small boy Ambrose, and he emerged from the family background in Indiana, where the family had moved, as a moody young man who swung between fits of depression in which he felt his inadequacy, and ebullitions that were equally disturbing to his fellows. The result of this family background was a screaming disapproval of everything that his parents stood for—religion, morality, thrift, and responsibility.

The lever that pried Bierce loose from his family was the Civil War, which broke out when he was 19. He enlisted in the Ninth Indiana Volunteers at the first call, and found in the army the school that his father could not afford. It is true that Bierce did attend Kentucky Military Institute for a few months, but one of his fellow students set the buildings on fire and the school was closed down.

In the army Bierce was a success, probably more successful than at any other point in his life. He was physically fearless, and the dangers of battle seem to have meant little to him. He was highly intelligent, and he was capable of a seriousness and single-mindedness that probably contrasted greatly with the indecisions of his fellow soldiers. He was commissioned an officer on the field—"obnoxious" was the term applied to him in the local Indiana newspaper upon reporting his promotion—and he eventually became a map officer on General Hazen's staff. He was wounded at Kenesaw Mountain, furloughed for a time, and discharged early in 1865.

Bierce served for a time as a Treasury agent watching for contraband in occupied Alabama, and then in 1866, after a brief and final visit to his family in Indiana, set out overland for the West Coast, traveling as a surveyor under his former chief and patron General Hazen. It was understood that an officer's commission would be waiting for him at the Presidio at San Francisco, but when he arrived, after a long, arduous expedition, he found only a commission for a second lieutenancy. Bierce had been discharged by error as a major rather than as a captain, and it is characteristic of his pride that he simply ignored the commission, neither acknowledging it nor declining it. He had been too gravely insulted.

In San Francisco Bierce decided to become a writer. What were his qualifications? He was young, quick to learn, willing to work hard, and he had a remarkable gift for coarse invective. He liked to read, he had a profound awe for learning, and he was willing to bide his time. In a very short while he became the protégé of James T. Watkins, a young Englishman who was then editor of the San Francisco *News-Letter and California Advertiser*. After having helped to conduct Bierce's education, Watkins left for New York, and through some mysterious process which has never been explained, Bierce became editor of a newspaper at the age of 26.

Newspaper life on the West Coast at this time was a sort of Roman games, where assorted beasts of prey battled one another, and every now and then bespattered the spectators with ordure or dragged them down. "Skunk" and "swindler," to parody Dr. Johnson, were in this area terms of fraternal reference. Apart from carrying on strongly felt personal enmities, business war and political struggle, newspapermen seemed to favor the theory that violence sold papers. They were right, of course, but the aftermath was sometimes fatal to them. Many a writer was assaulted or chased out of town, and murder was not uncommon: Charles de Young, one of the major newspaper publishers on the Coast, was murdered as the end result of slanderous articles.

Ambrose Bierce took to this life as a hog to a wallow, and in his early days set a level of viciousness and brutality seldom surpassed in American journalism, though many have imitated him. Enemies threatened him, and bets were taken upon his longevity; he simply took to carrying a pistol and using it upon occasion. Few people were either above or below his diatribes, and a calculated cruelty lay in his persistent attack at the person rather than the abuse. He was not subtle and not concerned with fair play, but he was at least impartial in ladling out abuse. He was intensely self-satisfied and highly moral where the morals of others were concerned, but the crimes that he denounced in his column for the next forty years or so were his own daily usage.

In 1871 Bierce married a girl as strong-minded and willful as himself, and received as a wedding present from his father-in-law (then a wealthy mining entrepreneur) funds for a stay in Europe. By spring 1872 Bierce and his wife found themselves settled in London, where the American colony currently included three Westerners: Bret Harte, Joaquin Miller, and Mark Twain. Through them Bierce joined the circles of George Sala, one of the more flamboyant journalists of the day, and Tom Hood, humorist and editor of *Fun*. It is perhaps significant that Bierce gravitated toward the second-line literary groups, rather than the higher circles. He always preferred to be a "big frog in a small puddle."

It was in England that the nickname "Bitter Bierce" and the image of Ambrose Bierce, Devil's Disciple, arose. This may have been a reaction to his surroundings, for Bierce resented being overshadowed by Harte and Miller, who were being lionized, while Twain openly sneered at him. Bierce may have regained his self-esteem by adding the acid of the professional cynic to the weapons of the violent journalist. He published some sardonic humor in *Fun*, put together a small volume of earlier journalism, and undertook to edit a rancorous periodical for the benefit of the exiled Empress Eugénie of France. But then his mother-in-law moved in, his money ran out, and in 1874 the Bierces returned to California.

Back in California, Bierce returned to journalism after an escapade at gold mining in the Black Hills of the Dakotas, and castigated others while his marriage gradually dissolved into recriminations. His father-in-law lost his money, Bierce found it difficult to support his family, and sought consolation outside his home—which merely made things worse. Three children appeared before he and his wife separated, and they turned out as sour as his marriage had been. One son was shot in later years in a ridiculous brawl over a girl, and the second son died of alcoholism and pneumonia. Bierce seldom saw his daughter after his separation from his wife.

Bierce had been living modestly in California for a time, contributing material to various small papers, drinking and enjoying himself, when one day in 1887 a slight, "fair young man," as he put it, "knocked at his door and cooed at him." It was William Randolph Hearst, offering Bierce a job. An agreement was soon reached: Bierce was to contribute his column "Prattle" to the Hearst papers, and editorial interference was to be minimal.

This was the beginning of an association that lasted for more than twenty years, despite quarrels and resignations. Bierce and Hearst eventually came to loathe each other, yet the reckless and vitriolic Bierce served well as one of Hearst's chief columnists. It has always been a mystery how Hearst managed to control Bierce, who was remarkably cantankerous, stubborn, hasty to judge and slow to change, yet also honest in strange ways. On the whole Hearst seems to have managed it easily enough: Bierce could always be depended upon to attack a fault or error when it was pointed out to him, and who is without sin?

Among Bierce's targets were immoral actresses and clergymen; robber barons; feminists; assorted politicians—he suffered the embarrassment of having demanded McKinley's assassination not long before the event, at which rival newspapers hinted that Czolgosz had been inspired by Bierce's work; bad poets, whom he delighted in roasting; bad novelists, whom he showered with lava;

religionists and atheists; farmers; socialists and union leaders; writers in dialect and regional novelists; opposition journalists and other enemies of Hearst's; successful people in all walks of life; and friends with whom he had quarreled. These categories eventually included almost everyone.

Bierce's greatest coup in journalism came in his share in defeating the notorious funding bill designed to benefit Leland Stanford. According to an earlier agreement between Stanford and the federal government, Stanford obtained the use of public lands for railways by paying a fixed rate, interest first, then principal. At the critical moment, the amount came to something like seventy-five million dollars, for Stanford had never bothered to make any payments at all. Stanford managed to have a bill introduced into Congress which would have funded this debt by bonds; this meant, for all practical purposes, forgiving it. News of the bill brought the Hearst empire down upon Stanford, and Bierce, then nearly 60, was selected in 1897 to go tȯ Washington to conduct the newspaper campaign against Stanford.

Stanford was one of the most unpopular of the robber barons, disliked even by his fellows. He seemed neither able to enjoy his wealth, nor to be able to let others enjoy it; he was animated solely by the desire for gain. He has been characterized as a "man with the soul of a crocodile." Stanford, in turn, held that every man had his price, and frankly approached Bierce and asked him if he could be bought. Bierce replied, "Yes." Stanford asked, "How much?" Bierce, his great moment arrived, replied, "Not a penny less than seventy-five million dollars, in a check payable to the Treasurer of the United States."

The funding bill was defeated, and Bierce was at the height of his reputation. But it was really too late. What seemed like the moment of triumph was really the peak beyond which the cliffs fall steep. He was over 60, an old man by now, and in many ways he had outlived his powers. He still considered himself the arbiter of taste on the West Coast, but all too often now was forced to see that the younger generation thought of him solely as a vicious journalist or ignored him.

After 1900 Bierce spent most of his time on the East Coast, probably to escape the distaste which the West had now come to have for him. He found in Washington a little of the former regard for "Major Bierce"; he issued his collected works through Walter Neale, an eccentric publisher, and he grew old disgracefully. His temper, always uncertain, grew worse, and his friends, long-suffering and patient, found his rages more and more difficult to bear. By the summer of 1913 he was old and tired beyond his 71 years. He had broken with Hearst, and had wrecked most of his personal relationships, including that with his brother Albert, who had always been his closest associate and most loving follower. Alcohol and asthma had retted his once vigorous physique. At this point he embarked upon the strange escapade that has done more to keep his name alive than any of his writings.

He announced that he was going to Mexico "with a pretty definite purpose . . . not at present disclosable." He entered Mexico, which was then convulsed in civil war, wrote one vague letter, and then disappeared. With Charley Ross and Colonel Fawcett he became one of the great vanishments of the modern world. People who cared little or nothing about his writings now found him a fascinating personality, and many books and articles have been written about his fate. What really happened? It is doubtful if we shall ever know.

Some say that the trip to Mexico was a blind, and that Bierce, under a medical death sentence, simply went off and committed suicide. One ingenious person felt that Bierce had leaped into the Grand Canyon, since this would be the logical place for a giant of American letters to leap. Another writer, even more ingenious, insisted that Bierce had slipped away to England, become an adviser to Lord Kitchener, and died with Kitchener. Still another theory is that Bierce went to Mexico to invite death on the battlefield.

The prevailing and sanest theory is that Bierce seriously wanted to cover Villa's movements as a war correspondent, but died in Mexico in one of the following ways: a natural death, or accidental death in battle, or execution because he insulted Villa. Like all other theories, however, these fail for lack of evidence. The perpetual stories of Mexicans who remember the quarrel between Villa and Bierce, or Bierce's burial on the battlefield, invariably peter out into uncertainties when investigated. In any case, the exact manner and moment of Bierce's death are not important now.

II

WHAT SORT of man was this Ambrose Bierce, at once so pathetic and so hateable? Physically, he was strikingly handsome, tall, erect even in his last years, light blond in his youth, ruddy and white-haired in his old age. He wore a heavy mustache, and his hair was often long. Women found him irresistible. He cultivated an air of damn-your-eyes defiance for the camera, and the camera was kind to him.

He was courtly and suave in manner, even when he was in his cups. Extremely soft-spoken, still gentler and even more urbane when he became angry, he bewildered strangers who had expected to find a roaring bully. Most people were greatly impressed with him upon first meeting, and most who remained to know him better came to dislike him intensely, although there were always masochistically loyal friends around. Bierce was immensely prickly, and sooner or later he would take offense at some slight, and hysterically angry letters would arrive.

Three men who knew Bierce well wrote biographical sketches about him. There was Adolphe de Castro (born Adolf Danziger), a German dentist and polyglot reciter, who collaborated with Bierce upon the translation of a bad German novel; George Sterling, long number-one disciple and drinking companion; and Walter Neale, the Washington publisher who issued Bierce's collected works. Their three accounts of Bierce are so different that it is hard at times to believe they refer to the same man.

De Castro, by anyone's standards a swindler, sharper, and liar (he even induced the painfully honest Bierce to act as a "front" for a publishing swindle) saw Bierce as master of a hypocrisy so enormous that it dwarfed all others; and de Castro admired it. At one time Bierce's son Leigh was in love with a California girl and, as the story goes, Bierce broke the romance, which he considered unsuitable, by telling Leigh that the girl was his illegitimate sister. What the exact truth was we shall never know, since there are many versions of the story, but de Castro claimed that he had been listening at the keyhole during the discussion and that Bierce created the illegitimacy at a moment's notice.

George Sterling, who combined flamboyant poetry with alcoholism and sexual exhibitionism, reported Bierce as an even greater alcoholic than himself, with stranger dimensions of sex. According to Sterling, Bierce, whose amours were legendary upon the Coast, had never disrobed before a woman. Neale, finally, who considered himself to be the last of the Southern aristocrats, found Bierce a paragon of Southern chivalry, even more snobbish and more intolerant than himself. All three men, in short, saw the image of their own personality, reflected and multiplied. This is an experience which many had with Bierce: he responded to one's weak side and showed then that his own was even worse.

Bierce did not mellow with age, and everyone agrees that by

the time of his disappearance he was a thoroughly unpleasant old man. Beneath his urbanity and clubroom courtesy, the old tiger brooded over injuries, and could slash out unexpected talons. Major Bierce (as he insisted upon being called) left life as a domineering, vindictive, suspicious old man.

There is a story, which to my knowledge has never been denied, that Bierce killed a man in Mexico to prove to Villa that he could be trusted. He killed his friendships in the same mixture of cold ruthlessness and passion. Before he left for Mexico, he wrote his brother Albert, who was closest to him, a letter almost paranoid in its fury; this letter is said to have hastened Albert's death. To continue the list of Bierce's character defects: he was a drunkard who used to boast of the men he had drunk under the table; he had suffered delirium tremens at least once. He was a hypocrite: he worked himself into paroxysms of righteous anger at the morals of others, yet lived with a succession of mistresses and left (it seems rather certain) illegitimate children. He waxed indignant at cant, yet he was a hired Cato who put his wrath at the disposal of his employer. "A paid skunk who stinks for gold," was the way one of his friends/enemies expressed it.

Despite this strong element of hypocrisy in one area, Bierce was honest to the point of painfulness in other ways. He refused to go along with Hearst's Cuban adventure, praising the Spaniards as gentlemen and calling the Cubans contemptible curs. Financially he was incorruptible. And there were moments when he was honest with himself, and could admit that he was not the grand scourge of the time, as he usually thought himself, but a failure in letters.

He was also a very lonely man. He could accept no bridges to others, unless they were of his own engineering, and as he grew older he demanded more and more of his acquaintances, more than he had any right to expect. He was always capable of retaining a few close friends, whom he loved, yet he could easily discard them if they showed too much individuality. He unquestionably loved his friend Tom Hood; he unquestionably loved his wife, even though he drove her away and refused a reconciliation out of stubbornness. He also loved his brother Albert, whom he discarded in rage. All through his life this same pattern emerged, of close relationships destroyed by emotional upheavals of the basest sort.

The same mixture of cruelty and occasional tenderness permeated smaller events. He could shoot dogs on sight, because he loathed their noise and smell and vulgarity, yet he felt a kinship with the smaller, weaker things of the woods. He would nurse young birds until they were able to fly, and he kept snakes, toads, and sick rats as pets. His daughter tells of a marvelous gift that he had with birds and wild animals. Bierce, she said, could go into a clearing in the wood, extend his arms, make calling noises, and the birds would come to sit upon his arms. Ambrose Bierce or Saint Francis of Assisi? I do not believe this story literally, but it has an aspect of a psychological truth, of an expression of the dualisms between good and evil that perpetually quarreled within him.

Bierce also spent a great deal of his time, without a thought of reward or payment, in correcting the manuscripts of fledgling authors, many of whom he never met. He served as grammar master in the rudiments of English composition and prosody to scores of young men and women who mailed manuscripts to him and asked for help; he gave his best to even the most unworthy. All that he asked was that they accept him as master and pay him a certain deference. There are many stories of little kindnesses that he did, just as there are many stories about young women whom he expected to go to bed with him because he had corrected their misspellings.

He was also one of the most ferocious critics of his day, and in his column he delighted in abusing flimsy poets and bad novelists. In this he was only partly like his model, Poe, for while Poe occasionally trampled bad poets, he was not slanderous, and could appreciate good work. Bierce was seldom capable of such objectivity, since to him greatness or success was in itself good cause for rancor and abuse. "There but for the grace of the Devil go I" was his sour feeling.

One of Bierce's weakest areas was associated with this desire to be the Master. Like Poe, again, he had the psychological need to seem omniscient, and had to be ready to express a strong opinion on any topic that might arise, although he was without Poe's solid ground of scholarship. He knew nothing of the sciences, yet would gravely discourse (sometimes very absurdly) on astronomy, physics, and biology. He knew no foreign languages except a little French and perhaps California backyard Spanish, yet spoke profusely about world literature. He had a limited knowledge and appreciation of English letters, yet set himself up as Grand Cham and arbiter to much of the younger generation of writers.

Why was Ambrose Bierce, then, Ambrose Bierce? There are many theories. His brother Albert, according to Sterling, claimed that Bierce's Civil War head injury had altered his character, but events before the injury make this questionable. Others have pointed to his barren life—formative years in the army, which he never outgrew; an unhappy marriage; the death of his two sons under sordid circumstances; literary frustration; and discontent with his job. Most of these factors, however, belong as readily to the category of effects as of causes. Others place the blame upon a bad biological organism and a miserable childhood.

Ambrose Bierce was a very complex man, and if this résumé of his life and my own reading of his character sound like a collection of paradoxes weighted heavily toward his negative side, it is because this aspect of his life emerges most strongly in his later fiction. I think that he was a man who began life with a very strong concatenation of evil potentialities, checked by an equally strong linkage of good. If the evil gradually grew stronger and overpowered the good, it is no matter for surprise. Ambrose Bierce was neither the first nor the last man to strike a half-pose of Satanism, and to end by being expelled by his pose. As Marlowe said of a similar person, "Cut is the branch that might have grown full straight."

III

THE GHOST stories of Ambrose Bierce are not the best in the English language, but they are among the most unusual. They embody a strange paradox: they are very stylized and written according to a very conscious theoretical pattern, and at the same time they are very personal, created out of the drives and fears of Ambrose Bierce. They have often been called too contrived, mechanical and artificial to be effective, and the criticism is not without validity; yet even their contrivance had its roots in a certain sincerity. The ideas which move his better stories moved him, and, indeed, in one form or another did much to wreck his life.

Bierce felt himself to be within the stream of supernatural fiction that began in the Gothic novel and ran through the Romantic short story and *nouvelle*. Much of his work is based upon Poe's, and he was unquestionably familiar with the general development of the whole supernatural form. His mentor Watkins of the *News-Letter* wrote to and about him: "The sort of sensation that waited upon Mrs. Radcliffe's and Monk Lewis's efforts affords some hint of the sort of career the new *Monk* and *Castle of Udolpho* would run. The work they did in stupid vaults you execute in the secret chambers of the soul, the poor limelight effects they worked upon a painted stage, you would sear with lightning on the face of nature. Your works would expand the human mind."

This is extravagant praise of Bierce and unnecessary denigration of the earlier writers in this genre, but it is a fair statement of what Bierce, in part at least, was trying to do. Much of this program, of course, had been anticipated by Poe, who equated the Gothic castle with the human psyche and used humor of the macabre in "Thou Art the Man." For Poe, however, these were but minor devices among many; for Bierce they were important. For Bierce the ultimate source of horror was the human mind; the foulest disgust emerged from conventional human relations; and the Gothic apparatus was simply a symbolization of this festering and decay.

Many of Bierce's stories are derivative in their subject matter: familiar tales of ghosts who were mistaken for living men until it was learned later that their "owners" had been dead at the time, trite stories of revenants who avenged themselves, and unconvincing tales of hypnotism and second sight. But beyond these there is a relatively small corpus of stories that are more individual and have more intimate connection with Ambrose Bierce. Among these are Civil War stories based upon the effects of death on the psyche and body, and stories of civilians, with the curious nexus of ideas that characteristically represent Bierce.

In these stories certain ideas were selected by Bierce to serve as horror-bearers: incest; the murder of a parent, with erotic overtones; the feeling of aloneness; the physical resurrection of the soulless and often malevolent dead; the power of a diseased mind to destroy itself; and the worthlessness of most human virtues. These themes are, of course, travesties in an order of reverse holiness of the religion in which Bierce had been reared, replacing love with hatred and immortality with the charnal truth about the grave.

There are sons in Bierce's stories who make incestuous love to their mothers, and sons who murder their fathers, either with detachment or with glee. There are dead things that refuse to stay buried and worry the living with their teeth—either the teeth of fear or the physical teeth of the corpse—and there are dead men who awaken and find something missing from themselves.

These themes obviously evoked emotion in Bierce, and were far more than an intellectually derived scheme to "make your flesh creep," for the same terror-symbols appear in the dreams that Bierce occasionally recorded, and his essay "Visions of the Night" reveals the same crystallization of emotion. Here there is an un-

charted death lurking in gloomy forests, a wanderer passing
through desert wastes (all alone, without friends), and death and
horror waiting for the long-traveled wanderer. The image of re-
birth plays a strong part, and the long-dead awaken into a life
that is only a fragment of humanity. The story "An Inhabitant of
Carcosa" would seem to have been written out of such dreams.

Much of Bierce's catalogue of horrors may now seem to us to be
raw-head-and-bloody-bones material, since our psychological and
cultural attitudes have changed greatly since Bierce's day. We
have come to recognize the relationship between love and hate,
and are likely to think carelessly, "Freud," when we read some of
Bierce's stories, without realizing that Bierce antedates Freud. We
have admitted ugliness into the canon of aesthetics and we are not
likely to fly into furies at Bierce's mockery of the Christian mythology. Also, we prefer more subtlety in our story-telling.

But it is always difficult to measure the emotional impact of
ideas upon readers of another time. Bierce's audiences seem to
have reacted as he would have wished, and he possibly saw this as
the validation of his mystique of horror. If we accept Bierce's
premise that there are certain ideas whose naked power is so
great as to make them fear-bearers, we can accept the emotional
basis of much of his fiction. If we accept, further, that the less
these archetypal ideas are encumbered with raiment, the stronger
they will be, we shall have accepted much of Bierce's aesthetic of
supernatural fiction. We may consider this an erroneous theory of
literature in both ends and means, but it is a possible theory.

One of the most characteristic, most curious aspects of Bierce's
supernatural fiction is its very heavy use of irony, which sometimes appears in the most unexpected ways, injected as a note of
sardonic, ghoulish humor into a situation of horror. In "The
Damned Thing," for example, the chapter headings read "One
does not always eat what is on the table" (referring to a corpse);
"What may happen in a field of wild oats" (referring to death
rather than to love); "A man though naked may be in rags" (referring to the fact that the dead man had been slashed to ribbons
by the invisible monster). This note enters in many of his stories,
where a calculated grotesqueness places subject matter and emotional overtones on opposite sides of the circle of emotions. There
is, indeed, a whole range of very heavily ironic stories written by
Bierce (mostly omitted from this collection) which have been
characterized as suicidal self-parodies.

It is by no means certain why Bierce used this device of irony so
fondly, for he must have known that he was destroying the emo-

tional mood he was otherwise trying to create. A partial answer may lie in the historical situation, back among the Romantic ironists in whose work Bierce was well-versed: Tieck, Hoffmann, Aytoun and the *Bon Gaultier Ballads,* and Heine. In typical Romantic theory, a constant self-parody and self-criticism, a handing of the artist's tools to the viewer, all demonstrate the artist's superiority; in this system of thought the cool, objective artist does not show complete mastery of his material as clearly as does the artist who plays captiously and whimsically with it. There are probably personal elements also involved in this use of irony: echoes of Bierce the fabulist—for with Bierce the fable often merges gradually into the supernatural story—who was accustomed to demonstrate his ferocity with cruel and violent endings that would destroy any pleasant mood the preparatory material had evoked.

Bierce is not always successful in his stories, and much of this failure lies in the limitations which he set upon his craft. He cared little about verisimilitude (except in his war stories) or the conventions of story telling (a strange neglect, what with his almost reactionary attitude toward points of grammar and word usage). His fiction is capsulated; material that another author might have developed into *nouvelles* or novels, Bierce usually compacted into short stories of a few hundred or a few thousand words. His critical articles reiterate his opinion that a novel is simply an easier way of writing a short story. To counterbalance Bierce's opinion, however, we should also mention the opinion of some of his contemporaries, who said that Bierce was unable to handle the structuring of story and personality required by the traditional novel, and had to confine himself to certain limits. According to this interpretation Bierce's critical theory is simply an unwitting disguise for his deficiencies.

As a result of these theories and deficiencies many of Bierce's stories lapse into curious half-symbolic situations, since very little humanity is present. The shabby aristocrats, the sleazy professional men, the half-mad poets, the perverts, the gleefully sadistic "Little Willie" types that abound in his stories are simply curious piles driven into the muck of life, around whom the sludge oozes, eating and corroding them.

Occasionally, however, these artificial limitations and accompanying experiments are surprisingly successful. Bierce's sparseness could intensify an emotional climax, and his disruption of conventional plot could lead to fictional techniques that did not reenter the workshop of the writer for many years. He could tell the same story in several different ways, through one lens after another, leaving to the reader the possibility of creating the drenching emotion by an act of mental synthesis, and through the perception of a psychopath he could write a curious sort of story that is superficially clear yet really very murky. The calculated ambiguity that pervades some of his better stories is likely to keep the reader puzzling for many hours.

These are the supernatural stories of Ambrose Bierce—a strange mixture of sincerity and contrivance, remarkable insights and astonishing stupidities, dazzling technique and leaden crudities, high-mindedness that often turns out to be simply vulgarity and coarseness in a bright uniform—all enacted in a strange bloody-skied land where cruelty and laughter are alternate doors to the same house of life.

Why did Bierce write these stories? The usual answers—for money or fame—do not really hold true. Poe, his greater predecessor, is on record as saying he wrote horror because it sold, but this was not true for Bierce. Bierce usually could not place his stories, lost interest in selling them after a few rejections, and eventually ended with publishing arrangements that were not too far removed from those of vanity presses. And yet approximately half of his fiction is in this supernatural vein.

Was it part of Bierce's perverse desire to shock at all times? There is some truth here, for Bierce, even more than G. B. Shaw, would sacrifice almost anything to arouse an emotion in his audience. And yet shock cannot be the whole purpose of Bierce's work, for to shock one must first print and Bierce never seemed to care greatly about publication.

Did the supernatural per se have any meaning for him? The answer seems to be no, not in the same sense that it has had for other writers of supernatural fiction. Bierce was avowedly an atheist or an agnostic, as the mood struck him, who violently rejected beliefs in survival after death. But, as is often the case, the total situation does not permit a simple answer. Bierce seems to have believed that he had a supernatural experience in England, when a wind-wraith rushed past him at the moment of Tom Hood's death. He often stated that this was Hood's spirit. And in his old age he collected stories of disappearances, especially those with adumbrations of the supernatural. Still, despite these two points it seems safe to say that Bierce was not really moved by a feeling of supernaturalism, whether religious like that of Maturin and M. R. James or occult-mystical like that of Machen and Blackwood.

We are gradually forced back upon the ancient (and often suspect) theory that writing eased some strange pressures within him, and that somehow he laxated his psyche by assaulting his own past, often in supernatural terms. I recognize that this same interpretation has been given to every literary figure since the days of Aristotle, but seldom are we faced with a person who so aptly embodies the theory of catharsis as Bierce. Paul Fatout in his definitive *Ambrose Bierce, The Devil's Lexicographer* has made a good case for finding reflections of Bierce's personal life in many of his stories.

IV

AMBROSE BIERCE's supernatural stories have been read by generations of American and British readers, for it is an unusual anthology of supernatural fiction that does not reprint at least one of his stories. "The Damned Thing," for example, has been anthologized at least eight times, and "The Middle Toe of the Right Foot" at least seven times, not counting collections of general fiction without a supernatural bias. The inclusion of general anthologies would probably triple or quadruple these figures.

Yet very few writers have paid Bierce the compliment of imitating him. In story technique and rationale of horror no major writer has ever followed his models. Perhaps this should not be surprising, for few writers would agree with Bierce's asceticism of narrative, and none, certainly, could relive his emotional experiences.

During Bierce's lifetime his work went very largely unheeded. The writers of run-of-the-mill ghost stories (as they appeared in *Temple Bar, Strand, London Illustrated News, Broadway Magazine,* etc.) wrote about very material Victorian ghosts and omens and cared nothing for Bierce's psychological interests. The major writers who overlapped with him in time progressed in different directions away from his work, and were unwilling to go along with Bierce's deliberate attempt to create as strong a horror story as possible. Of these writers, Algernon Blackwood, a gentle man who believed deeply in a personal blend of occultism and Buddhism, built his stories around mystical experiences and a sentimental *Naturphilosophie.* M. R. James, a Hellenistic scholar and historian, revealed the color in antiquarian lore and the persistence of ancient evil. Richard Garnett, librarian of the British Museum, and Vernon Lee, apologist for the Italian eighteenth century, found beauty in the quaint lore of strange lands and the arts, including the art of magic. Violet Hunt followed the complex webs of personal interrelationships and motivations of Henry James. Arthur Machen alternated between a project of deepening Stevenson's ideas and a highly personal amalgam of folklore, occultism, and ceremonial magic. W. H. Hodgson described evil forces surrounding the human island of safety, and Bram Stoker raided LeFanu and built thrillers around very complex plot situations. Even Bierce's most gifted protégé, Emma Dawson (the pathetic poet who is said to have starved to death in San Francisco), in her collection of ghost stories, *An Itinerant House,* shows little or no influence by Bierce.

It is only in externals that Bierce's influence can be seen. Robert W. Chambers, in his early work before he sank to writing costume romance, used some of Bierce's themes in *The King in Yellow* (1895), and drew motives from "An Inhabitant of Carcosa," which he quoted. And in the 1920's and early 1930's some of the *Weird Tales* coterie, like H. P. Lovecraft, turned to Bierce for suggestions. (Strangely enough, Adolphe de Castro, Bierce's old collaborator and friend/enemy, turned up in Providence, Rhode Island, where Lovecraft lived; the two men composed sonnets in a graveyard where Poe had once walked.) The *Weird Tales* authors copied mannerisms, but ignored the crude power and sensual drive that make Bierce still a living author. If today writers use Bierce's motives and techniques, it is not so much that they follow Bierce as that the cycle of literary fashion has come around very much to Bierce's central position.

Ambrose Bierce's ghost stories, despite some weaknesses, seem likely to be one of the three parts of his work that will survive. Some of his sardonic wit is still read, for a hot ferocity can be felt beneath the self-satisfaction and conditioned-reflex of his riposte. His Civil War stories are the best which were written by a participant, and please the 1950's and 1960's better than they did the 1890's. And a few of his better ghost stories will always be read. He may not have written the best ghost stories of his day, but in his best work he did write the most unusual. His stories are often remarkable for their economy of line and persistent hammering at a mystique of horror, and he occasionally struck some of the ultimates of human existence. He hit deeper and more brutally than his contemporaries, and if he sometimes fails in his purpose, he succeeds often enough to convey an abundance of chills to the reader.

E. F. BLEILER

New York, 1963

Contents

The Death of Halpin Frayser

I

For by death is wrought greater change than hath been shown. Whereas in general the spirit that removed cometh back upon occasion, and is sometimes seen of those in flesh (appearing in the form of the body it bore) yet it hath happened that the veritable body without the spirit hath walked. And it is attested of those encountering who have lived to speak thereon that a lich so raised up hath no natural affection, nor remembrance thereof, but only hate. Also, it is known that some spirits which in life were benign become by death evil altogether.—*Hali.*

ONE DARK night in midsummer a man waking from a dreamless sleep in a forest lifted his head from the earth, and staring a few moments into the blackness, said: "Catherine Larue." He said nothing more; no reason was known to him why he should have said so much.

The man was Halpin Frayser. He lived in St. Helena, but where he lives now is uncertain, for he is dead. One who practices sleeping in the woods with nothing under him but the dry leaves and the damp earth, and nothing over him but the branches from which the leaves have fallen and the sky from which the earth has fallen, cannot hope for great longevity, and Frayser had already attained the age of thirty-two. There are persons in this world, millions of persons, and far and away the best persons, who regard that as a very advanced age. They are the children. To those who view the voyage of life from the port of departure the bark that has accomplished any considerable distance appears already in close approach to the farther shore. However, it is not certain that Halpin Frayser came to his death by exposure.

He had been all day in the hills west of the Napa Valley, looking for doves and such small game as was in season. Late in the afternoon it had come on to be cloudy, and he had lost his bearings; and although he had only to go always downhill—everywhere the way to safety when one is lost—the absence of trails had so impeded him that he was overtaken by night while still in the forest. Unable in the darkness to penetrate the thickets of manzanita and other undergrowth, utterly bewildered and overcome with fatigue, he had lain down near the root of a large madroño and fallen into a dreamless sleep. It was hours later, in the very middle of the night, that one of God's mysterious messengers, gliding ahead of the incalculable host of his companions sweeping westward with the dawn line, pronounced the awakening word in the ear of the sleeper, who sat upright and spoke, he knew not why, a name, he knew not whose.

Halpin Frayser was not much of a philosopher, nor a scientist. The circumstance that, waking from a deep sleep at night in the midst of a forest, he had spoken aloud a name that he had not in memory and hardly had in mind did not arouse an enlightened curiosity to investigate the phenomenon. He thought it odd, and with a little perfunctory shiver, as if in deference to a seasonal presumption that the night was chill, he lay down again and went to sleep. But his sleep was no longer dreamless.

He thought he was walking along a dusty road that showed white in the gathering darkness of a summer night. Whence and whither it led, and why he traveled it, he did not know, though all seemed simple and natural, as is the way in dreams; for in the Land Beyond the Bed surprises cease from troubling and the judgment is at rest. Soon he came to a parting of the ways; leading from the highway was a road less traveled, having the appearance, indeed, of having been long abandoned, because, he thought, it led to something evil; yet he turned into it without hesitation, impelled by some imperious necessity.

As he pressed forward he became conscious that his way was haunted by invisible existences whom he could not definitely figure to his mind. From among the trees on either side he caught broken and incoherent whispers in a strange tongue which yet he partly understood. They seemed to him fragmentary utterances of a monstrous conspiracy against his body and soul.

It was now long after nightfall, yet the interminable forest through which he journeyed was lit with a wan glimmer having no point of diffusion, for in its mysterious lumination nothing cast a shadow. A shallow pool in the guttered depression of an old wheel rut, as from a recent rain, met his eye with a crimson gleam. He stooped and plunged his hand into it. It stained his fingers; it was blood! Blood, he then observed, was about him everywhere. The weeds growing rankly by the roadside showed it in blots and splashes on their big, broad leaves. Patches of dry dust between the wheelways were pitted and spattered as with a red rain. Defiling the trunks of the trees were broad maculations of crimson, and blood dripped like dew from their foliage.

All this he observed with a terror which seemed not incompatible with the fulfillment of a natural expectation. It seemed to him that it was all in expiation of some crime which, though conscious of his guilt, he could not rightly remember. To the menaces and mysteries of his surroundings the consciousness was an added horror. Vainly he sought by tracing life backward in memory, to reproduce the moment of his sin; scenes and incidents came crowding tumultuously into his mind, one picture effacing another, or commingling with it in confusion and obscurity, but nowhere could he catch a glimpse of what he sought. The failure augmented his terror; he felt as one who has murdered in the dark, not knowing whom nor why. So frightful was the situation—the mysterious light burned with so silent and awful a menace; the noxious plants, the trees that by common consent are invested with a melancholy or baleful character, so openly in his sight conspired against his peace; from overhead and all about came so audible and startling whispers and the sighs of creatures so obviously not of earth—that he could endure it no longer, and with a great effort to break some malign spell that bound his faculties to silence and inaction, he shouted with the full strength of his lungs! His voice broken, it seemed, into an infinite multitude of unfamiliar sounds, went babbling and stammering away into the distant reaches of the forest, died into silence, and all was as before. But he had made a beginning at resistance and was encouraged. He said:

"I will not submit unheard. There may be powers that are not malignant traveling this accursed road. I shall leave them a record and an appeal. I shall relate my wrongs, the persecutions that I endure—I, a helpless mortal, a penitent, an unoffending poet!" Halpin Frayser was a poet only as he was a penitent: in his dream.

Taking from his clothing a small red-leather pocketbook, one-half of which was leaved for memoranda, he discovered that he was without a pencil. He broke a twig from a bush, dipped it into a pool of blood and wrote rapidly. He had hardly touched the paper with the point of his twig when a low, wild peal of laughter broke out at a measureless distance away, and growing ever louder, seemed approaching ever nearer; a soulless, heartless, and unjoyous laugh, like that of the loon, solitary by the lakeside at midnight; a laugh which culminated in an unearthly shout close at hand, then died away by slow gradations, as if the accursed being that uttered it had withdrawn over the verge of the world whence it had come. But the man felt that this was not so—that it was nearby and had not moved.

A strange sensation began slowly to take possession of his body and his mind. He could not have said which, if any, of his senses was affected; he felt it rather as a consciousness—a mysterious mental assurance of some overpowering presence—some supernatural malevolence different in kind from the invisible existences that swarmed about him, and superior to them in power. He knew that it had uttered that hideous laugh. And now it seemed to be approaching him; from what direction he did not know—dared not conjecture. All his former fears were forgotten or merged in the gigantic terror that now held him in thrall. Apart from that, he had but one thought; to complete his written appeal to the benign powers who, traversing the haunted wood, might some time rescue him if he should be denied the blessing of annihilation. He wrote with terrible rapidity, the twig in his fingers rilling blood without renewal; but in the middle of a sentence his hands denied their service to his will, his arms fell to his sides, the book to the earth; and powerless to move or cry out, he found himself staring into the sharply drawn face and blank, dead eyes of his own mother, standing white and silent in the garments of the grave!

II

In his youth Halpin Frayser had lived with his parents in Nashville, Tennessee. The Fraysers were well-to-do, having a good position in such society as had survived the wreck wrought by civil war. Their children had the social and educational opportunities of their time and place, and had responded to good associations and instruction with agreeable manners and cultivated minds. Halpin being the youngest and not over-robust was perhaps a trifle "spoiled." He had the double disadvantage of a mother's assiduity and a father's neglect. Frayser *père* was what no Southern man of means is not—a politician. His country, or rather his section and State, made demands upon his time and attention so exacting that to those of his family he was compelled to turn an ear partly deafened by the thunder of the political captains and the shouting, his own included.

Young Halpin was of a dreamy, indolent and rather romantic turn, somewhat more addicted to literature than law, the profession to which he was bred. Among those of his relations who professed the modern faith of heredity it was well understood that in him the character of the late Myron Bayne, a maternal great-grandfather, had revisited the glimpses of the moon—by which orb Bayne had in his lifetime been sufficiently affected to be a poet of no small Colonial distinction. If not specially observed, it was observable that while a Frayser who was not the proud possessor of a sumptuous copy of the ancestral "poetical works" (printed at the family expense, and long ago withdrawn from an inhospitable market) was a rare Frayser indeed, there was an illogical indisposition to honor the great deceased in the person of his spiritual successor. Halpin was pretty generally deprecated as an intellectual black sheep who was likely at any moment to disgrace the flock by bleating in meter. The Tennessee Fraysers were a practical folk—not practical in the popular sense of devotion to sordid pursuits, but having a robust contempt for any qualities unfitting a man for the wholesome vocation of politics.

In justice to young Halpin it should be said that while in him were pretty faithfully reproduced most of the mental and moral characteristics ascribed by history and family tradition to the famous Colonial bard, his succession to the gift and faculty divine was purely inferential. Not only had he never been known to court the muse, but in truth he could not have written correctly a line of verse to save himself from the Killer of the Wise. Still, there was no knowing when the dormant faculty might wake and smite the lyre.

In the meantime the young man was rather a loose fish, anyhow. Between him and his mother was the most perfect sympathy, for secretly the lady was herself a devout disciple of the late and great Myron Bayne, though with the tact so generally and justly admired in her sex (despite the hardy calumniators who insist that it is essentially the same thing as cunning) she had always taken care to conceal her weakness from all eyes but those of him who shared it. Their common guilt in respect of that was an added tie between them. If in Halpin's youth his mother had "spoiled" him, he had assuredly done his part toward being spoiled. As he grew to such manhood as is attainable by a Southerner who does not care which way elections go, the attachment between him and his beautiful mother—whom from early childhood he had called Katy—became yearly stronger and more tender. In these two romantic natures was manifest in a signal way that neglected phenomenon, the dominance of the sexual element in all the relations of life, strengthening, softening, and beautifying even those of consanguinity. The two were nearly inseparable, and by strangers observing their manner were not infrequently mistaken for lovers.

Entering his mother's boudoir one day Halpin Frayser kissed her upon the forehead, toyed for a moment with a lock of her dark hair which had escaped from its confining pins, and said, with an obvious effort at calmness:

"Would you greatly mind, Katy, if I were called away to California for a few weeks?"

It was hardly needful for Katy to answer with her lips a question to which her telltale cheeks had made instant reply. Evidently she would greatly mind; and the tears, too, sprang into her large brown eyes as corroborative testimony.

"Ah, my son," she said, looking up into his face with infinite tenderness, "I should have known that this was coming. Did I not lie awake a half of the night weeping because, during the other half, Grandfather Bayne had come to me in a dream, and standing by his portrait—young, too, and handsome as that—pointed to yours on the same wall? And when I looked it seemed that I could not see the features; you had been painted with a face cloth, such as we put upon the dead. Your father has laughed at me, but you and I, dear, know that such things are not for nothing. And I saw below the edge of the cloth the marks of hands on your throat—forgive me, but we have not been used to keep such things from each other. Perhaps you have another interpretation. Perhaps it does not mean that you will go to California. Or maybe you will take me with you?"

It must be confessed that this ingenious interpretation of the dream in the light of newly discovered evidence did not wholly commend itself to the son's more logical mind; he had, for the moment at least, a conviction that it foreshadowed a more simple and immediate, if less tragic, disaster than a visit to the Pacific Coast. It was Halpin Frayser's impression that he was to be garroted on his native heath.

"Are there not medicinal springs in California?" Mrs. Frayser resumed before he had time to give her the true reading of the dream—"places where one recovers from rheumatism and neuralgia? Look—my fingers feel so stiff; and I am almost sure they have been giving me great pain while I slept."

She held out her hands for his inspection. What diagnosis of her case the young man may have thought it best to conceal with a smile the historian is unable to state, but for himself he feels bound to say that fingers looking less stiff, and showing fewer evidences of even insensible pain, have seldom been submitted for medical inspection by even the fairest patient desiring a prescription of unfamiliar scenes.

The outcome of it was that of these two odd persons having equally odd notions of duty, the one went to California, as the interest of his client required, and the other remained at home in compliance with a wish that her husband was scarcely conscious of entertaining.

While in San Francisco Halpin Frayser was walking one dark night along the water front of the city, when, with a suddenness that surprised and disconcerted him, he became a sailor. He was in fact "shanghaied" aboard a gallant, gallant ship, and sailed for a far countree. Nor did his misfortunes end with the voyage; for the ship was cast ashore on an island of the South Pacific, and it was six years afterward when the survivors were taken off by a venturesome trading schooner and brought back to San Francisco.

Though poor in purse, Frayser was no less proud in spirit than he had been in the years that seemed ages and ages ago. He would accept no assistance from strangers, and it was while living with a fellow survivor near the town of St. Helena, awaiting news and remittances from home, that he had gone gunning and dreaming.

III

The apparition confronting the dreamer in the haunted wood— the thing so like, yet so unlike his mother—was horrible! It stirred no love nor longing in his heart; it came unattended with pleasant memories of a golden past—inspired no sentiment of any kind; all the finer emotions were swallowed up in fear. He tried to turn and run from before it, but his legs were as lead; he was unable to lift his feet from the ground. His arms hung helpless at his sides; of his eyes only he retained control, and these he dared not remove from the lusterless orbs of the apparition, which he knew was not a soul without a body, but that most dreadful of all existences infesting that haunted wood —a body without a soul! In its blank stare was neither love, nor pity, nor intelligence—nothing to which to address an appeal for mercy. "An appeal will not lie," he thought, with an absurd reversion to professional slang, making the situation more horrible, as the fire of a cigar might light up a tomb.

For a time, which seemed so long that the world grew gray with age and sin, and the haunted forest, having fulfilled its purpose in this monstrous culmination of its terrors, vanished out of his consciousness with all its sights and sounds, the apparition stood within a pace, regarding him with the mindless malevolence of a wild brute; then thrust its hands forward and sprang upon him with appalling ferocity! The act released his physical energies without unfettering his will; his mind was still spellbound, but his powerful body and agile limbs, endowed with a blind, insensate life of their own, resisted stoutly and well. For an instant he seemed to see this unnatural contest between a dead intelligence and a breathing mechanism only as a spectator—such fancies are in dreams; then he regained his identity almost as if by a leap forward into his body, and the straining automaton had a directing will as alert and fierce as that of its hideous antagonist.

But what mortal can cope with a creature of his dream? The imagination creating the enemy is already vanquished; the combat's result is the combat's cause. Despite his struggles—despite his strength and activity, which seemed wasted in a void, he felt the cold fingers close upon his throat. Borne backward to the earth, he saw above him the dead and drawn face within a hand's breadth of his own, and then all was black. A sound as of the beating of distant drums—a murmur of swarming voices, a sharp, far cry signing all to silence, and Halpin Frayser dreamed that he was dead.

IV

A WARM, clear night had been followed by a morning of drenching fog. At about the middle of the afternoon of the preceding day a little whiff of light vapor—a mere thickening of the atmosphere, the ghost of a cloud—had been observed clinging to the western side of Mount St. Helena, away up along the barren altitudes near the summit. It was so thin, so diaphanous, so like a fancy made visible, that one would have said: "Look quickly! in a moment it will be gone."

In a moment it was visibly larger and denser. While with one edge it clung to the mountain, with the other it reached farther and farther out into the air above the lower slopes. At the same time it extended itself to north and south, joining small patches of mist that appeared to come out of the mountainside on exactly the same level, with an intelligent design to be absorbed. And so it grew and grew until the summit was shut out of view from the valley, and over the valley itself was an ever-extending canopy, opaque and gray. At Calistoga, which lies near the head of the valley and the foot of the mountain, there were a starless night and a sunless morning. The fog, sinking into the valley, had reached southward, swallowing up ranch after ranch, until it had blotted out the town of St. Helena, nine miles away. The dust in the road was laid; trees were adrip with moisture; birds sat silent in their coverts; the morning light was wan and ghastly, with neither color nor fire.

Two men left the town of St. Helena at the first glimmer of dawn, and walked along the road northward up the valley toward Calistoga. They carried guns on their shoulders, yet no one having knowledge of such matters could have mistaken them for hunters of bird or beast. They were a deputy sheriff from Napa and a detective from San Francisco—Holker and Jaralson, respectively. Their business was man-hunting.

"How far is it?" inquired Holker, as they strode along, their feet stirring white the dust beneath the damp surface of the road.

"The White Church? Only a half mile farther," the other answered. "By the way," he added, "it is neither white nor a church; it is an abandoned schoolhouse, gray with age and neglect. Religious services were once held in it—when it was white, and there is a graveyard that would delight a poet. Can you guess why I sent for you, and told you to come heeled?"

"Oh, I never have bothered you about things of that kind. I've always found you communicative when the time came. But if I may hazard a guess, you want me to help you arrest one of the corpses in the graveyard."

"You remember Branscom?" said Jaralson, treating his companion's wit with the inattention that it deserved.

"The chap who cut his wife's throat? I ought; I wasted a week's work on him and had my expenses for my trouble. There is a reward of five hundred dollars, but none of us ever got a sight of him. You don't mean to say——"

"Yes, I do. He has been under the noses of you fellows all the time. He comes by night to the old graveyard at the White Church."

"The devil! That's where they buried his wife."

"Well, you fellows might have had sense enough to suspect that he would return to her grave some time."

"The very last place that anyone would have expected him to return to."

"But you had exhausted all the other places. Learning your failure at them, I 'laid for him' there."

"And you found him?"

"Damn it! he found *me*. The rascal got the drop on me—regularly held me up and made me travel. It's God's mercy that he didn't go through me. Oh, he's a good one, and I fancy the half of that reward is enough for me if you're needy."

Holker laughed good-humoredly, and explained that his creditors were never more importunate.

"I wanted merely to show you the ground, and arrange a plan with you," the detective explained. "I thought it as well for us to be heeled, even in daylight."

"The man must be insane," said the deputy sheriff. "The reward is for his capture and conviction. If he's mad he won't be convicted."

Mr. Holker was so profoundly affected by that possible failure of justice that he involuntarily stopped in the middle of the road, then resumed his walk with abated zeal.

"Well, he looks it," assented Jaralson. "I'm bound to admit that a more unshaven, unshorn, unkempt, and uneverything wretch I never saw outside the ancient and honorable order of tramps. But I've gone in for him, and can't make up my mind to let go. There's glory in it for us, anyhow. Not another soul knows that he is this side of the Mountains of the Moon."

"All right," Holker said; "we will go and view the ground," and he added, in the words of a once favorite inscription for tombstones: " 'where you must shortly lie'—I mean, if old Branscom ever gets tired of you and your impertinent intrusion. By the way, I heard the other day that 'Branscom' was not his real name."

"What is?"

"I can't recall it. I had lost all interest in the wretch, and it did not fix itself in my memory—something like Pardee. The woman whose throat he had the bad taste to cut was a widow when he met her. She had come to California to look up some relatives—there are persons who will do that sometimes. But you know all that."

"Naturally."

"But not knowing the right name, by what happy inspiration did you find the right grave? The man who told me what the name was said it had been cut on the headboard."

"I don't know the right grave." Jaralson was apparently a trifle reluctant to admit his ignorance of so important a point of his plan. "I have been watching about the place generally. A part of our work this morning will be to identify that grave. Here is the White Church."

For a long distance the road had been bordered by fields on both sides, but now on the left there was a forest of oaks, madroños, and gigantic spruces whose lower parts only could be seen, dim and ghostly in the fog. The undergrowth was, in places, thick, but nowhere impenetrable. For some moments Holker saw nothing of the building, but as they turned into the woods it revealed itself in faint gray outline through the fog, looking huge and far away. A few steps more, and it was within an arm's length, distinct, dark with moisture, and insignificant in size. It had the usual country-schoolhouse form—belonged to the packing-box order of architecture; had an underpinning of stones, a moss-grown roof, and blank window spaces, whence both glass and sash had long departed. It was ruined, but not a ruin—a typical Californian substitute for what are known to guide-bookers abroad as "monuments of the past." With scarcely a glance at this uninteresting structure Jaralson moved on into the dripping undergrowth beyond.

"I will show you where he held me up," he said. "This is the graveyard."

Here and there among the bushes were small inclosures containing graves, sometimes no more than one. They were recognized as graves by the discolored stones or rotting boards at head and foot, leaning at all angles, some prostrate; by the ruined picket fences surrounding them; or, infrequently, by the mound itself showing its gravel through the fallen leaves. In many instances nothing marked the spot where lay the vestiges of some poor mortal—who, leaving "a large circle of sorrowing friends," had been left by them in turn—except a depression in the earth, more lasting than that in the spirits of the mourners. The paths, if any paths had been, were long obliterated; trees of a considerable size had been permitted to grow up from the graves and thrust aside with root or branch the inclosing fences. Over all was that air of abandonment and decay which seems nowhere so fit and significant as in a village of the forgotten dead.

As the two men, Jaralson leading, pushed their way through the growth of young trees, that enterprising man suddenly stopped and brought up his shotgun to the height of his breast, uttered a low note of warning, and stood motionless, his eyes fixed upon something ahead. As well as he could, obstructed by brush, his companion, though seeing nothing, imitated the posture and so stood, prepared for what might ensue. A moment later Jaralson moved cautiously forward, the other following.

Under the branches of an enormous spruce lay the dead body of a man. Standing silent above it they noted such particulars as first strike the attention—the face, the attitude, the clothing; whatever most promptly and plainly answers the unspoken question of a sympathetic curiosity.

The body lay upon its back, the legs wide apart. One arm was thrust upward, the other outward; but the latter was bent acutely, and the hand was near the throat. Both hands were tightly clenched. The whole attitude was that of desperate but ineffectual resistance to—what?

Nearby lay a shotgun and a game bag through the meshes of which was seen the plumage of shot birds. All about were evidences of a furious struggle; small sprouts of poison oak were bent and denuded of leaf and bark; dead and rotting leaves had been pushed into heaps and ridges on both sides of the legs by the action of other feet than theirs; alongside the hips were unmistakable impressions of human knees.

The nature of the struggle was made clear by a glance at the dead man's throat and face. While breast and hands were white, those were purple—almost black. The shoulders lay upon a low mound, and the head was turned back at an angle otherwise impossible, the expanded eyes staring blankly backward in a direction opposite to that of the feet. From the froth filling the open mouth the tongue protruded, black and swollen. The throat showed horrible contusions; not mere finger-marks, but bruises and lacerations wrought by two strong hands that must have buried themselves in the yielding flesh, maintaining their terrible grasp until long after death. Breast, throat, face, were wet; the clothing was saturated; drops of water, condensed from the fog, studded the hair and mustache.

All this the two men observed without speaking—almost at a glance. Then Holker said:

"Poor devil! he had a rough deal."

Jaralson was making a vigilant circumspection of the forest, his shotgun held in both hands and at full cock, his finger upon the trigger.

"The work of a maniac," he said, without withdrawing his eyes from the inclosing wood. "It was done by Branscom—Pardee."

Something half hidden by the disturbed leaves on the earth caught Holker's attention. It was a red-leather pocketbook. He picked it up and opened it. It contained leaves of white paper for memoranda, and upon the first leaf was the name "Halpin Frayser." Written in red on several succeeding leaves—scrawled as if in haste and barely legible—were the following lines, which Holker read aloud, while his companion continued scanning the dim gray confines of their narrow world and hearing matter of apprehension in the drip of water from every burdened branch:

Enthralled by some mysterious spell, I stood
In the lit gloom of an enchanted wood.
   The cypress there and myrtle twined their boughs,
Significant, in baleful brotherhood.

The brooding willow whispered to the yew;
Beneath, the deadly nightshade and the rue,
   With immortelles self-woven into strange
Funereal shapes, and horrid nettles grew.

No song of bird nor any drone of bees,
Nor light leaf lifted by the wholesome breeze:
   The air was stagnant all, and Silence was
A living thing that breathed among the trees.

Conspiring spirits whispered in the gloom,
Half-heard, the stilly secrets of the tomb.
   With blood the trees were all adrip; the leaves
Shone in the witch-light with a ruddy bloom.

I cried aloud!—the spell, unbroken still,
Rested upon my spirit and my will.
   Unsouled, unhearted, hopeless and forlorn,
I strove with monstrous presages of ill!

At last the viewless——

Holker ceased reading; there was no more to read. The manuscript broke off in the middle of a line.

"That sounds like Bayne," said Jaralson, who was something of a scholar in his way. He had abated his vigilance and stood looking down at the body.

"Who's Bayne?" Holker asked rather incuriously.

"Myron Bayne, a chap who flourished in the early years of the nation—more than a century ago. Wrote mighty dismal stuff; I have his collected works. That poem is not among them, but it must have been omitted by mistake."

"It is cold," said Holker; "let us leave here; we must have up the coroner from Napa."

Jaralson said nothing, but made a movement in compliance. Passing the end of the slight elevation of earth upon which the dead man's head and shoulders lay, his foot struck some hard substance under the rotting forest leaves, and he took the trouble to kick it into view. It was a fallen headboard, and painted on it were the hardly decipherable words, "Catherine Larue."

"Larue, Larue!" exclaimed Holker, with sudden animation. "Why, that is the real name of Branscom—not Pardee. And—bless my soul! how it all comes to me—the murdered woman's name had been Frayser!"

"There is some rascally mystery here," said Detective Jaralson. "I hate anything of that kind."

There came to them out of the fog—seemingly from a great distance—the sound of a laugh, a low, deliberate, soulless laugh, which had no more of joy than that of a hyena night-prowling in the desert; a laugh that rose by slow gradation, louder and louder, clearer, more distinct and terrible, until it seemed barely outside the narrow circle of their vision; a laugh so unnatural, so unhuman, so devilish, that it filled those hardy man-hunters with a sense of dread unspeakable! They did not move their weapons nor think of them; the menace of that horrible sound was not of the kind to be met with arms. As it had grown out of silence, so now it died away; from a culminating shout which had seemed almost in their ears, it drew itself away into the distance, until its failing notes, joyless and mechanical to the last, sank to silence at a measureless remove.

Moxon's Master

"ARE YOU serious?—do you really believe that a machine thinks?"

I got no immediate reply; Moxon was apparently intent upon the coals in the grate, touching them deftly here and there with the fire-poker till they signified a sense of his attention by a brighter glow. For several weeks I had been observing in him a growing habit of delay in answering even the most trivial of commonplace questions. His air, however, was that of preoccupation rather than deliberation: one might have said that he had "something on his mind."

Presently he said:

"What is a 'machine'? The word has been variously defined. Here is one definition from a popular dictionary: 'Any instrument or organization by which power is applied and made effective, or a desired effect produced.' Well, then, is not a man a machine? And you will admit that he thinks—or thinks he thinks."

"If you do not wish to answer my question," I said, rather testily, "why not say so?—all that you say is mere evasion. You know well enough that when I say 'machine' I do not mean a man, but something that man has made and controls."

"When it does not control him," he said, rising abruptly and looking out of a window, whence nothing was visible in the blackness of a stormy night. A moment later he turned about and with a smile said:

"I beg your pardon; I had no thought of evasion. I considered the dictionary man's unconscious testimony suggestive and worth something in the discussion. I can give your question a direct answer easily enough: I do believe that a machine thinks about the work that it is doing."

That was direct enough, certainly. It was not altogether pleasing, for it tended to confirm a sad suspicion that Moxon's devotion to study and work in his machine-shop had not been good for him. I knew, for one thing, that he suffered from insomnia, and that is no light affliction. Had it affected his mind? His re-

15

ply to my question seemed to me then evidence that it had; perhaps I should think differently about it now. I was younger then, and among the blessings that are not denied to youth is ignorance. Incited by that great stimulant to controversy, I said:

"And what, pray, does it think with—in the absence of a brain?"

The reply, coming with less than his customary delay, took his favorite form of counter-interrogation:

"With what does a plant think—in the absence of a brain?"

"Ah, plants also belong to the philosopher class! I should be pleased to know some of their conclusions; you may omit the premises."

"Perhaps," he replied, apparently unaffected by my foolish irony, "you may be able to infer their convictions from their acts. I will spare you the familiar examples of the sensitive mimosa, the several insectivorous flowers and those whose stamens bend down and shake their pollen upon the entering bee in order that he may fertilize their distant mates. But observe this. In an open spot in my garden I planted a climbing vine. When it was barely above the surface I set a stake into the soil a yard away. The vine at once made for it, but as it was about to reach it after several days I removed it a few feet. The vine at once altered its course, making an acute angle, and again made for the stake. This manœuvre was repeated several times, but finally, as if discouraged, the vine abandoned the pursuit and ignoring further attempts to divert it traveled to a small tree, further away, which it climbed.

"Roots of the eucalyptus will prolong themselves incredibly in search of moisture. A well-known horticulturist relates that one entered an old drain pipe and followed it until it came to a break, where a section of the pipe had been removed to make way for a stone wall that had been built across its course. The root left the drain and followed the wall until it found an opening where a stone had fallen out. It crept through and following the other side of the wall back to the drain, entered the unexplored part and resumed its journey."

"And all this?"

"Can you miss the significance of it? It shows the consciousness of plants. It proves that they think."

"Even if it did—what then? We were speaking, not of plants, but of machines. They may be composed partly of wood—wood that has no longer vitality—or wholly of metal. Is thought an attribute also of the mineral kingdom?"

"How else do you explain the phenomena, for example, of crystallization?"

"I do not explain them."

"Because you cannot without affirming what you wish to deny, namely, intelligent cooperation among the constituent elements of the crystals. When soldiers form lines, or hollow squares, you call it reason. When wild geese in flight take the form of a letter V you say instinct. When the homogeneous atoms of a mineral, moving freely in solution, arrange themselves into shapes mathematically perfect, or particles of frozen moisture into the symmetrical and beautiful forms of snowflakes, you have nothing to say. You have not even invented a name to conceal your heroic unreason."

Moxon was speaking with unusual animation and earnestness. As he paused I heard in an adjoining room known to me as his "machine-shop," which no one but himself was permitted to enter, a singular thumping sound, as of some one pounding upon a table with an open hand. Moxon heard it at the same moment and, visibly agitated, rose and hurriedly passed into the room whence it came. I thought it odd that any one else should be in there, and my interest in my friend—with doubtless a touch of unwarrantable curiosity—led me to listen intently, though, I am happy to say, not at the keyhole. There were confused sounds, as of a struggle or scuffle; the floor shook. I distinctly heard hard breathing and a hoarse whisper which said "Damn you!" Then all was silent, and presently Moxon reappeared and said, with a rather sorry smile:

"Pardon me for leaving you so abruptly. I have a machine in there that lost its temper and cut up rough."

Fixing my eyes steadily upon his left cheek, which was traversed by four parallel excoriations showing blood, I said:

"How would it do to trim its nails?"

I could have spared myself the jest; he gave it no attention, but seated himself in the chair that he had left and resumed the interrupted monologue as if nothing had occurred:

"Doubtless you do not hold with those (I need not name them to a man of your reading) who have taught that all matter is sentient, that every atom is a living, feeling, conscious being. *I* do. There is no such thing as dead, inert matter: it is all alive; all instinct with force, actual and potential; all sensitive to the same forces in its environment and susceptible to the contagion of higher and subtler ones residing in such superior organisms as it may be brought into relation with, as those of man when he is fashioning it into an instrument of his will. It absorbs something of his intelligence and purpose—more of them in proportion to the complexity of the resulting machine and that of its work.

"Do you happen to recall Herbert Spencer's definition of 'Life'? I read it thirty years ago. He may have altered it afterward, for anything I know, but in all that time I have been unable to think of a single word that could profitably be changed or added or removed. It seems to me not only the best definition, but the only possible one.

"'Life,' he says, 'is a definite combination of heterogeneous changes, both simultaneous and successive, in correspondence with external coexistences and sequences.'"

"That defines the phenomenon," I said, "but gives no hint of its cause."

"That," he replied, "is all that any definition can do. As Mill points out, we know nothing of cause except as an antecedent—nothing of effect except as a consequent. Of certain phenomena, one never occurs without another, which is dissimilar: the first in point of time we call cause, the second, effect. One who had many times seen a rabbit pursued by a dog, and had never seen rabbits and dogs otherwise, would think the rabbit the cause of the dog.

"But I fear," he added, laughing naturally enough, "that my rabbit is leading me a long way from the track of my legitimate quarry: I'm indulging in the pleasure of the chase for its own sake. What I want you to observe is that in Herbert Spencer's definition of 'life' the activity of a machine is included—there is nothing in the definition that is not applicable to it. According to this sharpest of observers and deepest of thinkers, if a man during his period of activity is alive, so is a machine when in operation. As an inventor and constructor of machines I know that to be true."

Moxon was silent for a long time, gazing absently into the fire. It was growing late and I thought it time to be going, but somehow I did not like the notion of leaving him in that isolated house, all alone except for the presence of some person of whose nature my conjectures could go no further than that it was unfriendly, perhaps malign. Leaning toward him and looking earnestly into his eyes while making a motion with my hand through the door of his workshop, I said:

"Moxon, whom have you in there?"

Somewhat to my surprise he laughed lightly and answered without hesitation:

"Nobody; the incident that you have in mind was caused by my folly in leaving a machine in action with nothing to act upon, while I undertook the interminable task of enlightening your understanding. Do you happen to know that Consciousness is the creature of Rhythm?"

"O bother them both!" I replied, rising and laying hold of my overcoat. "I'm going to wish you good night; and I'll add the hope that the machine which you inadvertently left in action will have her gloves on the next time you think it needful to stop her."

Without waiting to observe the effect of my shot I left the house.

Rain was falling, and the darkness was intense. In the sky beyond the crest of a hill toward which I groped my way along precarious plank sidewalks and across miry, unpaved streets I could see the faint glow of the city's lights, but behind me nothing was visible but a single window of Moxon's house. It glowed with what seemed to me a mysterious and fateful meaning. I knew it was an uncurtained aperture in my friend's "machine-shop," and I had little doubt that he had resumed the studies interrupted by his duties as my instructor in mechanical consciousness and the fatherhood of Rhythm. Odd, and in some degree humorous, as his convictions seemed to me at that time, I could not wholly divest myself of the feeling that they had some tragic relation to his life and character—perhaps to his destiny—although I no longer entertained the notion that they were the vagaries of a disordered mind. Whatever might be thought of his views, his exposition of them was too logical for that. Over and over, his last words came back to me: "Consciousness is the creature of Rhythm." Bald and terse as the statement was, I now found it infinitely alluring. At each recurrence it broadened in meaning and deepened in suggestion. Why, here (I thought) is something upon which to found a philosophy. If consciousness is the product of rhythm all things *are* conscious, for all have motion, and all motion is rhythmic. I wondered if Moxon knew the significance and breadth of his thought—the scope of this momentous generalization; or had he arrived at his philosophic faith by the tortuous and uncertain road of observation?

That faith was then new to me, and all Moxon's expounding

had failed to make me a convert; but now it seemed as if a great light shone about me, like that which fell upon Saul of Tarsus; and out there in the storm and darkness and solitude I experienced what Lewes calls "The endless variety and excitement of philosophic thought." I exulted in a new sense of knowledge, a new pride of reason. My feet seemed hardly to touch the earth; it was as if I were uplifted and borne through the air by invisible wings.

Yielding to an impulse to seek further light from him whom I now recognized as my master and guide, I had unconsciously turned about, and almost before I was aware of having done so found myself again at Moxon's door. I was drenched with rain, but felt no discomfort. Unable in my excitement to find the doorbell I instinctively tried the knob. It turned and, entering, I mounted the stairs to the room that I had so recently left. All was dark and silent; Moxon, as I had supposed, was in the adjoining room—the "machine-shop." Groping along the wall until I found the communicating door I knocked loudly several times, but got no response, which I attributed to the uproar outside, for the wind was blowing a gale and dashing the rain against the thin walls in sheets. The drumming upon the shingle roof spanning the unceiled room was loud and incessant.

I had never been invited into the machine-shop—had, indeed, been denied admittance, as had all others, with one exception, a skilled metal worker, of whom no one knew anything except that his name was Haley and his habit silence. But in my spiritual exaltation, discretion and civility were alike forgotten and I opened the door. What I saw took all philosophical speculation out of me in short order.

Moxon sat facing me at the farther side of a small table upon which a single candle made all the light that was in the room. Opposite him, his back toward me, sat another person. On the table between the two was a chessboard; the men were playing. I knew little of chess, but as only a few pieces were on the board it was obvious that the game was near its close. Moxon was intensely interested—not so much, it seemed to me, in the game as in his antagonist, upon whom he had fixed so intent a look that, standing though I did directly in the line of his vision, I was altogether unobserved. His face was ghastly white, and his eyes glittered like diamonds. Of his antagonist I had only a back view, but that was sufficient; I should not have cared to see his face.

He was apparently not more than five feet in height, with

proportions suggesting those of a gorilla—a tremendous breadth of shoulders, thick, short neck and broad, squat head, which had a tangled growth of black hair and was topped with a crimson fez. A tunic of the same color, belted tightly to the waist, reached the seat—apparently a box—upon which he sat; his legs and feet were not seen. His left forearm appeared to rest in his lap; he moved his pieces with his right hand, which seemed disproportionately long.

I had shrunk back and now stood a little to one side of the doorway and in shadow. If Moxon had looked farther than the face of his opponent he could have observed nothing now, except that the door was open. Something forbade me either to enter or to retire, a feeling—I know not how it came—that I was in the presence of an imminent tragedy and might serve my friend by remaining. With a scarcely conscious rebellion against the indelicacy of the act I remained.

The play was rapid. Moxon hardly glanced at the board before making his moves, and to my unskilled eye seemed to move the piece most convenient to his hand, his motions in doing so being quick, nervous and lacking in precision. The response of his antagonist, while equally prompt in the inception, was made with a slow, uniform, mechanical and, I thought, somewhat theatrical movement of the arm, that was a sore trial to my patience. There was something unearthly about it all, and I caught myself shuddering. But I was wet and cold.

Two or three times after moving a piece the stranger slightly inclined his head, and each time I observed that Moxon shifted his king. All at once the thought came to me that the man was dumb. And then that he was a machine—an automaton chessplayer! Then I remembered that Moxon had once spoken to me of having invented such a piece of mechanism, though I did not understand that it had actually been constructed. Was all his talk about the consciousness and intelligence of machines merely a prelude to eventual exhibition of this device—only a trick to intensify the effect of its mechanical action upon me in my ignorance of its secret?

A fine end, this, of all my intellectual transports—my "endless variety and excitement of philosophic thought!" I was about to retire in disgust when something occurred to hold my curiosity. I observed a shrug of the thing's great shoulders, as if it were irritated: and so natural was this—so entirely human—that in my new view of the matter it startled me. Nor was that all, for a moment later it struck the table sharply with its clenched hand. At that gesture Moxon seemed even more startled than I: he pushed his chair a little backward, as in alarm.

Presently Moxon, whose play it was, raised his hand high above the board, pounced upon one of his pieces like a sparrow-hawk and with the exclamation "checkmate!" rose quickly to his feet and stepped behind his chair. The automaton sat motionless.

The wind had now gone down, but I heard, at lessening intervals and progressively louder, the rumble and roll of thunder. In the pauses between I now became conscious of a low humming or buzzing which, like the thunder, grew momentarily louder and more distinct. It seemed to come from the body of the automaton, and was unmistakably a whirring of wheels. It gave me the impression of a disordered mechanism which had escaped the repressive and regulating action of some controlling part—an effect such as might be expected if a pawl should be jostled from the teeth of a ratchet-wheel. But before I had time for much conjecture as to its nature my attention was taken by the strange motions of the automaton itself. A slight but continuous convulsion appeared to have possession of it. In body and head it shook like a man with palsy or an ague chill, and the motion augmented every moment until the entire figure was in violent agitation. Suddenly it sprang to its feet and with a movement almost too quick for the eye to follow shot forward across table and chair, with both arms thrust forth to their full length—the posture and lunge of a diver. Moxon tried to throw himself backward out of reach, but he was too late: I saw the horrible thing's hands close upon his throat, his own clutch its wrists. Then the table was overturned, the candle thrown to the floor and extinguished, and all was black dark. But the noise of the struggle was dreadfully distinct, and most terrible of all were the raucous, squawking sounds made by the strangled man's efforts to breathe. Guided by the infernal hubbub, I sprang to the rescue of my friend, but had hardly taken a stride in the darkness when the whole room blazed with a blinding white light that burned into my brain and heart and memory a vivid picture of the combatants on the floor, Moxon underneath, his throat still in the clutch of those iron hands, his head forced backward, his eyes protruding, his mouth wide open and his tongue thrust out; and—horrible contrast!—upon the painted face of his assassin an expression of tranquil and profound thought, as in the solution of a problem in chess! This I observed, then all was blackness and silence.

Three days later I recovered consciousness in a hospital. As the memory of that tragic night slowly evolved in my ailing brain I recognized in my attendant Moxon's confidential workman, Haley. Responding to a look he approached, smiling.

"Tell me about it," I managed to say, faintly—"all about it."

"Certainly," he said; "you were carried unconscious from a burning house—Moxon's. Nobody knows how you came to be there. You may have to do a little explaining. The origin of the fire is a bit mysterious, too. My own notion is that the house was struck by lightning."

"And Moxon?"

"Buried yesterday—what was left of him."

Apparently this reticent person could unfold himself on occasion. When imparting shocking intelligence to the sick he was affable enough. After some moments of the keenest mental suffering I ventured to ask another question:

"Who rescued me?"

"Well, if that interests you—I did."

"Thank you, Mr. Haley, and may God bless you for it. Did you rescue, also, that charming product of your skill, the automaton chess-player that murdered its inventor?"

The man was silent a long time, looking away from me. Presently he turned and gravely said:

"Do you know that?"

"I do," I replied; "I saw it done."

That was many years ago. If asked today I should answer less confidently.

Beyond the Wall

MANY YEARS ago, on my way from Hongkong to New York, I passed a week in San Francisco. A long time had gone by since I had been in that city, during which my ventures in the Orient had prospered beyond my hope; I was rich and could afford to revisit my own country to renew my friendship with such of the companions of my youth as still lived and remembered me with the old affection. Chief of these, I hoped, was Mohun Dampier, an old schoolmate with whom I had held a desultory correspondence which had long ceased, as is the way of correspondence between men. You may have observed that the indisposition to write a merely social letter is in the ratio of the square of the distance between you and your correspondent. It is a law.

I remembered Dampier as a handsome, strong young fellow of scholarly tastes, with an aversion to work and a marked indifference to many of the things that the world cares for, including wealth, of which, however, he had inherited enough to put him beyond the reach of want. In his family, one of the oldest and most aristocratic in the country, it was, I think, a matter of pride that no member of it had ever been in trade nor politics, nor suffered any kind of distinction. Mohun was a trifle sentimental, and had in him a singular element of superstition, which led him to the study of all manner of occult subjects, although his sane mental health safeguarded him against fantastic and perilous faiths. He made daring incursions into the realm of the unreal without renouncing his residence in the partly surveyed and charted region of what we are pleased to call certitude.

The night of my visit to him was stormy. The Californian winter was on, and the incessant rain plashed in the deserted streets, or, lifted by irregular gusts of wind, was hurled against the houses with incredible fury. With no small difficulty my cabman found the right place, away out toward the ocean beach, in a sparsely populated suburb. The dwelling, a rather ugly one, apparently, stood in the center of its grounds, which as nearly as

24

I could make out in the gloom were destitute of either flowers or grass. Three or four trees, writhing and moaning in the torment of the tempest, appeared to be trying to escape from their dismal environment and take the chance of finding a better one out at sea. The house was a two-story brick structure with a tower, a story higher, at one corner. In a window of that was the only visible light. Something in the appearance of the place made me shudder, a performance that may have been assisted by a rill of rain-water down my back as I scuttled to cover in the doorway.

In answer to my note apprising him of my wish to call, Dampier had written, "Don't ring—open the door and come up." I did so. The staircase was dimly lighted by a single gas-jet at the top of the second flight. I managed to reach the landing without disaster and entered by an open door into the lighted square room of the tower. Dampier came forward in gown and slippers to receive me, giving me the greeting that I wished, and if I had held a thought that it might more fitly have been accorded me at the front door the first look at him dispelled any sense of his inhospitality.

He was not the same. Hardly past middle age, he had gone gray and had acquired a pronounced stoop. His figure was thin and angular, his face deeply lined, his complexion dead-white, without a touch of color. His eyes, unnaturally large, glowed with a fire that was almost uncanny.

He seated me, proffered a cigar, and with grave and obvious sincerity assured me of the pleasure that it gave him to meet me. Some unimportant conversation followed, but all the while I was dominated by a melancholy sense of the great change in him. This he must have perceived, for he suddenly said with a bright enough smile, "You are disappointed in me—*non sum qualis eram.*"

I hardly knew what to reply, but managed to say: "Why, really, I don't know: your Latin is about the same."

He brightened again. "No," he said, "being a dead language, it grows in appropriateness. But please have the patience to wait: where I am going there is perhaps a better tongue. Will you care to have a message in it?"

The smile faded as he spoke, and as he concluded he was looking into my eyes with a gravity that distressed me. Yet I would not surrender myself to his mood, nor permit him to see how deeply his prescience of death affected me.

"I fancy that it will be long," I said, "before human speech will cease to serve our need; and then the need, with its possibilities of service, will have passed."

He made no reply, and I too was silent, for the talk had taken a dispiriting turn, yet I knew not how to give it a more agreeable character. Suddenly, in a pause of the storm, when the dead silence was almost startling by contrast with the previous uproar, I heard a gentle tapping, which appeared to come from the wall behind my chair. The sound was such as might have been made by a human hand, not as upon a door by one asking admittance, but rather, I thought, as an agreed signal, an assurance of someone's presence in an adjoining room; most of us, I fancy, have had more experience of such communications than we should care to relate. I glanced at Dampier. If possibly there was something of amusement in the look he did not observe it. He appeared to have forgotten my presence, and was staring at the wall behind me with an expression in his eyes that I am unable to name, although my memory of it is as vivid today as was my sense of it then. The situation was embarrassing; I rose to take my leave. At this he seemed to recover himself.

"Please be seated," he said; "it is nothing—no one is there."

But the tapping was repeated, and with the same gentle, slow insistence as before.

"Pardon me," I said, "it is late. May I call tomorrow?"

He smiled—a little mechanically, I thought. "It is very delicate of you," said he, "but quite needless. Really, this is the only room in the tower, and no one is there. At least——" He left the sentence incomplete, rose, and threw up a window, the only opening in the wall from which the sound seemed to come. "See."

Not clearly knowing what else to do I followed him to the window and looked out. A street-lamp some little distance away gave enough light through the murk of the rain that was again falling in torrents to make it entirely plain that "no one was there." In truth there was nothing but the sheer blank wall of the tower.

Dampier closed the window and signing me to my seat resumed his own.

The incident was not in itself particularly mysterious; any one of a dozen explanations was possible (though none has occurred to me), yet it impressed me strangely, the more, perhaps, from my friend's effort to reassure me, which seemed to dignify it with a certain significance and importance. He had proved that no one was there, but in that fact lay all the interest; and he proffered no explanation. His silence was irritating and made me resentful.

"My good friend," I said, somewhat ironically, I fear, "I am not disposed to question your right to harbor as many spooks as you find agreeable to your taste and consistent with your notions of companionship; that is no business of mine. But being just a plain man of affairs, mostly of this world, I find spooks needless to my peace and comfort. I am going to my hotel, where my fellow-guests are still in the flesh."

It was not a very civil speech, but he manifested no feeling about it. "Kindly remain," he said. "I am grateful for your presence here. What you have heard to-night I believe myself to have heard twice before. Now I *know* it was no illusion. That is much to me—more than you know. Have a fresh cigar and a good stock of patience while I tell you the story."

The rain was now falling more steadily, with a low, monotonous susurration, interrupted at long intervals by the sudden slashing of the boughs of the trees as the wind rose and failed. The night was well advanced, but both sympathy and curiosity held me a willing listener to my friend's monologue, which I did not interrupt by a single word from beginning to end.

"Ten years ago," he said, "I occupied a ground-floor apartment in one of a row of houses, all alike, away at the other end of the town, on what we call Rincon Hill. This had been the best quarter of San Francisco, but had fallen into neglect and decay, partly because the primitive character of its domestic architecture no longer suited the maturing tastes of our wealthy citizens, partly because certain public improvements had made a wreck of it. The row of dwellings in one of which I lived stood a little way back from the street, each having a miniature garden, separated from its neighbors by low iron fences and bisected with mathematical precision by a box-bordered gravel walk from gate to door.

"One morning as I was leaving my lodging I observed a young girl entering the adjoining garden on the left. It was a warm day in June, and she was lightly gowned in white. From her shoulders hung a broad straw hat profusely decorated with flowers and wonderfully beribboned in the fashion of the time. My attention was not long held by the exquisite simplicity of her costume, for no one could look at her face and think of anything earthly. Do not fear; I shall not profane it by description; it was beautiful exceedingly. All that I had ever seen or dreamed of loveliness was in that matchless living picture by the hand of the Divine Artist. So deeply did it move me that, without a thought of the impropriety of the act, I unconsciously bared my head, as a devout Catholic or well-bred Protestant uncovers before an image of the Blessed Virgin. The maiden showed no displeasure; she merely turned her glorious dark eyes upon me with a look that made me catch my breath, and without other recognition of my act passed into the house. For a moment I stood motionless, hat in hand, painfully conscious of my rudeness, yet so dominated by the emotion inspired by that vision of incomparable beauty that my penitence was less poignant than it should have been. Then I went my way, leaving my heart behind. In the natural course of things I should probably have remained away until nightfall, but by the middle of the afternoon I was back in the little garden, affecting an interest in the few foolish flowers that I had never before observed. My hope was vain; she did not appear.

"To a night of unrest succeeded a day of expectation and disappointment, but on the day after, as I wandered aimlessly about the neighborhood, I met her. Of course I did not repeat my folly of uncovering, nor venture by even so much as too long a look to manifest an interest in her; yet my heart was beating audibly. I trembled and consciously colored as she turned her big black eyes upon me with a look of obvious recognition entirely devoid of boldness or coquetry.

"I will not weary you with particulars; many times afterward I met the maiden, yet never either addressed her or sought to fix her attention. Nor did I take any action toward making her acquaintance. Perhaps my forbearance, requiring so supreme an effort of self-denial, will not be entirely clear to you. That I was heels over head in love is true, but who can overcome his habit of thought, or reconstruct his character?

"I was what some foolish persons are pleased to call, and others, more foolish, are pleased to be called—an aristocrat; and despite her beauty, her charms and graces, the girl was not of my class. I had learned her name—which it is needless to speak —and something of her family. She was an orphan, a dependent niece of the impossible elderly fat woman in whose lodging-house she lived. My income was small and I lacked the talent for marrying; it is perhaps a gift. An alliance with that family would condemn me to its manner of life, part me from my books and studies, and in a social sense reduce me to the ranks. It is easy to deprecate such considerations as these and I have not retained myself for the defense. Let judgment be entered against me, but in strict justice all my ancestors for generations should be made co-defendants and I be permitted to plead in mitigation of punishment the imperious mandate of heredity. To a mésalliance of that kind every globule of my ancestral blood spoke in opposition. In brief, my tastes, habits, instinct, with whatever of reason my love had left me—all fought against it. Moreover, I was an irreclaimable sentimentalist, and found a subtle charm in an impersonal and spiritual relation which acquaintance might vulgarize and marriage would certainly dispel. No woman, I argued, is what this lovely creature seems. Love is a delicious dream; why should I bring about my own awakening?

"The course dictated by all this sense and sentiment was obvious. Honor, pride, prudence, preservation of my ideals—all commanded me to go away, but for that I was too weak. The utmost that I could do by a mighty effort of will was to cease meeting the girl, and that I did. I even avoided the chance encounters of the garden, leaving my lodging only when I knew that she had gone to her music lessons, and returning after nightfall. Yet all the while I was as one in a trance, indulging the most fascinating fancies and ordering my entire intellectual life in accordance with my dream. Ah, my friend, as one whose actions have a traceable relation to reason, you cannot know the fool's paradise in which I lived.

"One evening the devil put it into my head to be an unspeakable idiot. By apparently careless and purposeless questioning I learned from my gossipy landlady that the young woman's bedroom ajoined my own, a party-wall between. Yielding to a sudden and coarse impulse I gently rapped on the wall. There was no response, naturally, but I was in no mood to accept a rebuke. A madness was upon me and I repeated the folly, the offense, but again ineffectually, and I had the decency to desist.

"An hour later, while absorbed in some of my infernal studies, I heard, or thought I heard, my signal answered. Flinging down my books I sprang to the wall and as steadily as my beating heart would permit gave three slow taps upon it. This time the response was distinct, unmistakable: one, two, three—an exact repetition of my signal. That was all I could elicit, but it was enough—too much.

"The next evening, and for many evenings afterward, that folly went on, I always having 'the last word.' During the whole period I was deliriously happy, but with the perversity of my nature I persevered in my resolution not to see her. Then, as I should have expected, I got no further answers. 'She is disgusted,'

I said to myself, 'with what she thinks my timidity in making no more definite advances'; and I resolved to seek her and make her acquaintance and—what? I did not know, nor do I now know, what might have come of it. I know only that I passed days and days trying to meet her, and all in vain; she was invisible as well as inaudible. I haunted the streets where we had met, but she did not come. From my window I watched the garden in front of her house, but she passed neither in nor out. I fell into the deepest dejection, believing that she had gone away, yet took no steps to resolve my doubt by inquiry of my landlady, to whom, indeed, I had taken an unconquerable aversion from her having once spoken of the girl with less of reverence than I thought befitting.

"There came a fateful night. Worn out with emotion, irresolution and despondency, I had retired early and fallen into such sleep as was still possible to me. In the middle of the night something—some malign power bent upon the wrecking of my peace forever—caused me to open my eyes and sit up, wide awake and listening intently for I knew not what. Then I thought I heard a faint tapping on the wall—the mere ghost of the familiar signal. In a few moments it was repeated: one, two, three—no louder than before, but addressing a sense alert and strained to receive it. I was about to reply when the Adversary of Peace again intervened in my affairs with a rascally suggestion of retaliation. She had long and cruelly ignored me; now I would ignore her. Incredible fatuity—may God forgive it! All the rest of the night I lay awake, fortifying my obstinacy with shameless justifications and—listening.

"Late the next morning, as I was leaving the house, I met my landlady, entering.

" 'Good morning, Mr. Dampier,' she said. 'Have you heard the news?'

"I replied in words that I had heard no news; in manner, that I did not care to hear any. The manner escaped her observation.

" 'About the sick young lady next door,' she babbled on. 'What! you did not know? Why, she has been ill for weeks. And now——'

"I almost sprang upon her. 'And now,' I cried, 'now what?'

" 'She is dead.'

"That is not the whole story. In the middle of the night, as I learned later, the patient, awakening from a long stupor after a week of delirium, had asked—it was her last utterance—that her bed be moved to the opposite side of the room. Those in attendance had thought the request a vagary of her delirium, but had complied. And there the poor passing soul had exerted its failing will to restore a broken connection—a golden thread of sentiment between its innocence and a monstrous baseness owning a blind, brutal allegiance to the Law of Self.

"What reparation could I make? Are there masses that can be said for the repose of souls that are abroad such nights as this—spirits 'blown about by the viewless winds'—coming in the storm and darkness with signs and portents, hints of memory and presages of doom?

"This is the third visitation. On the first occasion I was too skeptical to do more than verify by natural methods the character of the incident; on the second, I responded to the signal after it had been several times repeated, but without result. Tonight's recurrence completes the 'fatal triad' expounded by Parapelius Necromantius. There is no more to tell."

When Dampier had finished his story I could think of nothing relevant that I cared to say, and to question him would have been a hideous impertinence. I rose and bade him good night in a way to convey to him a sense of my sympathy, which he silently acknowledged by a pressure of the hand. That night, alone with his sorrow and remorse, he passed into the Unknown.

The Damned Thing

I

ONE DOES NOT ALWAYS EAT
WHAT IS ON THE TABLE

BY THE light of a tallow candle which had been placed on one end of a rough table a man was reading something written in a book. It was an old account book, greatly worn; and the writing was not, apparently, very legible, for the man sometimes held the page close to the flame of the candle to get a stronger light on it. The shadow of the book would then throw into obscurity a half of the room, darkening a number of faces and figures; for besides the reader, eight other men were present. Seven of them sat against the rough log walls, silent, motionless, and the room being small, not very far from the table. By extending an arm any one of them could have touched the eighth man, who lay on the table, face upward, partly covered by a sheet, his arms at his sides. He was dead.

The man with the book was not reading aloud, and no one spoke; all seemed to be waiting for something to occur; the dead man only was without expectation. From the blank darkness outside came in, through the aperture that served for a window, all the ever unfamiliar noises of night in the wilderness— the long nameless note of a distant coyote; the stilly pulsing thrill of tireless insects in trees; strange cries of night birds, so different from those of the birds of day; the drone of great blundering beetles, and all that mysterious chorus of small sounds that seem always to have been but half heard when they have suddenly ceased, as if conscious of an indiscretion. But nothing of all this was noted in that company; its members were not overmuch addicted to idle interest in matters of no practical importance; that was obvious in every line of their rugged faces—obvious even in the dim light of the single candle. They were evidently men of the vicinity—farmers and woodsmen.

The person reading was a trifle different; one would have said of him that he was of the world, worldly, albeit there was that in his attire which attested a certain fellowship with the organisms of his environment. His coat would hardly have passed muster in San Francisco; his footgear was not of urban origin, and the hat that lay by him on the floor (he was the only one uncovered) was such that if one had considered it as an article of mere personal adornment he would have missed its meaning. In countenance the man was rather prepossessing, with just a hint of sternness; though that he may have assumed or cultivated, as appropriate to one in authority. For he was a coroner. It was by virtue of his office that he had possession of the book in which he was reading; it had been found among the dead man's effects—in his cabin, where the inquest was now taking place.

When the coroner had finished reading he put the book into his breast pocket. At that moment the door was pushed open and a young man entered. He, clearly, was not of mountain birth and breeding: he was clad as those who dwell in cities. His clothing was dusty, however, as from travel. He had, in fact, been riding hard to attend the inquest.

The coroner nodded; no one else greeted him.

"We have waited for you," said the coroner. "It is necessary to have done with this business to-night."

The young man smiled. "I am sorry to have kept you," he said. "I went away, not to evade your summons, but to post to my newspaper an account of what I suppose I am called back to relate."

The coroner smiled.

"The account that you posted to your newspaper," he said, "differs, probably, from that which you will give here under oath."

"That," replied the other, rather hotly and with a visible flush, "is as you please. I used manifold paper and have a copy of what I sent. It was not written as news, for it is incredible, but as fiction. It may go as a part of my testimony under oath."

"But you say it is incredible."

"That is nothing to you, sir, if I also swear that it is true."

The coroner was silent for a time, his eyes upon the floor. The men about the sides of the cabin talked in whispers, but seldom withdrew their gaze from the face of the corpse. Presently the coroner lifted his eyes and said: "We will resume the inquest."

The men removed their hats. The witness was sworn.

"What is your name?" the coroner asked.

"William Harker."

"Age?"

"Twenty-seven."

"You knew the deceased, Hugh Morgan?"

"Yes."

"You were with him when he died?"

"Near him."

"How did that happen—your presence, I mean?"

"I was visiting him at this place to shoot and fish. A part of my purpose, however, was to study him and his odd, solitary way of life. He seemed a good model for a character in fiction. I sometimes write stories."

"I sometimes read them."

"Thank you."

"Stories in general—not yours."

Some of the jurors laughed. Against a sombre background humor shows high lights. Soldiers in the intervals of battle laugh easily, and a jest in the death chamber conquers by surprise.

"Relate the circumstances of this man's death," said the coroner. "You may use any notes or memoranda that you please."

The witness understood. Pulling a manuscript from his breast pocket he held it near the candle and turning the leaves until he found the passage that he wanted began to read.

II

WHAT MAY HAPPEN IN A FIELD OF WILD OATS

". . . THE SUN had hardly risen when we left the house. We were looking for quail, each with a shotgun, but we had only one dog. Morgan said that our best ground was beyond a certain ridge that he pointed out, and we crossed it by a trail through the chaparral. On the other side was comparatively level ground, thickly covered with wild oats. As we emerged from the chaparral Morgan was but a few yards in advance. Suddenly we heard, at a little distance to our right and partly in front, a noise as of some animal thrashing about in the bushes, which we could see were violently agitated.

" 'We've started a deer,' I said. 'I wish we had brought a rifle.'

"Morgan, who had stopped and was intently watching the agitated chaparral, said nothing, but had cocked both barrels of his gun and was holding it in readiness to aim. I thought him a trifle excited, which surprised me, for he had a reputation for exceptional coolness, even in moments of sudden and imminent peril.

" 'O, come,' I said. 'You are not going to fill up a deer with quail-shot, are you?'

"Still he did not reply; but catching a sight of his face as he turned it slightly toward me I was struck by the intensity of his look. Then I understood that we had serious business in hand and my first conjecture was that we had 'jumped' a grizzly. I advanced to Morgan's side, cocking my piece as I moved.

"The bushes were now quiet and the sounds had ceased, but Morgan was as attentive to the place as before.

" 'What is it? What the devil is it?' I asked.

" 'That Damned Thing!' he replied, without turning his head. His voice was husky and unnatural. He trembled visibly.

"I was about to speak further, when I observed the wild oats near the place of the disturbance moving in the most inexplicable way. I can hardly describe it. It seemed as if stirred by a streak of wind, which not only bent it, but pressed it down—crushed it so that it did not rise; and this movement was slowly prolonging itself directly toward us.

"Nothing that I had ever seen had affected me so strangely as this unfamiliar and unaccountable phenomenon, yet I am unable to recall any sense of fear. I remember—and tell it here because, singularly enough, I recollected it then—that once in looking carelessly out of an open window I momentarily mistook a small tree close at hand for one of a group of larger trees at a little distance away. It looked the same size as the others, but being more distinctly and sharply defined in mass and detail seemed out of harmony with them. It was a mere falsification of the law of aërial perspective, but it startled, almost terrified me. We so rely upon the orderly operation of familiar natural laws that any seeming suspension of them is noted as a menace to our safety, a warning of unthinkable calamity. So now the apparently causeless movement of the herbage and the slow, undeviating approach of the line of disturbance were distinctly disquieting. My companion appeared actually frightened, and I could hardly credit my senses when I saw him suddenly throw his gun to his shoulder and fire both barrels at the agitated grain! Before the smoke of the discharge had cleared away I heard a loud savage cry—a scream like that of a wild animal—and flinging his gun upon the ground Morgan sprang away and ran swiftly from the spot. At the same instant I was thrown violently to the ground by the impact of something unseen in the smoke—some soft, heavy substance that seemed thrown against me with great force.

"Before I could get upon my feet and recover my gun, which seemed to have been struck from my hands, I heard Morgan crying out as if in mortal agony, and mingling with his cries were such hoarse, savage sounds as one hears from fighting dogs. Inexpressibly terrified, I struggled to my feet and looked in the direction of Morgan's retreat; and may Heaven in mercy spare me from another sight like that! At a distance of less than thirty yards was my friend, down upon one knee, his head thrown back at a frightful angle, hatless, his long hair in disorder and his whole body in violent movement from side to side, backward and forward. His right arm was lifted and seemed to lack the hand—at least, I could see none. The other arm was invisible. At times, as my memory now reports this extraordinary scene, I could discern but a part of his body; it was as if he had been partly blotted out—I cannot otherwise express it—then a shifting of his position would bring it all into view again.

"All this must have occurred within a few seconds, yet in that time Morgan assumed all the postures of a determined wrestler vanquished by superior weight and strength. I saw nothing but him, and him not always distinctly. During the entire incident his shouts and curses were heard, as if through an enveloping uproar of such sounds of rage and fury as I had never heard from the throat of man or brute!

"For a moment only I stood irresolute, then throwing down my gun I ran forward to my friend's assistance. I had a vague belief that he was suffering from a fit, or some form of convulsion. Before I could reach his side he was down and quiet. All sounds had ceased, but with a feeling of such terror as even these awful events had not inspired I now saw again the mysterious movement of the wild oats, prolonging itself from the trampled area about the prostrate man toward the edge of a wood. It was only when it had reached the wood that I was able to withdraw my eyes and look at my companion. He was dead."

III

A MAN THOUGH NAKED MAY BE IN RAGS

THE CORONER rose from his seat and stood beside the dead man. Lifting an edge of the sheet he pulled it away, exposing the entire body, altogether naked and showing in the candle-light a

claylike yellow. It had, however, broad maculations of bluish
black, obviously caused by extravasated blood from contusions.
The chest and sides looked as if they had been beaten with a
bludgeon. There were dreadful lacerations; the skin was torn in
strips and shreds.

The coroner moved round to the end of the table and undid
a silk handkerchief which had been passed under the chin and
knotted on the top of the head. When the handkerchief was
drawn away it exposed what had been the throat. Some of the
jurors who had risen to get a better view repented their curiosity
and turned away their faces. Witness Harker went to the open
window and leaned out across the sill, faint and sick. Dropping
the handkerchief upon the dead man's neck the coroner stepped
to an angle of the room and from a pile of clothing produced one
garment after another, each of which he held up a moment for
inspection. All were torn, and stiff with blood. The jurors did
not make a closer inspection. They seemed rather uninterested.
They had, in truth, seen all this before; the only thing that was
new to them being Harker's testimony.

"Gentlemen," the coroner said, "we have no more evidence, I
think. Your duty has been already explained to you; if there is
nothing you wish to ask you may go outside and consider your
verdict."

The foreman rose—a tall, bearded man of sixty, coarsely clad.

"I should like to ask one question, Mr. Coroner," he said.
"What asylum did this yer last witness escape from?"

"Mr. Harker," said the coroner, gravely and tranquilly, "from
what asylum did you last escape?"

Harker flushed crimson again, but said nothing, and the seven
jurors rose and solemnly filed out of the cabin.

"If you have done insulting me, sir," said Harker, as soon as
he and the officer were left alone with the dead man, "I suppose
I am at liberty to go?"

"Yes."

Harker started to leave, but paused, with his hand on the door
latch. The habit of his profession was strong in him—stronger
than his sense of personal dignity. He turned about and said:

"The book that you have there—I recognize it as Morgan's diary. You seemed greatly interested in it; you read in it while I
was testifying. May I see it? The public would like——"

"The book will cut no figure in this matter," replied the offi-
cial, slipping it into his coat pocket; "all the entries in it were
made before the writer's death."

As Harker passed out of the house the jury reentered and

stood about the table, on which the now covered corpse showed under the sheet with sharp definition. The foreman seated himself near the candle, produced from his breast pocket a pencil and scrap of paper and wrote rather laboriously the following verdict, which with various degrees of effort all signed:

"We, the jury, do find that the remains come to their death at the hands of a mountain lion, but some of us thinks, all the same, they had fits."

IV

AN EXPLANATION FROM THE TOMB

IN THE diary of the late Hugh Morgan are certain interesting entries having, possibly, a scientific value as suggestions. At the inquest upon his body the book was not put in evidence; possibly the coroner thought it not worth while to confuse the jury. The date of the first of the entries mentioned cannot be ascertained; the upper part of the leaf is torn away; the part of the entry remaining follows:

". . . would run in a half-circle, keeping his head turned always toward the centre, and again he would stand still, barking furiously. At last he ran away into the brush as fast as he could go. I thought at first that he had gone mad, but on returning to the house found no other alteration in his manner than what was obviously due to fear of punishment.

"Can a dog see with his nose? Do odors impress some cerebral centre with images of the thing that emitted them? . . .

"Sept. 2.—Looking at the stars last night as they rose above the crest of the ridge east of the house, I observed them successively disappear—from left to right. Each was eclipsed but an instant, and only a few at the same time, but along the entire length of the ridge all that were within a degree or two of the crest were blotted out. It was as if something had passed along between me and them; but I could not see it, and the stars were not thick enough to define its outline. Ugh! I don't like this." . . .

Several weeks' entries are missing, three leaves being torn from the book.

"Sept. 27.—It has been about here again—I find evidences of its presence every day. I watched again all last night in the same cover, gun in hand, double-charged with buckshot. In the morning the fresh footprints were there, as before. Yet I would have sworn that I did not sleep—indeed, I hardly sleep at all. It is terrible, insupportable! If these amazing experiences are real I shall go mad; if they are fanciful I am mad already.

"Oct. 3.—I shall not go—it shall not drive me away. No, this is *my* house, *my* land. God hates a coward. . . .

"Oct. 5.—I can stand it no longer; I have invited Harker to pass a few weeks with me—he has a level head. I can judge from his manner if he thinks me mad.

"Oct. 7—I have the solution of the mystery; it came to me last night—suddenly, as by revelation. How simple—how terribly simple!

"There are sounds that we cannot hear. At either end of the scale are notes that stir no chord of that imperfect instrument, the human ear. They are too high or too grave. I have observed a flock of blackbirds occupying an entire tree-top—the tops of several trees—and all in full song. Suddenly—in a moment—at absolutely the same instant—all spring into the air and fly away. How? They could not all see one another—whose tree-tops intervened. At no point could a leader have been visible to all. There must have been a signal of warning or command, high and shrill above the din, but by me unheard. I have observed, too, the same simultaneous flight when all were silent, among not only blackbirds, but other birds—quail, for example, widely separated by bushes—even on opposite sides of a hill.

"It is known to seamen that a school of whales basking or sporting on the surface of the ocean, miles apart, with the convexity of the earth between, will sometimes dive at the same instant—all gone out of sight in a moment. The signal has been sounded—too grave for the ear of the sailor at the masthead and his comrades on the deck—who nevertheless feel its vibrations in the ship as the stones of a cathedral are stirred by the bass of the organ.

"As with sounds, so with colors. At each end of the solar spectrum the chemist can detect the presence of what are known as 'actinic' rays. They represent colors—integral colors in the composition of light—which we are unable to discern. The human eye is an imperfect instrument; its range is but a few octaves of the real 'chromatic scale.' I am not mad; there are colors that we cannot see.

"And, God help me! the Damned Thing is of such a color!"

A Watcher by the Dead

I

In AN upper room of an unoccupied dwelling in the part of San Francisco known as North Beach lay the body of a man, under a sheet. The hour was near nine in the evening; the room was dimly lighted by a single candle. Although the weather was warm, the two windows, contrary to the custom which gives the dead plenty of air, were closed and the blinds drawn down. The furniture of the room consisted of but three pieces—an armchair, a small reading stand supporting the candle, and a long kitchen table, supporting the body of the man. All these, as also the corpse, seemed to have been recently brought in, for an observer, had there been one, would have seen that all were free from dust, whereas everything else in the room was pretty thickly coated with it, and there were cobwebs in the angles of the walls.

Under the sheet the outlines of the body could be traced, even the features, these having that unnaturally sharp definition which seems to belong to faces of the dead, but is really characteristic of those only that have been wasted by disease. From the silence of the room one would rightly have inferred that it was not in the front of the house, facing a street. It really faced nothing but a high breast of rock, the rear of the building being set into a hill.

As a neighboring church clock was striking nine with an indolence which seemed to imply such an indifference to the flight of time that one could hardly help wondering why it took the trouble to strike at all, the single door of the room was opened and a man entered, advancing toward the body. As he did so the door closed, apparently of its own volition; there was a grating, as of a key turned with difficulty, and the snap of the lock bolt as it shot into its socket. A sound of retiring footsteps in the passage outside ensued, and the man was to all appearance a prisoner. Advancing to the table, he stood a moment looking down at the body; then with a slight shrug of the shoulders walked over to one of the windows and hoisted the blind. The darkness outside was absolute, the panes were covered with dust, but by wiping this away he could see that the window was fortified with strong iron bars crossing it within a few inches of the glass and imbedded in the masonry on each side. He examined the other window. It was the same. He manifested no great curiosity in the matter, did not even so much as raise the sash. If he was a prisoner he was apparently a tractable one. Having completed his examination of the room, he seated himself in the arm-chair, took a book from his pocket, drew the stand with its candle alongside and began to read.

The man was young—not more than thirty—dark in complexion, smooth-shaven, with brown hair. His face was thin and high-nosed, with a broad forehead and a "firmness" of the chin and jaw which is said by those having it to denote resolution. The eyes were gray and steadfast, not moving except with definitive purpose. They were now for the greater part of the time fixed upon his book, but he occasionally withdrew them and turned them to the body on the table, not, apparently, from any dismal fascination which under such circumstances it might be supposed to exercise upon even a courageous person, nor with a conscious rebellion against the contrary influence which might dominate a timid one. He looked at it as if in his reading he had come upon something recalling him to a sense of his surroundings. Clearly this watcher by the dead was discharging his trust with intelligence and composure, as became him.

After reading for perhaps a half-hour he seemed to come to the end of a chapter and quietly laid away the book. He then rose and taking the reading-stand from the floor carried it into a corner of the room near one of the windows, lifted the candle from it and returned to the empty fireplace before which he had been sitting.

A moment later he walked over to the body on the table, lifted the sheet and turned it back from the head, exposing a mass of dark hair and a thin face-cloth, beneath which the features showed with even sharper definition than before. Shading his eyes by interposing his free hand between them and the candle, he stood looking at his motionless companion with a serious and tranquil regard. Satisfied with his inspection, he pulled the sheet over the face again and returning to the chair, took some matches off the candlestick, put them in the side pocket of his sack-coat and sat down. He then lifted the candle from its socket and looked at it critically, as if calculating how long it would last. It was barely two inches long; in another hour he would be in darkness. He replaced it in the candlestick and blew it out.

II

IN A physician's office in Kearny Street three men sat about a table, drinking punch and smoking. It was late in the evening, almost midnight, indeed, and there had been no lack of punch. The gravest of the three, Dr. Helberson, was the host—it was in his rooms they sat. He was about thirty years of age; the others were even younger; all were physicians.

"The superstitious awe with which the living regard the dead," said Dr. Helberson, "is hereditary and incurable. One needs no more be ashamed of it than of the fact that he inherits, for example, an incapacity for mathematics, or a tendency to lie."

The others laughed. "Oughtn't a man to be ashamed to lie?" asked the youngest of the three, who was in fact a medical student not yet graduated.

"My dear Harper, I said nothing about that. The tendency to lie is one thing; lying is another."

"But do you think," said the third man, "that this superstitious feeling, this fear of the dead, reasonless as we know it to be, is universal? I am myself not conscious of it."

"Oh, but it is 'in your system' for all that," replied Helberson; "it needs only the right conditions—what Shakespeare calls the 'confederate season'—to manifest itself in some very disagreeable way that will open your eyes. Physicians and soldiers are of course more nearly free from it than others."

"Physicians and soldiers!—why don't you add hangmen and headsmen? Let us have in all the assassin classes."

"No, my dear Mancher; the juries will not let the public executioners acquire sufficient familiarity with death to be altogether unmoved by it."

Young Harper, who had been helping himself to a fresh cigar at the sideboard, resumed his seat. "What would you consider conditions under which any man of woman born would become insupportably conscious of his share of our common weakness in this regard?" he asked, rather verbosely.

"Well, I should say that if a man were locked up all night with a corpse—alone—in a dark room—of a vacant house—with no bed covers to pull over his head—and lived through it without going altogether mad, he might justly boast himself not of woman born, nor yet, like Macduff, a product of Cæsarean section."

"I thought you never would finish piling up conditions," said Harper, "but I know a man who is neither a physician nor a soldier who will accept them all, for any stake you like to name."

"Who is he?"

"His name is Jarette—a stranger here; comes from my town in New York. I have no money to back him, but he will back himself with loads of it."

"How do you know that?"

"He would rather bet than eat. As for fear—I dare say he thinks it some cutaneous disorder, or possibly a particular kind of religious heresy."

"What does he look like?" Helberson was evidently becoming interested.

"Like Mancher, here—might be his twin brother."

"I accept the challenge," said Helberson, promptly.

"Awfully obliged to you for the compliment, I'm sure," drawled Mancher, who was growing sleepy. "Can't I get into this?"

"Not against me," Helberson said. "I don't want *your* money."

"All right," said Mancher; "I'll be the corpse."

The others laughed.

The outcome of this crazy conversation we have seen.

III

IN EXTINGUISHING his meagre allowance of candle Mr. Jarette's object was to preserve it against some unforeseen need. He may have thought, too, or half thought, that the darkness would be no worse at one time than another, and if the situation became insupportable it would be better to have a means of relief, or even release. At any rate it was wise to have a little reserve of light, even if only to enable him to look at his watch.

No sooner had he blown out the candle and set it on the floor at his side than he settled himself comfortably in the arm-chair, leaned back and closed his eyes, hoping and expecting to sleep. In this he was disappointed; he had never in his life felt less sleepy, and in a few minutes he gave up the attempt. But what could he do? He could not go groping about in absolute darkness at the risk of bruising himself—at the risk, too, of blundering against the table and rudely disturbing the dead. We all recognize their right to lie at rest, with immunity from all that is harsh and violent. Jarette almost succeeded in making himself believe that considerations of this kind restrained him from risking the collision and fixed him to the chair.

While thinking of this matter he fancied that he heard a faint sound in the direction of the table—what kind of sound he could hardly have explained. He did not turn his head. Why should he —in the darkness? But he listened—why should he not? And listening he grew giddy and grasped the arms of the chair for support. There was a strange ringing in his ears; his head seemed bursting; his chest was oppressed by the constriction of his clothing. He wondered why it was so, and whether these were symptoms of fear. Then, with a long and strong expiration, his chest appeared to collapse, and with the great gasp with which he refilled his exhausted lungs the vertigo left him and he knew that so intently had he listened that he had held his breath almost to suffocation. The revelation was vexatious; he arose, pushed away the chair with his foot and strode to the centre of the room. But one does not stride far in darkness; he began to grope, and finding the wall followed it to an angle, turned, followed it past the two windows and there in another corner came into violent contact with the reading-stand, overturning it. It made a clatter that startled him. He was annoyed. "How the devil could I have forgotten where it was?" he muttered, and groped his way along the third wall to the fireplace. "I must put things to rights," said he, feeling the floor for the candle.

Having recovered that, he lighted it and instantly turned his eyes to the table, where, naturally, nothing had undergone any change. The reading-stand lay unobserved upon the floor: he had forgotten to "put it to rights." He looked all about the room, dispersing the deeper shadows by movements of the candle in his hand, and crossing over to the door tested it by turning and pulling the knob with all his strength. It did not yield and this seemed to afford him a certain satisfaction; indeed, he secured it more firmly by a bolt which he had not before observed. Returning to his chair, he looked at his watch; it was half-past nine. With a start of surprise he held the watch at his ear. It had not stopped. The candle was now visibly shorter. He again extinguished it, placing it on the floor at his side as before.

Mr. Jarette was not at his ease; he was distinctly dissatisfied with his surroundings, and with himself for being so. "What have I to fear?" he thought. "This is ridiculous and disgraceful; I will not be so great a fool." But courage does not come of saying, "I will be courageous," nor of recognizing its appropriateness to the occasion. The more Jarette condemned himself, the more reason he gave himself for condemnation; the greater the number of variations which he played upon the simple theme of the harmlessness of the dead, the more insupportable grew the discord of his emotions. "What!" he cried aloud in the anguish of his spirit, "what! shall I, who have not a shade of superstition in my nature —I, who have no belief in immortality—I, who know (and never more clearly than now) that the after-life is the dream of a desire —shall I lose at once my bet, my honor and my self-respect, perhaps my reason, because certain savage ancestors dwelling in caves and burrows conceived the monstrous notion that the dead walk by night?—that——" Distinctly, unmistakably, Mr. Jarette heard behind him a light, soft sound of footfalls, deliberate, regular, successively nearer!

IV

JUST BEFORE daybreak the next morning Dr. Helberson and his young friend Harper were driving slowly through the streets of North Beach in the doctor's coupé.

"Have you still the confidence of youth in the courage or stolidity of your friend?" said the elder man. "Do you believe that I have lost this wager?"

"I *know* you have," replied the other, with enfeebling emphasis.

"Well, upon my soul, I hope so."

It was spoken earnestly, almost solemnly. There was a silence for a few moments.

"Harper," the doctor resumed, looking very serious in the shifting half-lights that entered the carriage as they passed the street lamps, "I don't feel altogether comfortable about this business. If your friend had not irritated me by the contemptuous manner in which he treated my doubt of his endurance—a purely physical quality—and by the cool incivility of his suggestion that the corpse be that of a physician, I should not have gone on with it. If anything should happen we are ruined, as I fear we deserve to be."

"What can happen? Even if the matter should be taking a serious turn, of which I am not at all afraid, Mancher has only to 'resurrect' himself and explain matters. With a genuine 'subject' from the dissecting-room, or one of your late patients, it might be different."

Dr. Mancher, then, had been as good as his promise; he was the "corpse."

Dr. Helberson was silent for a long time, as the carriage, at a snail's pace, crept along the same street it had traveled two or three times already. Presently he spoke: "Well, let us hope that Mancher, if he has had to rise from the dead, has been discreet about it. A mistake in that might make matters worse instead of better."

"Yes," said Harper, "Jarette would kill him. But, Doctor"—looking at his watch as the carriage passed a gas lamp—"it is nearly four o'clock at last."

A moment later the two had quitted the vehicle and were walking briskly toward the long-unoccupied house belonging to the doctor in which they had immured Mr. Jarette in accordance with the terms of the mad wager. As they neared it they met a man running. "Can you tell me," he cried, suddenly checking his speed, "where I can find a doctor?"

"What's the matter?" Helberson asked, non-committal.

"Go and see for yourself," said the man, resuming his running.

They hastened on. Arrived at the house, they saw several persons entering in haste and excitement. In some of the dwellings nearby and across the way the chamber windows were thrown up, showing a protrusion of heads. All heads were asking questions, none heeding the questions of the others. A few of the windows with closed blinds were illuminated; the inmates of those rooms were dressing to come down. Exactly opposite the door of the house that they sought a street lamp threw a yellow, insufficient light upon the scene, seeming to say that it could disclose a good deal more if it wished. Harper paused at the door and laid a hand upon his companion's arm. "It is all up with us, Doctor," he said in extreme agitation, which contrasted strangely with his free-and-easy words; "the game has gone against us all. Let's not go in there; I'm for lying low."

"I'm a physician," said Dr. Helberson, calmly; "there may be need of one."

They mounted the doorsteps and were about to enter. The door was open; the street lamp opposite lighted the passage into which it opened. It was full of men. Some had ascended the stairs at the farther end, and, denied admittance above, waited for better fortune. All were talking, none listening. Suddenly, on the upper landing there was a great commotion; a man had sprung out of a door and was breaking away from those endeavoring to detain him. Down through the mass of affrighted idlers he came, pushing them aside, flattening them against the wall on one side, or compelling them to cling to the rail on the other, clutching them by the throat, striking them savagely, thrusting them back down the stairs and walking over the fallen. His clothing was in disorder, he was without a hat. His eyes, wild and restless, had in them something more terrifying than his apparently superhuman strength. His face, smooth-shaven, was bloodless, his hair frost-white.

As the crowd at the foot of the stairs, having more freedom, fell away to let him pass Harper sprang forward. "Jarette! Jarette!" he cried.

Dr. Helberson seized Harper by the collar and dragged him back. The man looked into their faces without seeming to see them and sprang through the door, down the steps, into the street, and away. A stout policeman, who had had inferior success in conquering his way down the stairway, followed a moment later and started in pursuit, all the heads in the windows—those of women and children now—screaming in guidance.

The stairway being now partly cleared, most of the crowd having rushed down to the street to observe the flight and pursuit, Dr. Helberson mounted to the landing, followed by Harper. At a door in the upper passage an officer denied them admittance. "We are physicians," said the doctor, and they passed in. The room was full of men, dimly seen, crowded about a table. The newcomers edged their way forward and looked over the shoulders of those in the front rank. Upon the table, the lower limbs covered with a sheet, lay the body of a man, brilliantly illuminated by the beam of a bull's-eye lantern held by a policeman standing at the feet. The others, excepting those near the head—the officer himself—all were in darkness. The face of the body showed yellow, repulsive, horrible! The eyes were partly open and upturned and the jaw fallen; traces of froth defiled the lips, the chin, the cheeks. A tall man, evidently a doctor, bent over the body with his hand thrust under the shirt front. He withdrew it and placed two fingers in the open mouth. "This man has been about six hours dead," said he. "It is a case for the coroner."

He drew a card from his pocket, handed it to the officer and made his way toward the door.

"Clear the room—out, all!" said the officer, sharply, and the body disappeared as if it had been snatched away, as shifting the lantern he flashed its beam of light here and there against the faces of the crowd. The effect was amazing! The men, blinded, confused, almost terrified, made a tumultuous rush for the door, pushing, crowding, and tumbling over one another as they fled, like the hosts of Night before the shafts of Apollo. Upon the struggling, trampling mass the officer poured his light without pity and without cessation. Caught in the current, Helberson and Harper were swept out of the room and cascaded down the stairs into the street.

"Good God, Doctor! did I not tell you that Jarette would kill him?" said Harper, as soon as they were clear of the crowd.

"I believe you did," replied the other, without apparent emotion.

They walked on in silence, block after block. Against the graying east the dwellings of the hill tribes showed in silhouette. The familiar milk wagon was already astir in the streets; the baker's man would soon come upon the scene; the newspaper carrier was abroad in the land.

"It strikes me, youngster," said Helberson, "that you and I have been having too much of the morning air lately. It is unwholesome; we need a change. What do you say to a tour in Europe?"

"When?"

"I'm not particular. I should suppose that four o'clock this afternoon would be early enough."

"I'll meet you at the boat," said Harper.

V

SEVEN YEARS afterward these two men sat upon a bench in Madison Square, New York, in familiar conversation. Another man, who had been observing them for some time, himself unobserved, approached and, courteously lifting his hat from locks as white as frost, said: "I beg your pardon, gentlemen, but when you have killed a man by coming to life, it is best to change clothes with him, and at the first opportunity make a break for liberty."

Helberson and Harper exchanged significant glances. They were obviously amused. The former then looked the stranger kindly in the eye and replied:

"That has always been my plan. I entirely agree with you as to its advant——"

He stopped suddenly, rose and went white. He stared at the man, open-mouthed; he trembled visibly.

"Ah!" said the stranger, "I see that you are indisposed, Doctor. If you cannot treat yourself Dr. Harper can do something for you, I am sure."

"Who the devil are you?" said Harper, bluntly.

The stranger came nearer and, bending toward them, said in a whisper: "I call myself Jarette sometimes, but I don't mind telling you, for old friendship, that I am Dr. William Mancher."

The revelation brought Harper to his feet. "Mancher!" he cried; and Helberson added: "It is true, by God!"

"Yes," said the stranger, smiling vaguely, "it is true enough, no doubt."

He hesitated and seemed to be trying to recall something, then began humming a popular air. He had apparently forgotten their presence.

"Look here, Mancher," said the elder of the two, "tell us just what occurred that night—to Jarette, you know."

"Oh, yes, about Jarette," said the other. "It's odd I should have neglected to tell you—I tell it so often. You see I knew, by over-hearing him talking to himself, that he was pretty badly fright-ened. So I couldn't resist the temptation to come to life and have a bit of fun out of him—I couldn't really. That was all right, though certainly I did not think he would take it so seriously; I did not, truly. And afterward—well, it was a tough job changing places with him, and then—damn you! you didn't let me out!"

Nothing could exceed the ferocity with which these last words were delivered. Both men stepped back in alarm.

"We?—why—why," Helberson stammered, losing his self-pos-session utterly, "we had nothing to do with it."

"Didn't I say you were Drs. Hell-born and Sharper?" inquired the man, laughing.

"My name is Helberson, yes; and this gentleman is Mr. Har-per," replied the former, reassured by the laugh. "But we are not physicians now; we are—well, hang it, old man, we are gam-blers."

And that was the truth.

"A very good profession—very good, indeed; and, by the way, I hope Sharper here paid over Jarette's money like an honest stakeholder. A very good and honorable profession," he re-peated, thoughtfully, moving carelessly away; "but I stick to the old one. I am High Supreme Medical Officer of the Blooming-dale Asylum; it is my duty to cure the superintendent."

An Occurrence at Owl Creek Bridge

I

A MAN stood upon a railroad bridge in northern Alabama, looking down into the swift water twenty feet below. The man's hands were behind his back, the wrists bound with a cord. A rope closely encircled his neck. It was attached to a stout crosstimber above his head and the slack fell to the level of his knees. Some loose boards laid upon the sleepers supporting the metals of the railway supplied a footing for him and his executioners—two private soldiers of the Federal army, directed by a sergeant who in civil life may have been a deputy sheriff. At a short remove upon the same temporary platform was an officer in the uniform of his rank, armed. He was a captain. A sentinel at each end of the bridge stood with his rifle in the position known as "support," that is to say, vertical in front of the left shoulder, the hammer resting on the forearm thrown straight across the chest—a formal and unnatural position, enforcing an erect carriage of the body. It did not appear to be the duty of these two men to know what was occurring at the centre of the bridge; they merely blockaded the two ends of the foot planking that traversed it.

Beyond one of the sentinels nobody was in sight; the railroad ran straight away into a forest for a hundred yards, then, curving, was lost to view. Doubtless there was an outpost farther along. The other bank of the stream was open ground—a gentle acclivity topped with a stockade of vertical tree trunks, loopholed for rifles, with a single embrasure through which protruded the muzzle of a brass cannon commanding the bridge. Midway of the slope between bridge and fort were the spectators —a single company of infantry in line, at "parade rest," the butts of the rifles on the ground, the barrels inclining slightly backward against the right shoulder, the hands crossed upon the stock. A lieutenant stood at the right of the line, the point of his sword upon the ground, his left hand resting upon his right. Excepting the group of four at the centre of the bridge, not a man moved. The company faced the bridge, staring stonily, motionless. The sentinels, facing the banks of the stream, might have been statues to adorn the bridge. The captain stood with folded arms, silent, observing the work of his subordinates, but making no sign. Death is a dignitary who when he comes announced is to be received with formal manifestations of respect, even by those most familiar with him. In the code of military etiquette silence and fixity are forms of deference.

The man who was engaged in being hanged was apparently about thirty-five years of age. He was a civilian, if one might judge from his habit, which was that of a planter. His features were good—a straight nose, firm mouth, broad forehead, from which his long, dark hair was combed straight back, falling behind his ears to the collar of his well-fitting frock coat. He wore a mustache and pointed beard, but no whiskers; his eyes were large and dark gray, and had a kindly expression which one would hardly have expected in one whose neck was in the hemp. Evidently this was no vulgar assassin. The liberal military code makes provision for hanging many kinds of persons, and gentlemen are not excluded.

The preparations being complete, the two private soldiers stepped aside and each drew away the plank upon which he had been standing. The sergeant turned to the captain, saluted and placed himself immediately behind that officer, who in turn moved apart one pace. These movements left the condemned man and the sergeant standing on the two ends of the same plank, which spanned three of the cross-ties of the bridge. The end upon which the civilian stood almost, but not quite, reached a fourth. This plank had been held in place by the weight of the captain; it was now held by that of the sergeant. At a signal from the former the latter would step aside, the plank would tilt and the condemned man go down between two ties. The arrangement commended itself to his judgment as simple and effective. His face had not been covered nor his eyes bandaged. He looked a moment at his "unsteadfast footing," then let his gaze wander to the swirling water of the stream racing madly beneath his feet. A piece of dancing driftwood caught his attention and his eyes followed it down the current. How slowly it appeared to move! What a sluggish stream!

He closed his eyes in order to fix his last thoughts upon his

wife and children. The water, touched to gold by the early sun,
the brooding mists under the banks at some distance down the
stream, the fort, the soldiers, the piece of drift—all had dis-
tracted him. And now he became conscious of a new disturbance.
Striking through the thought of his dear ones was a sound which
he could neither ignore nor understand, a sharp, distinct, metal-
lic percussion like the stroke of a blacksmith's hammer upon the
anvil; it had the same ringing quality. He wondered what it
was, and whether immeasurably distant or nearby—it seemed
both. Its recurrence was regular, but as slow as the tolling of a
death knell. He awaited each stroke with impatience and—he
knew not why—apprehension. The intervals of silence grew progressively longer; the delays became maddening. With their
greater infrequency the sounds increased in strength and sharp-
ness. They hurt his ear like the thrust of a knife; he feared he
would shriek. What he heard was the ticking of his watch.

He unclosed his eyes and saw again the water below him. "If
I could free my hands," he thought, "I might throw off the noose
and spring into the stream. By diving I could evade the bullets
and, swimming vigorously, reach the bank, take to the woods
and get away home. My home, thank God, is as yet outside their
lines; my wife and little ones are still beyond the invader's farthest advance."

As these thoughts, which have here to be set down in words,
were flashed into the doomed man's brain rather than evolved
from it the captain nodded to the sergeant. The sergeant stepped
aside.

II

PEYTON FARQUHAR was a well-to-do planter, of an old and highly
respected Alabama family. Being a slave owner and like other
slave owners a politician he was naturally an original seces-
sionist and ardently devoted to the Southern cause. Circumstances of an imperious nature, which it is unnecessary to relate
here, had prevented him from taking service with the gallant
army that had fought the disastrous campaigns ending with the
fall of Corinth, and he chafed under the inglorious restraint,
longing for the release of his energies, the larger life of the soldier, the opportunity for distinction. That opportunity, he felt,
would come, as it comes to all in war time. Meanwhile he did
what he could. No service was too humble for him to perform
in aid of the South, no adventure too perilous for him to under-

take if consistent with the character of a civilian who was at heart a soldier, and who in good faith and without too much qualification assented to at least a part of the frankly villainous dictum that all is fair in love and war.

One evening while Farquhar and his wife were sitting on a rustic bench near the entrance to his grounds, a gray-clad soldier rode up to the gate and asked for a drink of water. Mrs. Farquhar was only too happy to serve him with her own white hands. While she was fetching the water her husband approached the dusty horseman and inquired eagerly for news from the front.

"The Yanks are repairing the railroads," said the man, "and are getting ready for another advance. They have reached the Owl Creek bridge, put it in order and built a stockade on the north bank. The commandant has issued an order, which is posted everywhere, declaring that any civilian caught interfering with the railroad, its bridges, tunnels or trains will be summarily hanged. I saw the order."

"How far is it to the Owl Creek bridge?" Farquhar asked.

"About thirty miles."

"Is there no force on this side the creek?"

"Only a picket post half a mile out, on the railroad, and a single sentinel at this end of the bridge."

"Suppose a man—a civilian and student of hanging—should elude the picket post and perhaps get the better of the sentinel," said Farquhar, smiling, "what could he accomplish?"

The soldier reflected. "I was there a month ago," he replied. "I observed that the flood of last winter had lodged a great quantity of driftwood against the wooden pier at this end of the bridge. It is now dry and would burn like tow."

The lady had now brought the water, which the soldier drank. He thanked her ceremoniously, bowed to her husband and rode away. An hour later, after nightfall, he repassed the plantation, going northward in the direction from which he had come. He was a Federal scout.

III

As PEYTON FARQUHAR fell straight downward through the bridge he lost consciousness and was as one already dead. From this state he was awakened—ages later, it seemed to him—by the pain of a sharp pressure upon his throat, followed by a sense of suffocation. Keen, poignant agonies seemed to shoot from his neck downward through every fibre of his body and limbs. These pains appeared to flash along well-defined lines of ramification and to beat with an inconceivably rapid periodicity. They seemed like streams of pulsating fire heating him to an intolerable temperature. As to his head, he was conscious of nothing but a feeling of fulness—of congestion. These sensations were unaccompanied by thought. The intellectual part of his nature was already effaced; he had power only to feel, and feeling was torment. He was conscious of motion. Encompassed in a luminous cloud, of which he was now merely the fiery heart, without material substance, he swung through unthinkable arcs of oscillation, like a vast pendulum. Then all at once, with terrible suddenness, the light about him shot upward with the noise of a loud plash; a frightful roaring was in his ears, and all was cold and dark. The power of thought was restored; he knew that the rope had broken and he had fallen into the stream. There was no additional strangulation; the noose about his neck was already suffocating him and kept the water from his lungs. To die of hanging at the bottom of a river!—the idea seemed to him ludicrous. He opened his eyes in the darkness and saw above him a gleam of light, but how distant, how inaccessible! He was still sinking, for the light became fainter and fainter until it was a mere glimmer. Then it began to grow and brighten, and he knew that he was rising toward the surface—knew it with reluctance, for he was now very comfortable. "To be hanged and drowned," he thought, "that is not so bad; but I do not wish to be shot. No; I will not be shot; that is not fair."

He was not conscious of an effort, but a sharp pain in his wrist apprised him that he was trying to free his hands. He gave the struggle his attention, as an idler might observe the feat of a juggler, without interest in the outcome. What splendid effort! —what magnificent, what superhuman strength! Ah, that was a fine endeavor! Bravo! The cord fell away; his arms parted and floated upward, the hands dimly seen on each side in the growing light. He watched them with a new interest as first one and then the other pounced upon the noose at his neck. They tore it away and thrust it fiercely aside, its undulations resembling those of a water-snake. "Put it back, put it back!" He thought he shouted these words to his hands, for the undoing of the noose had been succeeded by the direst pang that he had yet experienced. His neck ached horribly; his brain was on fire; his heart, which had been fluttering faintly, gave a great leap, trying to force itself out at his mouth. His whole body was racked and wrenched with an insupportable anguish! But his disobedient hands gave no heed to the command. They beat the water vigorously with quick, downward strokes, forcing him to the surface. He felt his head emerge; his eyes were blinded by the sunlight; his chest expanded convulsively, and with a supreme and crowning agony his lungs engulfed a great draught of air, which instantly he expelled in a shriek!

He was now in full possession of his physical senses. They were, indeed, preternaturally keen and alert. Something in the awful disturbance of his organic system had so exalted and refined them that they made record of things never before perceived. He felt the ripples upon his face and heard their separate sounds as they struck. He looked at the forest on the bank of the stream, saw the individual trees, the leaves and the veining of each leaf—saw the very insects upon them: the locusts, the brilliant-bodied flies, the gray spiders stretching their webs from twig to twig. He noted the prismatic colors in all the dewdrops upon a million blades of grass. The humming of the gnats that danced above the eddies of the stream, the beating of the dragon-flies' wings, the strokes of the water-spiders' legs, like oars which had lifted their boat—all these made audible music. A fish slid along beneath his eyes and he heard the rush of its body parting the water.

He had come to the surface facing down the stream; in a moment the visible world seemed to wheel slowly round, himself the pivotal point, and he saw the bridge, the fort, the soldiers upon the bridge, the captain, the sergeant, the two privates, his executioners. They were in silhouette against the blue sky. They shouted and gesticulated, pointing at him. The captain had drawn his pistol, but did not fire; the others were unarmed. Their movements were grotesque and horrible, their forms gigantic.

Suddenly he heard a sharp report and something struck the water smartly within a few inches of his head, spattering his face with spray. He heard a second report, and saw one of the sentinels with his rifle at his shoulder, a light cloud of blue smoke rising from the muzzle. The man in the water saw the eye of the man on the bridge gazing into his own through the sights of the rifle. He observed that it was a gray eye and remembered having read that gray eyes were keenest, and that all famous marksmen had them. Nevertheless, this one had missed.

A counter-swirl had caught Farquhar and turned him half round; he was again looking into the forest on the bank oppo-

site the fort. The sound of a clear, high voice in a monotonous
singsong now rang out behind him and came across the water
with a distinctness that pierced and subdued all other sounds,
even the beating of the ripples in his ears. Although no soldier,
he had frequented camps enough to know the dread significance
of that deliberate, drawling, aspirated chant; the lieutenant on
shore was taking a part in the morning's work. How coldly and
pitilessly—with what an even, calm intonation, presaging, and
enforcing tranquillity in the men—with what accurately measured intervals fell those cruel words:

"Attention, company! . . . Shoulder arms! . . . Ready! . . . Aim!
. . . Fire!"

Farquhar dived—dived as deeply as he could. The water
roared in his ears like the voice of Niagara, yet he heard the
dulled thunder of the volley and, rising again toward the surface, met shining bits of metal, singularly flattened, oscillating
slowly downward. Some of them touched him on the face and
hands, then fell away, continuing their descent. One lodged between his collar and neck; it was uncomfortably warm and he
snatched it out.

As he rose to the surface, gasping for breath, he saw that he
had been a long time under water; he was perceptibly farther
down stream—nearer to safety. The soldiers had almost finished
reloading; the metal ramrods flashed all at once in the sunshine as they were drawn from the barrels, turned in the air, and
thrust into their sockets. The two sentinels fired again, independently and ineffectually.

The hunted man saw all this over his shoulder; he was now
swimming vigorously with the current. His brain was as ener-
getic as his arms and legs; he thought with the rapidity of lightning.

"The officer," he reasoned, "will not make that martinet's er-
ror a second time. It is as easy to dodge a volley as a single shot.
He has probably already given the command to fire at will.
God help me, I cannot dodge them all!"

An appalling plash within two yards of him was followed by a
loud, rushing sound, *diminuendo,* which seemed to travel back
through the air to the fort and died in an explosion which
stirred the very river to its deeps! A rising sheet of water curved
over him, fell down upon him, blinded him, strangled him! The
cannon had taken a hand in the game. As he shook his head free
from the commotion of the smitten water he heard the deflected

shot humming through the air ahead, and in an instant it was cracking and smashing the branches in the forest beyond.

"They will not do that again," he thought; "the next time they will use a charge of grape. I must keep my eye upon the gun; the smoke will apprise me—the report arrives too late; it lags behind the missile. That is a good gun."

Suddenly he felt himself whirled round and round—spinning like a top. The water, the banks, the forests, the now distant bridge, fort and men—all were commingled and blurred. Objects were represented by their colors only; circular horizontal streaks of color—that was all he saw. He had been caught in a vortex and was being whirled on with a velocity of advance and gyration that made him giddy and sick. In a few moments he was flung upon the gravel at the foot of the left bank of the stream—the southern bank—and behind a projecting point which concealed him from his enemies. The sudden arrest of his motion, the abrasion of one of his hands on the gravel, restored him, and he wept with delight. He dug his fingers into the sand, threw it over himself in handfuls and audibly blessed it. It looked like diamonds, rubies, emeralds; he could think of nothing beautiful which it did not resemble. The trees upon the bank were giant garden plants; he noted a definite order in their arrangement, inhaled the fragrance of their blooms. A strange, roseate light shone through the spaces among their trunks and the wind made in their branches the music of æolian harps. He had no wish to perfect his escape—was content to remain in that enchanting spot until retaken.

A whiz and rattle of grapeshot among the branches high above his head roused him from his dream. The baffled cannoneer had fired him a random farewell. He sprang to his feet, rushed up the sloping bank, and plunged into the forest.

All that day he traveled, laying his course by the rounding sun. The forest seemed interminable; nowhere did he discover a break in it, not even a woodman's road. He had not known that he lived in so wild a region. There was something uncanny in the revelation.

By nightfall he was fatigued, footsore, famishing. The thought of his wife and children urged him on. At last he found a road which led him in what he knew to be the right direction. It was as wide and straight as a city street, yet it seemed untraveled. No fields bordered it, no dwelling anywhere. Not so much as the barking of a dog suggested human habitation. The black bodies of the trees formed a straight wall on both sides, terminating on the horizon in a point, like a diagram in a lesson in perspective. Overhead, as he looked up through this rift in the wood, shone great golden stars looking unfamiliar and grouped in strange constellations. He was sure they were arranged in some order which had a secret and malign significance. The wood on either side was full of singular noises, among which—once, twice, and again—he distinctly heard whispers in an unknown tongue.

His neck was in pain and lifting his hand to it he found it horribly swollen. He knew that it had a circle of black where the rope had bruised it. His eyes felt congested; he could no longer close them. His tongue was swollen with thirst; he relieved its fever by thrusting it forward from between his teeth into the cold air. How softly the turf had carpeted the untraveled avenue—he could no longer feel the roadway beneath his feet!

Doubtless, despite his suffering, he had fallen asleep while walking, for now he sees another scene—perhaps he has merely recovered from a delirium. He stands at the gate of his own home. All is as he left it, and all bright and beautiful in the morning sunshine. He must have traveled the entire night. As he pushes open the gate and passes up the wide white walk, he sees a flutter of female garments; his wife, looking fresh and cool and sweet, steps down from the veranda to meet him. At the bottom of the steps she stands waiting, with a smile of ineffable joy, an attitude of matchless grace and dignity. Ah, how beautiful she is! He springs forward with extended arms. As he is about to clasp her he feels a stunning blow upon the back of the neck; a blinding white light blazes all about him with a sound like the shock of a cannon—then all is darkness and silence!

Peyton Farquhar was dead; his body, with a broken neck, swung gently from side to side beneath the timbers of the Owl Creek bridge.

The Ways of Ghosts

PRESENT AT A HANGING

AN OLD man named Daniel Baker, living near Lebanon, Iowa, was suspected by his neighbors of having murdered a peddler who had obtained permission to pass the night at his house. This was in 1853, when peddling was more common in the Western country than it is now, and was attended with considerable danger. The peddler with his pack traversed the country by all manner of lonely roads, and was compelled to rely upon the country people for hospitality. This brought him into relation with queer characters, some of whom were not altogether scrupulous in their methods of making a living, murder being an acceptable means to that end. It occasionally occurred that a peddler with diminished pack and swollen purse would be traced to the lonely dwelling of some rough character and never could be traced beyond. This was so in the case of "old man Baker," as he was always called. (Such names are given in the western "settlements" only to elderly persons who are not esteemed; to the general disrepute of social unworth is affixed the special reproach of age.) A peddler came to his house and none went away—that is all that anybody knew.

Seven years later the Rev. Mr. Cummings, a Baptist minister well known in that part of the country, was driving by Baker's farm one night. It was not very dark: there was a bit of moon somewhere above the light veil of mist that lay along the earth. Mr. Cummings, who was at all times a cheerful person, was whistling a tune, which he would occasionally interrupt to speak a word of friendly encouragement to his horse. As he came to a little bridge across a dry ravine he saw the figure of a man standing upon it, clearly outlined against the gray background of a misty forest. The man had something strapped on his back and carried a heavy stick—obviously an itinerant peddler. His attitude had in it a suggestion of abstraction, like that of a sleepwalker. Mr. Cummings reined in his horse when he arrived in

59

front of him, gave him a pleasant salutation and invited him to a seat in the vehicle—"if you are going my way," he added. The man raised his head, looked him full in the face, but neither answered nor made any further movement. The minister, with good-natured persistence, repeated his invitation. At this the man threw his right hand forward from his side and pointed downward as he stood on the extreme edge of the bridge. Mr. Cummings looked past him, over into the ravine, saw nothing unusual and withdrew his eyes to address the man again. He had disappeared. The horse, which all this time had been uncommonly restless, gave at the same moment a snort of terror and started to run away. Before he had regained control of the animal the minister was at the crest of the hill a hundred yards along. He looked back and saw the figure again, at the same place and in the same attitude as when he had first observed it. Then for the first time he was conscious of a sense of the supernatural and drove home as rapidly as his willing horse would go.

On arriving at home he related his adventure to his family, and early the next morning, accompanied by two neighbors, John White Corwell and Abner Raiser, returned to the spot. They found the body of old man Baker hanging by the neck from one of the beams of the bridge, immediately beneath the spot where the apparition had stood. A thick coating of dust, slightly dampened by the mist, covered the floor of the bridge, but the only footprints were those of Mr. Cummings' horse.

In taking down the body the men disturbed the loose, friable earth of the slope below it, disclosing human bones already nearly uncovered by the action of water and frost. They were identified as those of the lost peddler. At the double inquest the coroner's jury found that Daniel Baker died by his own hand while suffering from temporary insanity, and that Samuel Morritz was murdered by some person or persons to the jury unknown.

A COLD GREETING

THIS IS a story told by the late Benson Foley of San Francisco:

"In the summer of 1881 I met a man named James H. Conway, a resident of Franklin, Tennessee. He was visiting San Francisco for his health, deluded man, and brought me a note of introduction from Mr. Lawrence Barting. I had known Barting as a captain in the Federal army during the civil war. At its close he had settled in Franklin, and in time became, I had reason to think, somewhat prominent as a lawyer. Barting had always seemed to me an honorable and truthful man, and the warm friendship which he expressed in his note for Mr. Conway was to me sufficient evidence that the latter was in every way worthy of my confidence and esteem. At dinner one day Conway told me that it had been solemnly agreed between him and Barting that the one who died first should, if possible, communicate with the other from beyond the grave, in some unmistakable way—just how, they had left (wisely, it seemed to me) to be decided by the deceased, according to the opportunities that his altered circumstances might present.

"A few weeks after the conversation in which Mr. Conway spoke of this agreement, I met him one day, walking slowly down Montgomery Street, apparently, from his abstracted air, in deep thought. He greeted me coldly with merely a movement of the head and passed on, leaving me standing on the walk, with half-proffered hand, surprised and naturally somewhat piqued. The next day I met him again in the office of the Palace Hotel, and seeing him about to repeat the disagreeable performance of the day before, intercepted him in a doorway, with a friendly salutation, and bluntly requested an explanation of his altered manner. He hesitated a moment; then, looking me frankly in the eyes, said:

" 'I do not think, Mr. Foley, that I have any longer a claim to your friendship, since Mr. Barting appears to have withdrawn his own from me—for what reason, I protest I do not know. If he has not already informed you he probably will do so.'

" 'But,' I replied, 'I have not heard from Mr. Barting.'

" 'Heard from him!' he repeated, with apparent surprise. 'Why, he is here. I met him yesterday ten minutes before meeting you. I gave you exactly the same greeting that he gave me. I met him again not a quarter of an hour ago, and his manner was precisely the same: he merely bowed and passed on. I shall not soon forget your civility to me. Good morning, or—as it may please you—farewell.'

"All this seemed to me singularly considerate and delicate behavior on the part of Mr. Conway.

"As dramatic situations and literary effects are foreign to my purpose I will explain at once that Mr. Barting was dead. He had died in Nashville four days before this conversation. Calling on Mr. Conway, I apprised him of our friend's death, showing him the letters announcing it. He was visibly affected in a way that forbade me to entertain a doubt of his sincerity.

" 'It seems incredible,' he said, after a period of reflection. 'I suppose I must have mistaken another man for Barting, and that man's cold greeting was merely a stranger's civil acknowledgment of my own. I remember, indeed, that he lacked Barting's mustache.'

" 'Doubtless it was another man,' I assented; and the subject was never afterward mentioned between us. But I had in my pocket a photograph of Barting, which had been inclosed in the letter from his widow. It had been taken a week before his death, and was without a mustache.

A WIRELESS MESSAGE

IN THE summer of 1896 Mr. William Holt, a wealthy manufacturer of Chicago, was living temporarily in a little town of central New York, the name of which the writer's memory has not retained. Mr. Holt had had "trouble with his wife," from whom he had parted a year before. Whether the trouble was anything more serious than "incompatibility of temper," he is probably the only living person that knows: he is not addicted to the vice of confidences. Yet he has related the incident herein set down to at least one person without exacting a pledge of secrecy. He is now living in Europe.

One evening he had left the house of a brother whom he was visiting, for a stroll in the country. It may be assumed—whatever the value of the assumption in connection with what is said to have occurred—that his mind was occupied with reflections on his domestic infelicities and the distressing changes that they had wrought in his life. Whatever may have been his thoughts, they so possessed him that he observed neither the lapse of time nor whither his feet were carrying him; he knew only that he had passed far beyond the town limits and was traversing a lonely region by a road that bore no resemblance to the one by which he had left the village. In brief, he was "lost."

Realizing his mischance, he smiled; central New York is not a region of perils, nor does one long remain lost in it. He turned about and went back the way that he had come. Before he had gone far he observed that the landscape was growing more distinct—was brightening. Everything was suffused with a soft, red glow in which he saw his shadow projected in the road before him. "The moon is rising," he said to himself. Then he remembered that it was about the time of the new moon, and if that tricksy orb was in one of its stages of visibility it had set long before. He stopped and faced about, seeking the source of the rapidly broadening light. As he did so, his shadow turned and lay along the road in front of him as before. The light still came from behind him. That was surprising; he could not understand. Again he turned, and again, facing successively to every point of the horizon. Always the shadow was before—always the light behind, "a still and awful red."

Holt was astonished—"dumfounded" is the word that he used in telling it—yet seems to have retained a certain intelligent curiosity. To test the intensity of the light whose nature and cause he could not determine, he took out his watch to see if he could make out the figures on the dial. They were plainly visible, and the hands indicated the hour of eleven o'clock and twenty-five minutes. At that moment the mysterious illumination suddenly flared to an intense, an almost blinding splendor, flushing the entire sky, extinguishing the stars and throwing the monstrous shadow of himself athwart the landscape. In that unearthly illumination he saw near him, but apparently in the air at a considerable elevation, the figure of his wife, clad in her nightclothing and holding to her breast the figure of his child. Her eyes were fixed upon his with an expression which he afterward professed himself unable to name or describe, further than that it was "not of this life."

The flare was momentary, followed by black darkness, in which, however, the apparition still showed white and motionless; then by insensible degrees it faded and vanished, like a bright image on the retina after the closing of the eyes. A peculiarity of the apparition, hardly noted at the time, but afterward recalled, was that it showed only the upper half of the woman's figure: nothing was seen below the waist.

The sudden darkness was comparative, not absolute, for gradually all objects of his environment became again visible.

In the dawn of the morning Holt found himself entering the village at a point opposite to that at which he had left it. He soon arrived at the house of his brother, who hardly knew him. He was wild-eyed, haggard, and gray as a rat. Almost incoherently, he related his night's experience.

"Go to bed, my poor fellow," said his brother, "and—wait. We shall hear more of this."

An hour later came the predestined telegram. Holt's dwelling in one of the suburbs of Chicago had been destroyed by fire. Her escape cut off by the flames, his wife had appeared at an upper window, her child in her arms. There she had stood, motionless, apparently dazed. Just as the firemen had arrived with a ladder, the floor had given way, and she was seen no more.

The moment of this culminating horror was eleven o'clock and twenty-five minutes, standard time.

AN ARREST

HAVING MURDERED his brother-in-law, Orrin Brower of Kentucky was a fugitive from justice. From the county jail where he had been confined to await his trial he had escaped by knocking down his jailer with an iron bar, robbing him of his keys and, opening the outer door, walking out into the night. The jailer being unarmed, Brower got no weapon with which to defend his recovered liberty. As soon as he was out of the town he had the folly to enter a forest; this was many years ago, when that region was wilder than it is now.

The night was pretty dark, with neither moon nor stars visible, and as Brower had never dwelt thereabout, and knew nothing of the lay of the land, he was, naturally, not long in losing himself. He could not have said if he were getting farther away from the town or going back to it—a most important matter to Orrin Brower. He knew that in either case a posse of citizens with a pack of bloodhounds would soon be on his track and his chance of escape was very slender; but he did not wish to assist in his own pursuit. Even an added hour of freedom was worth having.

Suddenly he emerged from the forest into an old road, and there before him saw, indistinctly, the figure of a man, motionless in the gloom. It was too late to retreat: the fugitive felt that at the first movement back toward the wood he would be, as he afterward explained, "filled with buckshot." So the two stood there like trees, Brower nearly suffocated by the activity of his own heart; the other—the emotions of the other are not recorded.

A moment later—it may have been an hour—the moon sailed into a patch of unclouded sky and the hunted man saw that visible embodiment of Law lift an arm and point significantly toward and beyond him. He understood. Turning his back to his captor, he walked submissively away in the direction indicated, looking to neither the right nor the left; hardly daring to breathe, his head and back actually aching with a prophecy of buckshot.

Brower was as courageous a criminal as ever lived to be hanged; that was shown by the conditions of awful personal peril in which he had coolly killed his brother-in-law. It is needless to relate them here; they came out at his trial, and the revelation of his calmness in confronting them came near to saving his neck. But what would you have?—when a brave man is beaten, he submits.

So they pursued their journey jailward along the old road through the woods. Only once did Brower venture a turn of the head: just once, when he was in deep shadow and he knew that the other was in moonlight, he looked backward. His captor was Burton Duff, the jailer, as white as death and bearing upon his brow the livid mark of the iron bar. Orrin Brower had no further curiosity.

Eventually they entered the town, which was all alight, but deserted; only the women and children remained, and they were off the streets. Straight toward the jail the criminal held his way. Straight up to the main entrance he walked, laid his hand upon the knob of the heavy iron door, pushed it open without command, entered and found himself in the presence of a half-dozen armed men. Then he turned. Nobody else entered.

On a table in the corridor lay the dead body of Burton Duff.

Some Haunted Houses

THE ISLE OF PINES

FOR MANY years there lived near the town of Gallipolis, Ohio, an old man named Herman Deluse. Very little was known of his history, for he would neither speak of it himself nor suffer others. It was a common belief among his neighbors that he had been a pirate—if upon any better evidence than his collection of boarding pikes, cutlasses, and ancient flintlock pistols, no one knew. He lived entirely alone in a small house of four rooms, falling rapidly into decay and never repaired further than was required by the weather. It stood on a slight elevation in the midst of a large, stony field overgrown with brambles, and cultivated in patches and only in the most primitive way. It was his only visible property, but could hardly have yielded him a living, simple and few as were his wants. He seemed always to have ready money, and paid cash for all his purchases at the village stores roundabout, seldom buying more than two or three times at the same place until after the lapse of a considerable time. He got no commendation, however, for this equitable distribution of his patronage; people were disposed to regard it as an ineffectual attempt to conceal his possession of so much money. That he had great hoards of ill-gotten gold buried somewhere about his tumble-down dwelling was not reasonably to be doubted by any honest soul conversant with the facts of local tradition and gifted with a sense of the fitness of things.

On the 9th of November, 1867, the old man died; at least his dead body was discovered on the 10th, and physicians testified that death had occurred about twenty-four hours previously—precisely how, they were unable to say; for the *post-mortem* examination showed every organ to be absolutely healthy, with no indication of disorder or violence. According to them, death must have taken place about noonday, yet the body was found in bed. The verdict of the coroner's jury was that he "came to his death by a visitation of God." The body was buried and the public administrator took charge of the estate.

A rigorous search disclosed nothing more than was already known about the dead man, and much patient excavation here and there about the premises by thoughtful and thrifty neighbors went unrewarded. The administrator locked up the house against the time when the property, real and personal, should be sold by law with a view to defraying, partly, the expenses of the sale.

The night of November 20 was boisterous. A furious gale stormed across the country, scourging it with desolating drifts of sleet. Great trees were torn from the earth and hurled across the roads. So wild a night had never been known in all that region, but toward morning the storm had blown itself out of breath and day dawned bright and clear. At about eight o'clock that morning the Rev. Henry Galbraith, a well-known and highly esteemed Lutheran minister, arrived on foot at his house, a mile and a half from the Deluse place. Mr. Galbraith had been for a month in Cincinnati. He had come up the river in a steamboat, and landing at Gallipolis the previous evening had immediately obtained a horse and buggy and set out for home. The violence of the storm had delayed him over night, and in the morning the fallen trees had compelled him to abandon his conveyance and continue his journey afoot.

"But where did you pass the night?" inquired his wife, after he had briefly related his adventure.

"With old Deluse at the 'Isle of Pines,' "* was the laughing reply; "and a glum enough time I had of it. He made no objection to my remaining, but not a word could I get out of him."

Fortunately for the interests of truth there was present at this conversation Mr. Robert Mosely Maren, a lawyer and *littérateur* of Columbus, the same who wrote the delightful "Mellowcraft Papers." Noting, but apparently not sharing, the astonishment caused by Mr. Galbraith's answer this ready-witted person checked by a gesture the exclamations that would naturally have followed, and tranquilly inquired: "How came you to go in there?"

This is Mr. Maren's version of Mr. Galbraith's reply:

"I saw a light moving about the house, and being nearly blinded by the sleet, and half frozen besides, drove in at the gate and put up my horse in the old rail stable, where it is now. I then rapped at the door, and getting no invitation went in

---

*The Isle of Pines was once a famous rendezvous of pirates.

without one. The room was dark, but having matches I found a candle and lit it. I tried to enter the adjoining room, but the door was fast, and although I heard the old man's heavy footsteps in there he made no response to my calls. There was no fire on the hearth, so I made one and laying [*sic*] down before it with my overcoat under my head, prepared myself for sleep. Pretty soon the door that I had tried silently opened and the old man came in, carrying a candle. I spoke to him pleasantly, apologizing for my intrusion, but he took no notice of me. He seemed to be searching for something, though his eyes were unmoved in their sockets. I wonder if he ever walks in his sleep. He took a circuit a part of the way round the room, and went out the same way he had come in. Twice more before I slept he came back into the room, acting precisely the same way, and departing as at first. In the intervals I heard him tramping all over the house, his footsteps distinctly audible in the pauses of the storm. When I woke in the morning he had already gone out."

Mr. Maren attempted some further questioning, but was unable longer to restrain the family's tongues; the story of Deluse's death and burial came out, greatly to the good minister's astonishment.

"The explanation of your adventure is very simple," said Mr. Maren. "I don't believe old Deluse walks in his sleep—not in his present one; but you evidently dream in yours."

And to this view of the matter Mr. Galbraith was compelled reluctantly to assent.

Nevertheless, a late hour of the next night found these two gentlemen, accompanied by a son of the minister, in the road in front of the old Deluse house. There was a light inside; it appeared now at one window and now at another. The three men advanced to the door. Just as they reached it there came from the interior a confusion of the most appalling sounds—the clash of weapons, steel against steel, sharp explosions as of firearms, shrieks of women, groans and the curses of men in combat! The investigators stood a moment, irresolute, frightened. Then Mr. Galbraith tried the door. It was fast. But the minister was a man of courage, a man, moreover, of Herculean strength. He retired a pace or two and rushed against the door, striking it with his right shoulder and bursting it from the frame with a loud crash. In a moment the three were inside. Darkness and silence! The only sound was the beating of their hearts.

Mr. Maren had provided himself with matches and a candle.

With some difficulty, begotten of his excitement, he made a light, and they proceeded to explore the place, passing from room to room. Everything was in orderly arrangement, as it had been left by the sheriff; nothing had been disturbed. A light coating of dust was everywhere. A back door was partly open, as if by neglect, and their first thought was that the authors of the awful revelry might have escaped. The door was opened, and the light of the candle shone through upon the ground. The expiring effort of the previous night's storm had been a light fall of snow; there were no footprints; the white surface was unbroken. They closed the door and entered the last room of the four that the house contained—that farthest from the road, in an angle of the building. Here the candle in Mr. Maren's hand was suddenly extinguished as by a draught of air. Almost immediately followed the sound of a heavy fall. When the candle had been hastily relighted young Mr. Galbraith was seen prostrate on the floor at a little distance from the others. He was dead. In one hand the body grasped a heavy sack of coins, which later examination showed to be all of old Spanish mintage. Directly over the body as it lay, a board had been torn from its fastenings in the wall, and from the cavity so disclosed it was evident that the bag had been taken.

Another inquest was held: another *post-mortem* examination failed to reveal a probable cause of death. Another verdict of "the visitation of God" left all at liberty to form their own conclusions. Mr. Maren contended that the young man died of excitement.

A FRUITLESS ASSIGNMENT

HENRY SAYLOR, who was killed in Covington, in a quarrel with Antonio Finch, was a reporter on the Cincinnati *Commercial*. In the year 1859 a vacant dwelling in Vine street, in Cincinnati, became the center of a local excitement because of the strange sights and sounds said to be observed in it nightly. According to the testimony of many reputable residents of the vicinity these were inconsistent with any other hypothesis than that the house was haunted. Figures with something singularly unfamiliar about them were seen by crowds on the sidewalk to pass in and out. No one could say just where they appeared upon the open lawn on their way to the front door by which they entered, nor at exactly what point they vanished as they came out; or, rather, while each spectator was positive enough about these matters, no two agreed. They were all similarly at variance in their descriptions of the figures themselves. Some of the bolder of the curious throng ventured on several evenings to stand upon the doorsteps to intercept them, or failing in this, get a nearer look at them. These courageous men, it was said, were unable to force the door by their united strength, and always were hurled from the steps by some invisible agency and severely injured; the door immediately afterward opening, apparently of its own volition, to admit or free some ghostly guest. The dwelling was known as the Roscoe house, a family of that name having lived there for some years, and then, one by one, disappeared, the last to leave being an old woman. Stories of foul play and successive murders had always been rife, but never were authenticated.

One day during the prevalence of the excitement Saylor presented himself at the office of the *Commercial* for orders. He received a note from the city editor which read as follows: "Go and pass the night alone in the haunted house in Vine street and if anything occurs worth while make two columns." Saylor obeyed his superior; he could not afford to lose his position on the paper.

Apprising the police of his intention, he effected an entrance through a rear window before dark, walked through the deserted rooms, bare of furniture, dusty and desolate, and seating himself at last in the parlor on an old sofa which he had dragged in from another room watched the deepening of the gloom as night came on. Before it was altogether dark the curious crowd had collected in the street, silent, as a rule, and expectant, with here and there a scoffer uttering his incredulity and courage with scornful remarks or ribald cries. None knew of the anxious watcher inside. He feared to make a light; the uncurtained windows would have betrayed his presence, subjecting him to insult, possibly to injury. Moreover, he was too conscientious to do anything to enfeeble his impressions and unwilling to alter any of the customary conditions under which the manifestations were said to occur.

It was now dark outside, but light from the street faintly illuminated the part of the room that he was in. He had set open every door in the whole interior, above and below, but all the outer ones were locked and bolted. Sudden exclamations from the crowd caused him to spring to the window and look out. He saw the figure of a man moving rapidly across the lawn toward the building—saw it ascend the steps; then a projection of the wall concealed it. There was a noise as of the opening and closing of the hall door; he heard quick, heavy footsteps along the passage—heard them ascend the stairs—heard them on the uncarpeted floor of the chamber immediately overhead.

Saylor promptly drew his pistol, and groping his way up the stairs entered the chamber, dimly lighted from the street. No one was there. He heard footsteps in an adjoining room and entered that. It was dark and silent. He struck his foot against some object on the floor, knelt by it, passed his hand over it. It was a human head—that of a woman. Lifting it by the hair this iron-nerved man returned to the half-lighted room below, carried it near the window and attentively examined it. While so engaged he was half conscious of the rapid opening and closing of the outer door, of footfalls sounding all about him. He raised his eyes from the ghastly object of his attention and saw himself the center of a crowd of men and women dimly seen; the room was thronged with them. He thought the people had broken in.

"Ladies and gentlemen," he said, coolly, "you see me under suspicious circumstances, but——" his voice was drowned in peals of laughter—such laughter as is heard in asylums for the insane. The persons about him pointed at the object in his hand and their merriment increased as he dropped it and it went rolling among their feet. They danced about it with gestures grotesque and attitudes obscene and indescribable. They struck it with their feet, urging it about the room from wall to wall; pushed and overthrew one another in their struggles to kick it; cursed and screamed and sang snatches of ribald songs as the battered head bounded about the room as if in terror and trying to escape. At last it shot out of the door into the hall, followed by all, with tumultuous haste. That moment the door closed with a sharp concussion. Saylor was alone, in dead silence.

Carefully putting away his pistol, which all the time he had held in his hand, he went to a window and looked out. The street was deserted and silent; the lamps were extinguished; the roofs and chimneys of the houses were sharply outlined against the dawn-light in the east. He left the house, the door yielding easily to his hand, and walked to the *Commercial* office. The city editor was still in his office—asleep. Saylor waked him and said: "I have been at the haunted house."

The editor stared blankly as if not wholly awake. "Good God!" he cried, "are you Saylor?"

"Yes—why not?"

The editor made no answer, but continued staring.

"I passed the night there—it seems," said Saylor.

"They say that things were uncommonly quiet out there," the editor said, trifling with a paper-weight upon which he had dropped his eyes. "Did anything occur?"

"Nothing whatever."

A VINE ON A HOUSE

ABOUT THREE miles from the little town of Norton, in Missouri, on the road leading to Maysville, stands an old house that was last occupied by a family named Harding. Since 1886 no one has lived in it, nor is anyone likely to live in it again. Time and the disfavor of persons dwelling thereabout are converting it into a rather picturesque ruin. An observer unacquainted with its history would hardly put it into the category of "haunted houses," yet in all the region round such is its evil reputation. Its windows are without glass, its doorways without doors; there are wide breaches in the shingle roof, and for lack of paint the weatherboarding is a dun gray. But these unfailing signs of the supernatural are partly concealed and greatly softened by the abundant foliage of a large vine overrunning the entire structure. This vine—of a species which no botanist has ever been able to name—has an important part in the story of the house.

The Harding family consisted of Robert Harding, his wife Matilda, Miss Julia Went, who was her sister, and two young children. Robert Harding was a silent, cold-mannered man who made no friends in the neighborhood and apparently cared to make none. He was about forty years old, frugal and industrious, and made a living from the little farm which is now overgrown with brush and brambles. He and his sister-in-law were rather tabooed by their neighbors, who seemed to think that they were seen too frequently together—not entirely their fault, for at these times they evidently did not challenge observation. The moral code of rural Missouri is stern and exacting.

Mrs. Harding was a gentle, sad-eyed woman, lacking a left foot.

At some time in 1884 it became known that she had gone to visit her mother in Iowa. That was what her husband said in reply to inquiries, and his manner of saying it did not encourage further questioning. She never came back, and two years later, without selling his farm or anything that was his, or appointing an agent to look after his interests, or removing his household goods, Harding, with the rest of the family, left the country. Nobody knew whither he went; nobody at that time cared. Naturally, whatever was movable about the place soon disappeared and the deserted house became "haunted" in the manner of its kind.

One summer evening, four or five years later, the Rev. J. Gruber, of Norton, and a Maysville attorney named Hyatt met on horseback in front of the Harding place. Having business matters to discuss, they hitched their animals and going to the house sat on the porch to talk. Some humorous reference to the somber reputation of the place was made and forgotten as soon as uttered, and they talked of their business affairs until it grew almost dark. The evening was oppressively warm, the air stagnant.

Presently both men started from their seats in surprise: a long vine that covered half the front of the house and dangled its branches from the edge of the porch above them was visibly and audibly agitated, shaking violently in every stem and leaf.

"We shall have a storm," Hyatt exclaimed.

Gruber said nothing, but silently directed the other's attention to the foliage of adjacent trees, which showed no movement; even the delicate tips of the boughs silhouetted against the clear sky were motionless. They hastily passed down the steps to what had been a lawn and looked upward at the vine, whose entire length was now visible. It continued in violent agitation, yet they could discern no disturbing cause.

"Let us leave," said the minister.

And leave they did. Forgetting that they had been traveling in opposite directions, they rode away together. They went to Norton, where they related their strange experience to several discreet friends. The next evening, at about the same hour, accompanied by two others whose names are not recalled, they were again on the porch of the Harding house, and again the mysterious phenomenon occurred: the vine was violently agitated while under the closest scrutiny from root to tip, nor did their combined strength applied to the trunk serve to still it. After an hour's observation they retreated, no less wise, it is thought, than when they had come.

No great time was required for these singular facts to rouse the curiosity of the entire neighborhood. By day and by night crowds of persons assembled at the Harding house "seeking a sign." It does not appear that any found it, yet so credible were the witnesses mentioned that none doubted the reality of the "manifestations" to which they testified.

By either a happy inspiration or some destructive design, it was one day proposed—nobody appeared to know from whom the suggestion came—to dig up the vine, and after a good deal of debate this was done. Nothing was found but the root, yet nothing could have been more strange!

For five or six feet from the trunk, which had at the surface of the ground a diameter of several inches, it ran downward, single and straight, into a loose, friable earth; then it divided and sub-divided into rootlets, fibers and filaments, most curiously inter-woven. When carefully freed from soil they showed a singular formation. In their ramifications and doublings back upon them-selves they made a compact network, having in size and shape an amazing resemblance to the human figure. Head, trunk and limbs were there; even the fingers and toes were distinctly de-fined; and many professed to see in the distribution and arrange-ment of the fibers in the globular mass representing the head a grotesque suggestion of a face. The figure was horizontal; the smaller roots had begun to unite at the breast.

In point of resemblance to the human form this image was imperfect. At about ten inches from one of the knees, the *cilia* forming that leg had abruptly doubled backward and inward upon their course of growth. The figure lacked the left foot.

There was but one inference—the obvious one; but in the en-suing excitement as many courses of action were proposed as there were incapable counselors. The matter was settled by the sheriff of the county, who as the lawful custodian of the aban-doned estate ordered the root replaced and the excavation filled with the earth that had been removed.

Later inquiry brought out only one fact of relevancy and sig-nificance: Mrs. Harding had never visited her relatives in Iowa, nor did they know that she was supposed to have done so.

Of Robert Harding and the rest of his family nothing is known. The house retains its evil reputation, but the replanted vine is as orderly and well-behaved a vegetable as a nervous per-son could wish to sit under of a pleasant night, when the katy-dids grate out their immemorial revelation and the distant whippoorwill signifies his notion of what ought to be done about it.

AT OLD MAN ECKERT'S

PHILIP ECKERT lived for many years in an old, weather-stained wooden house about three miles from the little town of Marion, in Vermont. There must be quite a number of persons living who remember him, not unkindly, I trust, and know something of the story that I am about to tell.

"Old Man Eckert," as he was always called, was not of a sociable disposition and lived alone. As he was never known to speak of his own affairs nobody thereabout knew anything of his past, nor of his relatives if he had any. Without being particularly ungracious or repellent in manner or speech, he managed somehow to be immune to impertinent curiosity, yet exempt from the evil repute with which it commonly revenges itself when baffled; so far as I know, Mr. Eckert's renown as a reformed assassin or a retired pirate of the Spanish Main had not reached any ear in Marion. He got his living cultivating a small and not very fertile farm.

One day he disappeared and a prolonged search by his neighbors failed to turn him up or throw any light upon his whereabouts or whyabouts. Nothing indicated preparation to leave: all was as he might have left it to go to the spring for a bucket of water. For a few weeks little else was talked of in that region; then "old man Eckert" became a village tale for the ear of the stranger. I do not know what was done regarding his property—the correct legal thing, doubtless. The house was standing, still vacant and conspicuously unfit, when I last heard of it, some twenty years afterward.

Of course it came to be considered "haunted," and the customary tales were told of moving lights, dolorous sounds and startling apparitions. At one time, about five years after the disappearance, these stories of the supernatural became so rife, or through some attesting circumstances seemed so important, that some of Marion's most serious citizens deemed it well to investigate, and to that end arranged for a night session on the premises. The parties to this undertaking were John Holcomb, an apothecary; Wilson Merle, a lawyer; and Andrus C. Palmer, the teacher of the public school, all men of consequence and repute. They were to meet at Holcomb's house at eight o'clock in the evening of the appointed day and go together to the scene of their vigil, where certain arrangements for their comfort, a provision of fuel and the like, for the season was winter, had been already made.

Palmer did not keep the engagement, and after waiting a half-hour for him the others went to the Eckert house without him. They established themselves in the principal room, before a glowing fire, and without other light than it gave, awaited events. It had been agreed to speak as little as possible: they did not even renew the exchange of views regarding the defection of Palmer, which had occupied their minds on the way.

Probably an hour had passed without incident when they

heard (not without emotion, doubtless) the sound of an opening door in the rear of the house, followed by footfalls in the room adjoining that in which they sat. The watchers rose to their feet, but stood firm, prepared for whatever might ensue. A long silence followed—how long neither would afterward undertake to say. Then the door between the two rooms opened and a man entered.

It was Palmer. He was pale, as if from excitement—as pale as the others felt themselves to be. His manner, too, was singularly distrait: he neither responded to their salutations nor so much as looked at them, but walked slowly across the room in the light of the failing fire and opening the front door passed out into the darkness.

It seems to have been the first thought of both men that Palmer was suffering from fright—that something seen, heard or imagined in the back room had deprived him of his senses. Acting on the same friendly impulse both ran after him through the open door. But neither they nor anyone ever again saw or heard of Andrus Palmer!

This much was ascertained the next morning. During the session of Messrs. Holcomb and Merle at the "haunted house" a new snow had fallen to a depth of several inches upon the old. In this snow Palmer's trail from his lodging in the village to the back door of the Eckert house was conspicuous. But there it ended: from the front door nothing led away but the tracks of the two men who swore that he preceded them. Palmer's disappearance was as complete as that of "old man Eckert" himself—whom, indeed, the editor of the local paper somewhat graphically accused of having "reached out and pulled him in."

THE SPOOK HOUSE

ON THE road leading north from Manchester, in eastern Kentucky, to Booneville, twenty miles away, stood, in 1862, a wooden plantation house of a somewhat better quality than most of the dwellings in that region. The house was destroyed by fire in the year following—probably by some stragglers from the retreating column of General George W. Morgan, when he was driven from Cumberland Gap to the Ohio river by General Kirby Smith. At the time of its destruction, it had for four or five years been vacant. The fields about it were overgrown with brambles, the fences gone, even the few negro quarters, and outhouses gener-

ally, fallen partly into ruin by neglect and pillage; for the Negroes and poor whites of the vicinity found in the building and
fences an abundant supply of fuel, of which they availed themselves without hesitation, openly and by daylight. By daylight
alone; after nightfall no human being except passing strangers
ever went near the place.

It was known as the "Spook House." That it was tenanted by
evil spirits, visible, audible and active, no one in all that region
doubted any more than he doubted what he was told of Sundays
by the traveling preacher. Its owner's opinion of the matter was
unknown; he and his family had disappeared one night and no
trace of them had ever been found. They left everything—household goods, clothing, provisions, the horses in the stable, the cows
in the field, the Negroes in the quarters—all as it stood; nothing
was missing—except a man, a woman, three girls, a boy and a
babe! It was not altogether surprising that a plantation where
seven human beings could be simultaneously effaced and nobody the wiser should be under some suspicion.

One night in June, 1859, two citizens of Frankfort, Col. J. C.
McArdle, a lawyer, and Judge Myron Veigh, of the State Mili-
tia, were driving from Booneville to Manchester. Their business was so important that they decided to push on, despite the
darkness and the mutterings of an approaching storm, which
eventually broke upon them just as they arrived opposite the
"Spook House." The lightning was so incessant that they easily
found their way through the gateway and into a shed, where
they hitched and unharnessed their team. They then went to the
house, through the rain, and knocked at all the doors without
getting any response. Attributing this to the continuous uproar
of the thunder they pushed at one of the doors, which yielded.
They entered without further ceremony and closed the door.
That instant they were in darkness and silence. Not a gleam of
the lightning's unceasing blaze penetrated the windows or crev-
ices; not a whisper of the awful tumult without reached them
there. It was as if they had suddenly been stricken blind and
deaf, and McArdle afterward said that for a moment he believed
himself to have been killed by a stroke of lightning as he crossed
the threshold. The rest of this adventure can as well be related
in his own words, from the Frankfort *Advocate* of August 6, 1876:

"When I had somewhat recovered from the dazing effect of the
transition from uproar to silence, my first impulse was to reopen
the door which I had closed, and from the knob of which I was
not conscious of having removed my hand; I felt it distinctly,

still in the clasp of my fingers. My notion was to ascertain by stepping again into the storm whether I had been deprived of sight and hearing. I turned the door-knob and pulled open the door. It led into another room!

"This apartment was suffused with a faint greenish light, the source of which I could not determine, making everything distinctly visible, though nothing was sharply defined. Everything, I say, but in truth the only objects within the blank stone walls of that room were human corpses. In number they were perhaps eight or ten—it may well be understood that I did not truly count them. They were of different ages, or rather sizes, from infancy up, and of both sexes. All were prostrate on the floor, excepting one, apparently a young woman, who sat up, her back supported by an angle of the wall. A babe was clasped in the arms of another and older woman. A half-grown lad lay face downward across the legs of a full-bearded man. One or two were nearly naked, and the hand of a young girl held the fragment of a gown which she had torn open at the breast. The bodies were in various stages of decay, all greatly shrunken in face and figure. Some were but little more than skeletons.

"While I stood stupefied with horror by this ghastly spectacle and still holding open the door, by some unaccountable perversity my attention was diverted from the shocking scene and concerned itself with trifles and details. Perhaps my mind, with an instinct of self-preservation, sought relief in matters which would relax its dangerous tension. Among other things, I observed that the door that I was holding open was of heavy iron plates, riveted. Equidistant from one another and from the top and bottom, three strong bolts protruded from the beveled edge. I turned the knob and they were retracted flush with the edge; released it, and they shot out. It was a spring lock. On the inside there was no knob, nor any kind of projection—a smooth surface of iron.

"While noting these things with an interest and attention which it now astonishes me to recall, I felt myself thrust aside, and Judge Veigh, whom in the intensity and vicissitudes of my feelings I had altogether forgotten, pushed by me into the room. 'For God's sake,' I cried, 'do not go in there! Let us get out of this dreadful place!'

"He gave no heed to my entreaties, but (as fearless a gentleman as lived in all the South) walked quickly to the center of the room, knelt beside one of the bodies for a closer examination and tenderly raised its blackened and shriveled head in his hands. A strong disagreeable odor came through the doorway, completely overpowering me. My senses reeled; I felt myself falling, and in clutching at the edge of the door for support pushed it shut with a sharp click!

"I remember no more: six weeks later I recovered my reason in a hotel at Manchester, whither I had been taken by strangers the next day. For all these weeks I had suffered from a nervous fever, attended with constant delirium. I had been found lying in the road several miles away from the house; but how I had escaped from it to get there I never knew. On recovery, or as soon as my physicians permitted me to talk, I inquired the fate of Judge Veigh, whom (to quiet me, as I now know) they represented as well and at home.

"No one believed a word of my story, and who can wonder? And who can imagine my grief when, arriving at my home in Frankfort two months later, I learned that Judge Veigh had never been heard of since that night? I then regretted bitterly the pride which since the first few days after the recovery of my reason had forbidden me to repeat my discredited story and insist upon its truth.

"With all that afterward occurred—the examination of the house; the failure to find any room corresponding to that which I have described; the attempt to have me adjudged insane, and my triumph over my accusers—the readers of the *Advocate* are familiar. After all these years I am still confident that excavations which I have neither the legal right to undertake nor the wealth to make would disclose the secret of the disappearance of my unhappy friend, and possibly of the former occupants and owners of the deserted and now destroyed house. I do not despair of yet bringing about such a search, and it is a source of deep grief to me that it has been delayed by the undeserved hostility and unwise incredulity of the family and friends of the late Judge Veigh."

Colonel McArdle died in Frankfort on the thirteenth day of December, in the year 1879.

THE OTHER LODGERS

"In order to take that train," said Colonel Levering, sitting in the Waldorf-Astoria hotel, "you will have to remain nearly all night in Atlanta. That is a fine city, but I advise you not to put up at the Breathitt House, one of the principal hotels. It is an old wooden building in urgent need of repairs. There are breaches in the walls that you could throw a cat through. The bedrooms have no locks on the doors, no furniture but a single chair in each, and a bedstead without bedding—just a mattress. Even these meager accommodations you cannot be sure that you will have in monopoly; you must take your chance of being stowed in with a lot of others. Sir, it is a most abominable hotel.

"The night that I passed in it was an uncomfortable night. I got in late and was shown to my room on the ground floor by an apologetic night-clerk with a tallow candle, which he considerately left with me. I was worn out by two days and a night of hard railway travel and had not entirely recovered from a gunshot wound in the head, received in an altercation. Rather than look for better quarters I lay down on the mattress without removing my clothing and fell asleep.

"Along toward morning I awoke. The moon had risen and was shining in at the uncurtained window, illuminating the room with a soft, bluish light which seemed, somehow, a bit spooky, though I dare say it had no uncommon quality; all moonlight is that way if you will observe it. Imagine my surprise and indignation when I saw the floor occupied by at least a dozen other lodgers! I sat up, earnestly damning the management of that unthinkable hotel, and was about to spring from the bed to go and make trouble for the night-clerk—him of the apologetic manner and the tallow candle—when something in the situation affected me with a strange indisposition to move. I suppose I was what a story-writer might call 'frozen with terror.' For those men were obviously all dead!

"They lay on their backs, disposed orderly along three sides of the room, their feet to the walls—against the other wall, farthest from the door, stood my bed and the chair. All the faces were covered, but under their white cloths the features of the two bodies that lay in the square patch of moonlight near the window showed in sharp profile as to nose and chin.

"I thought this a bad dream and tried to cry out, as one does in a nightmare, but could make no sound. At last, with a desperate effort I threw my feet to the floor and passing between the two rows of clouted faces and the two bodies that lay nearest the door, I escaped from the infernal place and ran to the office. The night-clerk was there, behind the desk, sitting in the dim light of another tallow candle—just sitting and staring. He did not rise: my abrupt entrance produced no effect upon him, though I must have looked a veritable corpse myself. It occurred to me then that I had not before really observed the fellow. He was a little chap, with a colorless face and the whitest, blankest eyes I ever saw. He had no more expression than the back of my hand. His clothing was a dirty gray.

" 'Damn you!' I said; 'what do you mean?'

"Just the same, I was shaking like a leaf in the wind and did not recognize my own voice.

The night-clerk rose, bowed (apologetically) and—well, he was no longer there, and at that moment I felt a hand laid upon my shoulder from behind. Just fancy that if you can! Unspeakably frightened, I turned and saw a portly, kind-faced gentleman, who asked:

" 'What is the matter, my friend?'

"I was not long in telling him, but before I made an end of it he went pale himself. 'See here,' he said, 'are you telling the truth?'

"I had now got myself in hand and terror had given place to indignation. 'If you dare to doubt it,' I said, 'I'll hammer the life out of you!'

" 'No,' he replied, 'don't do that; just sit down till I tell you. This is not a hotel. It used to be; afterward it was a hospital. Now it is unoccupied, awaiting a tenant. The room that you mention was the dead-room—there were always plenty of dead. The fellow that you call the night clerk used to be that, but later he booked the patients as they were brought in. I don't understand his being here. He has been dead a few weeks.'

" 'And who are you?' I blurted out.

" 'Oh, I look after the premises. I happened to be passing just now, and seeing a light in here came in to investigate. Let us have a look into that room,' he added, lifting the sputtering candle from the desk.

" 'I'll see you at the devil first!' said I, bolting out of the door into the street.

"Sir, that Breathitt House, in Atlanta, is a beastly place! Don't you stop there."

"God forbid! Your account of it certainly does not suggest comfort. By the way, Colonel, when did all that occur?"

"In September, 1864—shortly after the siege."

THE THING AT NOLAN

To THE south of where the road between Leesville and Hardy, in the State of Missouri, crosses the east fork of May Creek stands an abandoned house. Nobody has lived in it since the summer of

1879, and it is fast going to pieces. For some three years before the date mentioned above, it was occupied by the family of Charles May, from one of whose ancestors the creek near which it stands took its name. Mr. May's family consisted of a wife, an adult son and two young girls. The son's name was John—the names of the daughters are unknown to the writer of this sketch.

John May was of a morose and surly disposition, not easily moved to anger, but having an uncommon gift of sullen, implacable hate. His father was quite otherwise; of a sunny, jovial disposition, but with a quick temper like a sudden flame kindled in a wisp of straw, which consumes it in a flash and is no more. He cherished no resentments, and his anger gone, was quick to make overtures for reconciliation. He had a brother living nearby who was unlike him in respect of all this, and it was a current witticism in the neighborhood that John had inherited his disposition from his uncle.

One day a misunderstanding arose between father and son, harsh words ensued, and the father struck the son full in the face with his fist. John quietly wiped away the blood that followed the blow, fixed his eyes upon the already penitent offender and said with cold composure, "You will die for that."

The words were overheard by two brothers named Jackson, who were approaching the men at the moment; but seeing them engaged in a quarrel they retired, apparently unobserved. Charles May afterward related the unfortunate occurrence to his wife and explained that he had apologized to the son for the hasty blow, but without avail; the young man not only rejected his overtures, but refused to withdraw his terrible threat. Nevertheless, there was no open rupture of relations: John continued living with the family, and things went on very much as before.

One Sunday morning in June, 1879, about two weeks after what has been related, May senior left the house immediately after breakfast, taking a spade. He said he was going to make an excavation at a certain spring in a wood about a mile away, so that the cattle could obtain water. John remained in the house for some hours, variously occupied in shaving himself, writing letters and reading a newspaper. His manner was very nearly what it usually was; perhaps he was a trifle more sullen and surly.

At two o'clock he left the house. At five, he returned. For some reason not connected with any interest in his movements, and which is not now recalled, the time of his departure and that of his return were noted by his mother and sisters, as was attested at his trial for murder. It was observed that his clothing was wet in spots, as if (so the prosecution afterward pointed out) he had been removing blood-stains from it. His manner was strange, his look wild. He complained of illness, and going to his room took to his bed.

May senior did not return. Later that evening the nearest neighbors were aroused, and during that night and the following day a search was prosecuted through the wood where the spring was. It resulted in little but the discovery of both men's foot-prints in the clay about the spring. John May in the meantime had grown rapidly worse with what the local physician called brain fever, and in his delirium raved of murder, but did not say whom he conceived to have been murdered, nor whom he imagined to have done the deed. But his threat was recalled by the brothers Jackson and he was arrested on suspicion and a deputy sheriff put in charge of him at his home. Public opinion ran strongly against him and but for his illness he would prob-ably have been hanged by a mob. As it was, a meeting of the neighbors was held on Tuesday and a committee appointed to watch the case and take such action at any time as circumstances might seem to warrant.

On Wednesday all was changed. From the town of Nolan, eight miles away, came a story which put a quite different light on the matter. Nolan consisted of a school house, a blacksmith's shop, a "store" and a half-dozen dwellings. The store was kept by one Henry Odell, a cousin of the elder May. On the afternoon of the Sunday of May's disappearance Mr. Odell and four of his neigh-bors, men of credibility, were sitting in the store smoking and talking. It was a warm day; and both the front and the back door were open. At about three o'clock Charles May, who was well known to three of them, entered at the front door and passed out at the rear. He was without hat or coat. He did not look at them, nor return their greeting, a circumstance which did not surprise, for he was evidently seriously hurt. Above the left eye-brow was a wound—a deep gash from which the blood flowed, covering the whole left side of the face and neck and saturating his light-gray shirt. Oddly enough, the thought uppermost in the minds of all was that he had been fighting and was going to the brook directly at the back of the store, to wash himself.

Perhaps there was a feeling of delicacy—a backwoods etiquette which restrained them from following him to offer assistance; the court records, from which, mainly, this narrative is drawn, are silent as to anything but the fact. They waited for him to return, but he did not return.

Bordering the brook behind the store is a forest extending for six miles back to the Medicine Lodge Hills. As soon as it became known in the neighborhood of the missing man's dwelling that he had been seen in Nolan there was a marked alteration in public sentiment and feeling. The vigilance committee went out of existence without the formality of a resolution. Search along the wooded bottom lands of May Creek was stopped and nearly the entire male population of the region took to beating the bush about Nolan and in the Medicine Lodge Hills. But of the missing man no trace was found.

One of the strangest circumstances of this strange case is the formal indictment and trial of a man for murder of one whose body no human being professed to have seen—one not known to be dead. We are all more or less familiar with the vagaries and eccentricities of frontier law, but this instance, it is thought, is unique. However that may be, it is of record that on recovering from his illness John May was indicted for the murder of his missing father. Counsel for the defense appears not to have demurred and the case was tried on its merits. The prosecution was spiritless and perfunctory; the defense easily established—with regard to the deceased—an *alibi*. If during the time in which John May must have killed Charles May, if he killed him at all, Charles May was miles away from where John May must have been, it is plain that the deceased must have come to his death at the hands of someone else.

John May was acquitted, immediately left the country, and has never been heard of from that day. Shortly afterward his mother and sisters removed to St. Louis. The farm having passed into the possession of a man who owns the land adjoining, and has a dwelling of his own, the May house has ever since been vacant, and has the somber reputation of being haunted.

One day after the May family had left the country, some boys, playing in the woods along May Creek, found concealed under a mass of dead leaves, but partly exposed by the rooting of hogs, a spade, nearly new and bright, except for a spot on one edge, which was rusted and stained with blood. The implement had the initials C. M. cut into the handle.

This discovery renewed, in some degree, the public excitement of a few months before. The earth near the spot where the spade was found was carefully examined, and the result was the finding of the dead body of a man. It had been buried under two or three feet of soil and the spot covered with a layer of dead leaves and twigs. There was but little decomposition, a fact attributed to some preservative property in the mineral-bearing soil.

Above the left eyebrow was a wound—a deep gash from which blood had flowed, covering the whole left side of the face and neck and saturating the light-gray shirt. The skull had been cut through by the blow. The body was that of Charles May.

But what was it that passed through Mr. Odell's store at Nolan?

"Mysterious Disappearances"

THE DIFFICULTY OF CROSSING A FIELD

ONE MORNING in July, 1854, a planter named Williamson, living six miles from Selma, Alabama, was sitting with his wife and a child on the veranda of his dwelling. Immediately in front of the house was a lawn, perhaps fifty yards in extent between the house and public road, or, as it was called, the "pike." Beyond this road lay a close-cropped pasture of some ten acres, level and without a tree, rock, or any natural or artificial object on its surface. At the time there was not even a domestic animal in the field. In another field, beyond the pasture, a dozen slaves were at work under an overseer.

Throwing away the stump of a cigar, the planter rose, saying: "I forgot to tell Andrew about those horses." Andrew was the overseer.

Williamson strolled leisurely down the gravel walk, plucking a flower as he went, passed across the road and into the pasture, pausing a moment as he closed the gate leading into it, to greet a passing neighbor, Armour Wren, who lived on an adjoining plantation. Mr. Wren was in an open carriage with his son James, a lad of thirteen. When he had driven some two hundred yards from the point of meeting, Mr. Wren said to his son: "I forgot to tell Mr. Williamson about those horses."

Mr. Wren had sold to Mr. Williamson some horses, which were to have been sent for that day, but for some reason not now remembered it would be inconvenient to deliver them until the morrow. The coachman was directed to drive back, and as the vehicle turned Williamson was seen by all three, walking leisurely across the pasture. At that moment one of the coach horses stumbled and came near falling. It had no more than fairly recovered itself when James Wren cried: "Why, Father, what has become of Mr. Williamson?"

It is not the purpose of this narrative to answer that question.

Mr. Wren's strange account of the matter, given under oath in the course of legal proceedings relating to the Williamson estate, here follows:

"My son's exclamation caused me to look toward the spot where I had seen the deceased [*sic*] an instant before, but he was not there, nor was he anywhere visible. I cannot say that at the moment I was greatly startled, or realized the gravity of the occurrence, though I thought it singular. My son, however, was greatly astonished and kept repeating his question in different forms until we arrived at the gate. My black boy Sam was similarly affected, even in a greater degree, but I reckon more by my son's manner than by anything he had himself observed. [This sentence in the testimony was stricken out.] As we got out of the carriage at the gate of the field, and while Sam was hanging [*sic*] the team to the fence, Mrs. Williamson, with her child in her arms and followed by several servants, came running down the walk in great excitement, crying: 'He is gone, he is gone! O God! what an awful thing!' and many other such exclamations, which I do not distinctly recollect. I got from them the impression that they related to something more than the mere disappearance of her husband, even if that had occurred before her eyes. Her manner was wild, but not more so, I think, than was natural under the circumstances. I have no reason to think she had at that time lost her mind. I have never since seen nor heard of Mr. Williamson."

This testimony, as might have been expected, was corroborated in almost every particular by the only other eye-witness (if that is a proper term)—the lad James. Mrs. Williamson had lost her reason and the servants were, of course, not competent to testify. The boy James Wren had declared at first that he *saw* the disappearance, but there is nothing of this in his testimony given in court. None of the field hands working in the field to which Williamson was going had seen him at all, and the most rigorous search of the entire plantation and adjoining country failed to supply a clew. The most monstrous and grotesque fictions, originating with the blacks, were current in that part of the State for many years, and probably are to this day; but what has been here related is all that is certainly known of the matter. The courts decided that Williamson was dead, and his estate was distributed according to law.

AN UNFINISHED RACE

JAMES BURNE WORSON was a shoemaker who lived in Leamington, Warwickshire, England. He had a little shop in one of the by-ways leading off the road to Warwick. In his humble sphere he was esteemed an honest man, although like many of his class in English towns he was somewhat addicted to drink. When in liquor he would make foolish wagers. On one of these too frequent occasions he was boasting of his prowess as a pedestrian and athlete, and the outcome was a match against nature. For a stake of one sovereign he undertook to run all the way to Coventry and back, a distance of something more than forty miles. This was on the 3d day of September in 1873. He set out at once, the man with whom he had made the bet—whose name is not remembered—accompanied by Barham Wise, a linen draper, and Hamerson Burns, a photographer, I think, following in a light cart or wagon.

For several miles Worson went on very well, at an easy gait, without apparent fatigue, for he had really great powers of endurance and was not sufficiently intoxicated to enfeeble them. The three men in the wagon kept a short distance in the rear, giving him occasional friendly "chaff" or encouragement, as the spirit moved them. Suddenly—in the very middle of the roadway, not a dozen yards from them, and with their eyes full upon him—the man seemed to stumble, pitched headlong forward, uttered a terrible cry and vanished! He did not fall to the earth —he vanished before touching it. No trace of him was ever discovered.

After remaining at and about the spot for some time, with aimless irresolution, the three men returned to Leamington, told their astonishing story and were afterward taken into custody. But they were of good standing, had always been considered truthful, were sober at the time of the occurrence, and nothing ever transpired to discredit their sworn account of their extraordinary adventure, concerning the truth of which, nevertheless, public opinion was divided, throughout the United Kingdom. If they had something to conceal, their choice of means is certainly one of the most amazing ever made by sane human beings.

CHARLES ASHMORE'S TRAIL

THE FAMILY of Christian Ashmore consisted of his wife, his mother, two grown daughters, and a son of sixteen years. They lived in Troy, New York, were well-to-do, respectable persons, and had many friends, some of whom, reading these lines, will doubtless learn for the first time the extraordinary fate of the young man. From Troy the Ashmores moved in 1871 or 1872 to Richmond, Indiana, and a year or two later to the vicinity of Quincy, Illinois, where Mr. Ashmore bought a farm and lived on it. At some little distance from the farmhouse was a spring with a constant flow of clear, cold water, whence the family derived its supply for domestic use at all seasons.

On the evening of the 9th of November in 1878, at about nine o'clock, young Charles Ashmore left the family circle about the hearth, took a tin bucket and started toward the spring. As he did not return, the family became uneasy, and going to the door by which he had left the house, his father called without receiving an answer. He then lighted a lantern and with the eldest daughter, Martha, who insisted on accompanying him, went in search. A light snow had fallen, obliterating the path, but making the young man's trail conspicuous; each footprint was plainly defined. After going a little more than half-way—perhaps seventy-five yards—the father, who was in advance, halted, and elevating his lantern stood peering intently into the darkness ahead.

"What is the matter, Father?" the girl asked.

This was the matter: the trail of the young man had abruptly ended, and all beyond was smooth, unbroken snow. The last footprints were as conspicuous as any in the line; the very nailmarks were distinctly visible. Mr. Ashmore looked upward, shading his eyes with his hat held between them and the lantern. The stars were shining; there was not a cloud in the sky; he was denied the explanation which had suggested itself, doubtful as it would have been—a new snowfall with a limit so plainly defined. Taking a wide circuit round the ultimate tracks, so as to leave them undisturbed for further examination, the man proceeded to the spring, the girl following, weak and terrified. Neither had spoken a word of what both had observed. The spring was covered with ice, hours old.

Returning to the house they noted the appearance of the snow on both sides of the trail its entire length. No tracks led away from it.

The morning light showed nothing more. Smooth, spotless, unbroken, the shallow snow lay everywhere.

Four days later the grief-stricken mother herself went to the spring for water. She came back and related that in passing the spot where the footprints had ended she had heard the voice of her son and had been eagerly calling to him, wandering about the place, as she had fancied the voice to be now in one direction, now in another, until she was exhausted with fatigue and emotion. Questioned as to what the voice had said, she was unable to tell, yet averred that the words were perfectly distinct. In a moment the entire family was at the place, but nothing was heard, and the voice was believed to be an hallucination caused by the mother's great anxiety and her disordered nerves. But for months afterward, at irregular intervals of a few days, the voice was heard by the several members of the family, and by others. All declared it unmistakably the voice of Charles Ashmore; all agreed that it seemed to come from a great distance, faintly, yet with entire distinctness of articulation; yet none could determine its direction, nor repeat its words. The intervals of silence grew longer and longer, the voice fainter and farther, and by midsummer it was heard no more.

If anybody knows the fate of Charles Ashmore it is probably his mother. She is dead.

SCIENCE TO THE FRONT

IN CONNECTION with this subject of "mysterious disappearance" —of which every memory is stored with abundant example—it is pertinent to note the belief of Dr. Hern, of Leipsic; not by way of explanation, unless the reader may choose to take it so, but because of its intrinsic interest as a singular speculation. This distinguished scientist has expounded his views in a book entitled "Verschwinden und Seine Theorie," which has attracted some attention, "particularly," says one writer, "among the followers of Hegel, and mathematicians who hold to the actual existence of a so-called non-Euclidean space—that is to say, of space which has more dimensions than length, breadth, and thickness—space in which it would be possible to tie a knot in an endless cord and to turn a rubber ball inside out without 'a solution of its continuity,' or in other words, without breaking or cracking it."

Dr. Hern believes that in the visible world there are void places—*vacua,* and something more—holes, as it were, through which animate and inanimate objects may fall into the invisible world and be seen and heard no more. The theory is something like this: Space is pervaded by luminiferous ether, which is a material thing—as much a substance as air or water, though almost infinitely more attenuated. All force, all forms of energy must be propagated in this; every process must take place in it which takes place at all. But let us suppose that cavities exist in this otherwise universal medium, as caverns exist in the earth, or cells in a Swiss cheese. In such a cavity there would be absolutely nothing. It would be such a vacuum as cannot be artificially produced; for if we pump the air from a receiver there remains the luminiferous ether. Through one of these cavities light could not pass, for there would be nothing to bear it. Sound could not come from it; nothing could be felt in it. It would not have a single one of the conditions necessary to the action of any of our senses. In such a void, in short, nothing whatever could occur. Now, in the words of the writer before quoted—the learned doctor himself nowhere puts it so concisely: "A man inclosed in such a closet could neither see nor be seen; neither hear nor be heard; neither feel nor be felt; neither live nor die, for both life and death are processes which can take place only where there is force, and in empty space no force could exist." Are these the awful conditions (some will ask) under which the friends of the lost are to think of them as existing, and doomed forever to exist?

Baldly and imperfectly as here stated, Dr. Hern's theory, in so far as it professes to be an adequate explanation of "mysterious disappearances," is open to many obvious objections; to fewer as he states it himself in the "spacious volubility" of his book. But even as expounded by its author it does not explain, and in truth is incompatible with some incidents of, the occurrences related in these memoranda: for example, the sound of Charles Ashmore's voice. It is not my duty to indue facts and theories with affinity.

A. B.

The Man and the Snake

It is of veritabyll report, and attested of so many that there be nowe of wyse and learned none to gaynsaye it, that ye serpente hys eye hath a magnetick propertie that whosoe falleth into its svasion is drawn forwards in despyte of his wille, and perisheth miserabyll by ye creature hys byte.

STRETCHED AT ease upon a sofa, in gown and slippers, Harker Brayton smiled as he read the foregoing sentence in old Morryster's *Marvells of Science.* "The only marvel in the matter," he said to himself, "is that the wise and learned in Morryster's day should have believed such nonsense as is rejected by most of even the ignorant in ours."

A train of reflection followed—for Brayton was a man of thought—and he unconsciously lowered his book without altering the direction of his eyes. As soon as the volume had gone below the line of sight, something in an obscure corner of the room recalled his attention to his surroundings. What he saw, in the shadow under his bed, was two small points of light, apparently about an inch apart. They might have been reflections of the gas jet above him, in metal nail heads; he gave them but little thought and resumed his reading. A moment later something —some impulse which it did not occur to him to analyze—impelled him to lower the book again and seek for what he saw before. The points of light were still there. They seemed to have become brighter than before, shining with a greenish lustre that he had not at first observed. He thought, too, that they might have moved a trifle—were somewhat nearer. They were still too much in shadow, however, to reveal their nature and origin to an indolent attention, and again he resumed his reading. Suddenly something in the text suggested a thought that made him start and drop the book for the third time to the side of the sofa, whence, escaping from his hand, it fell sprawling to the floor, back upward. Brayton, half-risen, was staring intently into the obscurity beneath the bed, where the points of light shone with, it seemed to him, an added fire. His attention was now fully aroused, his gaze eager and imperative. It disclosed, almost directly under the foot-rail of the bed, the coils of a large serpent —the points of light were its eyes! Its horrible head, thrust flatly forth from the innermost coil and resting upon the outermost, was directed straight toward him, the definition of the wide, brutal jaw and the idiot-like forehead serving to show the direction of its malevolent gaze. The eyes were no longer merely luminous points; they looked into his own with a meaning, a malign significance.

II

A SNAKE in a bedroom of a modern city dwelling of the better sort is, happily, not so common a phenomenon as to make explanation altogether needless. Harker Brayton, a bachelor of thirty-five, a scholar, idler and something of an athlete, rich, popular and of sound health, had returned to San Francisco from all manner of remote and unfamiliar countries. His tastes, always a trifle luxurious, had taken on an added exuberance from long privation; and the resources of even the Castle Hotel being inadequate to their perfect gratification, he had gladly accepted the hospitality of his friend, Dr. Druring, the distinguished scientist. Dr. Druring's house, a large, old-fashioned one in what is now an obscure quarter of the city, had an outer and visible aspect of proud reserve. It plainly would not associate with the contiguous elements of its altered environment, and appeared to have developed some of the eccentricities which come of isolation. One of these was a "wing," conspicuously irrelevant in point of architecture, and no less rebellious in matter of purpose; for it was a combination of laboratory, menagerie and museum. It was here that the doctor indulged the scientific side of his nature in the study of such forms of animal life as engaged his interest and comforted his taste—which, it must be confessed, ran rather to the lower types. For one of the higher nimbly and sweetly to recommend itself unto his gentle senses it had at least to retain certain rudimentary characteristics allying it to such "dragons of the prime" as toads and snakes. His scientific sympathies were distinctly reptilian; he loved nature's vulgarians and described himself as the Zola of zoölogy. His wife and daughters not having the advantage to share his enlightened curiosity regarding the works and ways of our ill-starred fellow-creatures, were with needless austerity excluded from what he called the Snakery and doomed to companionship with their own kind, though to soften the rigors of their lot he had permitted them out of his great wealth to outdo the reptiles in the gorgeousness of their surroundings and to shine with a superior splendor.

Architecturally and in point of "furnishing" the Snakery had a severe simplicity befitting the humble circumstances of its occupants, many of whom, indeed, could not safely have been intrusted with the liberty that is necessary to the full enjoyment of luxury, for they had the troublesome peculiarity of being alive. In their own apartments, however, they were under as little personal restraint as was compatible with their protection from the baneful habit of swallowing one another; and, as Brayton had thoughtfully been apprised, it was more than a tradition that some of them had at divers times been found in parts of the premises where it would have embarrassed them to explain their presence. Despite the Snakery and its uncanny associations—to which, indeed, he gave little attention—Brayton found life at the Druring mansion very much to his mind.

III

BEYOND A smart shock of surprise and a shudder of mere loathing Mr. Brayton was not greatly affected. His first thought was to ring the call bell and bring a servant; but although the bell cord dangled within easy reach he made no movement toward it; it had occurred to his mind that the act might subject him to the suspicion of fear, which he certainly did not feel. He was more keenly conscious of the incongruous nature of the situation than affected by its perils; it was revolting, but absurd.

The reptile was of a species with which Brayton was unfamiliar. Its length he could only conjecture; the body at the largest visible part seemed about as thick as his forearm. In what way was it dangerous, if in any way? Was it venomous? Was it a constrictor? His knowledge of nature's danger signals did not enable him to say; he had never deciphered the code.

If not dangerous the creature was at least offensive. It was *de trop*—"matter out of place"—an impertinence. The gem was unworthy of the setting. Even the barbarous taste of our time and country, which had loaded the walls of the room with pictures, the floor with furniture and the furniture with bric-a-brac, had not quite fitted the place for this bit of the savage life of the jungle. Besides—insupportable thought!—the exhalations of its breath mingled with the atmosphere which he himself was breathing.

These thoughts shaped themselves with greater or less definition in Brayton's mind and begot action. The process is what we
call consideration and decision. It is thus that we are wise and
unwise. It is thus that the withered leaf in an autumn breeze
shows greater or less intelligence than its fellows, falling upon
the land or upon the lake. The secret of human action is an open
one: something contracts our muscles. Does it matter if we give
to the preparatory molecular changes the name of will?

Brayton rose to his feet and prepared to back softly away from
the snake, without disturbing it if possible, and through the
door. Men retire so from the presence of the great, for greatness
is power and power is a menace. He knew that he could walk
backward without error. Should the monster follow, the taste
which had plastered the walls with paintings had consistently
supplied a rack of murderous Oriental weapons from which he
could snatch one to suit the occasion. In the meantime the snake's
eyes burned with a more pitiless malevolence than before.

Brayton lifted his right foot free of the floor to step backward.
That moment he felt a strong aversion to doing so.

"I am accounted brave," he thought; "is bravery, then, no
more than pride? Because there are none to witness the shame
shall I retreat?"

He was steadying himself with his right hand upon the back
of a chair, his foot suspended.

"Nonsense!" he said aloud; "I am not so great a coward as to
fear to seem to myself afraid."

He lifted the foot a little higher by slightly bending the knee
and thrust it sharply to the floor—an inch in front of the other!
He could not think how that occurred. A trial with the left foot
had the same result; it was again in advance of the right. The
hand upon the chair back was grasping it; the arm was straight,
reaching somewhat backward. One might have said that he was
reluctant to lose his hold. The snake's malignant head was still
thrust forth from the inner coil as before, the neck level. It had
not moved, but its eyes were now electric sparks, radiating an in-
finity of luminous needles.

The man had an ashy pallor. Again he took a step forward,
and another, partly dragging the chair, which when finally released fell upon the floor with a crash. The man groaned; the
snake made neither sound nor motion, but its eyes were two dazzling suns. The reptile itself was wholly concealed by them.
They gave off enlarging rings of rich and vivid colors, which at
their greatest expansion successively vanished like soap-bubbles; they seemed to approach his very face, and anon were an

immeasurable distance away. He heard, somewhere, the continuous throbbing of a great drum, with desultory bursts of far music, inconceivably sweet, like the tones of an æolian harp. He knew it for the sunrise melody of Memnon's statue, and thought he stood in the Nileside reeds hearing with exalted sense that immortal anthem through the silence of the centuries.

The music ceased; rather, it became by insensible degrees the distant roll of a retreating thunder-storm. A landscape, glittering with sun and rain, stretched before him, arched with a vivid rainbow framing in its giant curve a hundred visible cities. In the middle distance a vast serpent, wearing a crown, reared its head out of its voluminous convolutions and looked at him with his dead mother's eyes. Suddenly this enchanting landscape seemed to rise swiftly upward like the drop scene at a theatre, and vanished in a blank. Something struck him a hard blow upon the face and breast. He had fallen to the floor; the blood ran from his broken nose and his bruised lips. For a time he was dazed and stunned, and lay with closed eyes, his face against the floor. In a few moments he had recovered, and then knew that this fall, by withdrawing his eyes, had broken the spell that held him. He felt that now, by keeping his gaze averted, he would be able to retreat. But the thought of the serpent within a few feet of his head, yet unseen—perhaps in the very act of springing upon him and throwing its coils about his throat—was too horrible! He lifted his head, stared again into those baleful eyes and was again in bondage.

The snake had not moved and appeared somewhat to have lost its power upon the imagination; the gorgeous illusions of a few moments before were not repeated. Beneath that flat and brainless brow its black, beady eyes simply glittered as at first with an expression unspeakably malignant. It was as if the creature, assured of its triumph, had determined to practise no more alluring wiles.

Now ensued a fearful scene. The man, prone upon the floor, within a yard of his enemy, raised the upper part of his body upon his elbows, his head thrown back, his legs extended to their full length. His face was white between its stains of blood; his eyes were strained open to their uttermost expansion. There was froth upon his lips; it dropped off in flakes. Strong convulsions ran through his body, making almost serpentile undulations. He bent himself at the waist, shifting his legs from side to side. And every movement left him a little nearer to the snake. He thrust his hands forward to brace himself back, yet constantly advanced upon his elbows.

IV

DR. DRURING and his wife sat in the library. The scientist was in rare good humor.

"I have just obtained by exchange with another collector," he said, "a splendid specimen of the *ophiophagus*."

"And what may that be?" the lady inquired with a somewhat languid interest.

"Why, bless my soul, what profound ignorance! My dear, a man who ascertains after marriage that his wife does not know Greek is entitled to a divorce. The *ophiophagus* is a snake that eats other snakes."

"I hope it will eat all yours," she said, absently shifting the lamp. "But how does it get the other snakes? By charming them, I suppose."

"That is just like you, dear," said the doctor, with an affectation of petulance. "You know how irritating to me is any allusion to that vulgar superstition about a snake's power of fascination."

The conversation was interrupted by a mighty cry, which rang through the silent house like the voice of a demon shouting in a tomb! Again and yet again it sounded, with terrible distinctness. They sprang to their feet, the man confused, the lady pale and speechless with fright. Almost before the echoes of the last cry had died away the doctor was out of the room, springing up the stairs two steps at a time. In the corridor in front of Brayton's chamber he met some servants who had come from the upper floor. Together they rushed at the door without knocking. It was unfastened and gave way. Brayton lay upon his stomach on the floor, dead. His head and arms were partly concealed under the foot-rail of the bed. They pulled the body away, turning it upon the back. The face was daubed with blood and froth, the eyes were wide open, staring—a dreadful sight!

"Died in a fit," said the scientist, bending his knee and placing his hand upon the heart. While in that position, he chanced to look under the bed. "Good God!" he added, "how did this thing get in here?"

He reached under the bed, pulled out the snake and flung it, still coiled, to the center of the room, whence with a harsh, shuffling sound it slid across the polished floor till stopped by the wall, where it lay without motion. It was a stuffed snake; its eyes were two shoe buttons.

The Suitable Surroundings

THE NIGHT

ONE MIDSUMMER night a farmer's boy living about ten miles from the city of Cincinnati was following a bridle path through a dense and dark forest. He had lost himself while searching for some missing cows, and near midnight was a long way from home, in a part of the country with which he was unfamiliar. But he was a stout-hearted lad, and knowing his general direction from his home, he plunged into the forest without hesitation, guided by the stars. Coming into the bridle path, and observing that it ran in the right direction, he followed it.

The night was clear, but in the woods it was exceedingly dark. It was more by the sense of touch than by that of sight that the lad kept the path. He could not, indeed, very easily go astray; the undergrowth on both sides was so thick as to be almost impenetrable. He had gone into the forest a mile or more when he was surprised to see a feeble gleam of light shining through the foliage skirting the path on his left. The sight of it startled him and set his heart beating audibly.

"The old Breede house is somewhere about here," he said to himself. "This must be the other end of the path which we reach it by from our side. Ugh! what should a light be doing there?"

Nevertheless, he pushed on. A moment later he had emerged from the forest into a small, open space, mostly upgrown to brambles. There were remnants of a rotting fence. A few yards from the trail, in the middle of the "clearing," was the house from which the light came, through an unglazed window. The window had once contained glass, but that and its supporting frame had long ago yielded to missiles flung by hands of venturesome boys to attest alike their courage and their hostility to the supernatural; for the Breede house bore the evil reputation of being haunted. Possibly it was not, but even the hardiest sceptic could not deny that it was deserted—which in rural regions is much the same thing.

Looking at the mysterious dim light shining from the ruined window the boy remembered with apprehension that his own hand had assisted at the destruction. His penitence was of course poignant in proportion to its tardiness and inefficacy. He half expected to be set upon by all the unworldly and bodiless malevolences whom he had outraged by assisting to break alike their windows and their peace. Yet this stubborn lad, shaking in every limb, would not retreat. The blood in his veins was strong and rich with the iron of the frontiersman. He was but two removes from the generation that had subdued the Indian. He started to pass the house.

As he was going by he looked in at the blank window space and saw a strange and terrifying sight,—the figure of a man seated in the centre of the room, at a table upon which lay some loose sheets of paper. The elbows rested on the table, the hands supporting the head, which was uncovered. On each side the fingers were pushed into the hair. The face showed dead-yellow in the light of a single candle a little to one side. The flame illuminated that side of the face, the other was in deep shadow. The man's eyes were fixed upon the blank window space with a stare in which an older and cooler observer might have discerned something of apprehension, but which seemed to the lad altogether soulless. He believed the man to be dead.

The situation was horrible, but not without its fascination. The boy stopped to note it all. He was weak, faint and trembling; he could feel the blood forsaking his face. Nevertheless, he set his teeth and resolutely advanced to the house. He had no conscious intention—it was the mere courage of terror. He thrust his white face forward into the illuminated opening. At that instant a strange, harsh cry, a shriek, broke upon the silence of the night—the note of a screech-owl. The man sprang to his feet, overturning the table and extinguishing the candle. The boy took to his heels.

THE DAY BEFORE

"Good-morning, Colston. I am in luck, it seems. You have often said that my commendation of your literary work was mere civility, and here you find me absorbed—actually merged—in your latest story in the *Messenger*. Nothing less shocking than your touch upon my shoulder would have roused me to consciousness."

"The proof is stronger than you seem to know," replied the man addressed: "so keen is your eagerness to read my story that you are willing to renounce selfish considerations and forego all the pleasure that you could get from it."

"I don't understand you," said the other, folding the newspaper that he held and putting it into his pocket. "You writers are a queer lot, anyhow. Come, tell me what I have done or omitted in this matter. In what way does the pleasure that I get, or might get, from your work depend on me?"

"In many ways. Let me ask you how you would enjoy your breakfast if you took it in this streetcar. Suppose the phonograph so perfected as to be able to give you an entire opera, —singing, orchestration, and all; do you think you would get much pleasure out of it if you turned it on at your office during business hours? Do you really care for a serenade by Schubert when you hear it fiddled by an untimely Italian on a morning ferryboat? Are you always cocked and primed for enjoyment? Do you keep every mood on tap, ready to any demand? Let me remind you, sir, that the story which you have done me the honor to begin as a means of becoming oblivious to the discomfort of this car is a ghost story!"

"Well?"

"Well! Has the reader no duties corresponding to his privileges? You have paid five cents for that newspaper. It is yours. You have the right to read it when and where you will. Much of what is in it is neither helped nor harmed by time and place and mood; some of it actually requires to be read at once— while it is fizzing. But my story is not of that character. It is not 'the very latest advices' from Ghostland. You are not expected to keep yourself *au courant* with what is going on in the realm of spooks. The stuff will keep until you have leisure to put yourself into the frame of mind appropriate to the sentiment of the piece—which I respectfully submit that you cannot do in a streetcar, even if you are the only passenger. The solitude is not of the right sort. An author has rights which the reader is bound to respect."

"For specific example?"

"The right to the reader's undivided attention. To deny him this is immoral. To make him share your attention with the rattle of a streetcar, the moving panorama of the crowds on the sidewalks, and the buildings beyond—with any of the thousands of distractions which make our customary environment—is to treat him with gross injustice. By God, it is infamous!"

The speaker had risen to his feet and was steadying himself by one of the straps hanging from the roof of the car. The other man looked up at him in sudden astonishment, wondering how so trivial a grievance could seem to justify so strong language. He saw that his friend's face was uncommonly pale and that his eyes glowed like living coals.

"You know what I mean," continued the writer, impetuously crowding his words—"you know what I mean, Marsh. My stuff in this morning's *Messenger* is plainly subheaded 'A Ghost Story.' That is ample notice to all. Every honorable reader will understand it as prescribing by implication the conditions under which the work is to be read."

The man addressed as Marsh winced a trifle, then asked with a smile: "What conditions? You know that I am only a plain business man who cannot be supposed to understand such things. How, when, where should I read your ghost story?"

"In solitude—at night—by the light of a candle. There are certain emotions which a writer can easily enough excite—such as compassion or merriment. I can move you to tears or laughter under almost any circumstances. But for my ghost story to be effective you must be made to feel fear—at least a strong sense of the supernatural—and that is a difficult matter. I have a right to expect that if you read me at all you will give me a chance; that you will make yourself accessible to the emotion that I try to inspire."

The car had now arrived at its terminus and stopped. The trip just completed was its first for the day and the conversation of the two early passengers had not been interrupted. The streets were yet silent and desolate; the house tops were just touched by the rising sun. As they stepped from the car and walked away together Marsh narrowly eyed his companion, who was reported, like most men of uncommon literary ability, to be addicted to various destructive vices. That is the revenge which dull minds take upon bright ones in resentment of their superiority. Mr. Colston was known as a man of genius. There are honest souls who believe that genius is a mode of excess. It was known that Colston did not drink liquor, but many said that he ate opium. Something in his appearance that morning—a certain wildness of the eyes, an unusual pallor, a thickness and rapidity of speech—were taken by Mr. Marsh to confirm the report. Nevertheless, he had not the self-denial to abandon a subject which he found interesting, however it might excite his friend.

"Do you mean to say," he began, "that if I take the trouble to observe your directions—place myself in the conditions that you demand: solitude, night and a tallow candle—you can with your ghostly work give me an uncomfortable sense of the supernatural, as you call it? Can you accelerate my pulse, make me start at sudden noises, send a nervous chill along my spine and cause my hair to rise?"

Colston turned suddenly and looked him squarely in the eyes as they walked. "You would not dare—you have not the courage," he said. He emphasized the words with a contemptuous gesture. "You are brave enough to read me in a streetcar, but —in a deserted house—alone—in the forest—at night! Bah! I have a manuscript in my pocket that would kill you."

Marsh was angry. He knew himself courageous, and the words stung him. "If you know such a place," he said, "take me there to-night and leave me your story and a candle. Call for me when I've had time enough to read it and I'll tell you the entire plot and—kick you out of the place."

That is how it occurred that the farmer's boy, looking in at an unglazed window of the Breede house, saw a man sitting in the light of a candle.

THE DAY AFTER

LATE IN the afternoon of the next day three men and a boy approached the Breede house from that point of the compass toward which the boy had fled the preceding night. The men were in high spirits; they talked very loudly and laughed. They made facetious and good-humored ironical remarks to the boy about his adventure, which evidently they did not believe in. The boy accepted their raillery with seriousness, making no reply. He had a sense of the fitness of things and knew that one who professes to have seen a dead man rise from his seat and blow out a candle is not a credible witness.

Arriving at the house and finding the door unlocked, the party of investigators entered without ceremony. Leading out of the passage into which this door opened was another on the right and one on the left. They entered the room on the left— the one which had the blank front window. Here was the dead body of a man.

It lay partly on one side, with the forearm beneath it, the cheek on the floor. The eyes were wide open; the stare was not an agreeable thing to encounter. The lower jaw had fallen; a little pool of saliva had collected beneath the mouth. An over-thrown table, a partly burned candle, a chair and some paper with writing on it were all else that the room contained. The men looked at the body, touching the face in turn. The boy gravely stood at the head, assuming a look of ownership. It was the proudest moment of his life. One of the men said to him, "You're a good 'un"—a remark which was received by the two others with nods of acquiescence. It was Scepticism apolo-gizing to Truth. Then one of the men took from the floor the sheet of manuscript and stepped to the window, for already the evening shadows were glooming the forest. The song of the whip-poor-will was heard in the distance and a monstrous beetle sped by the window on roaring wings and thundered away out of hearing. The man read:

THE MANUSCRIPT

"BEFORE COMMITTING the act which, rightly or wrongly, I have resolved on and appearing before my Maker for judgment, I, James R. Colston, deem it my duty as a journalist to make a statement to the public. My name is, I believe, tolerably well known to the people as a writer of tragic tales, but the somber-est imagination never conceived anything so tragic as my own life and history. Not in incident: my life has been destitute of adventure and action. But my mental career has been lurid with experiences such as kill and damn. I shall not recount them here—some of them are written and ready for publication else-where. The object of these lines is to explain to whomsoever may be interested that my death is voluntary—my own act. I shall die at twelve o'clock on the night of the 15th of July— a significant anniversary to me, for it was on that day, and at that hour, that my friend in time and eternity, Charles Breede, performed his vow to me by the same act which his fidelity to our pledge now entails upon me. He took his life in his little house in the Copeton woods. There was the customary verdict of 'temporary insanity.' Had I testified at that inquest—had I told all I knew, they would have called *me* mad!"

Here followed an evidently long passage which the man read-ing read to himself only. The rest he read aloud.

"I have still a week of life in which to arrange my worldly affairs and prepare for the great change. It is enough, for I have but few affairs and it is now four years since death became an imperative obligation.

"I shall bear this writing on my body; the finder will please hand it to the coroner.

"JAMES R. COLSTON.

"P. S.—Willard Marsh, on this fatal fifteenth day of July I hand you this manuscript, to be opened and read under the conditions agreed upon, and at the place which I designated. I forego my intention to keep it on my body to explain the manner of my death, which is not important. It will serve to explain the manner of yours. I am to call for you during the night to receive assurance that you have read the manuscript. You know me well enough to expect me. But, my friend, it *will be after twelve o'clock*. May God have mercy on our souls!

"J. R. C."

Before the man who was reading this manuscript had finished, the candle had been picked up and lighted. When the reader had done, he quietly thrust the paper against the flame and despite the protestations of the others held it until it was burnt to ashes. The man who did this, and who afterward placidly endured a severe reprimand from the coroner, was a son-in-law of the late Charles Breede. At the inquest nothing could elicit an intelligent account of what the paper had contained.

FROM "THE TIMES"

"YESTERDAY THE Commissioners of Lunacy committed to the asylum Mr. James R. Colston, a writer of some local reputation, connected with the *Messenger*. It will be remembered that on the evening of the 15th inst. Mr. Colston was given into custody by one of his fellow-lodgers in the Baine House, who had observed him acting very suspiciously, baring his throat and whetting a razor—occasionally trying its edge by actually cutting through the skin of his arm, etc. On being handed over to the police, the unfortunate man made a desperate resistance, and has ever since been so violent that it has been necessary to keep him in a strait-jacket. Most of our esteemed contemporary's other writers are still at large."

The Eyes of the Panther

I

ONE DOES NOT ALWAYS MARRY WHEN INSANE

A MAN and a woman—nature had done the grouping—sat on a rustic seat, in the late afternoon. The man was middle-aged, slender, swarthy, with the expression of a poet and the complexion of a pirate—a man at whom one would look again. The woman was young, blonde, graceful, with something in her figure and movements suggesting the word "lithe." She was habited in a gray gown with odd brown markings in the texture. She may have been beautiful; one could not readily say, for her eyes denied attention to all else. They were gray-green, long and narrow, with an expression defying analysis. One could only know that they were disquieting. Cleopatra may have had such eyes.

The man and the woman talked.

"Yes," said the woman, "I love you, God knows! But marry you, no. I cannot, will not."

"Irene, you have said that many times, yet always have denied me a reason. I've a right to know, to understand, to feel and prove my fortitude if I have it. Give me a reason."

"For loving you?"

The woman was smiling through her tears and her pallor. That did not stir any sense of humor in the man.

"No; there is no reason for that. A reason for not marrying me. I've a right to know. I must know. I will know!"

He had risen and was standing before her with clenched hands, on his face a frown—it might have been called a scowl. He looked as if he might attempt to learn by strangling her. She smiled no more—merely sat looking up into his face with a fixed, set regard that was utterly without emotion or sentiment. Yet it had something in it that tamed his resentment and made him shiver.

"You are determined to have my reason?" she asked in a tone

105

that was entirely mechanical—a tone that might have been her look made audible.

"If you please—if I'm not asking too much."

Apparently this lord of creation was yielding some part of his dominion over his co-creature.

"Very well, you shall know: I am insane."

The man started, then looked incredulous and was conscious that he ought to be amused. But, again, the sense of humor failed him in his need and despite his disbelief he was profoundly disturbed by that which he did not believe. Between our convictions and our feelings there is no good understanding.

"That is what the physicians would say," the woman continued—"if they knew. I might myself prefer to call it a case of 'possession.' Sit down and hear what I have to say."

The man silently resumed his seat beside her on the rustic bench by the wayside. Over against them on the eastern side of the valley the hills were already sunset-flushed and the stillness all about was of that peculiar quality that foretells the twilight. Something of its mysterious and significant solemnity had imparted itself to the man's mood. In the spiritual, as in the material world, are signs and presages of night. Rarely meeting her look, and whenever he did so conscious of the indefinable dread with which, despite their feline beauty, her eyes always affected him, Jenner Brading listened in silence to the story told by Irene Marlowe. In deference to the reader's possible prejudice against the artless method of an unpracticed historian the author ventures to substitute his own version for hers.

II

A ROOM MAY BE TOO NARROW FOR THREE, THOUGH ONE IS OUTSIDE

In a little log house containing a single room sparely and rudely furnished, crouching on the floor against one of the walls, was a woman, clasping to her breast a child. Outside, a dense unbroken forest extended for many miles in every direction. This was at night and the room was black dark: no human eye could have discerned the woman and the child. Yet they were observed, narrowly, vigilantly, with never even a momentary slackening of attention; and that is the pivotal fact upon which this narrative turns.

Charles Marlowe was of the class, now extinct in this country, of woodmen pioneers—men who found their most acceptable surroundings in sylvan solitudes that stretched along the eastern slope of the Mississippi Valley, from the Great Lakes to the Gulf of Mexico. For more than a hundred years these men pushed ever westward, generation after generation, with rifle and ax, reclaiming from Nature and her savage children here and there an isolated acreage for the plow, no sooner reclaimed than surrendered to their less venturesome but more thrifty successors. At last they burst through the edge of the forest into the open country and vanished as if they had fallen over a cliff. The woodman pioneer is no more; the pioneer of the plains—he whose easy task it was to subdue for occupancy two-thirds of the country in a single generation—is another and inferior creation. With Charles Marlowe in the wilderness, sharing the dangers, hardships and privations of that strange, unprofitable life, were his wife and child, to whom, in the manner of his class, in which the domestic virtues were a religion, he was passionately attached. The woman was still young enough to be comely, new enough to the awful isolation of her lot to be cheerful. By withholding the large capacity for happiness which the simple satisfactions of the forest life could not have filled, Heaven had dealt honorably with her. In her light household tasks, her child, her husband and her few foolish books, she found abundant provision for her needs.

One morning in midsummer Marlowe took down his rifle from the wooden hooks on the wall and signified his intention of getting game.

"We've meat enough," said the wife; "please don't go out to-day. I dreamed last night, O, such a dreadful thing! I cannot recollect it, but I'm almost sure that it will come to pass if you go out."

It is painful to confess that Marlowe received this solemn statement with less of gravity than was due to the mysterious nature of the calamity foreshadowed. In truth, he laughed.

"Try to remember," he said. "Maybe you dreamed that Baby had lost the power of speech."

The conjecture was obviously suggested by the fact that Baby, clinging to the fringe of his hunting-coat with all her ten pudgy thumbs was at that moment uttering her sense of the situation in a series of exultant goo-goos inspired by sight of her father's raccoon-skin cap.

The woman yielded: lacking the gift of humor she could not hold out against his kindly badinage. So, with a kiss for the mother and a kiss for the child, he left the house and closed the door upon his happiness forever.

At nightfall he had not returned. The woman prepared supper and waited. Then she put Baby to bed and sang softly to her until she slept. By this time the fire on the hearth, at which she had cooked supper, had burned out and the room was lighted by a single candle. This she afterward placed in the open window as a sign and welcome to the hunter if he should approach from that side. She had thoughtfully closed and barred the door against such wild animals as might prefer it to an open window—of the habits of beasts of prey in entering a house uninvited she was not advised, though with true female prevision she may have considered the possibility of their entrance by way of the chimney. As the night wore on she became not less anxious, but more drowsy, and at last rested her arms upon the bed by the child and her head upon the arms. The candle in the window burned down to the socket, sputtered and flared a moment and went out unobserved; for the woman slept and dreamed.

In her dreams she sat beside the cradle of a second child. The first one was dead. The father was dead. The home in the forest was lost and the dwelling in which she lived was unfamiliar. There were heavy oaken doors, always closed, and outside the windows, fastened into the thick stone walls, were iron bars, obviously (so she thought) a provision against Indians. All this she noted with an infinite self-pity, but without surprise—an emotion unknown in dreams. The child in the cradle was invisible under its coverlet which something impelled her to remove. She did so, disclosing the face of a wild animal! In the shock of this dreadful revelation the dreamer awoke, trembling in the darkness of her cabin in the wood.

As a sense of her actual surroundings came slowly back to her she felt for the child that was not a dream, and assured herself by its breathing that all was well with it; nor could she forbear to pass a hand lightly across its face. Then, moved by some impulse for which she probably could not have accounted, she rose and took the sleeping babe in her arms, holding it close against her breast. The head of the child's cot was against the wall to which the woman now turned her back as she stood. Lifting her eyes she saw two bright objects starring the darkness with a reddish-green glow. She took them to be two coals on the hearth, but with her returning sense of direction came the disquieting consciousness that they were not in that quarter of the room, moreover were too high, being nearly at the level of the eyes—of her own eyes. For these were the eyes of a panther.

The beast was at the open window directly opposite and not five paces away. Nothing but those terrible eyes was visible, but in the dreadful tumult of her feelings as the situation disclosed itself to her understanding she somehow knew that the animal was standing on its hinder feet, supporting itself with its paws on the window-ledge. That signified a malign interest—not the mere gratification of an indolent curiosity. The consciousness of the attitude was an added horror, accentuating the menace of those awful eyes, in whose steadfast fire her strength and courage were alike consumed. Under their silent questioning she shuddered and turned sick. Her knees failed her, and by degrees, instinctively striving to avoid a sudden movement that might bring the beast upon her, she sank to the floor, crouched against the wall and tried to shield the babe with her trembling body without withdrawing her gaze from the luminous orbs that were killing her. No thought of her husband came to her in her agony—no hope nor suggestion of rescue or escape. Her capacity for thought and feeling had narrowed to the dimensions of a single emotion—fear of the animal's spring, of the impact of its body, the buffeting of its great arms, the feel of its teeth in her throat, the mangling of her babe. Motionless now and in absolute silence, she awaited her doom, the moments growing to hours, to years, to ages; and still those devilish eyes maintained their watch.

RETURNING TO his cabin late at night with a deer on his shoulders Charles Marlowe tried the door. It did not yield. He knocked; there was no answer. He laid down his deer and went round to the window. As he turned the angle of the building he fancied he heard a sound as of stealthy footfalls and a rustling in the undergrowth of the forest, but they were too slight for certainty, even to his practised ear. Approaching the window, and to his surprise finding it open, he threw his leg over the sill and entered. All was darkness and silence. He groped his way to the fire-place, struck a match and lit a candle.

Then he looked about. Cowering on the floor against a wall was his wife, clasping his child. As he sprang toward her she rose and broke into laughter, long, loud, and mechanical, devoid of gladness and devoid of sense—the laughter that is not out of keeping with the clanking of a chain. Hardly knowing what he did he extended his arms. She laid the babe in them. It was dead—pressed to death in its mother's embrace.

III

THE THEORY OF THE DEFENSE

THAT IS what occurred during a night in a forest, but not all of it did Irene Marlowe relate to Jenner Brading; not all of it was known to her. When she had concluded the sun was below the horizon and the long summer twilight had begun to deepen in the hollows of the land. For some moments Brading was silent, expecting the narrative to be carried forward to some definite connection with the conversation introducing it; but the narrator was as silent as he, her face averted, her hands clasping and unclasping themselves as they lay in her lap, with a singular suggestion of an activity independent of her will.

"It is a sad, a terrible story," said Brading at last, "but I do not understand. You call Charles Marlowe father; that I know. That he is old before his time, broken by some great sorrow, I have seen, or thought I saw. But, pardon me, you said that you—that you——"

"That I am insane," said the girl, without a movement of head or body.

"But, Irene, you say—please, dear, do not look away from me—you say that the child was dead, not demented."

"Yes, that one—I am the second. I was born three months after that night, my mother being mercifully permitted to lay down her life in giving me mine."

Brading was again silent; he was a trifle dazed and could not at once think of the right thing to say. Her face was still turned away. In his embarrassment he reached impulsively toward the hands that lay closing and unclosing in her lap, but something—he could not have said what—restrained him. He then remembered, vaguely, that he had never altogether cared to take her hand.

"Is it likely," she resumed, "that a person born under such circumstances is like others—is what you call sane?"

Brading did not reply; he was preoccupied with a new thought that was taking shape in his mind—what a scientist would have called an hypothesis; a detective, a theory. It might throw an added light, albeit a lurid one, upon such doubt of her sanity as her own assertion had not dispelled.

The country was still new and, outside the villages, sparsely populated. The professional hunter was still a familiar figure, and among his trophies were heads and pelts of the larger kinds of game. Tales variously credible of nocturnal meetings with savage animals in lonely roads were sometimes current, passed through the customary stages of growth and decay, and were forgotten. A recent addition to these popular apocrypha, originating, apparently, by spontaneous generation in several households, was of a panther which had frightened some of their members by looking in at windows by night. The yarn had caused its little ripple of excitement—had even attained to the distinction of a place in the local newspaper; but Brading had given it no attention. Its likeness to the story to which he had just listened now impressed him as perhaps more than accidental. Was it not possible that the one story had suggested the other—that finding congenial conditions in a morbid mind and a fertile fancy, it had grown to the tragic tale that he had heard?

Brading recalled certain circumstances of the girl's history and disposition, of which, with love's incuriosity, he had hitherto been heedless—such as her solitary life with her father, at whose house no one, apparently, was an acceptable visitor, and her strange fear of the night, by which those who knew her best accounted for her never being seen after dark. Surely in such a mind imagination once kindled might burn with a lawless flame, penetrating and enveloping the entire structure. That she was mad, though the conviction gave him the acutest pain, he could no longer doubt; she had only mistaken an effect of her mental disorder for its cause, bringing into imaginary relation with her own personality the vagaries of the local myth-makers. With some vague intention of testing his new "theory," and no very definite notion of how to set about it he said, gravely, but with hesitation:

"Irene, dear, tell me—I beg you will not take offence, but tell me——"

"I have told you," she interrupted, speaking with a passionate earnestness that he had not known her to show—"I have already told you that we cannot marry; is anything else worth saying?"

Before he could stop her she had sprung from her seat and without another word or look was gliding away among the trees toward her father's house. Brading had risen to detain her; he stood watching her in silence until she had vanished in the gloom. Suddenly he started as if he had been shot; his face took on an expression of amazement and alarm: in one of the black shadows into which she had disappeared he had caught a quick, brief glimpse of shining eyes! For an instant he was dazed and irresolute; then he dashed into the wood after her, shouting: "Irene, Irene, look out! The panther! The panther!"

In a moment he had passed through the fringe of forest into open ground and saw the girl's gray skirt vanishing into her father's door. No panther was visible.

IV

AN APPEAL TO THE CONSCIENCE OF GOD

JENNER BRADING, attorney-at-law, lived in a cottage at the edge of the town. Directly behind the dwelling was the forest. Being a bachelor, and therefore, by the Draconian moral code of the time and place denied the services of the only species of domestic servant known thereabout, the "hired girl," he boarded at the village hotel, where also was his office. The woodside cottage was merely a lodging maintained—at no great cost, to be sure—as an evidence of prosperity and respectability. It would hardly do for one to whom the local newspaper had pointed with pride as "the foremost jurist of his time" to be "homeless," albeit he may sometimes have suspected that the words "home" and "house" were not strictly synonymous. Indeed, his consciousness of the disparity and his will to harmonize it were matters of logical inference, for it was generally reported that soon after the cottage was built its owner had made a futile venture in the direction of marriage—had, in truth, gone so far as to be rejected by the beautiful but eccentric daughter of Old Man Marlowe, the recluse. This was publicly believed because he had told it himself and she had not—a reversal of the usual order of things which could hardly fail to carry conviction.

Brading's bedroom was at the rear of the house, with a single window facing the forest. One night he was awakened by a noise at that window; he could hardly have said what it was like. With a little thrill of the nerves he sat up in bed and laid hold of the revolver which, with a forethought most commendable in one addicted to the habit of sleeping on the ground floor with an open window, he had put under his pillow. The room was in absolute darkness, but being unterrified he knew where to direct his eyes, and there he held them, awaiting in silence what further might occur. He could now dimly discern the aperture—a square of lighter black. Presently there appeared at its lower edge two gleaming eyes that burned with a malignant lustre inexpressibly terrible! Brading's heart gave a great jump, then seemed to stand still. A chill passed along his spine and through his hair; he felt the blood forsake his cheeks. He could not have cried out —not to save his life; but being a man of courage he would not, to save his life, have done so if he had been able. Some trepidation his coward body might feel, but his spirit was of sterner stuff. Slowly the shining eyes rose with a steady motion that seemed an approach, and slowly rose Brading's right hand, holding the pistol. He fired!

Blinded by the flash and stunned by the report, Brading nevertheless heard, or fancied that he heard, the wild, high scream of the panther, so human in sound, so devilish in suggestion. Leaping from the bed he hastily clothed himself and, pistol in hand, sprang from the door, meeting two or three men who came running up from the road. A brief explanation was followed by a cautious search of the house. The grass was wet with dew; beneath the window it had been trodden and partly leveled for a wide space, from which a devious trail, visible in the light of a lantern, led away into the bushes. One of the men stumbled and fell upon his hands, which as he rose and rubbed them together were slippery. On examination they were seen to be red with blood.

An encounter, unarmed, with a wounded panther was not agreeable to their taste; all but Brading turned back. He, with lantern and pistol, pushed courageously forward into the wood. Passing through a difficult undergrowth he came into a small opening, and there his courage had its reward, for there he found the body of his victim. But it was no panther. What it was is told, even to this day, upon a weather-worn headstone in the village churchyard, and for many years was attested daily at the graveside by the bent figure and sorrow-seamed face of Old Man Marlowe, to whose soul, and to the soul of his strange, unhappy child, peace. Peace and reparation.

The Famous Gilson Bequest

IT WAS rough on Gilson. Such was the terse, cold, but not altogether unsympathetic judgment of the better public opinion at Mammon Hill—the dictum of respectability. The verdict of the opposite, or rather the opposing, element—the element that lurked red-eyed and restless about Moll Gurney's "deadfall," while respectability took it with sugar at Mr. Jo. Bentley's gorgeous "saloon"—was to pretty much the same general effect, though somewhat more ornately expressed by the use of picturesque expletives, which it is needless to quote. Virtually, Mammon Hill was a unit on the Gilson question. And it must be confessed that in a merely temporal sense all was not well with Mr. Gilson. He had that morning been led into town by Mr. Brentshaw and publicly charged with horse stealing; the sheriff meantime busying himself about The Tree with a new manila rope and Carpenter Pete being actively employed between drinks upon a pine box about the length and breadth of Mr. Gilson. Society having rendered its verdict, there remained between Gilson and eternity only the decent formality of a trial.

These are the short and simple annals of the prisoner: He had recently been a resident of New Jerusalem, on the north fork of the Little Stony, but had come to the newly discovered placers of Mammon Hill immediately before the "rush" by which the former place was depopulated. The discovery of the new diggings had occurred opportunely for Mr. Gilson, for it had only just before been intimated to him by a New Jerusalem vigilance committee that it would better his prospects in, and for, life to go somewhere; and the list of places to which he could safely go did not include any of the older camps; so he naturally established himself at Mammon Hill. Being eventually followed thither by all his judges, he ordered his conduct with considerable circumspection, but as he had never been known to do an honest day's work at any industry sanctioned by the stern local code of morality except draw poker he was still an object of suspicion. Indeed, it was conjectured that he was the author of the many dar-

114

ing depredations that had recently been committed with pan
and brush on the sluice boxes.

Prominent among those in whom this suspicion had ripened
into a steadfast conviction was Mr. Brentshaw. At all seasonable
and unseasonable times Mr. Brentshaw avowed his belief in
Mr. Gilson's connection with these unholy midnight enterprises,
and his own willingness to prepare a way for the solar beams
through the body of any one who might think it expedient to ut-
ter a different opinion—which, in his presence, no one was more
careful not to do than the peace-loving person most concerned.
Whatever may have been the truth of the matter, it is certain
that Gilson frequently lost more "clean dust" at Jo. Bentley's faro
table than it was recorded in local history that he had ever honestly earned at draw poker in all the days of the camp's existence. But at last Mr. Bentley—fearing, it may be, to lose the
more profitable patronage of Mr. Brentshaw—peremptorily refused to let Gilson copper the queen, intimating at the same
time, in his frank, forthright way, that the privilege of losing
money at "this bank" was a blessing appertaining to, proceeding
logically from, and coterminous with, a condition of notorious
commercial righteousness and social good repute.

The Hill thought it high time to look after a person whom its
most honored citizen had felt it his duty to rebuke at a considerable personal sacrifice. The New Jerusalem contingent, particularly, began to abate something of the toleration begotten of
amusement at their own blunder in exiling an objectionable
neighbor from the place which they had left to the place whither
they had come. Mammon Hill was at last of one mind. Not
much was said, but that Gilson must hang was "in the air." But
at this critical juncture in his affairs he showed signs of an altered life if not a changed heart. Perhaps it was only that "the
bank" being closed against him he had no further use for gold
dust. Anyhow the sluice boxes were molested no more forever.
But it was impossible to repress the abounding energies of such
a nature as his, and he continued, possibly from habit, the tortuous courses which he had pursued for profit of Mr. Bentley. After
a few tentative and resultless undertakings in the way of highway robbery—if one may venture to designate road-agency by so
harsh a name—he made one or two modest essays in horse-herd-
ing, and it was in the midst of a promising enterprise of this
character, and just as he had taken the tide in his affairs at its
flood, that he made shipwreck. For on a misty, moonlight night
Mr. Brentshaw rode up alongside a person who was evidently

leaving that part of the country, laid a hand upon the halter connecting Mr. Gilson's wrist with Mr. Harper's bay mare, tapped
him familiarly on the cheek with the barrel of a navy revolver
and requested the pleasure of his company in a direction opposite to that in which he was traveling.

It was indeed rough on Gilson.

On the morning after his arrest he was tried, convicted, and
sentenced. It only remains, so far as concerns his earthly career,
to hang him, reserving for more particular mention his last will
and testament, which, with great labor, he contrived in prison,
and in which, probably from some confused and imperfect notion
of the rights of captors, he bequeathed everything he owned to
his "lawfle execketer," Mr. Brentshaw. The bequest, however,
was made conditional on the legatee taking the testator's body
from The Tree and "planting it white."

So Mr. Gilson was—I was about to say "swung off," but I fear
there has been already something too much of slang in this
straightforward statement of facts; besides, the manner in which
the law took its course is more accurately described in the terms
employed by the judge in passing sentence: Mr. Gilson was
"strung up."

In due season Mr. Brentshaw, somewhat touched, it may well
be, by the empty compliment of the bequest, repaired to The
Tree to pluck the fruit thereof. When taken down the body was
found to have in its waistcoat pocket a duly attested codicil to
the will already noted. The nature of its provisions accounted for
the manner in which it had been withheld, for had Mr. Brentshaw previously been made aware of the conditions under which
he was to succeed to the Gilson estate he would indubitably
have declined the responsibility. Briefly stated, the purport of the
codicil was as follows:

Whereas, at divers times and in sundry places, certain persons
had asserted that during his life the testator had robbed their
sluice boxes; therefore, if during the five years next succeeding
the date of this instrument any one should make proof of such assertion before a court of law, such person was to receive as reparation the entire personal and real estate of which the testator
died seized and possessed, minus the expenses of court and a
stated compensation to the executor, Henry Clay Brentshaw; provided, that if more than one person made such proof the estate
was to be equally divided between or among them. But in case
none should succeed in so establishing the testator's guilt, then
the whole property, minus court expenses, as aforesaid, should

go to the said Henry Clay Brentshaw for his own use, as stated in the will.

The syntax of this remarkable document was perhaps open to critical objection, but that was clearly enough the meaning of it. The orthography conformed to no recognized system, but being mainly phonetic it was not ambiguous. As the probate judge remarked, it would take five aces to beat it. Mr. Brentshaw smiled good-humoredly, and after performing the last sad rites with amusing ostentation, had himself duly sworn as executor and conditional legatee under the provisions of a law hastily passed (at the instance of the member from the Mammon Hill district) by a facetious legislature; which law was afterward discovered to have created also three or four lucrative offices and authorized the expenditure of a considerable sum of public money for the construction of a certain railway bridge that with greater advantage might perhaps have been erected on the line of some actual railway.

Of course Mr. Brentshaw expected neither profit from the will nor litigation in consequence of its unusual provisions; Gilson, although frequently "flush," had been a man whom assessors and tax collectors were well satisfied to lose no money by. But a careless and merely formal search among his papers revealed title deeds to valuable estates in the East and certificates of deposit for incredible sums in banks less severely scrupulous than that of Mr. Jo. Bentley.

The astounding news got abroad directly, throwing the Hill into a fever of excitement. The Mammon Hill *Patriot,* whose editor had been a leading spirit in the proceedings that resulted in Gilson's departure from New Jerusalem, published a most complimentary obituary notice of the deceased, and was good enough to call attention to the fact that his degraded contemporary, the Squaw Gulch *Clarion,* was bringing virtue into contempt by beslavering with flattery the memory of one who in life had spurned the vile sheet as a nuisance from his door. Undeterred by the press, however, claimants under the will were not slow in presenting themselves with their evidence; and great as was the Gilson estate it appeared conspicuously paltry considering the vast number of sluice boxes from which it was averred to have been obtained. The country rose as one man!

Mr. Brentshaw was equal to the emergency. With a shrewd application of humble auxiliary devices, he at once erected above the bones of his benefactor a costly monument, overtopping every rough headboard in the cemetery, and on this he judiciously caused to be inscribed an epitaph of his own composing, eulogizing the honesty, public spirit and cognate virtues of him who slept beneath, "a victim to the unjust aspersions of Slander's viper brood."

Moreover, he employed the best legal talent in the Territory to defend the memory of his departed friend, and for five long years the Territorial courts were occupied with litigation growing out of the Gilson bequest. To fine forensic abilities Mr. Brentshaw opposed abilities more finely forensic; in bidding for purchasable favors he offered prices which utterly deranged the market; the judges found at his hospitable board entertainment for man and beast, the like of which had never been spread in the Territory; mendacious witnesses he confronted with witnesses of superior mendacity.

Nor was the battle confined to the temple of the blind goddess —it invaded the press, the pulpit, the drawing-room. It raged in the mart, the exchange, the school; in the gulches, and on the street corners. And upon the last day of the memorable period to which legal action under the Gilson will was limited, the sun went down upon a region in which the moral sense was dead, the social conscience callous, the intellectual capacity dwarfed, enfeebled, and confused! But Mr. Brentshaw was victorious all along the line.

On that night it so happened that the cemetery in one corner of which lay the now honored ashes of the late Milton Gilson, Esq., was partly under water. Swollen by incessant rains, Cat Creek had spilled over its banks an angry flood which, after scooping out unsightly hollows wherever the soil had been disturbed, had partly subsided, as if ashamed of the sacrilege, leaving exposed much that had been piously concealed. Even the famous Gilson monument, the pride and glory of Mammon Hill, was no longer a standing rebuke to the "viper brood"; succumbing to the sapping current it had toppled prone to earth. The ghoulish flood had exhumed the poor, decayed pine coffin, which now lay half-exposed, in pitiful contrast to the pompous monolith which, like a giant note of admiration, emphasized the disclosure.

To this depressing spot, drawn by some subtle influence he had sought neither to resist nor analyze, came Mr. Brentshaw. An altered man was Mr. Brentshaw. Five years of toil, anxiety, and wakefulness had dashed his black locks with streaks and patches of gray, bowed his fine figure, drawn sharp and angular his face, and debased his walk to a doddering shuffle. Nor had this lustrum of fierce contention wrought less upon his heart and intellect. The careless good humor that had prompted him to accept the trust of the dead man had given place to a fixed habit of melancholy. The firm, vigorous intellect had overripened into the mental mellowness of second childhood. His broad understanding had narrowed to the accommodation of a single idea; and in place of the quiet, cynical incredulity of former days, there was in him a haunting faith in the supernatural, that flitted and fluttered about his soul, shadowy, batlike, ominous of insanity. Unsettled in all else, his understanding clung to one conviction with the tenacity of a wrecked intellect. That was an unshaken belief in the entire blamelessness of the dead Gilson. He had so often sworn to this in court and asserted it in private conversation—had so frequently and so triumphantly established it by testimony that had come expensive to him (for that very day he had paid the last dollar of the Gilson estate to Mr. Jo. Bentley, the last witness to the Gilson good character)—that it had become to him a sort of religious faith. It seemed to him the one great central and basic truth of life—the sole serene verity in a world of lies.

On that night, as he seated himself pensively upon the prostrate monument, trying by the uncertain moonlight to spell out the epitaph which five years before he had composed with a chuckle that memory had not recorded, tears of remorse came into his eyes as he remembered that he had been mainly instrumental in compassing by a false accusation this good man's death; for during some of the legal proceedings, Mr. Harper, for a consideration (forgotten) had come forward and sworn that in the little transaction with his bay mare the deceased had acted in strict accordance with the Harperian wishes, confidentially communicated to the deceased and by him faithfully concealed at the cost of his life. All that Mr. Brentshaw had since done for the dead man's memory seemed pitifully inadequate—most mean, paltry, and debased with selfishness!

As he sat there, torturing himself with futile regrets, a faint shadow fell across his eyes. Looking toward the moon, hanging low in the west, he saw what seemed a vague, watery cloud obscuring her; but as it moved so that her beams lit up one side of it he perceived the clear, sharp outline of a human figure. The apparition became momentarily more distinct, and grew, visibly; it was drawing near. Dazed as were his senses, half locked up with terror and confounded with dreadful imaginings, Mr. Brentshaw yet could but perceive, or think he perceived, in this unearthly shape a strange similitude to the mortal part of the late Milton Gilson, as that person had looked when taken from The Tree five years before. The likeness was indeed complete, even to the full, stony eyes, and a certain shadowy circle about the neck. It was without coat or hat, precisely as Gilson had been when laid in his poor, cheap casket by the not ungentle hands of Carpenter Pete—for whom some one had long since performed the same neighborly office. The spectre, if such it was, seemed to bear something in its hands which Mr. Brentshaw could not clearly make out. It drew nearer, and paused at last beside the coffin containing the ashes of the late Mr. Gilson, the lid of which was awry, half disclosing the uncertain interior. Bending over this, the phantom seemed to shake into it from a basin some dark substance of dubious consistency, then glided stealthily back to the lowest part of the cemetery. Here the retiring flood had stranded a number of open coffins, about and among which it gurgled with low sobbings and stilly whispers. Stooping over one of these, the apparition carefully brushed its contents into the basin, then returning to its own casket, emptied the vessel into that, as before. This mysterious operation was repeated at every exposed coffin, the ghost sometimes dipping its laden basin into the running water, and gently agitating it to free it of the baser clay, always hoarding the residuum in its own private box. In short, the immortal part of the late Milton Gilson was cleaning up the dust of its neighbors and providently adding the same to its own.

Perhaps it was a phantasm of a disordered mind in a fevered body. Perhaps it was a solemn farce enacted by pranking existences that throng the shadows lying along the border of another world. God knows; to us is permitted only the knowledge that when the sun of another day touched with a grace of gold the ruined cemetery of Mammon Hill his kindliest beam fell upon the white, still face of Henry Brentshaw, dead among the dead.

An Adventure at Brownville*

I TAUGHT a little country school near Brownville, which, as every one knows who has had the good luck to live there, is the capital of a considerable expanse of the finest scenery in California. The town is somewhat frequented in summer by a class of persons whom it is the habit of the local journal to call "pleasure seekers," but who by a juster classification would be known as "the sick and those in adversity." Brownville itself might rightly enough be described, indeed, as a summer place of last resort. It is fairly well endowed with boarding-houses, at the least pernicious of which I performed twice a day (lunching at the schoolhouse) the humble rite of cementing the alliance between soul and body. From this "hostelry" (as the local journal preferred to call it when it did not call it a "caravanserai") to the schoolhouse the distance by the wagon road was about a mile and a half; but there was a trail, very little used, which led over an intervening range of low, heavily wooded hills, considerably shortening the distance. By this trail I was returning one evening later than usual. It was the last day of the term and I had been detained at the schoolhouse until almost dark, preparing an account of my stewardship for the trustees—two of whom, I proudly reflected, would be able to read it, and the third (an instance of the dominion of mind over matter) would be overruled in his customary antagonism to the schoolmaster of his own creation.

I had gone not more than a quarter of the way when, finding an interest in the antics of a family of lizards which dwelt thereabout and seemed full of reptilian joy for their immunity from the ills incident to life at the Brownville House, I sat upon a fallen tree to observe them. As I leaned wearily against a branch of the gnarled old trunk the twilight deepened in the somber woods and the faint new moon began casting visible shadows and gilding the leaves of the trees with a tender but ghostly light.

I heard the sound of voices—a woman's, angry, impetuous, ris-

*This story was written in collaboration with Miss Ina Lillian Peterson, to whom is rightly due the credit for whatever merit it may have.

121

ing against deep masculine tones, rich and musical. I strained my eyes, peering through the dusky shadows of the wood, hoping to get a view of the intruders on my solitude, but could see no one. For some yards in each direction I had an uninterrupted view of the trail, and knowing of no other within a half mile thought the persons heard must be approaching from the wood at one side. There was no sound but that of the voices, which were now so distinct that I could catch the words. That of the man gave me an impression of anger, abundantly confirmed by the matter spoken.

"I will have no threats; you are powerless, as you very well know. Let things remain as they are or, by God! you shall both suffer for it."

"What do you mean?"—this was the voice of the woman, a cultivated voice, the voice of a lady. "You would not—murder us."

There was no reply, at least none that was audible to me. During the silence I peered into the wood in hope to get a glimpse of the speakers, for I felt sure that this was an affair of gravity in which ordinary scruples ought not to count. It seemed to me that the woman was in peril; at any rate the man had not disavowed a willingness to murder. When a man is enacting the rôle of potential assassin he has not the right to choose his audience.

After some little time I saw them, indistinct in the moonlight among the trees. The man, tall and slender, seemed clothed in black; the woman wore, as nearly as I could make out, a gown of gray stuff. Evidently they were still unaware of my presence in the shadow, though for some reason when they renewed their conversation they spoke in lower tones and I could no longer understand. As I looked the woman seemed to sink to the ground and raise her hands in supplication, as is frequently done on the stage and never, so far as I knew, anywhere else, and I am now not altogether sure that it was done in this instance. The man fixed his eyes upon her; they seemed to glitter bleakly in the moonlight with an expression that made me apprehensive that he would turn them upon me. I do not know by what impulse I was moved, but I sprang to my feet out of the shadow. At that instant the figures vanished. I peered in vain through the spaces among the trees and clumps of undergrowth. The night wind rustled the leaves; the lizards had retired early, reptiles of exemplary habits. The little moon was already slipping behind a black hill in the west.

I went home, somewhat disturbed in mind, half doubting that

I had heard or seen any living thing excepting the lizards. It all seemed a trifle odd and uncanny. It was as if among the several phenomena, objective and subjective, that made the sum total of the incident there had been an uncertain element which had diffused its dubious character over all—had leavened the whole mass with unreality. I did not like it.

At the breakfast table the next morning there was a new face; opposite me sat a young woman at whom I merely glanced as I took my seat. In speaking to the high and mighty female personage who condescended to seem to wait upon us, this girl soon invited my attention by the sound of her voice, which was like, yet not altogether like, the one still murmuring in my memory of the previous evening's adventure. A moment later another girl, a few years older, entered the room and sat at the left of the other, speaking to her a gentle "good morning." By *her* voice I was startled: it was without doubt the one of which the first girl's had reminded me. Here was the lady of the sylvan incident sitting bodily before me, "in her habit as she lived."

Evidently enough the two were sisters. With a nebulous kind of apprehension that I might be recognized as the mute inglorious hero of an adventure which had in my consciousness and conscience something of the character of eavesdropping, I allowed myself only a hasty cup of the lukewarm coffee thoughtfully provided by the prescient waitress for the emergency, and left the table. As I passed out of the house into the grounds I heard a rich, strong male voice singing an aria from "Rigoletto." I am bound to say that it was exquisitely sung, too, but there was something in the performance that displeased me, I could say neither what nor why, and I walked rapidly away.

Returning later in the day I saw the elder of the two young women standing on the porch and near her a tall man in black clothing—the man whom I had expected to see. All day the desire to know something of these persons had been uppermost in my mind and I now resolved to learn what I could of them in any way that was neither dishonorable nor low.

The man was talking easily and affably to his companion, but at the sound of my footsteps on the gravel walk he ceased, and turning about looked me full in the face. He was apparently of middle age, dark and uncommonly handsome. His attire was faultless, his bearing easy and graceful, the look which he turned upon me open, free, and devoid of any suggestion of rudeness. Nevertheless it affected me with a distinct emotion which on subsequent analysis in memory appeared to be compounded of hatred and dread—I am unwilling to call it fear. A second later the man and woman had disappeared. They seemed to have a trick of disappearing. On entering the house, however, I saw them through the open doorway of the parlor as I passed; they had merely stepped through a window which opened down to the floor.

Cautiously "approached" on the subject of her new guests my landlady proved not ungracious. Restated with, I hope, some small reverence for English grammar the facts were these: the two girls were Pauline and Eva Maynard of San Francisco; the elder was Pauline. The man was Richard Benning, their guardian, who had been the most intimate friend of their father, now deceased. Mr. Benning had brought them to Brownville in the hope that the mountain climate might benefit Eva, who was thought to be in danger of consumption.

Upon these short and simple annals the landlady wrought an embroidery of eulogium which abundantly attested her faith in Mr. Benning's will and ability to pay for the best that her house afforded. That he had a good heart was evident to her from his devotion to his two beautiful wards and his really touching solicitude for their comfort. The evidence impressed me as insufficient and I silently found the Scotch verdict, "Not proven."

Certainly Mr. Benning was most attentive to his wards. In my strolls about the country I frequently encountered them—sometimes in company with other guests of the hotel—exploring the gulches, fishing, rifle shooting, and otherwise wiling away the monotony of country life; and although I watched them as closely as good manners would permit I saw nothing that would in any way explain the strange words that I had overheard in the wood. I had grown tolerably well acquainted with the young ladies and could exchange looks and even greetings with their guardian without actual repugnance.

A month went by and I had almost ceased to interest myself in their affairs when one night our entire little community was thrown into excitement by an event which vividly recalled my experience in the forest.

This was the death of the elder girl, Pauline.

The sisters had occupied the same bedroom on the third floor of the house. Waking in the gray of the morning Eva had found Pauline dead beside her. Later, when the poor girl was weeping beside the body amid a throng of sympathetic if not very considerate persons, Mr. Benning entered the room and appeared to be about to take her hand. She drew away from the side of the dead and moved slowly toward the door.

"It is you," she said—"you who have done this. You—you—you!"

"She is raving," he said in a low voice. He followed her, step by step, as she retreated, his eyes fixed upon hers with a steady gaze in which there was nothing of tenderness nor of compassion. She stopped; the hand that she had raised in accusation fell to her side, her dilated eyes contracted visibly, the lids slowly dropped over them, veiling their strange wild beauty, and she stood motionless and almost as white as the dead girl lying near. The man took her hand and put his arm gently about her shoulders, as if to support her. Suddenly she burst into a passion of tears and clung to him as a child to its mother. He smiled with a smile that affected me most disagreeably—perhaps any kind of smile would have done so—and led her silently out of the room.

There was an inquest—and the customary verdict: the deceased, it appeared, came to her death through "heart disease." It was before the invention of heart *failure,* though the heart of poor Pauline had indubitably failed. The body was embalmed and taken to San Francisco by some one summoned thence for the purpose, neither Eva nor Benning accompanying it. Some of the hotel gossips ventured to think that very strange, and a few hardy spirits went so far as to think it very strange indeed; but the good landlady generously threw herself into the breach, saying it was owing to the precarious nature of the girl's health. It is not of record that either of the two persons most affected and apparently least concerned made any explanation.

One evening about a week after the death I went out upon the veranda of the hotel to get a book that I had left there. Under some vines shutting out the moonlight from a part of the space I saw Richard Benning, for whose apparition I was prepared by having previously heard the low, sweet voice of Eva Maynard, whom also I now discerned, standing before him with one hand raised to his shoulder and her eyes, as nearly as I could judge, gazing upward into his. He held her disengaged hand and his head was bent with a singular dignity and grace. Their attitude was that of lovers, and as I stood in deep shadow to observe I felt even guiltier than on that memorable night in the wood. I was about to retire, when the girl spoke, and the contrast between her words and her attitude was so surprising that I remained, because I had merely forgotten to go away.

"You will take my life," she said, "as you did Pauline's. I know your intention as well as I know your power, and I ask nothing, only that you finish your work without needless delay and let me be at peace."

He made no reply—merely let go the hand that he was holding, removed the other from his shoulder, and turning away descended the steps leading to the garden and disappeared in the shrubbery. But a moment later I heard, seemingly from a great distance, his fine clear voice in a barbaric chant, which as I listened brought before some inner spiritual sense a consciousness of some far, strange land peopled with beings having forbidden powers. The song held me in a kind of spell, but when it had died away I recovered and instantly perceived what I thought an opportunity. I walked out of my shadow to where the girl stood. She turned and stared at me with something of the look, it seemed to me, of a hunted hare. Possibly my intrusion had frightened her.

"Miss Maynard," I said, "I beg you to tell me who that man is and the nature of his power over you. Perhaps this is rude in me, but it is not a matter for idle civilities. When a woman is in danger any man has a right to act."

She listened without visible emotion—almost I thought without interest, and when I had finished she closed her big blue eyes as if unspeakably weary.

"You can do nothing," she said.

I took hold of her arm, gently shaking her as one shakes a person falling into a dangerous sleep.

"You must rouse yourself," I said; "something must be done and you must give me leave to act. You have said that that man killed your sister, and I believe it—that he will kill you, and I believe that."

She merely raised her eyes to mine.

"Will you not tell me all?" I added.

"There is nothing to be done, I tell you—nothing. And if I could do anything I would not. It does not matter in the least. We shall be here only two days more; we go away then, oh, so far! If you have observed anything, I beg you to be silent."

"But this is madness, girl." I was trying by rough speech to break the deadly repose of her manner. "You have accused him of murder. Unless you explain these things to me I shall lay the matter before the authorities."

This roused her, but in a way that I did not like. She lifted her head proudly and said: "Do not meddle, sir, in what does not concern you. This is my affair, Mr. Moran, not yours."

"It concerns every person in the country—in the world," I answered, with equal coldness. "If you had no love for your sister I, at least, am concerned for you."

"Listen," she interrupted, leaning toward me. "I loved her, yes, God knows! But more than that—beyond all, beyond expression, I love *him*. You have overheard a secret, but you shall not make use of it to harm him. I shall deny all. Your word against mine—it will be that. Do you think your 'authorities' will believe you?"

She was now smiling like an angel and, God help me! I was heels over head in love with her! Did she, by some of the many methods of divination known to her sex, read my feelings? Her whole manner had altered.

"Come," she said, almost coaxingly, "promise that you will not be impolite again." She took my arm in the most friendly way. "Come, I will walk with you. He will not know—he will remain away all night."

Up and down the veranda we paced in the moonlight, she seemingly forgetting her recent bereavement, cooing and murmuring girlwise of every kind of nothing in all Brownville; I silent, consciously awkward and with something of the feeling of being concerned in an intrigue. It was a revelation—this most charming and apparently blameless creature coolly and confessedly deceiving the man for whom a moment before she had acknowledged and shown the supreme love which finds even death an acceptable endearment.

"Truly," I thought in my inexperience, "here is something new under the moon."

And the moon must have smiled.

Before we parted I had exacted a promise that she would walk with me the next afternoon—before going away forever—to the Old Mill, one of Brownville's revered antiquities, erected in 1860.

"If he is not about," she added gravely, as I let go the hand she had given me at parting, and of which, may the good saints forgive me, I strove vainly to repossess myself when she had said it —so charming, as the wise Frenchman has pointed out, do we find woman's infidelity when we are its objects, not its victims. In apportioning his benefactions that night the Angel of Sleep overlooked me.

The Brownville House dined early, and after dinner the next day Miss Maynard, who had not been at table, came to me on the veranda, attired in the demurest of walking costumes, saying not a word. "He" was evidently "not about." We went slowly up the road that led to the Old Mill. She was apparently not strong and at times took my arm, relinquishing it and taking it again rather capriciously, I thought. Her mood, or rather her succession of moods, was as mutable as skylight in a rippling sea. She jested as if she had never heard of such a thing as death, and laughed on the lightest incitement, and directly afterward would sing a few bars of some grave melody with such tenderness of expression that I had to turn away my eyes lest she should see the evidence of her success in art, if art it was, not artlessness, as then I was compelled to think it. And she said the oddest things in the most unconventional way, skirting sometimes unfathomable abysms of thought, where I had hardly the courage to set foot. In short, she was fascinating in a thousand and fifty different ways, and at every step I executed a new and profounder emotional folly, a hardier spiritual indiscretion, incurring fresh liability to arrest by the constabulary of conscience for infractions of my own peace.

Arriving at the mill, she made no pretense of stopping, but turned into a trail leading through a field of stubble toward a creek. Crossing by a rustic bridge we continued on the trail, which now led uphill to one of the most picturesque spots in the country. The Eagle's Nest, it was called—the summit of a cliff that rose sheer into the air to a height of hundreds of feet above the forest at its base. From this elevated point we had a noble view of another valley and of the opposite hills flushed with the last rays of the setting sun. As we watched the light escaping to higher and higher planes from the encroaching flood of shadow filling the valley we heard footsteps, and in another moment were joined by Richard Benning.

"I saw you from the road," he said carelessly; "so I came up."

Being a fool, I neglected to take him by the throat and pitch him into the treetops below, but muttered some polite lie instead. On the girl the effect of his coming was immediate and unmistakable. Her face was suffused with the glory of love's transfiguration: the red light of the sunset had not been more obvious in her eyes than was now the lovelight that replaced it.

"I am so glad you came!" she said, giving him both her hands; and, God help me! it was manifestly true.

Seating himself upon the ground he began a lively dissertation upon the wild flowers of the region, a number of which he had with him. In the middle of a facetious sentence he suddenly ceased speaking and fixed his eyes upon Eva, who leaned against the stump of a tree, absently plaiting grasses. She lifted her eyes in a startled way to his, as if she had *felt* his look. She then rose, cast away her grasses, and moved slowly away from him. He also rose, continuing to look at her. He had still in his hand the bunch of flowers. The girl turned, as if to speak, but said nothing. I recall clearly now something of which I was but half-conscious then—the dreadful contrast between the smile upon her lips and the terrified expression in her eyes as she met his steady and imperative gaze. I know nothing of how it happened, nor how it was that I did not sooner understand; I only know that with the smile of an angel upon her lips and that look of terror in her beautiful eyes Eva Maynard sprang from the cliff and shot crashing into the tops of the pines below!

How and how long afterward I reached the place I cannot say, but Richard Benning was already there, kneeling beside the dreadful thing that had been a woman.

"She is dead—quite dead," he said coldly. "I will go to town for assistance. Please do me the favor to remain."

He rose to his feet and moved away, but in a moment had stopped and turned about.

"You have doubtless observed, my friend," he said, "that this was entirely her own act. I did not rise in time to prevent it, and you, not knowing her mental condition—you could not, of course, have suspected."

His manner maddened me.

"You are as much her assassin," I said, "as if your damnable hands had cut her throat."

He shrugged his shoulders without reply and, turning, walked away. A moment later I heard, through the deepening shadows of the wood into which he had disappeared, a rich, strong, baritone voice singing *"La donna è mobile,"* from "Rigoletto."

An Inhabitant of Carcosa

For there be divers sorts of death—some wherein the body re-maineth; and in some it vanisheth quite away with the spirit. This commonly occurreth only in solitude (such is God's will) and, none seeing the end, we say the man is lost, or gone on a long journey—which indeed he hath; but sometimes it hath happened in sight of many, as abundant testimony showeth. In one kind of death the spirit also dieth, and this it hath been known to do while yet the body was in vigor for many years. Sometimes, as is veritably at-tested, it dieth with the body, but after a season is raised up again in that place where the body did decay.

PONDERING THESE words of Hali (whom God rest) and question-ing their full meaning, as one who, having an intimation, yet doubts if there be not something behind, other than that which he has discerned, I noted not whither I had strayed until a sud-den chill wind striking my face revived in me a sense of my sur-roundings. I observed with astonishment that everything seemed unfamiliar. On every side of me stretched a bleak and desolate expanse of plain, covered with a tall overgrowth of sere grass, which rustled and whistled in the autumn wind with heaven knows what mysterious and disquieting suggestion. Protruded at long intervals above it, stood strangely shaped and somber-colored rocks, which seemed to have an understanding with one another and to exchange looks of uncomfortable significance, as if they had reared their heads to watch the issue of some fore-seen event. A few blasted trees here and there appeared as lead-ers in this malevolent conspiracy of silent expectation.

The day, I thought, must be far advanced, though the sun was invisible; and although sensible that the air was raw and chill my consciousness of that fact was rather mental than physical—I had no feeling of discomfort. Over all the dismal landscape a canopy of low, lead-colored clouds hung like a visible curse. In all this there were a menace and a portent—a hint of evil, an in-timation of doom. Bird, beast, or insect there was none. The wind sighed in the bare branches of the dead trees and the gray grass bent to whisper its dread secret to the earth; but no other sound nor motion broke the awful repose of that dismal place.

I observed in the herbage a number of weather-worn stones, evidently shaped with tools. They were broken, covered with moss and half sunken in the earth. Some lay prostrate, some leaned at various angles, none was vertical. They were obviously headstones of graves, though the graves themselves no longer existed as either mounds or depressions; the years had leveled all. Scattered here and there, more massive blocks showed where some pompous tomb or ambitious monument had once flung its feeble defiance at oblivion. So old seemed these relics, these vestiges of vanity and memorials of affection and piety, so battered and worn and stained—so neglected, deserted, forgotten the place, that I could not help thinking myself the discoverer of the burial-ground of a prehistoric race of men whose very name was long extinct.

Filled with these reflections, I was for some time heedless of the sequence of my own experiences, but soon I thought, "How came I hither?" A moment's reflection seemed to make this all clear and explain at the same time, though in a disquieting way, the singular character with which my fancy had invested all that I saw or heard. I was ill. I remembered now that I had been prostrated by a sudden fever, and that my family had told me that in my periods of delirium I had constantly cried out for liberty and air, and had been held in bed to prevent my escape out-of-doors. Now I had eluded the vigilance of my attendants and had wandered hither to—to where? I could not conjecture. Clearly I was at a considerable distance from the city where I dwelt—the ancient and famous city of Carcosa.

No signs of human life were anywhere visible nor audible; no rising smoke, no watchdog's bark, no lowing of cattle, no shouts of children at play—nothing but that dismal burial-place with its air of mystery and dread, due to my own disordered brain. Was I not becoming again delirious, there beyond human aid? Was it not indeed *all* an illusion of my madness? I called aloud the names of my wives and sons, reached out my hands in search of theirs, even as I walked among the crumbling stones and in the withered grass.

A noise behind me caused me to turn about. A wild animal— a lynx—was approaching. The thought came to me: If I break down here in the desert—if the fever return and I fail, this beast will be at my throat. I sprang toward it, shouting. It trotted tranquilly by within a hand's breadth of me and disappeared behind a rock.

A moment later a man's head appeared to rise out of the ground a short distance away. He was ascending the farther slope of a low hill whose crest was hardly to be distinguished from the general level. His whole figure soon came into view against the background of gray cloud. He was half naked, half clad in skins. His hair was unkempt, his beard long and ragged. In one hand he carried a bow and arrow; the other held a blazing torch with a long trail of black smoke. He walked slowly and with caution, as if he feared falling into some open grave concealed by the tall grass. This strange apparition surprised but did not alarm, and taking such a course as to intercept him I met him almost face to face, accosting him with the familiar salutation, "God keep you."

He gave no heed, nor did he arrest his pace.

"Good stranger," I continued, "I am ill and lost. Direct me, I beseech you, to Carcosa."

The man broke into a barbarous chant in an unknown tongue, passing on and away.

An owl on the branch of a decayed tree hooted dismally and was answered by another in the distance. Looking upward, I saw through a sudden rift in the clouds Aldebaran and the Hyades! In all this there was a hint of night—the lynx, the man with the torch, the owl. Yet I saw—I saw even the stars in absence of the darkness. I saw, but was apparently not seen nor heard. Under what awful spell did I exist?

I seated myself at the root of a great tree, seriously to consider what it were best to do. That I was mad I could no longer doubt, yet recognized a ground of doubt in the conviction. Of fever I had no trace. I had, withal, a sense of exhilaration and vigor altogether unknown to me—a feeling of mental and physical exaltation. My senses seemed all alert; I could feel the air as a ponderous substance; I could hear the silence.

A great root of the giant tree against whose trunk I leaned as I sat held inclosed in its grasp a slab of stone, a part of which protruded into a recess formed by another root. The stone was thus partly protected from the weather, though greatly decomposed. Its edges were worn round, its corners eaten away, its surface deeply furrowed and scaled. Glittering particles of mica were visible in the earth about it—vestiges of its decomposition. This stone had apparently marked the grave out of which the tree had sprung ages ago. The tree's exacting roots had robbed the grave and made the stone a prisoner.

A sudden wind pushed some dry leaves and twigs from the uppermost face of the stone; I saw the low-relief letters of an inscription and bent to read it. God in Heaven! *my* name in full!—the date of *my* birth!—the date of *my* death!

A level shaft of light illuminated the whole side of the tree as I sprang to my feet in terror. The sun was rising in the rosy east. I stood between the tree and his broad red disk—no shadow darkened the trunk!

A chorus of howling wolves saluted the dawn. I saw them sitting on their haunches, singly and in groups, on the summits of irregular mounds and tumuli filling a half of my desert prospect and extending to the horizon. And then I knew that these were ruins of the ancient and famous city of Carcosa.

———————

Such are the facts imparted to the medium Bayrolles by the spirit Hoseib Alar Robardin.

The Secret of Macarger's Gulch

NORTHWESTWARDLY FROM Indian Hill, about nine miles as the crow flies, is Macarger's Gulch. It is not much of a gulch—a mere depression between two wooded ridges of inconsiderable height. From its mouth up to its head—for gulches, like rivers, have an anatomy of their own—the distance does not exceed two miles, and the width at bottom is at only one place more than a dozen yards; for most of the distance on either side of the little brook which drains it in winter, and goes dry in the early spring, there is no level ground at all; the steep slopes of the hills, covered with an almost impenetrable growth of manzanita and chamiso, are parted by nothing but the width of the water course. No one but an occasional enterprising hunter of the vicinity ever goes into Macarger's Gulch, and five miles away it is unknown, even by name. Within that distance in any direction are far more conspicuous topographical features without names, and one might try in vain to ascertain by local inquiry the origin of the name of this one.

About midway between the head and the mouth of Macarger's Gulch, the hill on the right as you ascend is cloven by another gulch, a short dry one, and at the junction of the two is a level space of two or three acres, and there a few years ago stood an old board house containing one small room. How the component parts of the house, few and simple as they were, had been assembled at that almost inaccessible point is a problem in the solution of which there would be greater satisfaction than advantage. Possibly the creek bed is a reformed road. It is certain that the gulch was at one time pretty thoroughly prospected by miners, who must have had some means of getting in with at least pack animals carrying tools and supplies; their profits, apparently, were not such as would have justified any considerable outlay to connect Macarger's Gulch with any center of civilization enjoying the distinction of a sawmill. The house, however, was there, most of it. It lacked a door and a window frame, and the chimney of mud and stones had fallen into an unlovely heap, overgrown with rank weeds. Such humble furniture as there may once have been and much of the lower weatherboarding, had served as fuel in the camp fires of hunters; as had also, probably, the curbing of an old well, which at the time I write of existed in the form of a rather wide but not very deep depression nearby.

One afternoon in the summer of 1874, I passed up Macarger's Gulch from the narrow valley into which it opens, by following the dry bed of the brook. I was quail-shooting and had made a bag of about a dozen birds by the time I had reached the house described, of whose existence I was until then unaware. After rather carelessly inspecting the ruin I resumed my sport, and having fairly good success prolonged it until near sunset, when it occurred to me that I was a long way from any human habitation —too far to reach one by nightfall. But in my game bag was food, and the old house would afford shelter, if shelter were needed on a warm and dewless night in the foothills of the Sierra Nevada, where one may sleep in comfort on the pine needles, without covering. I am fond of solitude and love the night, so my resolution to "camp out" was soon taken, and by the time that it was dark I had made my bed of boughs and grasses in a corner of the room and was roasting a quail at a fire that I had kindled on the hearth. The smoke escaped out of the ruined chimney, the light illuminated the room with a kindly glow, and as I ate my simple meal of plain bird and drank the remains of a bottle of red wine which had served me all the afternoon in place of the water which the region did not supply, I experienced a sense of comfort which better fare and accommodations do not always give.

Nevertheless, there was something lacking. I had a sense of comfort, but not of security. I detected myself staring more frequently at the open doorway and blank window than I could find warrant for doing. Outside these apertures all was black, and I was unable to repress a certain feeling of apprehension as my fancy pictured the outer world and filled it with unfriendly entities, natural and supernatural—chief among which, in their respective classes, were the grizzly bear, which I knew was occasionally still seen in that region, and the ghost, which I had reason to think was not. Unfortunately, our feelings do not always respect the law of probabilities, and to me that evening, the possible and the impossible were equally disquieting.

Everyone who has had experience in the matter must have observed that one confronts the actual and imaginary perils of the night with far less apprehension in the open air than in a house with an open doorway. I felt this now as I lay on my leafy couch in a corner of the room next to the chimney and permitted my fire to die out. So strong became my sense of the presence of something malign and menacing in the place, that I found myself almost unable to withdraw my eyes from the opening, as in the deepening darkness it became more and more indistinct. And when the last little flame flickered and went out I grasped the shotgun which I had laid at my side and actually turned the muzzle in the direction of the now invisible entrance, my thumb on one of the hammers, ready to cock the piece, my breath suspended, my muscles rigid and tense. But later I laid down the weapon with a sense of shame and mortification. What did I fear, and why?—I, to whom the night had been

> a more familiar face
> Than that of man—

I, in whom that element of hereditary superstition from which none of us is altogether free had given to solitude and darkness and silence only a more alluring interest and charm! I was unable to comprehend my folly, and losing in the conjecture the thing conjectured of, I fell asleep. And then I dreamed.

I was in a great city in a foreign land—a city whose people were of my own race, with minor differences of speech and costume; yet precisely what these were I could not say; my sense of them was indistinct. The city was dominated by a great castle upon an overlooking height whose name I knew, but could not speak. I walked through many streets, some broad and straight with high, modern buildings, some narrow, gloomy, and tortuous, between the gables of quaint old houses whose overhanging stories, elaborately ornamented with carvings in wood and stone, almost met above my head.

I sought someone whom I had never seen, yet knew that I should recognize when found. My quest was not aimless and fortuitous; it had a definite method. I turned from one street into another without hesitation and threaded a maze of intricate passages, devoid of the fear of losing my way.

Presently I stopped before a low door in a plain stone house which might have been the dwelling of an artisan of the better sort, and without announcing myself, entered. The room, rather sparely furnished, and lighted by a single window with small diamond-shaped panes, had but two occupants; a man and a woman. They took no notice of my intrusion, a circumstance which, in the manner of dreams, appeared entirely natural. They were not conversing; they sat apart, unoccupied and sullen.

The woman was young and rather stout, with fine large eyes and a certain grave beauty; my memory of her expression is exceedingly vivid, but in dreams one does not observe the details of faces. About her shoulders was a plaid shawl. The man was older, dark, with an evil face made more forbidding by a long scar extending from near the left temple diagonally downward into the black mustache; though in my dreams it seemed rather to haunt the face as a thing apart—I can express it no otherwise—than to belong to it. The moment that I found the man and woman I knew them to be husband and wife.

What followed, I remember indistinctly; all was confused and inconsistent—made so, I think, by gleams of consciousness. It was as if two pictures, the scene of my dream, and my actual surroundings, had been blended, one overlying the other, until the former, gradually fading, disappeared, and I was broad awake in the deserted cabin, entirely and tranquilly conscious of my situation.

My foolish fear was gone, and opening my eyes I saw that my fire, not altogether burned out, had revived by the falling of a stick and was again lighting the room. I had probably slept only a few minutes, but my commonplace dream had somehow so strongly impressed me that I was no longer drowsy; and after a little while I rose, pushed the embers of my fire together, and lighting my pipe proceeded in a rather ludicrously methodical way to meditate upon my vision.

It would have puzzled me then to say in what respect it was worth attention. In the first moment of serious thought that I gave to the matter I recognized the city of my dream as Edinburgh, where I had never been; so if the dream was a memory it was a memory of pictures and description. The recognition somehow deeply impressed me; it was as if something in my mind insisted rebelliously against will and reason on the importance of all this. And that faculty, whatever it was, asserted also a control of my speech. "Surely," I said aloud, quite involuntarily, "the MacGregors must have come here from Edinburgh."

At the moment, neither the substance of this remark nor the fact of my making it, surprised me in the least; it seemed entirely natural that I should know the name of my dreamfolk and something of their history. But the absurdity of it all soon dawned upon me: I laughed aloud, knocked the ashes from my pipe and again stretched myself upon my bed of boughs and grass, where I lay staring absently into my failing fire, with no further thought of either my dream or my surroundings. Suddenly the single remaining flame crouched for a moment, then, springing upward, lifted itself clear of its embers and expired in air. The darkness was absolute.

At that instant—almost, it seemed, before the gleam of the blaze had faded from my eyes—there was a dull, dead sound, as of some heavy body falling upon the floor, which shook beneath me as I lay. I sprang to a sitting posture and groped at my side for my gun; my notion was that some wild beast had leaped in through the open window. While the flimsy structure was still shaking from the impact I heard the sound of blows, the scuffling of feet upon the floor, and then—it seemed to come from almost within reach of my hand, the sharp shrieking of a woman in mortal agony. So horrible a cry I had never heard nor conceived; it utterly unnerved me; I was conscious for a moment of nothing but my own terror! Fortunately my hand now found the weapon of which it was in search, and the familiar touch somewhat restored me. I leaped to my feet, straining my eyes to pierce the darkness. The violent sounds had ceased, but more terrible than these, I heard, at what seemed long intervals, the faint intermittent gasping of some living, dying thing!

As my eyes grew accustomed to the dim light of the coals in the fireplace, I saw first the shapes of the door and window, looking blacker than the black of the walls. Next, the distinction between wall and floor became discernible, and at last I was sensible to the form and full expanse of the floor from end to end and side to side. Nothing was visible and the silence was unbroken.

With a hand that shook a little, the other still grasping my gun, I restored my fire and made a critical examination of the place. There was nowhere any sign that the cabin had been entered. My own tracks were visible in the dust covering the floor, but there were no others. I relit my pipe, provided fresh fuel by ripping a thin board or two from the inside of the house—I did not care to go into the darkness out of doors—and passed the rest of the night smoking and thinking, and feeding my fire; not for added years of life would I have permitted that little flame to expire again.

SOME YEARS afterward I met in Sacramento a man named Morgan, to whom I had a note of introduction from a friend in San Francisco. Dining with him one evening at his home I observed various "trophies" upon the wall, indicating that he was fond of shooting. It turned out that he was, and in relating some of his feats he mentioned having been in the region of my adventure.

"Mr. Morgan," I asked abruptly, "do you know a place up there called Macarger's Gulch?"

"I have good reason to," he replied; "it was I who gave to the newspapers, last year, the accounts of the finding of the skeleton there."

I had not heard of it; the accounts had been published, it appeared, while I was absent in the East.

"By the way," said Morgan, "the name of the gulch is a corruption; it should have been called 'MacGregor's.' My dear," he added, speaking to his wife, "Mr. Elderson has upset his wine."

That was hardly accurate—I had simply dropped it, glass and all.

"There was an old shanty once in the gulch," Morgan resumed when the ruin wrought by my awkwardness had been repaired, "but just previously to my visit it had been blown down, or rather blown away, for its *débris* was scattered all about, the very floor being parted, plank from plank. Between two of the sleepers still in position I and my companion observed the remnant of a plaid shawl, and examining it found that it was wrapped about the shoulders of the body of a woman, of which but little remained besides the bones, partly covered with fragments of clothing, and brown dry skin. But we will spare Mrs. Morgan," he added with a smile. The lady had indeed exhibited signs of disgust rather than sympathy.

"It is necessary to say, however," he went on, "that the skull was fractured in several places, as by blows of some blunt instrument; and that instrument itself—a pick-handle, still stained with blood —lay under the boards nearby."

Mr. Morgan turned to his wife. "Pardon me, my dear," he said with affected solemnity, "for mentioning these disagreeable particulars, the natural though regrettable incidents of a conjugal quarrel—resulting, doubtless, from the luckless wife's insubordination."

"I ought to be able to overlook it," the lady replied with composure; "you have so many times asked me to in those very words."

I thought he seemed rather glad to go on with his story.

"From these and other circumstances," he said, "the coroner's jury found that the deceased, Janet MacGregor, came to her death from blows inflicted by some person to the jury unknown;

but it was added that the evidence pointed strongly to her husband, Thomas MacGregor, as the guilty person. But Thomas MacGregor has never been found nor heard of. It was learned that the couple came from Edinburgh, but not—my dear, do you not observe that Mr. Elderson's boneplate has water in it?"

I had deposited a chicken bone in my finger bowl.

"In a little cupboard I found a photograph of MacGregor, but it did not lead to his capture."

"Will you let me see it?" I said.

The picture showed a dark man with an evil face made more forbidding by a long scar extending from near the temple diagonally downward into the black mustache.

"By the way, Mr. Elderson," said my affable host, "may I know why you asked about 'Macarger's Gulch'?"

"I lost a mule near there once," I replied, "and the mischance has—has quite—upset me."

"My dear," said Mr. Morgan, with the mechanical intonation of an interpreter translating, "the loss of Mr. Elderson's mule has peppered his coffee."

The Moonlit Road

I

STATEMENT OF JOEL HETMAN, JR.

I AM the most unfortunate of men. Rich, respected, fairly well educated and of sound health—with many other advantages usually valued by those having them and coveted by those who have them not—I sometimes think that I should be less unhappy if they had been denied me, for then the contrast between my outer and my inner life would not be continually demanding a painful attention. In the stress of privation and the need of effort I might sometimes forget the somber secret ever baffling the conjecture that it compels.

I am the only child of Joel and Julia Hetman. The one was a well-to-do country gentleman, the other a beautiful and accomplished woman to whom he was passionately attached with what I now know to have been a jealous and exacting devotion. The family home was a few miles from Nashville, Tennessee, a large, irregularly built dwelling of no particular order of architecture, a little way off the road, in a park of trees and shrubbery.

At the time of which I write I was nineteen years old, a student at Yale. One day I received a telegram from my father of such urgency that in compliance with its unexplained demand I left at once for home. At the railway station in Nashville a distant relative awaited me to apprise me of the reason for my recall: my mother had been barbarously murdered—why and by whom none could conjecture, but the circumstances were these:

My father had gone to Nashville, intending to return the next afternoon. Something prevented his accomplishing the business in hand, so he returned on the same night, arriving just before the dawn. In his testimony before the coroner he explained that having no latchkey and not caring to disturb the sleeping servants, he had, with no clearly defined intention, gone round to the rear of the house. As he turned an angle of the building, he heard a sound as of a door gently closed, and saw in the darkness, indistinctly, the figure of a man, which instantly disappeared among the trees of the lawn. A hasty pursuit and brief search of the grounds in the belief that the trespasser was some one secretly visiting a servant proving fruitless, he entered at the unlocked door and mounted the stairs to my mother's chamber. Its door was open, and stepping into black darkness he fell headlong over some heavy object on the floor. I may spare myself the details; it was my poor mother, dead of strangulation by human hands!

Nothing had been taken from the house, the servants had heard no sound, and excepting those terrible finger-marks upon the dead woman's throat—dear God! that I might forget them! —no trace of the assassin was ever found.

I gave up my studies and remained with my father, who, naturally, was greatly changed. Always of a sedate, taciturn disposition, he now fell into so deep a dejection that nothing could hold his attention, yet anything—a footfall, the sudden closing of a door—aroused in him a fitful interest; one might have called it an apprehension. At any small surprise of the senses he would start visibly and sometimes turn pale, then relapse into a melancholy apathy deeper than before. I suppose he was what is called a "nervous wreck." As to me, I was younger then than now— there is much in that. Youth is Gilead, in which is balm for every wound. Ah, that I might again dwell in that enchanted land! Unacquainted with grief, I knew not how to appraise my bereavement; I could not rightly estimate the strength of the stroke.

One night, a few months after the dreadful event, my father and I walked home from the city. The full moon was about three hours above the eastern horizon; the entire countryside had the solemn stillness of a summer night; our footfalls and the ceaseless song of the katydids were the only sound, aloof. Black shadows of bordering trees lay athwart the road, which, in the short reaches between, gleamed a ghostly white. As we approached the gate to our dwelling, whose front was in shadow, and in which no light shone, my father suddenly stopped and clutched my arm, saying, hardly above his breath:

"God! God! what is that?"

"I hear nothing," I replied.

"But see—see!" he said, pointing along the road, directly ahead.

I said: "Nothing is there. Come, Father, let us go in—you are ill."

He had released my arm and was standing rigid and motionless in the center of the illuminated roadway, staring like one bereft of sense. His face in the moonlight showed a pallor and fixity inexpressibly distressing. I pulled gently at his sleeve, but he had forgotten my existence. Presently he began to retire backward, step by step, never for an instant removing his eyes from what he saw, or thought he saw. I turned half round to follow, but stood irresolute. I do not recall any feeling of fear, unless a sudden chill was its physical manifestation. It seemed as if an icy wind had touched my face and enfolded my body from head to foot; I could feel the stir of it in my hair.

At that moment my attention was drawn to a light that suddenly streamed from an upper window of the house: one of the servants, awakened by what mysterious premonition of evil who can say, and in obedience to an impulse that she was never able to name, had lit a lamp. When I turned to look for my father he was gone, and in all the years that have passed no whisper of his fate has come across the borderland of conjecture from the realm of the unknown.

II

STATEMENT OF CASPAR GRATTAN

TO-DAY I am said to live; to-morrow, here in this room, will lie a senseless shape of clay that all too long was I. If anyone lift the cloth from the face of that unpleasant thing it will be in gratification of a mere morbid curiosity. Some, doubtless, will go further and inquire, "Who was he?" In this writing I supply the only answer that I am able to make—Caspar Grattan. Surely, that should be enough. The name has served my small need for more than twenty years of a life of unknown length. True, I gave it to myself, but lacking another I had the right. In this world one must have a name; it prevents confusion, even when it does not establish identity. Some, though, are known by numbers, which also seem inadequate distinctions.

One day, for illustration, I was passing along a street of a city, far from here, when I met two men in uniform, one of whom, half pausing and looking curiously into my face, said to his companion, "That man looks like 767." Something in the number seemed familiar and horrible. Moved by an uncontrollable impulse, I sprang into a side street and ran until I fell exhausted in a country lane.

I have never forgotten that number, and always it comes to memory attended by gibbering obscenity, peals of joyless laughter, the clang of iron doors. So I say a name, even if self-bestowed, is better than a number. In the register of the potter's field I shall soon have both. What wealth!

Of him who shall find this paper I must beg a little consideration. It is not the history of my life; the knowledge to write that is denied me. This is only a record of broken and apparently unrelated memories, some of them as distinct and sequent as brilliant beads upon a thread, others remote and strange, having the character of crimson dreams with interspaces blank and black—witch-fires glowing still and red in a great desolation.

Standing upon the shore of eternity, I turn for a last look landward over the course by which I came. There are twenty years of footprints fairly distinct, the impressions of bleeding feet. They lead through poverty and pain, devious and unsure, as of one staggering beneath a burden—

Remote, unfriended, melancholy, slow.

Ah, the poet's prophecy of Me—how admirable, how dreadfully admirable!

Backward beyond the beginning of this *via dolorosa*—this epic of suffering with episodes of sin—I see nothing clearly; it comes out of a cloud. I know that it spans only twenty years, yet I am an old man.

One does not remember one's birth—one has to be told. But with me it was different; life came to me full-handed and dowered me with all my faculties and powers. Of a previous existence I know no more than others, for all have stammering intimations that may be memories and may be dreams. I know only that my first consciousness was of maturity in body and mind—a consciousness accepted without surprise or conjecture. I merely found myself walking in a forest, half-clad, footsore, unutterably weary and hungry. Seeing a farmhouse, I approached and asked for food, which was given me by one who inquired my name. I did not know, yet knew that all had names. Greatly embarrassed, I retreated, and night coming on, lay down in the forest and slept.

The next day I entered a large town which I shall not name. Nor shall I recount further incidents of the life that is now to end —a life of wandering, always and everywhere haunted by an overmastering sense of crime in punishment of wrong and of terror in punishment of crime. Let me see if I can reduce it to narrative.

I seem once to have lived near a great city, a prosperous planter, married to a woman whom I loved and distrusted. We had, it sometimes seems, one child, a youth of brilliant parts and promise. He is at all times a vague figure, never clearly drawn, frequently altogether out of the picture.

One luckless evening it occurred to me to test my wife's fidelity in a vulgar, commonplace way familiar to everyone who has acquaintance with the literature of fact and fiction. I went to the city, telling my wife that I should be absent until the following afternoon. But I returned before daybreak and went to the rear of the house, purposing to enter by a door with which I had secretly so tampered that it would seem to lock, yet not actually fasten. As I approached it, I heard it gently open and close, and saw a man steal away into the darkness. With murder in my heart, I sprang after him, but he had vanished without even the bad luck of identification. Sometimes now I cannot even persuade myself that it was a human being.

Crazed with jealousy and rage, blind and bestial with all the elemental passions of insulted manhood, I entered the house and sprang up the stairs to the door of my wife's chamber. It was closed, but having tampered with its lock also, I easily entered and despite the black darkness soon stood by the side of her bed. My groping hands told me that although disarranged it was unoccupied.

"She is below," I thought, "and terrified by my entrance has evaded me in the darkness of the hall."

With the purpose of seeking her I turned to leave the room, but took a wrong direction—the right one! My foot struck her, cowering in a corner of the room. Instantly my hands were at her throat, stifling a shriek, my knees were upon her struggling body; and there in the darkness, without a word of accusation or reproach, I strangled her till she died!

There ends the dream. I have related it in the past tense, but the present would be the fitter form, for again and again the somber tragedy reenacts itself in my consciousness—over and over I lay the plan, I suffer the confirmation, I redress the wrong. Then all is blank; and afterward the rains beat against the grimy window-panes, or the snows fall upon my scant attire, the wheels rattle in the squalid streets where my life lies in poverty and mean employment. If there is ever sunshine I do not recall it; if there are birds they do not sing.

There is another dream, another vision of the night. I stand among the shadows in a moonlit road. I am aware of another presence, but whose I cannot rightly determine. In the shadow of a great dwelling I catch the gleam of white garments; then the figure of a woman confronts me in the road—my murdered wife! There is death in the face; there are marks upon the throat. The eyes are fixed on mine with an infinite gravity which is not reproach, nor hate, nor menace, nor anything less terrible than recognition. Before this awful apparition I retreat in terror—a terror that is upon me as I write. I can no longer rightly shape the words. See! they—

Now I am calm, but truly there is no more to tell: the incident ends where it began—in darkness and in doubt.

Yes, I am again in control of myself: "the captain of my soul." But that is not respite; it is another stage and phase of expiation. My penance, constant in degree, is mutable in kind: one of its variants is tranquillity. After all, it is only a life-sentence. "To Hell for life"—that is a foolish penalty: the culprit chooses the duration of his punishment. To-day my term expires.

To each and all, the peace that was not mine.

III

STATEMENT OF THE LATE JULIA HETMAN, THROUGH THE MEDIUM BAYROLLES

I HAD retired early and fallen almost immediately into a peaceful sleep, from which I awoke with that indefinable sense of peril which is, I think, a common experience in that other, earlier life. Of its unmeaning character, too, I was entirely persuaded, yet that did not banish it. My husband, Joel Hetman, was away from home; the servants slept in another part of the house. But these were familiar conditions; they had never before distressed me. Nevertheless, the strange terror grew so insupportable that conquering my reluctance to move I sat up and lit the lamp at my bedside. Contrary to my expectation this gave me no relief;

the light seemed rather an added danger, for I reflected that it would shine out under the door, disclosing my presence to whatever evil thing might lurk outside. You that are still in the flesh, subject to horrors of the imagination, think what a monstrous fear that must be which seeks in darkness security from malevolent existences of the night. That is to spring to close quarters with an unseen enemy—the strategy of despair!

Extinguishing the lamp I pulled the bedclothing about my head and lay trembling and silent, unable to shriek, forgetful to pray. In this pitiable state I must have lain for what you call hours—with us there are no hours, there is no time.

At last it came—a soft, irregular sound of footfalls on the stairs! They were slow, hesitant, uncertain, as of something that did not see its way; to my disordered reason all the more terrifying for that, as the approach of some blind and mindless malevolence to which is no appeal. I even thought that I must have left the hall lamp burning and the groping of this creature proved it a monster of the night. This was foolish and inconsistent with my previous dread of the light, but what would you have? Fear has no brains; it is an idiot. The dismal witness that it bears and the cowardly counsel that it whispers are unrelated. We know this well, we who have passed into the Realm of Terror, who skulk in eternal dusk among the scenes of our former lives, invisible even to ourselves and one another, yet hiding forlorn in lonely places; yearning for speech with our loved ones, yet dumb, and as fearful of them as they of us. Sometimes the disability is removed, the law suspended: by the deathless power of love or hate we break the spell—we are seen by those whom we would warn, console, or punish. What form we seem to them to bear we know not; we know only that we terrify even those whom we most wish to comfort, and from whom we most crave tenderness and sympathy.

Forgive, I pray you, this inconsequent digression by what was once a woman. You who consult us in this imperfect way—you do not understand. You ask foolish questions about things unknown and things forbidden. Much that we know and could impart in our speech is meaningless in yours. We must communicate with you through a stammering intelligence in that small fraction of our language that you yourselves can speak. You think that we are of another world. No, we have knowledge of no world but yours, though for us it holds no sunlight, no warmth, no music, no laughter, no song of birds, nor any companionship. O God! what a thing it is to be a ghost, cowering and shivering in an altered world, a prey to apprehension and despair!

No, I did not die of fright: the Thing turned and went away. I heard it go down the stairs, hurriedly, I thought, as if itself in sudden fear. Then I rose to call for help. Hardly had my shaking hand found the door-knob when—merciful heaven!—I heard it returning. Its footfalls as it remounted the stairs were rapid, heavy and loud; they shook the house. I fled to an angle of the wall and crouched upon the floor. I tried to pray. I tried to call the name of my dear husband. Then I heard the door thrown open. There was an interval of unconsciousness, and when I revived I felt a strangling clutch upon my throat—felt my arms feebly beating against something that bore me backward—felt my tongue thrusting itself from between my teeth! And then I passed into this life.

No, I have no knowledge of what it was. The sum of what we knew at death is the measure of what we know afterward of all that went before. Of this existence we know many things, but no new light falls upon any page of that; in memory is written all of it that we can read. Here are no heights of truth overlooking the confused landscape of that dubitable domain. We still dwell in the Valley of the Shadow, lurk in its desolate places, peering from brambles and thickets at its mad, malign inhabitants. How should we have new knowledge of that fading past?

What I am about to relate happened on a night. We know when it is night, for then you retire to your houses and we can venture from our places of concealment to move unafraid about our old homes, to look in at the windows, even to enter and gaze upon your faces as you sleep. I had lingered long near the dwelling where I had been so cruelly changed to what I am, as we do while any that we love or hate remain. Vainly I had sought some method of manifestation, some way to make my continued existence and my great love and poignant pity understood by my husband and son. Always if they slept they would wake, or if in my desperation I dared approach them when they were awake, would turn toward me the terrible eyes of the living, frightening me by the glances that I sought from the purpose that I held.

On this night I had searched for them without success, fearing to find them; they were nowhere in the house, nor about the moonlit lawn. For, although the sun is lost to us forever, the moon, full-orbed or slender, remains to us. Sometimes it shines by night, sometimes by day, but always it rises and sets, as in that other life.

I left the lawn and moved in the white light and silence along the road, aimless and sorrowing. Suddenly I heard the voice of my poor husband in exclamations of astonishment, with that of my son in reassurance and dissuasion; and there by the shadow of a group of trees they stood—near, so near! Their faces were toward me, the eyes of the elder man fixed upon mine. He saw me —at last, at last, he saw me! In the consciousness of that, my terror fled as a cruel dream. The death-spell was broken: Love had conquered Law! Mad with exultation I shouted—I *must* have shouted, "He sees, he sees: he will understand!" Then, controlling myself, I moved forward, smiling and consciously beautiful, to offer myself to his arms, to comfort him with endearments, and, with my son's hand in mine, to speak words that should restore the broken bonds between the living and the dead.

Alas! alas! his face went white with fear, his eyes were as those of a hunted animal. He backed away from me, as I advanced, and at last turned and fled into the wood—whither, it is not given to me to know.

To my poor boy, left doubly desolate, I have never been able to impart a sense of my presence. Soon he, too, must pass to this Life Invisible and be lost to me forever.

The Haunted Valley

I

HOW TREES ARE FELLED IN CHINA

A HALF-MILE north from Jo. Dunfer's on the road from Hutton's to
Mexican Hill, the highway dips into a sunless ravine which
opens out on either hand in a half-confidential manner, as if it
had a secret to impart at some more convenient season. I never
used to ride through it without looking first to the one side and
then to the other, to see if the time had arrived for the revelation.
If I saw nothing—and I never did see anything—there was no
feeling of disappointment, for I knew the disclosure was merely
withheld temporarily for some good reason which I had no right
to question. That I should one day be taken into full confidence
I no more doubted than I doubted the existence of Jo. Dunfer
himself, through whose premises the ravine ran.

It was said that Jo. had once undertaken to erect a cabin in
some remote part of it, but for some reason had abandoned the
enterprise and constructed his present hermaphrodite habitation, half residence and half groggery, at the roadside, upon an
extreme corner of his estate; as far away as possible, as if on purpose to show how radically he had changed his mind.

This Jo. Dunfer—or, as he was familiarly known in the neighborhood, Whisky Jo.—was a very important personage in those
parts. He was apparently about forty years of age, a long, shock-
headed fellow, with a corded face, a gnarled arm and a knotty
hand like a bunch of prison-keys. He was a hairy man, with a
stoop in his walk, like that of one who is about to spring upon
something and rend it.

Next to the peculiarity to which he owed his local appellation,
Mr. Dunfer's most obvious characteristic was a deep-seated an-
tipathy to the Chinese. I saw him once in a towering rage because one of his herdsmen had permitted a travel-heated Asian
to slake his thirst at the horse trough in front of the saloon end

150

of Jo.'s establishment. I ventured faintly to remonstrate with Jo. for his unchristian spirit, but he merely explained that there was nothing about Chinamen in the New Testament, and strode away to wreak his displeasure upon his dog, which also, I suppose, the inspired scribes had overlooked.

Some days afterward, finding him sitting alone in his barroom, I cautiously approached the subject, when, greatly to my relief, the habitual austerity of his expression visibly softened into something that I took for condescension.

"You young Easterners," he said, "are a mile-and-a-half too good for this country, and you don't catch on to our play. People who don't know a Chileño from a Kanaka can afford to hang out liberal ideas about Chinese immigration, but a fellow that has to fight for his bone with a lot of mongrel coolies hasn't any time for foolishness."

This long consumer, who had probably never done an honest day's work in his life, sprung the lid of a Chinese tobacco-box and with thumb and forefinger forked out a wad like a small haycock. Holding this reinforcement within supporting distance he fired away with renewed confidence.

"They're a flight of devouring locusts, and they're going for everything green in this God blest land, if you want to know."

Here he pushed his reserve into the breach and when his gabble-gear was again disengaged resumed his uplifting discourse.

"I had one of them on this ranch five years ago, and I'll tell you about it, so that you can see the nub of this whole question. I didn't pan out particularly well those days—drank more whisky than was prescribed for me and didn't seem to care for my duty as a patriotic American citizen; so I took that pagan in, as a kind of cook. But when I got religion over at the Hill and they talked of running me for the Legislature it was given to me to see the light. But what was I to do? If I gave him the go somebody else would take him, and mightn't treat him white. *What* was I to do? What would any good Christian do, especially one new to the trade and full to the neck with the brotherhood of Man and the fatherhood of God?"

Jo. paused for a reply, with an expression of unstable satisfaction, as of one who has solved a problem by a distrusted method. Presently he rose and swallowed a glass of whisky from a full bottle on the counter, then resumed his story.

"Besides, he didn't count for much—didn't know anything and gave himself airs. They all do that. I said him nay, but he muled it through on that line while he lasted; but after turning the

other cheek seventy and seven times I doctored the dice so that
he didn't last forever. And I'm almighty glad I had the sand to
do it."

Jo.'s gladness, which somehow did not impress me, was duly
and ostentatiously celebrated at the bottle.

"About five years ago I started in to stick up a shack. That was
before this one was built, and I put it in another place. I set Ah
Wee and a little cuss named Gopher to cutting the timber. Of
course I didn't expect Ah Wee to help much, for he had a face
like a day in June and big black eyes—I guess maybe they were
the damn'dest eyes in this neck o' woods."

While delivering this trenchant thrust at common sense Mr.
Dunfer absently regarded a knot-hole in the thin board partition
separating the bar from the living-room, as if that were one of
the eyes whose size and color had incapacitated his servant for
good service.

"Now you Eastern galoots won't believe anything against the
yellow devils," he suddenly flamed out with an appearance of
earnestness not altogether convincing, "but I tell you that Chink
was the perversest scoundrel outside San Francisco. The miserable pig-tail Mongolian went to hewing away at the saplings all
round the stems, like a worm o' the dust gnawing a radish. I
pointed out his error as patiently as I knew how, and showed him
how to cut them on two sides, so as to make them fall right; but
no sooner would I turn my back on him, like this"—and he
turned it on me, amplifying the illustration by taking some more
liquor—"than he was at it again. It was just this way: while I
looked at him, *so*"—regarding me rather unsteadily and with evident complexity of vision—"he was all right; but when I looked
away, *so*"—taking a long pull at the bottle—"he defied me. Then
I'd gaze at him reproachfully, *so*, and butter wouldn't have
melted in his mouth."

Doubtless Mr. Dunfer honestly intended the look that he fixed
upon me to be merely reproachful, but it was singularly fit to
arouse the gravest apprehension in any unarmed person incurring it; and as I had lost all interest in his pointless and interminable narrative, I rose to go. Before I had fairly risen, he had
again turned to the counter, and with a barely audible "so," had
emptied the bottle at a gulp.

Heavens! what a yell! It was like a Titan in his last, strong
agony. Jo. staggered back after emitting it, as a cannon recoils
from its own thunder, and then dropped into his chair, as if he
had been "knocked in the head" like a beef—his eyes drawn side-

wise toward the wall, with a stare of terror. Looking in the same
direction, I saw that the knot-hole in the wall had indeed become
a human eye—a full, black eye, that glared into my own with an
entire lack of expression more awful than the most devilish glitter. I think I must have covered my face with my hands to shut
out the horrible illusion, if such it was, and Jo.'s little white
man-of-all-work coming into the room broke the spell, and I
walked out of the house with a sort of dazed fear that *delirium
tremens* might be infectious. My horse was hitched at the water-
ing-trough, and untying him I mounted and gave him his head,
too much troubled in mind to note whither he took me.

I did not know what to think of all this, and like every one who
does not know what to think I thought a great deal, and to little
purpose. The only reflection that seemed at all satisfactory, was,
that on the morrow I should be some miles away, with a strong
probability of never returning.

A sudden coolness brought me out of my abstraction, and looking up I found myself entering the deep shadows of the ravine.
The day was stifling; and this transition from the pitiless, visible
heat of the parched fields to the cool gloom, heavy with pungency
of cedars and vocal with twittering of the birds that had been
driven to its leafy asylum, was exquisitely refreshing. I looked
for my mystery, as usual, but not finding the ravine in a communicative mood, dismounted, led my sweating animal into the undergrowth, tied him securely to a tree and sat down upon a rock
to meditate.

I began bravely by analyzing my pet superstition about the
place. Having resolved it into its constituent elements I arranged
them in convenient troops and squadrons, and collecting all the
forces of my logic bore down upon them from impregnable
premises with the thunder of irresistible conclusions and a great
noise of chariots and general intellectual shouting. Then, when
my big mental guns had overturned all opposition, and were
growling almost inaudibly away on the horizon of pure speculation, the routed enemy straggled in upon their rear, massed silently into a solid phalanx, and captured me, bag and baggage.
An indefinable dread came upon me. I rose to shake it off, and
began threading the narrow dell by an old, grass-grown cow-
path that seemed to flow along the bottom, as a substitute for the
brook that Nature had neglected to provide.

The trees among which the paths straggled were ordinary,
well-behaved plants, a trifle perverted as to trunk and eccentric
as to bough, but with nothing unearthly in their general aspect.

A few loose bowlders, which had detached themselves from the sides of the depression to set up an independent existence at the bottom, had dammed up the pathway, here and there, but their stony repose had nothing in it of the stillness of death. There was a kind of death-chamber hush in the valley, it is true, and a mysterious whisper above: the wind was just fingering the tops of the trees—that was all.

I had not thought of connecting Jo. Dunfer's drunken narrative with what I now sought, and only when I came into a clear space and stumbled over the level trunks of some small trees did I have the revelation. This was the site of the abandoned "shack." The discovery was verified by noting that some of the rotting stumps were hacked all round, in a most unwoodmanlike way, while others were cut straight across, and the butt ends of the corresponding trunks had the blunt wedge-form given by the axe of a master.

The opening among the trees was not more than thirty paces across. At one side was a little knoll—a natural hillock, bare of shrubbery but covered with wild grass, and on this, standing out of the grass, the headstone of a grave!

I do not remember that I felt anything like surprise at this discovery. I viewed that lonely grave with something of the feeling that Columbus must have had when he saw the hills and headlands of the New World. Before approaching it I leisurely completed my survey of the surroundings. I was even guilty of the affectation of winding my watch at that unusual hour, and with needless care and deliberation. Then I approached my mystery.

The grave—a rather short one—was in somewhat better repair than was consistent with its obvious age and isolation, and my eyes, I dare say, widened a trifle at a clump of unmistakable garden flowers showing evidence of recent watering. The stone had clearly enough done duty once as a doorstep. In its front was carved, or rather dug, an inscription. It read thus:

AH WEE—CHINAMAN.

Age unknown. Worked for Jo. Dunfer.
This monument is erected by him to keep the Chink's
memory green. Likewise as a warning to Celestials
not to take on airs. Devil take 'em!
She Was a Good Egg.

I cannot adequately relate my astonishment at this uncommon inscription! The meagre but sufficient identification of the deceased; the impudent candor of confession; the brutal anathema;

the ludicrous change of sex and sentiment—all marked this record as the work of one who must have been at least as much demented as bereaved. I felt that any further disclosure would be
a paltry anti-climax, and with an unconscious regard for dramatic effect turned squarely about and walked away. Nor did I
return to that part of the county for four years.

II

WHO DRIVES SANE OXEN SHOULD HIMSELF BE SANE

"Gee-up, there, old Fuddy-Duddy!"

This unique adjuration came from the lips of a queer little
man perched upon a wagonful of firewood, behind a brace of
oxen that were hauling it easily along with a simulation of
mighty effort which had evidently not imposed on their lord and
master. As that gentleman happened at the moment to be staring me squarely in the face as I stood by the roadside it was not
altogether clear whether he was addressing me or his beasts; nor
could I say if they were named Fuddy and Duddy and were both
subjects of the imperative verb "to gee-up." Anyhow the command produced no effect on us, and the queer little man removed his eyes from mine long enough to spear Fuddy and
Duddy alternately with a long pole, remarking, quietly but with
feeling: "Dern your skin," as if they enjoyed that integument in
common. Observing that my request for a ride took no attention,
and finding myself falling slowly astern, I placed one foot upon
the inner circumference of a hind wheel and was slowly elevated
to the level of the hub, whence I boarded the concern, *sans céré-
monie,* and scrambling forward seated myself beside the driver
—who took no notice of me until he had administered another
indiscriminate castigation to his cattle, accompanied with the advice to "buckle down, you derned Incapable!" Then, the master
of the outfit (or rather the former master, for I could not suppress
a whimsical feeling that the entire establishment was my lawful
prize) trained his big, black eyes upon me with an expression
strangely, and somewhat unpleasantly, familiar, laid down his
rod—which neither blossomed nor turned into a serpent, as I
half expected—folded his arms, and gravely demanded, "W'at
did you do to W'isky?"

My natural reply would have been that I drank it, but there

was something about the query that suggested a hidden significance, and something about the man that did not invite a shallow jest. And so, having no other answer ready, I merely held my
tongue, but felt as if I were resting under an imputation of guilt,
and that my silence was being construed into a confession.

Just then a cold shadow fell upon my cheek, and caused me to
look up. We were descending into my ravine! I can not describe
the sensation that came upon me: I had not seen it since it un-
bosomed itself four years before, and now I felt like one to whom
a friend has made some sorrowing confession of crime long past,
and who has basely deserted him in consequence. The old memories of Jo. Dunfer, his fragmentary revelation, and the unsatis-
fying explanatory note by the headstone, came back with singular distinctness. I wondered what had become of Jo., and—I
turned sharply round and asked my prisoner. He was intently
watching his cattle, and without withdrawing his eyes replied:

"Gee-up, old Terrapin! He lies aside of Ah Wee up the gulch.
Like to see it? They always come back to the spot—I've been ex-
pectin' you. H-woa!"

At the enunciation of the aspirate, Fuddy-Duddy, the incapable terrapin, came to a dead halt, and before the vowel had
died away up the ravine had folded up all his eight legs and lain
down in the dusty road, regardless of the effect upon his derned
skin. The queer little man slid off his seat to the ground and
started up the dell without deigning to look back to see if I was
following. But I was.

It was about the same season of the year, and at near the same
hour of the day, as my last visit. The jays clamored loudly, and
the trees whispered darkly, as before; and I somehow traced in
the two sounds a fanciful analogy to the open boastfulness of Mr.
Jo. Dunfer's mouth and the mysterious reticence of his manner,
and to the mingled hardihood and tenderness of his sole literary
production—the epitaph. All things in the valley seemed un-
changed, excepting the cow-path, which was almost wholly overgrown with weeds. When we came out into the "clearing," however, there was change enough. Among the stumps and trunks
of the fallen saplings, those that had been hacked "China fashion" were no longer distinguishable from those that were cut
" 'Melican way." It was as if the Old-World barbarism and the
New-World civilization had reconciled their differences by the
arbitration of an impartial decay—as is the way of civiliza-
tions. The knoll was there, but the Hunnish brambles had over-

run and all but obliterated its effete grasses; and the patrician
garden-violet had capitulated to his plebeian brother—perhaps
had merely reverted to his original type. Another grave—a long,
robust mound—had been made beside the first, which seemed to
shrink from the comparison; and in the shadow of a new headstone the old one lay prostrate, with its marvelous inscription il-
legible by accumulation of leaves and soil. In point of literary
merit the new was inferior to the old—was even repulsive in its
terse and savage jocularity:

JO. DUNFER. DONE FOR.

I turned from it with indifference, and brushing away the
leaves from the tablet of the dead pagan restored to light the
mocking words which, fresh from their long neglect, seemed to
have a certain pathos. My guide, too, appeared to take on an
added seriousness as he read it, and I fancied that I could detect
beneath his whimsical manner something of manliness, almost of
dignity. But while I looked at him his former aspect, so subtly
unhuman, so tantalizingly familiar, crept back into his big eyes,
repellant and attractive. I resolved to make an end of the mystery if possible.

"My friend," I said, pointing to the smaller grave, "did Jo.
Dunfer murder that Chinaman?"

He was leaning against a tree and looking across the open
space into the top of another, or into the blue sky beyond. He
neither withdrew his eyes, nor altered his posture as he slowly replied:

"No, sir; he justifiably homicided him."

"Then he really did kill him."

"Kill 'im? I should say he did, rather. Doesn't everybody know
that? Didn't he stan' up before the coroner's jury and confess it?
And didn't they find a verdict of 'Came to 'is death by a wholesome Christian sentiment workin' in the Caucasian breast'? An'
didn't the church at the Hill turn W'isky down for it? And didn't
the sovereign people elect him Justice of the Peace to get even on
the gospelers? I don't know where you were brought up."

"But did Jo. do that because the Chinaman did not, or would
not, learn to cut down trees like a white man?"

"Sure!—it stan's so on the record, which makes it true an' legal.
My knowin' better doesn't make any difference with legal truth;
it wasn't my funeral and I wasn't invited to deliver an oration.
But the fact is, W'isky was jealous o' *me*"—and the little wretch

actually swelled out like a turkey cock and made a pretense of adjusting an imaginary neck-tie, noting the effect in the palm of his hand, held up before him to represent a mirror.

"Jealous of *you*!" I repeated with ill-mannered astonishment.

"That's what I said. Why not?—don't I look all right?"

He assumed a mocking attitude of studied grace, and twitched the wrinkles out of his threadbare waistcoat. Then, suddenly dropping his voice to a low pitch of singular sweetness, he continued:

"W'isky thought a lot o' that Chink; nobody but me knew how 'e doted on 'im. Couldn't bear 'im out of 'is sight, the derned protoplasm! And w'en 'e came down to this clearin' one day an' found him an' me neglectin' our work—him asleep an' me grapplin' a tarantula out of 'is sleeve—W'isky laid hold of my axe and let us have it, good an' hard! I dodged just then, for the spider bit me, but Ah Wee got it bad in the side an' tumbled about like anything. W'isky was just weighin' me out one w'en 'e saw the spider fastened on my finger; then 'e knew he'd made a jackass of 'imself. He threw away the axe and got down on 'is knees alongside of Ah Wee, who gave a last little kick and opened 'is eyes—he had eyes like mine—an' puttin' up 'is hands drew down W'isky's ugly head and held it there w'ile 'e stayed. That wasn't long, for a tremblin' ran through 'im and 'e gave a bit of a moan an' beat the game."

During the progress of the story the narrator had become transfigured. The comic, or rather, the sardonic element was all out of him, and as he painted that strange scene it was with difficulty that I kept my composure. And this consummate actor had somehow so managed me that the sympathy due to his *dramatis personæ* was given to himself. I stepped forward to grasp his hand, when suddenly a broad grin danced across his face and with a light, mocking laugh he continued:

"W'en W'isky got 'is nut out o' that 'e was a sight to see! All his fine clothes—he dressed mighty blindin' those days—were spoiled everlastin'! 'Is hair was towsled and his face—what I could see of it—was whiter than the ace of lilies. 'E stared once at me, and looked away as if I didn't count; an' then there were shootin' pains chasin' one another from my bitten finger into my head, and it was Gopher to the dark. That's why I wasn't at the inquest."

"But why did you hold your tongue afterward?" I asked.

"It's that kind of tongue," he replied, and not another word would he say about it.

"After that W'isky took to drinkin' harder an' harder, and was rabider an' rabider anti-coolie, but I don't think 'e was ever particularly glad that 'e dispelled Ah Wee. He didn't put on so much dog about it w'en we were alone as w'en he had the ear of a derned Spectacular Extravaganza like you. 'E put up that headstone and gouged the inscription accordin' to his varyin' moods. It took 'im three weeks, workin' between drinks. I gouged his in one day."

"When did Jo. die?" I asked rather absently. The answer took my breath:

"Pretty soon after I looked at him through that knot-hole, w'en you had put something in his w'isky, you derned Borgia!"

Recovering somewhat from my surprise at this astounding charge, I was half-minded to throttle the audacious accuser, but was restrained by a sudden conviction that came to me in the light of a revelation. I fixed a grave look upon him and asked, as calmly as I could: "And when did you go luny?"

"Nine years ago!" he shrieked, throwing out his clenched hands—"nine years ago, w'en that big brute killed the woman who loved him better than she did me!—me who had followed 'er from San Francisco, where 'e won 'er at draw poker!—me who had watched over 'er for years w'en the scoundrel she belonged to was ashamed to acknowledge 'er and treat 'er white!—me who for her sake kept 'is cussed secret till it ate 'im up!—me who w'en you poisoned the beast fulfilled 'is last request to lay 'im alongside 'er and give 'im a stone to the head of 'im! And I've never since seen 'er grave till now, for I didn't want to meet 'im here."

"Meet him? Why, Gopher, my poor fellow, he is dead!"

"That's why I'm afraid of 'im."

I followed the little wretch back to his wagon and wrung his hand at parting. It was now nightfall, and as I stood there at the roadside in the deepening gloom, watching the blank outlines of the receding wagon, a sound was borne to me on the evening wind—a sound as of a series of vigorous thumps—and a voice came out of the night:

"Gee-up, there, you derned old Geranium."

A Jug of Sirup

THIS NARRATIVE begins with the death of its hero. Silas Deemer died on the 16th day of July, 1863, and two days later his remains were buried. As he had been personally known to every man, woman and well-grown child in the village, the funeral, as the local newspaper phrased it, "was largely attended." In accordance with a custom of the time and place, the coffin was opened at the graveside and the entire assembly of friends and neighbors filed past, taking a last look at the face of the dead. And then, before the eyes of all, Silas Deemer was put into the ground. Some of the eyes were a trifle dim, but in a general way it may be said that at that interment there was lack of neither observance nor observation; Silas was indubitably dead, and none could have pointed out any ritual delinquency that would have justified him in coming back from the grave. Yet if human testimony is good for anything (and certainly it once put an end to witchcraft in and about Salem) he came back.

I forgot to state that the death and burial of Silas Deemer occurred in the little village of Hillbrook, where he had lived for thirty-one years. He had been what is known in some parts of the Union (which is admittedly a free country) as a "merchant"; that is to say, he kept a retail shop for the sale of such things as are commonly sold in shops of that character. His honesty had never been questioned, so far as is known, and he was held in high esteem by all. The only thing that could be urged against him by the most censorious was a too close attention to business. It was not urged against him, though many another, who manifested it in no greater degree, was less leniently judged. The business to which Silas was devoted was mostly his own—that, possibly, may have made a difference.

At the time of Deemer's death nobody could recollect a single day, Sundays excepted, that he had not passed in his "store," since he had opened it more than a quarter-century before. His health having been perfect during all that time, he had been unable to discern any validity in whatever may or might have been urged to lure him astray from his counter; and it is related that once when he was summoned to the county seat as a witness in an important law case and did not attend, the lawyer who had the hardihood to move that he be "admonished" was solemnly informed that the Court regarded the proposal with "surprise." Judicial surprise being an emotion that attorneys are not commonly ambitious to arouse, the motion was hastily withdrawn and an agreement with the other side effected as to what Mr. Deemer would have said if he had been there—the other side pushing its advantage to the extreme and making the supposititious testimony distinctly damaging to the interests of its proponents. In brief, it was the general feeling in all that region that Silas Deemer was the one immobile verity of Hillbrook, and that his translation in space would precipitate some dismal public ill or strenuous calamity.

Mrs. Deemer and two grown daughters occupied the upper rooms of the building, but Silas had never been known to sleep elsewhere than on a cot behind the counter of the store. And there, quite by accident, he was found one night, dying, and passed away just before the time for taking down the shutters. Though speechless, he appeared conscious, and it was thought by those who knew him best that if the end had unfortunately been delayed beyond the usual hour for opening the store the effect upon him would have been deplorable.

Such had been Silas Deemer—such the fixity and invariety of his life and habit, that the village humorist (who had once attended college) was moved to bestow upon him the sobriquet of "Old Ibidem," and, in the first issue of the local newspaper after the death, to explain without offence that Silas had taken "a day off." It was more than a day, but from the record it appears that well within a month Mr. Deemer made it plain that he had not the leisure to be dead.

One of Hillbrook's most respected citizens was Alvan Creede, a banker. He lived in the finest house in town, kept a carriage and was a most estimable man variously. He knew something of the advantages of travel, too, having been frequently in Boston, and once, it was thought, in New York, though he modestly disclaimed that glittering distinction. The matter is mentioned here merely as a contribution to an understanding of Mr. Creede's worth, for either way it is creditable to him—to his intelligence if he had put himself, even temporarily, into contact with metropolitan culture; to his candor if he had not.

One pleasant summer evening at about the hour of ten Mr.

Creede, entering at his garden gate, passed up the gravel walk, which looked very white in the moonlight, mounted the stone steps of his fine house and pausing a moment inserted his latch-key in the door. As he pushed this open he met his wife, who was crossing the passage from the parlor to the library. She greeted him pleasantly and pulling the door further back held it for him to enter. Instead he turned and, looking about his feet in front of the threshold, uttered an exclamation of surprise.

"Why!—what the devil," he said, "has become of that jug?"

"What jug, Alvan?" his wife inquired, not very sympathetically.

"A jug of maple sirup—I brought it along from the store and set it down here to open the door. What the——"

"There, there, Alvan, please don't swear again," said the lady, interrupting. Hillbrook, by the way, is not the only place in Christendom where a vestigial polytheism forbids the taking in vain of the Evil One's name.

The jug of maple sirup which the easy ways of village life had permitted Hillbrook's foremost citizen to carry home from the store was not there.

"Are you quite sure, Alvan?"

"My dear, do you suppose a man does not know when he is carrying a jug? I bought that sirup at Deemer's as I was passing. Deemer himself drew it and lent me the jug, and I——"

The sentence remains to this day unfinished. Mr. Creede staggered into the house, entered the parlor and dropped into an arm-chair, trembling in every limb. He had suddenly remembered that Silas Deemer was three weeks dead.

Mrs. Creede stood by her husband, regarding him with surprise and anxiety.

"For Heaven's sake," she said, "what ails you?"

Mr. Creede's ailment having no obvious relation to the interests of the better land he did not apparently deem it necessary to expound it on that demand; he said nothing—merely stared. There were long moments of silence broken by nothing but the measured ticking of the clock, which seemed somewhat slower than usual, as if it were civilly granting them an extension of time in which to recover their wits.

"Jane, I have gone mad—that is it." He spoke thickly and hurriedly. "You should have told me; you must have observed my symptoms before they became so pronounced that I have observed them myself. I thought I was passing Deemer's store; it was open and lit up—that is what I thought; of course it is never open now. Silas Deemer stood at his desk behind the counter. My God, Jane, I saw him as distinctly as I see you. Remembering that you had said you wanted some maple sirup, I went in and bought some—that is all—I bought two quarts of maple sirup from Silas Deemer, who is dead and underground, but nevertheless drew that sirup from a cask and handed it to me in a jug. He talked with me, too, rather gravely, I remember, even more so than was his way, but not a word of what he said can I now recall. But I saw him—good Lord, I saw and talked with him—and he is dead! So I thought, but I'm mad, Jane, I'm as crazy as a beetle; and you have kept it from me."

This monologue gave the woman time to collect what faculties she had.

"Alvan," she said, "you have given no evidence of insanity, believe me. This was undoubtedly an illusion—how should it be anything else? That would be too terrible! But there is no insanity; you are working too hard at the bank. You should not have attended the meeting of directors this evening; any one could see that you were ill; I knew something would occur."

It may have seemed to him that the prophecy had lagged a bit, awaiting the event, but he said nothing of that, being concerned with his own condition. He was calm now, and could think coherently.

"Doubtless the phenomenon was subjective," he said, with a somewhat ludicrous transition to the slang of science. "Granting the possibility of spiritual apparition and even materialization, yet the apparition and materialization of a half-gallon brown clay jug—a piece of coarse, heavy pottery evolved from nothing— that is hardly thinkable."

As he finished speaking, a child ran into the room—his little daughter. She was clad in a bedgown. Hastening to her father she threw her arms about his neck, saying: "You naughty papa, you forgot to come in and kiss me. We heard you open the gate and got up and looked out. And, papa dear, Eddy says mayn't he have the little jug when it is empty?"

As the full import of that revelation imparted itself to Alvan Creede's understanding he visibly shuddered. For the child could not have heard a word of the conversation.

The estate of Silas Deemer being in the hands of an administrator who had thought it best to dispose of the "business," the store had been closed ever since the owner's death, the goods having been removed by another "merchant" who had purchased them *en bloc*. The rooms above were vacant as well, for the widow and daughters had gone to another town.

On the evening immediately after Alvan Creede's adventure (which had somehow "got out") a crowd of men, women and children thronged the sidewalk opposite the store. That the place was haunted by the spirit of the late Silas Deemer was now well known to every resident of Hillbrook, though many affected disbelief. Of these the hardiest, and in a general way the youngest, threw stones against the front of the building, the only part accessible, but carefully missed the unshuttered windows. Incredulity had not grown to malice. A few venturesome souls crossed the street and rattled the door in its frame; struck matches and held them near the window; attempted to view the black interior. Some of the spectators invited attention to their wit by shouting and groaning and challenging the ghost to a footrace.

After a considerable time had elapsed without any manifestation, and many of the crowd had gone away, all those remaining began to observe that the interior of the store was suffused with a dim, yellow light. At this all demonstrations ceased; the intrepid souls about the door and windows fell back to the opposite side of the street and were merged in the crowd; the small boys ceased throwing stones. Nobody spoke above his breath; all whispered excitedly and pointed to the now steadily growing light. How long a time had passed since the first faint glow had been observed none could have guessed, but eventually the illumination was bright enough to reveal the whole interior of the store; and there, standing at his desk behind the counter, Silas Deemer was distinctly visible!

The effect upon the crowd was marvelous. It began rapidly to melt away at both flanks, as the timid left the place. Many ran as fast as their legs would let them; others moved off with greater dignity, turning occasionally to look backward over the shoulder. At last a score or more, mostly men, remained where they were, speechless, staring, excited. The apparition inside gave them no attention; it was apparently occupied with a book of accounts.

Presently three men left the crowd on the sidewalk as if by a common impulse and crossed the street. One of them, a heavy man, was about to set his shoulder against the door when it opened, apparently without human agency, and the courageous investigators passed in. No sooner had they crossed the threshold than they were seen by the awed observers outside to be acting in the most unaccountable way. They thrust out their hands before them, pursued devious courses, came into violent collision with the counter, with boxes and barrels on the floor, and with one another. They turned awkwardly hither and thither and seemed trying to escape, but unable to retrace their steps. Their voices were heard in exclamations and curses. But in no way did the apparition of Silas Deemer manifest an interest in what was going on.

By what impulse the crowd was moved none ever recollected, but the entire mass—men, women, children, dogs—made a simultaneous and tumultuous rush for the entrance. They congested the doorway, pushing for precedence—resolving themselves at length into a line and moving up step by step. By some subtle spiritual or physical alchemy observation had been transmuted into action—the sight-seers had become participants in the spectacle—the audience had usurped the stage.

To the only spectator remaining on the other side of the street —Alvan Creede, the banker—the interior of the store with its inpouring crowd continued in full illumination; all the strange things going on there were clearly visible. To those inside all was black darkness. It was as if each person as he was thrust in at the door had been stricken blind, and was maddened by the mischance. They groped with aimless imprecision, tried to force their way out against the current, pushed and elbowed, struck at random, fell and were trampled, rose and trampled in their turn. They seized one another by the garments, the hair, the beard—fought like animals, cursed, shouted, called one another opprobrious and obscene names. When, finally, Alvan Creede had seen the last person of the line pass into that awful tumult the light that had illuminated it was suddenly quenched and all was as black to him as to those within. He turned away and left the place.

In the early morning a curious crowd had gathered about "Deemer's." It was composed partly of those who had run away the night before, but now had the courage of sunshine, partly of honest folk going to their daily toil. The door of the store stood open; the place was vacant, but on the walls, the floor, the furniture, were shreds of clothing and tangles of hair. Hillbrook militant had managed somehow to pull itself out and had gone home to medicine its hurts and swear that it had been all night in bed. On the dusty desk, behind the counter, was the sales-book.

The entries in it, in Deemer's handwriting, had ceased on the 16th day of July, the last of his life. There was no record of a later sale to Alvan Creede.

That is the entire story—except that men's passions having subsided and reason having resumed its immemorial sway, it was confessed in Hillbrook that, considering the harmless and honorable character of his first commercial transaction under the new conditions, Silas Deemer, deceased, might properly have been suffered to resume business at the old stand without mobbing. In that judgment the local historian from whose unpublished work these facts are compiled had the thoughtfulness to signify his concurrence.

The Night-Doings at "Deadman's"

A Story That Is Untrue

IT WAS a singularly sharp night, and clear as the heart of a diamond. Clear nights have a trick of being keen. In darkness you may be cold and not know it; when you see, you suffer. This night was bright enough to bite like a serpent. The moon was moving mysteriously along behind the giant pines crowning the South Mountain, striking a cold sparkle from the crusted snow, and bringing out against the black west the ghostly outlines of the Coast Range, beyond which lay the invisible Pacific. The snow had piled itself, in the open spaces along the bottom of the gulch, into long ridges that seemed to heave, and into hills that appeared to toss and scatter spray. The spray was sunlight, twice reflected: dashed once from the moon, once from the snow.

In this snow many of the shanties of the abandoned mining camp were obliterated, (a sailor might have said they had gone down) and at irregular intervals it had overtopped the tall trestles which had once supported a river called a flume; for, of course, "flume" is *flumen*. Among the advantages of which the mountains cannot deprive the gold-hunter is the privilege of speaking Latin. He says of his dead neighbor, "He has gone up the flume." This is not a bad way to say, "His life has returned to the Fountain of Life."

While putting on its armor against the assaults of the wind, this snow had neglected no coign of vantage. Snow pursued by the wind is not wholly unlike a retreating army. In the open field it ranges itself in ranks and battalions; where it can get a foothold it makes a stand; where it can take cover it does so. You may see whole platoons of snow cowering behind a bit of broken wall. The devious old road, hewn out of the mountainside, was full of it. Squadron upon squadron had struggled to es-

cape by this line, when suddenly pursuit had ceased. A more desolate and dreary spot than Deadman's Gulch in a winter midnight it is impossible to imagine. Yet Mr. Hiram Beeson
elected to live there, the sole inhabitant.

Away up the side of the North Mountain his little pine-log
shanty projected from its single pane of glass a long, thin beam
of light, and looked not altogether unlike a black beetle fastened
to the hillside with a bright new pin. Within it sat Mr. Beeson
himself, before a roaring fire, staring into its hot heart as if he
had never before seen such a thing in all his life. He was not a
comely man. He was gray; he was ragged and slovenly in his attire; his face was wan and haggard; his eyes were too bright. As
to his age, if one had attempted to guess it, one might have said
forty-seven, then corrected himself and said seventy-four. He was
really twenty-eight. Emaciated he was; as much, perhaps, as he
dared be, with a needy undertaker at Bentley's Flat and a new
and enterprising coroner at Sonora. Poverty and zeal are an upper and a nether millstone. It is dangerous to make a third in
that kind of sandwich.

As Mr. Beeson sat there, with his ragged elbows on his ragged
knees, his lean jaws buried in his lean hands, and with no apparent intention of going to bed, he looked as if the slightest movement would tumble him to pieces. Yet during the last hour he
had winked no fewer than three times.

There was a sharp rapping at the door. A rap at that time of
night and in that weather might have surprised an ordinary
mortal who had dwelt two years in the gulch without seeing a
human face, and could not fail to know that the country was im-
passable; but Mr. Beeson did not so much as pull his eyes out of
the coals. And even when the door was pushed open he only
shrugged a little more closely into himself, as one does who is expecting something that he would rather not see. You may observe
this movement in women when, in a mortuary chapel, the coffin
is borne up the aisle behind them.

But when a long old man in a blanket overcoat, his head tied
up in a handkerchief and nearly his entire face in a muffler, wearing green goggles and with a complexion of glittering whiteness
where it could be seen, strode silently into the room, laying a
hard, gloved hand on Mr. Beeson's shoulder, the latter so far forgot himself as to look up with an appearance of no small astonishment; whomever he may have been expecting, he had evidently not counted on meeting anyone like this. Nevertheless,
the sight of this unexpected guest produced in Mr. Beeson the

following sequence: a feeling of astonishment; a sense of gratification; a sentiment of profound good will. Rising from his seat, he took the knotty hand from his shoulder, and shook it up and down with a fervor quite unaccountable; for in the old man's aspect was nothing to attract, much to repel. However, attraction is too general a property for repulsion to be without it. The most attractive object in the world is the face we instinctively cover with a cloth. When it becomes still more attractive—fascinating —we put seven feet of earth above it.

"Sir," said Mr. Beeson, releasing the old man's hand, which fell passively against his thigh with a quiet clack, "it is an extremely disagreeable night. Pray be seated; I am very glad to see you."

Mr. Beeson spoke with an easy good breeding that one would hardly have expected, considering all things. Indeed, the contrast between his appearance and his manner was sufficiently surprising to be one of the commonest of social phenomena in the mines. The old man advanced a step toward the fire, glowing cavernously in the green goggles. Mr. Beeson resumed:

"You bet your life I am!"

Mr. Beeson's elegance was not too refined; it had made reasonable concessions to local taste. He paused a moment, letting his eyes drop from the muffled head of his guest, down along the row of moldy buttons confining the blanket overcoat, to the greenish cowhide boots powdered with snow, which had begun to melt and run along the floor in little rills. He took an inventory of his guest, and appeared satisfied. Who would not have been? Then he continued:

"The cheer I can offer you is, unfortunately, in keeping with my surroundings; but I shall esteem myself highly favored if it is your pleasure to partake of it, rather than seek better at Bentley's Flat."

With a singular refinement of hospitable humility Mr. Beeson spoke as if a sojourn in his warm cabin on such a night, as compared with walking fourteen miles up to the throat in snow with a cutting crust, would be an intolerable hardship. By way of reply, his guest unbuttoned the blanket overcoat. The host laid fresh fuel on the fire, swept the hearth with the tail of a wolf, and added:

"But *I* think you'd better skedaddle."

The old man took a seat by the fire, spreading his broad soles to the heat without removing his hat. In the mines the hat is seldom removed except when the boots are. Without further remark Mr. Beeson also seated himself in a chair which had been a barrel, and which, retaining much of its original character, seemed to have been designed with a view to preserving his dust if it should please him to crumble. For a moment there was silence; then, from somewhere among the pines, came the snarling yelp of a coyote; and simultaneously the door rattled in its frame. There was no other connection between the two incidents than that the coyote has an aversion to storms, and the wind was rising; yet there seemed somehow a kind of supernatural conspiracy between the two, and Mr. Beeson shuddered with a vague sense of terror. He recovered himself in a moment and again addressed his guest.

"There are strange doings here. I will tell you everything, and then if you decide to go I shall hope to accompany you over the worst of the way; as far as where Baldy Peterson shot Ben Hike—I dare say you know the place."

The old man nodded emphatically, as intimating not merely that he did, but that he did indeed.

"Two years ago," began Mr. Beeson, "I, with two companions, occupied this house; but when the rush to the Flat occurred we left, along with the rest. In ten hours the Gulch was deserted. That evening, however, I discovered I had left behind me a valuable pistol (that is it) and returned for it, passing the night here alone, as I have passed every night since. I must explain that a few days before we left, our Chinese domestic had the misfortune to die while the ground was frozen so hard that it was impossible to dig a grave in the usual way. So, on the day of our hasty departure, we cut through the floor there, and gave him such burial as we could. But before putting him down I had the extremely bad taste to cut off his pigtail and spike it to that beam above his grave, where you may see it at this moment, or, preferably, when warmth has given you leisure for observation.

"I stated, did I not, that the Chinaman came to his death from natural causes? I had, of course, nothing to do with that, and returned through no irresistible attraction, or morbid fascination, but only because I had forgotten a pistol. This is clear to you, is it not, sir?"

The visitor nodded gravely. He appeared to be a man of few words, if any. Mr. Beeson continued:

"According to the Chinese faith, a man is like a kite: he cannot go to heaven without a tail. Well, to shorten this tedious story—which, however, I thought it my duty to relate—on that night, while I was here alone and thinking of anything but him, that Chinaman came back for his pigtail.

"He did not get it."

At this point Mr. Beeson relapsed into blank silence. Perhaps he was fatigued by the unwonted exercise of speaking; perhaps he had conjured up a memory that demanded his undivided attention. The wind was now fairly abroad, and the pines along the mountain-side sang with singular distinctness. The narrator continued:

"You say you do not see much in that, and I must confess I do not myself.

"But he keeps coming!"

There was another long silence, during which both stared into the fire without the movement of a limb. Then Mr. Beeson broke out, almost fiercely, fixing his eyes on what he could see of the impassive face of his auditor:

"Give it him? Sir, in this matter I have no intention of troubling anyone for advice. You will pardon me, I am sure"—here he became singularly persuasive—"but I have ventured to nail that pigtail fast, and have assumed the somewhat onerous obligation of guarding it. So it is quite impossible to act on your considerate suggestion.

"Do you play me for a Modoc?"

Nothing could exceed the sudden ferocity with which he thrust this indignant remonstrance into the ear of his guest. It was as if he had struck him on the side of the head with a steel gauntlet. It was a protest, but it was a challenge. To be mistaken for a coward—to be played for a Modoc: these two expressions are one. Sometimes it is a Chinaman. Do you play me for a Chinaman? is a question frequently addressed to the ear of the suddenly dead.

Mr. Beeson's buffet produced no effect, and after a moment's pause, during which the wind thundered in the chimney like the sound of clods upon a coffin, he resumed:

"But, as you say, it is wearing me out. I feel that the life of the last two years has been a mistake—a mistake that corrects itself; you see how. The grave! No; there is no one to dig it. The ground is frozen, too. But you are very welcome. You may say at Bentley's—but that is not important. It was very tough to cut: they braid silk into their pigtails. Kwaagh."

Mr. Beeson was speaking with his eyes shut, and he wandered. His last word was a snore. A moment later he drew a long breath, opened his eyes with an effort, made a single remark, and fell into a deep sleep. What he said was this:

"They are swiping my dust!"

Then the aged stranger, who had not uttered one word since his arrival, arose from his seat and deliberately laid off his outer clothing, looking as angular in his flannels as the late Signorina Festorazzi, an Irish woman, six feet in height, and weighing fifty-six pounds, who used to exhibit herself in her chemise to the people of San Francisco. He then crept into one of the "bunks," having first placed a revolver in easy reach, according to the custom of the country. This revolver he took from a shelf, and it was the one which Mr. Beeson had mentioned as that for which he had returned to the Gulch two years before.

In a few moments Mr. Beeson awoke, and seeing that his guest had retired he did likewise. But before doing so he approached the long, plaited wisp of pagan hair and gave it a powerful tug, to assure himself that it was fast and firm. The two beds—mere shelves covered with blankets not overclean—faced each other from opposite sides of the room, the little square trap door that had given access to the Chinaman's grave being midway between. This, by the way, was crossed by a double row of spike-heads. In his resistance to the supernatural, Mr. Beeson had not disdained the use of material precautions.

The fire was now low, the flames burning bluely and petu-lantly, with occasional flashes, projecting spectral shadows on the walls—shadows that moved mysteriously about, now dividing, now uniting. The shadow of the pendent queue, however, kept moodily apart, near the roof at the further end of the room, looking like a note of admiration. The song of the pines outside had now risen to the dignity of a triumphal hymn. In the pauses the silence was dreadful.

It was during one of these intervals that the trap in the floor be-gan to lift. Slowly and steadily it rose, and slowly and steadily rose the swaddled head of the old man in the bunk to observe it. Then, with a clap that shook the house to its foundation, it was thrown clean back, where it lay with its unsightly spikes pointing threateningly upward. Mr. Beeson awoke, and without rising, pressed his fingers into his eyes. He shuddered; his teeth chat-tered. His guest was now reclining on one elbow, watching the proceedings with the goggles that glowed like lamps.

Suddenly a howling gust of wind swooped down the chimney, scattering ashes and smoke in all directions, for a moment obscur-ing everything. When the firelight again illuminated the room there was seen, sitting gingerly on the edge of a stool by the hearthside, a swarthy little man of prepossessing appearance and dressed with faultless taste, nodding to the old man with a friendly and engaging smile. "From San Francisco, evidently," thought Mr. Beeson, who having somewhat recovered from his fright was groping his way to a solution of the evening's events.

But now another actor appeared upon the scene. Out of the square black hole in the middle of the floor protruded the head of the departed Chinaman, his glassy eyes turned upward in their angular slits and fastened on the dangling queue above with a look of yearning unspeakable. Mr. Beeson groaned, and again spread his hands upon his face. A mild odor of opium pervaded the place. The phantom, clad only in a short blue tunic quilted and silken but covered with grave-mold, rose slowly, as if pushed by a weak spiral spring. Its knees were at the level of the floor, when with a quick upward impulse like the silent leaping of a flame it grasped the queue with both hands, drew up its body and took the tip in its horrible yellow teeth. To this it clung in a seeming frenzy, grimacing ghastly, surging and plunging from side to side in its efforts to disengage its property from the beam, but uttering no sound. It was like a corpse artificially convulsed by means of a galvanic battery. The contrast between its superhuman activity and its silence was no less than hideous!

Mr. Beeson cowered in his bed. The swarthy little gentleman uncrossed his legs, beat an impatient tattoo with the toe of his boot and consulted a heavy gold watch. The old man sat erect and quietly laid hold of the revolver.

Bang!

Like a body cut from the gallows the Chinaman plumped into the black hole below, carrying his tail in his teeth. The trap door turned over, shutting down with a snap. The swarthy little gentleman from San Francisco sprang nimbly from his perch, caught something in the air with his hat, as a boy catches a butterfly, and vanished into the chimney as if drawn up by suction.

From away somewhere in the outer darkness floated in through the open door a faint, far cry—a long, sobbing wail, as of a child death-strangled in the desert, or a lost soul borne away by the Adversary. It may have been the coyote.

In the early days of the following spring a party of miners on their way to new diggings passed along the Gulch, and straying through the deserted shanties found in one of them the body of Hiram Beeson, stretched upon a bunk, with a bullet hole through the heart. The ball had evidently been fired from the opposite side of the room, for in one of the oaken beams overhead was a shallow blue dint, where it had struck a knot and been deflected downward to the breast of its victim. Strongly attached to the same beam was what appeared to be an end of a rope of braided horsehair, which had been cut by the bullet in its passage to the knot. Nothing else of interest was noted, excepting a suit of moldy and incongruous clothing, several articles of which were afterward identified by respectable witnesses as those in which certain deceased citizens of Deadman's had been buried years before. But it is not easy to understand how that could be, unless, indeed, the garments had been worn as a disguise by Death himself—which is hardly credible.

The Middle Toe of the Right Foot

I

IT IS well known that the old Manton house is haunted. In all the rural district near about, and even in the town of Marshall, a mile away, not one person of unbiased mind entertains a doubt of it; incredulity is confined to those opinionated persons who will be called "cranks" as soon as the useful word shall have penetrated the intellectual demesne of the Marshall *Advance*. The evidence that the house is haunted is of two kinds: the testimony of disinterested witnesses who have had ocular proof, and that of the house itself. The former may be disregarded and ruled out on any of the various grounds of objection which may be urged against it by the ingenious; but facts within the observation of all are material and controlling.

In the first place, the Manton house has been unoccupied by mortals for more than ten years, and with its outbuildings is slowly falling into decay—a circumstance which in itself the judicious will hardly venture to ignore. It stands a little way off the loneliest reach of the Marshall and Harriston road, in an opening which was once a farm and is still disfigured with strips of rotting fence and half covered with brambles overrunning a stony and sterile soil long unacquainted with the plow. The house itself is in tolerably good condition, though badly weatherstained and in dire need of attention from the glazier, the smaller male population of the region having attested in the manner of its kind its disapproval of dwelling without dwellers. It is two stories in height, nearly square, its front pierced by a single doorway flanked on each side by a window boarded up to the very top. Corresponding windows above, not protected, serve to admit light and rain to the rooms of the upper floor. Grass and weeds grow pretty rankly all about, and a few shade trees, somewhat the worse for wind, and leaning all in one direction, seem to be making a concerted effort to run away. In short, as the Marshall town humorist explained in the columns of the *Advance,* "the proposition that the Manton house is badly haunted is the only logical conclusion from the premises." The fact that in this dwelling Mr. Manton thought it expedient one night some ten years ago to rise and cut the throats of his wife and two small children, removing at once to another part of the country, has no doubt done its share in directing public attention to the fitness of the place for supernatural phenomena.

To this house, one summer evening, came four men in a wagon. Three of them promptly alighted, and the one who had been driving hitched the team to the only remaining post of what had been a fence. The fourth remained seated in the wagon. "Come," said one of his companions, approaching him, while the others moved away in the direction of the dwelling— "this is the place."

The man addressed did not move. "By God!" he said harshly, "this is a trick, and it looks to me as if you were in it."

"Perhaps I am," the other said, looking him straight in the face and speaking in a tone which had something of contempt in it. "You will remember, however, that the choice of place was with your own assent left to the other side. Of course if you are afraid of spooks——"

"I am afraid of nothing," the man interrupted with another oath, and sprang to the ground. The two then joined the others at the door, which one of them had already opened with some difficulty, caused by rust of lock and hinge. All entered. Inside it was dark, but the man who had unlocked the door produced a candle and matches and made a light. He then unlocked a door on their right as they stood in the passage. This gave them entrance to a large, square room that the candle but dimly lighted. The floor had a thick carpeting of dust, which partly muffled their footfalls. Cobwebs were in the angles of the walls and depended from the ceiling like strips of rotting lace, making undulatory movements in the disturbed air. The room had two windows in adjoining sides, but from neither could anything be seen except the rough inner surfaces of boards a few inches from the glass. There was no fireplace, no furniture; there was nothing: besides the cobwebs and the dust, the four men were the only objects there which were not a part of the structure.

Strange enough they looked in the yellow light of the candle. The one who had so reluctantly alighted was especially spectacular—he might have been called sensational. He was of middle age, heavily built, deep chested and broad shouldered. Looking at his figure, one would have said that he had a giant's strength; at his features, that he would use it like a giant. He was clean shaven, his hair rather closely cropped and gray. His low forehead was seamed with wrinkles above the eyes, and over the nose these became vertical. The heavy black brows followed the same law, saved from meeting only by an upward turn at what would otherwise have been the point of contact. Deeply sunken beneath these, glowed in the obscure light a pair of eyes of uncertain color, but obviously enough too small. There was something forbidding in their expression, which was not bettered by the cruel mouth and wide jaw. The nose was well enough, as noses go; one does not expect much of noses. All that was sinister in the man's face seemed accentuated by an unnatural pallor—he appeared altogether bloodless.

The appearance of the other men was sufficiently commonplace: they were such persons as one meets and forgets that he met. All were younger than the man described, between whom and the eldest of the others, who stood apart, there was apparently no kindly feeling. They avoided looking at each other.

"Gentlemen," said the man holding the candle and keys, "I believe everything is right. Are you ready, Mr. Rosser?"

The man standing apart from the group bowed and smiled.

"And you, Mr. Grossmith?"

The heavy man bowed and scowled.

"You will be pleased to remove your outer clothing."

Their hats, coats, waistcoats and neckwear were soon removed and thrown outside the door, in the passage. The man with the candle now nodded, and the fourth man—he who had urged Grossmith to leave the wagon—produced from the pocket of his overcoat two long, murderous-looking bowie-knives, which he drew now from their leather scabbards.

"They are exactly alike," he said, presenting one to each of the two principals—for by this time the dullest observer would have understood the nature of this meeting. It was to be a duel to the death.

Each combatant took a knife, examined it critically near the candle and tested the strength of blade and handle across his lifted knee. Their persons were then searched in turn, each by the second of the other.

"If it is agreeable to you, Mr. Grossmith," said the man holding the light, "you will place yourself in that corner."

He indicated the angle of the room farthest from the door,

whither Grossmith retired, his second parting from him with a grasp of the hand which had nothing of cordiality in it. In the angle nearest the door Mr. Rosser stationed himself, and after a whispered consultation his second left him, joining the other near the door. At that moment the candle was suddenly extinguished, leaving all in profound darkness. This may have been done by a draught from the opened door; whatever the cause, the effect was startling.

"Gentlemen," said a voice which sounded strangely unfamiliar in the altered condition affecting the relations of the senses—"gentlemen, you will not move until you hear the closing of the outer door."

A sound of trampling ensued, then the closing of the inner door; and finally the outer one closed with a concussion which shook the entire building.

A few minutes afterward a belated farmer's boy met a light wagon which was being driven furiously toward the town of Marshall. He declared that behind the two figures on the front seat stood a third, with its hands upon the bowed shoulders of the others, who appeared to struggle vainly to free themselves from its grasp. This figure, unlike the others, was clad in white, and had undoubtedly boarded the wagon as it passed the haunted house. As the lad could boast a considerable former experience with the supernatural thereabouts his word had the weight justly due to the testimony of an expert. The story (in connection with the next day's events) eventually appeared in the *Advance,* with some slight literary embellishments and a concluding intimation that the gentlemen referred to would be allowed the use of the paper's columns for their version of the night's adventure. But the privilege remained without a claimant.

II

THE EVENTS that led up to this "duel in the dark" were simple enough. One evening three young men of the town of Marshall were sitting in a quiet corner of the porch of the village hotel, smoking and discussing such matters as three educated young men of a Southern village would naturally find interesting. Their names were King, Sancher and Rosser. At a little distance, within easy hearing, but taking no part in the conversation, sat a fourth. He was a stranger to the others. They merely knew that on his arrival by the stage-coach that afternoon he had written in the hotel register the name Robert Grossmith. He had not been observed to speak to anyone except the hotel clerk. He seemed, indeed, singularly fond of his own company—or, as the *personnel* of the *Advance* expressed it, "grossly addicted to evil associations." But then it should be said in justice to the stranger that the *personnel* was himself of a too convivial disposition fairly to judge one differently gifted, and had, moreover, experienced a slight rebuff in an effort at an "interview."

"I hate any kind of deformity in a woman," said King, "whether natural or—acquired. I have a theory that any physical defect has its correlative mental and moral defect."

"I infer, then," said Rosser, gravely, "that a lady lacking the moral advantage of a nose would find the struggle to become Mrs. King an arduous enterprise."

"Of course you may put it that way," was the reply; "but, seriously, I once threw over a most charming girl on learning quite accidentally that she had suffered amputation of a toe. My conduct was brutal if you like, but if I had married that girl I should have been miserable for life and should have made her so."

"Whereas," said Sancher, with a light laugh, "by marrying a gentleman of more liberal views she escaped with a parted throat."

"Ah, you know to whom I refer. Yes, she married Manton, but I don't know about his liberality; I'm not sure but he cut her throat because he discovered that she lacked that excellent thing in woman, the middle toe of the right foot."

"Look at that chap!" said Rosser in a low voice, his eyes fixed upon the stranger.

That chap was obviously listening intently to the conversation.

"Damn his impudence!" muttered King—"what ought we to do?"

"That's an easy one," Rosser replied, rising. "Sir," he continued, addressing the stranger, "I think it would be better if you would remove your chair to the other end of the veranda. The presence of gentlemen is evidently an unfamiliar situation to you."

The man sprang to his feet and strode forward with clenched hands, his face white with rage. All were now standing. Sancher stepped between the belligerents.

"You are hasty and unjust," he said to Rosser; "this gentleman has done nothing to deserve such language."

But Rosser would not withdraw a word. By the custom of the country and the time there could be but one outcome to the quarrel.

"I demand the satisfaction due to a gentleman," said the stranger, who had become more calm. "I have not an acquaintance in this region. Perhaps you, sir," bowing to Sancher, "will be kind enough to represent me in this matter."

Sancher accepted the trust—somewhat reluctantly it must be confessed, for the man's appearance and manner were not at all to his liking. King, who during the colloquy had hardly removed his eyes from the stranger's face and had not spoken a word, consented with a nod to act for Rosser, and the upshot of it was that, the principals having retired, a meeting was arranged for the next evening. The nature of the arrangements has been already disclosed. The duel with knives in a dark room was once a commoner feature of Southwestern life than it is likely to be again. How thin a veneering of "chivalry" covered the essential brutality of the code under which such encounters were possible we shall see.

III

IN THE blaze of a midsummer noonday the old Manton house was hardly true to its traditions. It was of the earth, earthy. The sunshine caressed it warmly and affectionately, with evident disregard of its bad reputation. The grass greening all the expanse in its front seemed to grow, not rankly, but with a natural and joyous exuberance, and the weeds blossomed quite like plants. Full of charming lights and shadows and populous with pleasant-voiced birds, the neglected shade trees no longer struggled to run away, but bent reverently beneath their burdens of sun and song. Even in the glassless upper windows was an expression of peace and contentment, due to the light within. Over the stony fields the visible heat danced with a lively tremor incompatible with the gravity which is an attribute of the supernatural.

Such was the aspect under which the place presented itself to Sheriff Adams and two other men who had come out from Marshall to look at it. One of these men was Mr. King, the sheriff's deputy; the other, whose name was Brewer, was a brother of the late Mrs. Manton. Under a beneficent law of the State relating to property which has been for a certain period abandoned by an owner whose residence cannot be ascertained, the sheriff was legal custodian of the Manton farm and appurtenances thereunto belonging. His present visit was in mere perfunctory compliance with some order of a court in which Mr. Brewer had an action to get possession of the property as heir to his deceased sister. By a mere coincidence, the visit was made on the day after the night that Deputy King had unlocked the house for another and very different purpose. His presence now was not of his own choosing: he had been ordered to accompany his superior and at the moment could think of nothing more prudent than simulated alacrity in obedience to the command.

Carelessly opening the front door, which to his surprise was not locked, the sheriff was amazed to see, lying on the floor of the passage into which it opened, a confused heap of men's apparel. Examination showed it to consist of two hats, and the same number of coats, waistcoats and scarves, all in a remarkably good state of preservation, albeit somewhat defiled by the dust in which they lay. Mr. Brewer was equally astonished, but Mr. King's emotion is not of record. With a new and lively interest in his own actions the sheriff now unlatched and pushed open a door on the right, and the three entered. The room was apparently vacant—no; as their eyes became accustomed to the dimmer light something was visible in the farthest angle of the wall. It was a human figure—that of a man crouching close in the corner. Something in the attitude made the intruders halt when they had barely passed the threshold. The figure more and more clearly defined itself. The man was upon one knee, his back in the angle of the wall, his shoulders elevated to the level of his ears, his hands before his face, palms outward, the fingers spread and crooked like claws; the white face turned upward on the retracted neck had an expression of unutterable fright, the mouth half open, the eyes incredibly expanded. He was stone dead. Yet, with the exception of a bowie-knife, which had evidently fallen from his own hand, not another object was in the room.

In thick dust that covered the floor were some confused footprints near the door and along the wall through which it opened. Along one of the adjoining walls, too, past the boarded-up windows, was the trail made by the man himself in reaching his corner. Instinctively in approaching the body the three men followed that trail. The sheriff grasped one of the outthrown arms; it was as rigid as iron, and the application of a gentle force rocked the entire body without altering the relation of its parts. Brewer, pale with excitement, gazed intently into the distorted face. "God of mercy!" he suddenly cried, "it is Manton!"

"You are right," said King, with an evident attempt at calmness: "I knew Manton. He then wore a full beard and his hair long, but this is he."

He might have added: "I recognized him when he challenged Rosser. I told Rosser and Sancher who he was before we played him this horrible trick. When Rosser left this dark room at our heels, forgetting his outer clothing in the excitement, and driving away with us in his shirt sleeves—all through the discreditable proceedings we knew whom we were dealing with, murderer and coward that he was!"

But nothing of this did Mr. King say. With his better light he was trying to penetrate the mystery of the man's death. That he had not once moved from the corner where he had been stationed; that his posture was that of neither attack nor defense; that he had dropped his weapon; that he had obviously perished of sheer horror of something that he *saw*—these were circumstances which Mr. King's disturbed intelligence could not rightly comprehend.

Groping in intellectual darkness for a clew to his maze of doubt, his gaze, directed mechanically downward in the way of one who ponders momentous matters, fell upon something which, there, in the light of day and in the presence of living companions, affected him with terror. In the dust of years that lay thick upon the floor—leading from the door by which they had entered, straight across the room to within a yard of Manton's crouching corpse—were three parallel lines of footprints—light but definite impressions of bare feet, the outer ones those of small children, the inner a woman's. From the point at which they ended they did not return; they pointed all one way. Brewer, who had observed them at the same moment, was leaning forward in an attitude of rapt attention, horribly pale.

"Look at that!" he cried, pointing with both hands at the nearest print of the woman's right foot, where she had apparently stopped and stood. "The middle toe is missing—it was Gertrude!"

Gertrude was the late Mrs. Manton, sister to Mr. Brewer.

John Bartine's Watch

A Story by a Physician

THE EXACT time? Good God! my friend, why do you insist? One would think—but what does it matter; it is easily bedtime—isn't that near enough? But, here, if you must set your watch, take mine and see for yourself."

With that he detached his watch—a tremendously heavy, old-fashioned one—from the chain, and handed it to me; then turned away, and walking across the room to a shelf of books, began an examination of their backs. His agitation and evident distress surprised me; they appeared reasonless. Having set my watch by his, I stepped over to where he stood and said, "Thank you."

As he took his timepiece and reattached it to the guard I observed that his hands were unsteady. With a tact upon which I greatly prided myself, I sauntered carelessly to the sideboard and took some brandy and water; then, begging his pardon for my thoughtlessness, asked him to have some and went back to my seat by the fire, leaving him to help himself, as was our custom. He did so and presently joined me at the hearth, as tranquil as ever.

This odd little incident occurred in my apartment, where John Bartine was passing an evening. We had dined together at the club, had come home in a cab and—in short, everything had been done in the most prosaic way; and why John Bartine should break in upon the natural and established order of things to make himself spectacular with a display of emotion, apparently for his own entertainment, I could nowise understand. The more I thought of it, while his brilliant conversational gifts were commending themselves to my inattention, the more curious I grew, and of course had no difficulty in persuading myself that my curiosity was friendly solicitude. That is the disguise that curiosity usually assumes to evade resentment. So I ruined one of the finest sentences of his disregarded monologue by cutting it short without ceremony.

"John Bartine," I said, "you must try to forgive me if I am wrong, but with the light that I have at present I cannot concede your right to go all to pieces when asked the time o' night. I cannot admit that it is proper to experience a mysterious reluctance to look your own watch in the face and to cherish in my presence, without explanation, painful emotions which are denied to me, and which are none of my business."

To this ridiculous speech Bartine made no immediate reply, but sat looking gravely into the fire. Fearing that I had offended I was about to apologize and beg him to think no more about the matter, when looking me calmly in the eyes he said:

"My dear fellow, the levity of your manner does not at all disguise the hideous impudence of your demand; but happily I had already decided to tell you what you wish to know, and no manifestation of your unworthiness to hear it shall alter my decision. Be good enough to give me your attention and you shall hear all about the matter.

"This watch," he said, "had been in my family for three generations before it fell to me. Its original owner, for whom it was made, was my great-grandfather, Bramwell Olcott Bartine, a wealthy planter of Colonial Virginia, and as stanch a Tory as ever lay awake nights contriving new kinds of maledictions for the head of Mr. Washington, and new methods of aiding and abetting good King George. One day this worthy gentleman had the deep misfortune to perform for his cause a service of capital importance which was not recognized as legitimate by those who suffered its disadvantages. It does not matter what it was, but among its minor consequences was my excellent ancestor's arrest one night in his own house by a party of Mr. Washington's rebels. He was permitted to say farewell to his weeping family, and was then marched away into the darkness which swallowed him up forever. Not the slenderest clew to his fate was ever found. After the war the most diligent inquiry and the offer of large rewards failed to turn up any of his captors or any fact concerning his disappearance. He had disappeared, and that was all."

Something in Bartine's manner that was not in his words— I hardly knew what it was—prompted me to ask:

"What is your view of the matter—of the justice of it?"

"My view of it," he flamed out, bringing his clenched hand down upon the table as if he had been in a public house dicing with blackguards—"my view of it is that it was a characteristically dastardly assassination by that damned traitor, Washington, and his ragamuffin rebels!"

For some minutes nothing was said: Bartine was recovering his temper, and I waited. Then I said:

"Was that all?"

"No—there was something else. A few weeks after my great-grandfather's arrest his watch was found lying on the porch at the front door of his dwelling. It was wrapped in a sheet of letter paper bearing the name of Rupert Bartine, his only son, my grandfather. I am wearing that watch."

Bartine paused. His usually restless black eyes were staring fixedly into the grate, a point of red light in each, reflected from the glowing coals. He seemed to have forgotten me. A sudden threshing of the branches of a tree outside one of the windows, and almost at the same instant a rattle of rain against the glass, recalled him to a sense of his surroundings. A storm had risen, heralded by a single gust of wind, and in a few moments the steady plash of the water on the pavement was distinctly heard. I hardly know why I relate this incident; it seemed somehow to have a certain significance and relevancy which I am unable now to discern. It at least added an element of seriousness, almost solemnity. Bartine resumed:

"I have a singular feeling toward this watch—a kind of affection for it; I like to have it about me, though partly from its weight, and partly for a reason I shall now explain, I seldom carry it. The reason is this: Every evening when I have it with me I feel an unaccountable desire to open and consult it, even if I can think of no reason for wishing to know the time. But if I yield to it, the moment my eyes rest upon the dial I am filled with a mysterious apprehension—a sense of imminent calamity. And this is the more insupportable the nearer it is to eleven o'clock—by this watch, no matter what the actual hour may be. After the hands have registered eleven the desire to look is gone; I am entirely indifferent. Then I can consult the thing as often as I like, with no more emotion than you feel in looking at your own. Naturally I have trained myself not to look at that watch in the evening before eleven; nothing could induce me. Your insistence this evening upset me a trifle. I felt very much as I suppose an opium-eater might feel if his yearning for his special and particular kind of hell were re-enforced by opportunity and advice.

"Now that is my story, and I have told it in the interest of your trumpery science; but if on any evening hereafter you observe me wearing this damnable watch, and you have the thoughtfulness to ask me the hour, I shall beg leave to put you to the inconvenience of being knocked down."

His humor did not amuse me. I could see that in relating his delusion he was again somewhat disturbed. His concluding smile was positively ghastly, and his eyes had resumed something more than their old restlessness; they shifted hither and thither about the room with apparent aimlessness and I fancied had taken on a wild expression, such as is sometimes observed in cases of dementia. Perhaps this was my own imagination, but at any rate I was now persuaded that my friend was afflicted with a most singular and interesting monomania. Without, I trust, any abatement of my affectionate solicitude for him as a friend, I began to regard him as a patient, rich in possibilities of profitable study. Why not? Had he not described his delusion in the interest of science? Ah, poor fellow, he was doing more for science than he knew: not only his story but himself was in evidence. I should cure him if I could, of course, but first I should make a little experiment in psychology—nay, the experiment itself might be a step in his restoration.

"That is very frank and friendly of you, Bartine," I said cordially, "and I'm rather proud of your confidence. It is all very odd, certainly. Do you mind showing me the watch?"

He detached it from his waistcoat, chain and all, and passed it to me without a word. The case was of gold, very thick and strong, and singularly engraved. After closely examining the dial and observing that it was nearly twelve o'clock, I opened it at the back and was interested to observe an inner case of ivory, upon which was painted a miniature portrait in that exquisite and delicate manner which was in vogue during the eighteenth century.

"Why, bless my soul!" I exclaimed, feeling a sharp artistic delight—"how under the sun did you get that done? I thought miniature painting on ivory was a lost art."

"That," he replied, gravely smiling, "is not I; it is my excellent great-grandfather, the late Bramwell Olcott Bartine, Esquire, of Virginia. He was younger then than later—about my age, in fact. It is said to resemble me; do you think so?"

"Resemble you? I should say so! Barring the costume, which I supposed you to have assumed out of compliment to the art— or for *vraisemblance,* so to say—and the no mustache, that portrait is you in every feature, line, and expression."

No more was said at that time. Bartine took a book from the table and began reading. I heard outside the incessant plash of the rain in the street. There were occasional hurried footfalls on the sidewalks; and once a slower, heavier tread seemed to cease at my door—a policeman, I thought, seeking shelter in the doorway. The boughs of the trees tapped significantly on the window panes, as if asking for admittance. I remember it all through these years and years of a wiser, graver life.

Seeing myself unobserved, I took the old-fashioned key that dangled from the chain and quickly turned back the hands of the watch a full hour; then, closing the case, I handed Bartine his property and saw him replace it on his person.

"I think you said," I began, with assumed carelessness, "that after eleven the sight of the dial no longer affects you. As it is now nearly twelve"—looking at my own timepiece—"perhaps, if you don't resent my pursuit of proof, you will look at it now."

He smiled good-humoredly, pulled out the watch again, opened it, and instantly sprang to his feet with a cry that Heaven has not had the mercy to permit me to forget! His eyes, their blackness strikingly intensified by the pallor of his face, were fixed upon the watch, which he clutched in both hands. For some time he remained in that attitude without uttering another sound; then, in a voice that I should not have recognized as his, he said:

"Damn you! it is two minutes to eleven!"

I was not unprepared for some such outbreak, and without rising replied, calmly enough:

"I beg your pardon; I must have misread your watch in setting my own by it."

He shut the case with a sharp snap and put the watch in his pocket. He looked at me and made an attempt to smile, but his lower lip quivered and he seemed unable to close his mouth. His hands, also, were shaking, and he thrust them, clenched, into the pockets of his sack-coat. The courageous spirit was manifestly endeavoring to subdue the coward body. The effort was too great; he began to sway from side to side, as from vertigo, and before I could spring from my chair to support him his knees gave way and he pitched awkwardly forward and fell upon his face. I sprang to assist him to rise; but when John Bartine rises we shall all rise.

The *post-mortem* examination disclosed nothing; every organ was normal and sound. But when the body had been prepared for burial a faint dark circle was seen to have developed around the neck; at least I was so assured by several persons who said they saw it, but of my own knowledge I cannot say if that was true.

Nor can I set limitations to the law of heredity. I do not know that in the spiritual world a sentiment or emotion may not survive the heart that held it, and seek expression in a kindred life, ages removed. Surely, if I were to guess at the fate of Bramwell Olcott Bartine, I should guess that he was hanged at eleven o'clock in the evening, and that he had been allowed several hours in which to prepare for the change.

As to John Bartine, my friend, my patient for five minutes, and—Heaven forgive me!—my victim for eternity, there is no more to say. He is buried, and his watch with him—I saw to that. May God rest his soul in Paradise, and the soul of his Virginian ancestor, if, indeed, they are two souls.

The Stranger

A MAN stepped out of the darkness into the little illuminated circle about our failing campfire and seated himself upon a rock.

"You are not the first to explore this region," he said, gravely.

Nobody controverted his statement; he was himself proof of its truth, for he was not of our party and must have been somewhere near when we camped. Moreover, he must have companions not far away; it was not a place where one would be living or traveling alone. For more than a week we had seen, besides ourselves and our animals, only such living things as rattlesnakes and horned toads. In an Arizona desert one does not long coexist with only such creatures as these: one must have pack animals, supplies, arms—"an outfit." And all these imply comrades. It was perhaps a doubt as to what manner of men this unceremonious stranger's comrades might be, together with something in his words interpretable as a challenge, that caused every man of our half-dozen "gentlemen adventurers" to rise to a sitting posture and lay his hand upon a weapon—an act signifying, in that time and place, a policy of expectation. The stranger gave the matter no attention and began again to speak in the same deliberate, uninflected monotone in which he had delivered his first sentence:

"Thirty years ago Ramon Gallegos, William Shaw, George W. Kent and Berry Davis, all of Tucson, crossed the Santa Catalina mountains and traveled due west, as nearly as the configuration of the country permitted. We were prospecting and it was our intention, if we found nothing, to push through to the Gila river at some point near Big Bend, where we understood there was a settlement. We had a good outfit but no guide—just Ramon Gallegos, William Shaw, George W. Kent and Berry Davis.

The man repeated the names slowly and distinctly, as if to fix them in the memories of his audience, every member of which was now attentively observing him, but with a slackened apprehension regarding his possible companions somewhere in the darkness that seemed to enclose us like a black wall; in the man-

189

ner of this volunteer historian was no suggestion of an unfriendly purpose. His act was rather that of a harmless lunatic than an enemy. We were not so new to the country as not to know that the solitary life of many a plainsman had a tendency to develop eccentricities of conduct and character not always easily distinguishable from mental aberration. A man is like a tree: in a forest of his fellows he will grow as straight as his generic and individual nature permits; alone in the open, he yields to the deforming stresses and tortions that environ him. Some such thoughts were in my mind as I watched the man from the shadow of my hat, pulled low to shut out the firelight. A witless fellow, no doubt, but what could he be doing there in the heart of a desert?

Having undertaken to tell this story, I wish that I could describe the man's appearance; that would be a natural thing to do. Unfortunately, and somewhat strangely, I find myself unable to do so with any degree of confidence, for afterward no two of us agreed as to what he wore and how he looked; and when I try to set down my own impressions they elude me. Anyone can tell some kind of story; narration is one of the elemental powers of the race. But the talent for description is a gift.

Nobody having broken silence the visitor went on to say:

"This country was not then what it is now. There was not a ranch between the Gila and the Gulf. There was a little game here and there in the mountains, and near the infrequent waterholes grass enough to keep our animals from starvation. If we should be so fortunate as to encounter no Indians we might get through. But within a week the purpose of the expedition had altered from discovery of wealth to preservation of life. We had gone too far to go back, for what was ahead could be no worse than what was behind; so we pushed on, riding by night to avoid Indians and the intolerable heat, and concealing ourselves by day as best we could. Sometimes, having exhausted our supply of wild meat and emptied our casks, we were days without food or drink; then a water-hole or a shallow pool in the bottom of an arroyo so restored our strength and sanity that we were able to shoot some of the wild animals that sought it also. Sometimes it was a bear, sometimes an antelope, a coyote, a cougar—that was as God pleased; all were food.

"One morning as we skirted a mountain range, seeking a practicable pass, we were attacked by a band of Apaches who had followed our trail up a gulch—it is not far from here. Knowing that they outnumbered us ten to one, they took none of their usual cowardly precautions, but dashed upon us at a gallop, firing and yelling. Fighting was out of the question: we urged our feeble animals up the gulch as far as there was footing for a hoof, then threw ourselves out of our saddles and took to the chaparral on one of the slopes, abandoning our entire outfit to the enemy. But we retained our rifles, every man—Ramon Gallegos, William Shaw, George W. Kent and Berry Davis."

"Same old crowd," said the humorist of our party. He was an Eastern man, unfamiliar with the decent observances of social intercourse. A gesture of disapproval from our leader silenced him and the stranger proceeded with his tale:

"The savages dismounted also, and some of them ran up the gulch beyond the point at which we had left it, cutting off further retreat in that direction and forcing us on up the side. Unfortunately the chaparral extended only a short distance up the slope, and as we came into the open ground above we took the fire of a dozen rifles; but Apaches shoot badly when in a hurry, and God so willed it that none of us fell. Twenty yards up the slope, beyond the edge of the brush, were vertical cliffs, in which, directly in front of us, was a narrow opening. Into that we ran, finding ourselves in a cavern about as large as an ordinary room in a house. Here for a time we were safe: a single man with a repeating rifle could defend the entrance against all the Apaches in the land. But against hunger and thirst we had no defense. Courage we still had, but hope was a memory.

"Not one of those Indians did we afterward see, but by the smoke and glare of their fires in the gulch we knew that by day and by night they watched with ready rifles in the edge of the bush—knew that if we made a sortie not a man of us would live to take three steps into the open. For three days, watching in turn, we held out before our suffering became insupportable. Then—it was the morning of the fourth day—Ramon Gallegos said:

" 'Senores, I know not well of the good God and what please him. I have live without religion, and I am not acquaint with that of you. Pardon, senores, if I shock you, but for me the time is come to beat the game of the Apache.'

"He knelt upon the rock floor of the cave and pressed his pistol against his temple. 'Madre de Dios,' he said, 'comes now the soul of Ramon Gallegos.'

"And so he left us—William Shaw, George W. Kent and Berry Davis.

"I was the leader: it was for me to speak.

" 'He was a brave man,' I said—'he knew when to die, and

how. It is foolish to go mad from thirst and fall by Apache bullets, or be skinned alive—it is in bad taste. Let us join Ramon Gallegos.'

" 'That is right,' said William Shaw.

" 'That is right,' said George W. Kent.

"I straightened the limbs of Ramon Gallegos and put a handkerchief over his face. Then William Shaw said: 'I should like to look like that—a little while.'

"And George W. Kent said that he felt that way, too.

" 'It shall be so,' I said: 'the red devils will wait a week. William Shaw and George W. Kent, draw and kneel.'

"They did so and I stood before them.

" 'Almighty God, our Father,' said I.

" 'Almighty God, our Father,' said William Shaw.

" 'Almighty God, our Father,' said George W. Kent.

" 'Forgive us our sins,' said I.

" 'Forgive us our sins,' said they.

" 'And receive our souls.'

" 'And receive our souls.'

" 'Amen!'

" 'Amen!'

"I laid them beside Ramon Gallegos and covered their faces."

There was a quick commotion on the opposite side of the campfire: one of our party had sprung to his feet, pistol in hand.

"And you!" he shouted—"*you* dared to escape?—you dare to be alive? You cowardly hound, I'll send you to join them if I hang for it!"

But with the leap of a panther the captain was upon him, grasping his wrist. "Hold it in, Sam Yountsey, hold it in!"

We were now all upon our feet—except the stranger, who sat motionless and apparently inattentive. Some one seized Yountsey's other arm.

"Captain," I said, "there is something wrong here. This fellow is either a lunatic or merely a liar—just a plain, everyday liar whom Yountsey has no call to kill. If this man was of that party it had five members, one of whom—probably himself—he has not named."

"Yes," said the captain, releasing the insurgent, who sat down, "there is something—unusual. Years ago four dead bodies of white men, scalped and shamefully mutilated, were found about the mouth of that cave. They are buried there; I have seen the graves—we shall all see them to-morrow."

The stranger rose, standing tall in the light of the expiring fire, which in our breathless attention to his story we had neglected to keep going.

"There were four," he said—"Ramon Gallegos, William Shaw, George W. Kent and Berry Davis."

With this reiterated roll-call of the dead he walked into the darkness and we saw him no more.

At that moment one of our party, who had been on guard, strode in among us, rifle in hand and somewhat excited.

"Captain," he said, "for the last half-hour three men have been standing out there on the mesa." He pointed in the direction taken by the stranger. "I could see them distinctly, for the moon is up, but as they had no guns and I had them covered with mine I thought it was their move. They have made none, but, damn it! they have got on to my nerves."

"Go back to your post, and stay till you see them again," said the captain. "The rest of you lie down again, or I'll kick you all into the fire."

The sentinel obediently withdrew, swearing, and did not return. As we were arranging our blankets the fiery Yountsey said: "I beg your pardon, Captain, but who the devil do you take them to be?"

"Ramon Gallegos, William Shaw and George W. Kent."

"But how about Berry Davis? I ought to have shot him."

"Quite needless; you couldn't have made him any deader. Go to sleep."

Visions of the Night

I HOLD the belief that the Gift of Dreams is a valuable literary endowment—that if by some art not now understood the elusive fancies that it supplies could be caught and fixed and made to serve we should have a literature "exceeding fair." In captivity and domestication the gift could doubtless be wonderfully improved, as animals bred to service acquire new capacities and powers. By taming our dreams we shall double our working hours and our most fruitful labor will be done in sleep. Even as matters are, Dreamland is a tributary province, as witness "Kubla Khan."

What is a dream? A loose and lawless collocation of memories—a disorderly succession of matters once present in the waking consciousness. It is a resurrection of the dead, pell-mell—ancient and modern, the just and the unjust—springing from their cracked tombs, each "in his habit as he lived," pressing forward confusedly to have an audience of the Master of the Revel, and snatching one another's garments as they run. Master? No; he has abdicated his authority and they have their will of him; his own is dead and does not rise with the rest. His judgment, too, is gone, and with it the capacity to be surprised. Pained he may be and pleased, terrified and charmed, but wonder he can not feel. The monstrous, the preposterous, the unnatural—these all are simple, right and reasonable. The ludicrous does not amuse, nor the impossible amaze. The dreamer is your only true poet; he is "of imagination all compact."

Imagination is merely memory. Try to imagine something that you have never observed, experienced, heard of or read about. Try to conceive an animal, for example, without body, head, limbs or tail—a house without walls or roof. But, when awake, having assistance of will and judgment, we can somewhat control and direct; we can pick and choose from memory's store, taking that which serves, excluding, though sometimes with difficulty, what is not to the purpose; asleep, our fancies "inherit us." They come so grouped, so blended and compounded the one

194

with another, so wrought of one another's elements, that the whole seems new; but the old familiar units of conception are there, and none beside. Waking or sleeping, we get from imagination nothing new but new adjustments: "the stuff that dreams are made on" has been gathered by the physical senses and stored in memory, as squirrels hoard nuts. But one, at least, of the senses contributes nothing to the fabric of the dream: no one ever dreamed an odor. Sight, hearing, feeling, possibly taste, are all workers, making provision for our nightly entertainment; but Sleep is without a nose. It surprises that those keen observers, the ancient poets, did not so describe the drowsy god, and that their obedient servants, the ancient sculptors, did not so represent him. Perhaps these latter worthies, working for posterity, reasoned that time and mischance would inevitably revise their work in this regard, conforming it to the facts of nature.

Who can so relate a dream that it shall seem one? No poet has so light a touch. As well try to write the music of an æolian harp. There is a familiar species of the genus Bore (*Penetrator intolerabilis*) who having read a story—perhaps by some master of style—is at the pains elaborately to expound its plot for your edification and delight; then thinks, good soul, that now you need not read it. "Under substantially similar circumstances and conditions" (as the interstate commerce law hath it) I should not be guilty of the like offence; but I purpose herein to set forth the plots of certain dreams of my own, the "circumstances and conditions" being, as I conceive, dissimilar in this, that the dreams themselves are not accessible to the reader. In endeavoring to make record of their poorer part I do not indulge the hope of a higher success. I have no salt to put upon the tail of a dream's elusive spirit.

I was walking at dusk through a great forest of unfamiliar trees. Whence and whither I did not know. I had a sense of the vast extent of the wood, a consciousness that I was the only living thing in it. I was obsessed by some awful spell in expiation of a forgotten crime committed, as I vaguely surmised, against the sunrise. Mechanically and without hope, I moved under the arms of the giant trees along a narrow trail penetrating the haunted solitudes of the forest. I came at length to a brook that flowed darkly and sluggishly across my path, and saw that it was blood. Turning to the right, I followed it up a considerable distance, and soon came to a small circular opening in the forest, filled with a dim, unreal light, by which I saw in the center of the opening a deep tank of white marble. It was filled with blood, and the stream that I had followed up was its outlet. All round the tank, between it and the enclosing forest—a space of perhaps ten feet in breadth, paved with immense slabs of marble—were dead bodies of men—a score; though I did not count them I knew that the number had some significant and portentous relation to my crime. Possibly they marked the time, in centuries, since I had committed it. I only recognized the fitness of the number, and knew it without counting. The bodies were naked and arranged symmetrically around the central tank, radiating from it like spokes of a wheel. The feet were outward, the heads hanging over the edge of the tank. Each lay upon its back, its throat cut, blood slowly dripping from the wound. I looked on all this unmoved. It was a natural and necessary result of my offence, and did not affect me; but there was something that filled me with apprehension and terror—a monstrous pulsation, beating with a slow, inevitable recurrence. I do not know which of the senses it addressed, or if it made its way to the consciousness through some avenue unknown to science and experience. The pitiless regularity of this vast rhythm was maddening. I was conscious that it pervaded the entire forest, and was a manifestation of some gigantic and implacable malevolence.

Of this dream I have no further recollection. Probably, overcome by a terror which doubtless had its origin in the discomfort of an impeded circulation, I cried out and was awakened by the sound of my own voice.

The dream whose skeleton I shall now present occurred in my early youth. I could not have been more than sixteen. I am considerably more now, yet I recall the incidents as vividly as when the vision was "of an hour's age" and I lay cowering beneath the bedcovering and trembling with terror from the memory.

I was alone on a boundless level in the night—in my bad dreams I am always alone and it is usually night. No trees were anywhere in sight, no habitations of men, no streams nor hills. The earth seemed to be covered with a short, coarse vegetation that was black and stubbly, as if the plain had been swept by fire. My way was broken here and there as I went forward with I know not what purpose by small pools of water occupying shallow depressions, as if the fire had been succeeded by rain. These pools were on every side, and kept vanishing and appearing again, as heavy dark clouds drove athwart those parts of the sky which they reflected, and passing on disclosed again the steely glitter of the stars, in whose cold light the waters shone with a black luster. My course lay toward the west, where low along the horizon burned a crimson light beneath long strips of cloud, giving that effect of measureless distance that I have since learned to look for in Doré's pictures, where every touch of his hand has laid a portent and a curse. As I moved I saw outlined against this uncanny background a silhouette of battlements and towers which, expanding with every mile of my journey, grew at last to an unthinkable height and breadth, till the building subtended a wide angle of vision, yet seemed no nearer than before. Heartless and hopeless I struggled on over the blasted and forbidding plain, and still the mighty structure grew until I could no longer compass it with a look, and its towers shut out the stars directly overhead; then I passed in at an open portal, between columns of cyclopean masonry whose single stones were larger than my father's house.

Within all was vacancy; everything was coated with the dust of desertion. A dim light—the lawless light of dreams, sufficient unto itself—enabled me to pass from corridor to corridor, and from room to room, every door yielding to my hand. In the rooms it was a long walk from wall to wall; of no corridor did I ever reach an end. My footfalls gave out that strange, hollow sound that is never heard but in abandoned dwellings and tenanted tombs. For hours I wandered in this awful solitude, conscious of a seeking purpose, yet knowing not what I sought. At last, in what I conceived to be an extreme angle of the building, I entered a room of the ordinary dimensions, having a single window. Through this I saw the same crimson light still lying along the horizon in the measureless reaches of the west, like a visible doom, and knew it for the lingering fire of eternity. Looking upon the red menace of its sullen and sinister glare, there came to me the dreadful truth which years later as an extravagant fancy I endeavored to express in verse:

> Man is long ages dead in every zone,
> The angels all are gone to graves unknown;
> The devils, too, are cold enough at last,
> And God lies dead before the great white throne!

The light was powerless to dispel the obscurity of the room, and it was some time before I discovered in the farthest angle the outlines of a bed, and approached it with a prescience of ill. I felt that here somehow the bad business of my adventure was to end with some horrible climax, yet could not resist the spell that urged me to the fulfilment. Upon the bed, partly clothed, lay the dead body of a human being. It lay upon its back, the arms straight along the sides. By bending over it, which I did with loathing but no fear, I could see that it was dreadfully decomposed. The ribs protruded from the leathern flesh; through the skin of the sunken belly could be seen the protuberances of the spine. The face was black and shriveled and the lips, drawn away from the yellow teeth, cursed it with a ghastly grin. A fulness under the closed lids seemed to indicate that the eyes had survived the general wreck; and this was true, for as I bent above them they slowly opened and gazed into mine with a tranquil, steady regard. Imagine my horror how you can—no words of mine can assist the conception; the eyes were my own! That vestigial fragment of a vanished race—that unspeakable thing which neither time nor eternity had wholly effaced—that hateful and abhorrent scrap of mortality, still sentient after the death of God and the angels, was I!

There are dreams that repeat themselves. Of this class is one of my own,* which seems sufficiently singular to justify its narration, though truly I fear the reader will think the realms of sleep are anything but a happy hunting-ground for my night-wandering soul. This is not true; the greater number of my incursions into dreamland, and I suppose those of most others, are attended with the happiest results. My imagination returns to the body like a bee to the hive, loaded with spoil which, reason assisting, is transmuted to honey and stored away in the cells of memory to be a joy forever. But the dream which I am about to relate has a double character; it is strangely dreadful in the experience, but the horror it inspires is so ludicrously disproportionate to the one incident producing it, that in retrospection the fantasy amuses.

I am passing through an open glade in a thinly wooded country. Through the belt of scattered trees that bound the irregular space there are glimpses of cultivated fields and the homes of strange intelligences. It must be near daybreak, for the moon, nearly at full, is low in the west, showing blood-red through the mists with which the landscape is fantastically freaked. The grass about my feet is heavy with dew, and the whole scene is that of a morning in early summer, glimmering in the unfamiliar light of a setting full moon. Near my path is a horse, visibly and audibly cropping the herbage. It lifts its head as I am about to pass, regards me motionless for a moment, then walks toward me. It is milk-white, mild of mien and amiable in look. I say to myself: "This horse is a gentle soul," and pause to caress it. It keeps its

---

*At my suggestion the late Flora Macdonald Shearer put this drama into sonnet form in her book of poems, *The Legend of Aulus.*

eyes fixed upon my own, approaches and speaks to me in a human voice, with human words. This does not surprise, but terrifies, and instantly I return to this our world.

The horse always speaks my own tongue, but I never know what it says. I suppose I vanish from the land of dreams before it finishes expressing what it has in mind, leaving it, no doubt, as greatly terrified by my sudden disappearance as I by its manner of accosting me. I would give value to know the purport of its communication.

Perhaps some morning I shall understand—and return no more to this our world.

CATALOGUE OF DOVER BOOKS

Books Explaining Science and Mathematics

WHAT IS SCIENCE?, N. Campbell. The role of experiment and measurement, the function of mathematics, the nature of scientific laws, the difference between laws and theories, the limitations of science, and many similarly provocative topics are treated clearly and without technicalities by an eminent scientist. "Still an excellent introduction to scientific philosophy," H. Margenau in PHYSICS TODAY. "A first-rate primer . . . deserves a wide audience," SCIENTIFIC AMERICAN. 192pp. 5⅜ x 8.   S43 Paperbound **$1.25**

THE NATURE OF PHYSICAL THEORY, P. W. Bridgman. A Nobel Laureate's clear, non-technical lectures on difficulties and paradoxes connected with frontier research on the physical sciences. Concerned with such central concepts as thought, logic, mathematics, relativity, probability, wave mechanics, etc. he analyzes the contributions of such men as Newton, Einstein, Bohr, Heisenberg, and many others. "Lucid and entertaining . . . recommended to anyone who wants to get some insight into current philosophies of science," THE NEW PHILOSOPHY. Index. xi + 138pp. 5⅜ x 8.   S33 Paperbound **$1.25**

EXPERIMENT AND THEORY IN PHYSICS, Max Born. A Nobel Laureate examines the nature of experiment and theory in theoretical physics and analyzes the advances made by the great physicists of our day: Heisenberg, Einstein, Bohr, Planck, Dirac, and others. The actual process of creation is detailed step-by-step by one who participated. A fine examination of the scientific method at work. 44pp. 5⅜ x 8.   S308 Paperbound **75¢**

THE PSYCHOLOGY OF INVENTION IN THE MATHEMATICAL FIELD, J. Hadamard. The reports of such men as Descartes, Pascal, Einstein, Poincaré, and others are considered in this investigation of the method of idea-creation in mathematics and other sciences and the thinking process in general. How do ideas originate? What is the role of the unconscious? What is Poincaré's forgetting hypothesis? are some of the fascinating questions treated. A penetrating analysis of Einstein's thought processes concludes the book. xiii + 145pp. 5⅜ x 8.   T107 Paperbound **$1.25**

THE NATURE OF LIGHT AND COLOUR IN THE OPEN AIR, M. Minnaert. Why are shadows sometimes blue, sometimes green, or other colors depending on the light and surroundings? What causes mirages? Why do multiple suns and moons appear in the sky? Professor Minnaert explains these unusual phenomena and hundreds of others in simple, easy-to-understand terms based on optical laws and the properties of light and color. No mathematics is required but artists, scientists, students, and everyone fascinated by these "tricks" of nature will find thousands of useful and amazing pieces of information. 200 illustrations; 42 photos. xvi + 362pp. 5⅜ x 8.   T196 Paperbound **$2.00**

THE UNIVERSE OF LIGHT, W. Bragg. Sir William Bragg, Nobel Laureate and great modern physicist, is also well known for his powers of clear exposition. Here he analyzes all aspects of light for the layman: lenses, reflection, refraction, the optics of vision, x-rays, the photoelectric effect, etc. He tells you what causes the color of spectra, rainbows, and soap bubbles, how magic mirrors work, and much more. Dozens of simple experiments are described. Preface. Index. 199 line drawings and photographs, including 2 full-page color plates. x + 283pp. 5⅜ x 8.   T538 Paperbound **$1.85**

SOAP-BUBBLES: THEIR COLOURS AND THE FORCES THAT MOULD THEM, C. V. Boys. For continuing popularity and validity as scientific primer, few books can match this volume of easily-followed experiments, explanations. Lucid exposition of complexities of liquid films, surface tension and related phenomena, bubbles' reaction to heat, motion, music, magnetic fields. Experiments with capillary attraction, soap bubbles on frames, composite bubbles, liquid cylinders and jets, bubbles other than soap, etc. Wonderful introduction to scientific method, natural laws that have many ramifications in areas of modern physics. Only complete edition in print. New Introduction by S. Z. Lewin, New York University. 83 illustrations; 1 full-page color plate. xii + 190pp. 5⅜ x 8½.   T542 Paperbound **95¢**

THE STORY OF X-RAYS FROM RONTGEN TO ISOTOPES, A. R. Bleich, M.D. This book, by a member of the American College of Radiology, gives the scientific explanation of x-rays, their applications in medicine, industry and art, and their danger (and that of atmospheric radiation) to the individual and the species. You learn how radiation therapy is applied against cancer, how x-rays diagnose heart disease and other ailments, how they are used to examine mummies for information on diseases of early societies, and industrial materials for hidden weaknesses. 54 illustrations show x-rays of flowers, bones, stomach, gears with flaws, etc. 1st publication. Index. xix + 186pp. 5⅜ x 8. **T622 Paperbound $1.35**

SPINNING TOPS AND GYROSCOPIC MOTION, John Perry. A classic elementary text of the dynamics of rotation — the behavior and use of rotating bodies such as gyroscopes and tops. In simple, everyday English you are shown how quasi-rigidity is induced in discs of paper, smoke rings, chains, etc., by rapid motions; why a gyrostat falls and why a top rises; precession; how the earth's motion affects climate; and many other phenomena. Appendix on practical use of gyroscopes. 62 figures. 128pp. 5⅜ x 8. **T416 Paperbound $1.00**

SNOW CRYSTALS, W. A. Bentley, M. J. Humphreys. For almost 50 years W. A. Bentley photographed snow flakes in his laboratory in Jericho, Vermont; in 1931 the American Meteorological Society gathered together the best of his work, some 2400 photographs of snow flakes, plus a few ice flowers, windowpane frosts, dew, frozen rain, and other ice formations. Pictures were selected for beauty and scientific value. A very valuable work to anyone in meteorology, cryology; most interesting to layman; extremely useful for artist who wants beautiful, crystalline designs. All copyright free. Unabridged reprint of 1931 edition. 2453 illustrations. 227pp. 8 x 10½. **T287 Paperbound $3.00**

A DOVER SCIENCE SAMPLER, edited by George Barkin. A collection of brief, non-technical passages from 44 Dover Books Explaining Science for the enjoyment of the science-minded browser. Includes work of Bertrand Russell, Poincaré, Laplace, Max Born, Galileo, Newton; material on physics, mathematics, metallurgy, anatomy, astronomy, chemistry, etc. You will be fascinated by Martin Gardner's analysis of the sincere pseudo-scientist, Moritz's account of Newton's absentmindedness, Bernard's examples of human vivisection, etc. Illustrations from the Diderot Pictorial Encyclopedia and De Re Metallica. 64 pages. **FREE**

THE STORY OF ATOMIC THEORY AND ATOMIC ENERGY, J. G. Feinberg. A broader approach to subject of nuclear energy and its cultural implications than any other similar source. Very readable, informal, completely non-technical text. Begins with first atomic theory, 600 B.C. and carries you through the work of Mendelejeff, Röntgen, Madame Curie, to Einstein's equation and the A-bomb. New chapter goes through thermonuclear fission, binding energy, other events up to 1959. Radioactive decay and radiation hazards, future benefits, work of Bohr, moderns, hundreds more topics. "Deserves special mention . . . not only authoritative but thoroughly popular in the best sense of the word," Saturday Review. Formerly, "The Atom Story." Expanded with new chapter. Three appendixes. Index. 34 illustrations. vii + 243pp. 5⅜ x 8. **T625 Paperbound $1.45**

THE STRANGE STORY OF THE QUANTUM, AN ACCOUNT FOR THE GENERAL READER OF THE GROWTH OF IDEAS UNDERLYING OUR PRESENT ATOMIC KNOWLEDGE, B. Hoffmann. Presents lucidly and expertly, with barest amount of mathematics, the problems and theories which led to modern quantum physics. Dr. Hoffmann begins with the closing years of the 19th century, when certain trifling discrepancies were noticed, and with illuminating analogies and examples takes you through the brilliant concepts of Planck, Einstein, Pauli, Broglie, Bohr, Schroedinger, Heisenberg, Dirac, Sommerfeld, Feynman, etc. This edition includes a new, long postscript carrying the story through 1958. "Of the books attempting an account of the history and contents of our modern atomic physics which have come to my attention, this is the best," H. Margenau, Yale University, in "American Journal of Physics." 32 tables and line illustrations. Index. 275pp. 5⅜ x 8. **T518 Paperbound $1.50**

SPACE AND TIME, E. Borel. Written by a versatile mathematician of world renown with his customary lucidity and precision, this introduction to relativity for the layman presents scores of examples, analogies, and illustrations that open up new ways of thinking about space and time. It covers abstract geometry and geographical maps, continuity and topology, the propagation of light, the special theory of relativity, the general theory of relativity, theoretical researches, and much more. Mathematical notes. 2 Indexes. 4 Appendices. 15 figures. xvi + 243pp. 5⅜ x 8. **T592 Paperbound $1.45**

FROM EUCLID TO EDDINGTON: A STUDY OF THE CONCEPTIONS OF THE EXTERNAL WORLD, Sir Edmund Whittaker. A foremost British scientist traces the development of theories of natural philosophy from the western rediscovery of Euclid to Eddington, Einstein, Dirac, etc. The inadequacy of classical physics is contrasted with present day attempts to understand the physical world through relativity, non-Euclidean geometry, space curvature, wave mechanics, etc. 5 major divisions of examination: Space; Time and Movement; the Concepts of Classical Physics; the Concepts of Quantum Mechanics; the Eddington Universe. 212pp. 5⅜ x 8. **T491 Paperbound $1.35**

Nature, Biology

NATURE RECREATION: Group Guidance for the Out-of-doors, William Gould Vinal. Intended for both the uninitiated nature instructor and the education student on the college level, this complete "how-to" program surveys the entire area of nature education for the young. Philosophy of nature recreation; requirements, responsibilities, important information for group leaders; nature games; suggested group projects; conducting meetings and getting discussions started; etc. Scores of immediately applicable teaching aids, plus completely updated sources of information, pamphlets, field guides, recordings, etc. Bibliography. 74 photographs. + 310pp. 5⅜ x 8½. T1015 Paperbound **$1.75**

HOW TO KNOW THE WILD FLOWERS, Mrs. William Starr Dana. Classic nature book that has introduced thousands to wonders of American wild flowers. Color-season principle of organization is easy to use, even by those with no botanical training, and the genial, refreshing discussions of history, folklore, uses of over 1,000 native and escape flowers, foliage plants are informative as well as fun to read. Over 170 full-page plates, collected from several editions, may be colored in to make permanent records of finds. Revised to conform with 1950 edition of Gray's Manual of Botany. xlii + 438pp. 5⅜ x 8½. T332 Paperbound **$1.85**

HOW TO KNOW THE FERNS, F. T. Parsons. Ferns, among our most lovely native plants, are all too little known. This classic of nature lore will enable the layman to identify almost any American fern he may come across. After an introduction on the structure and life of ferns, the 57 most important ferns are fully pictured and described (arranged upon a simple identification key). Index of Latin and English names. 61 illustrations and 42 full-page plates. xiv + 215pp. 5⅜ x 8. T740 Paperbound **$1.35**

MANUAL OF THE TREES OF NORTH AMERICA, Charles Sprague Sargent. Still unsurpassed as most comprehensive, reliable study of North American tree characteristics, precise locations and distribution. By dean of American dendrologists. Every tree native to U.S., Canada, Alaska, 185 genera, 717 species, described in detail—leaves, flowers, fruit, winterbuds, bark, wood, growth habits etc. plus discussion of varieties and local variants, immaturity variations. Over 100 keys, including unusual 11-page analytical key to genera, aid in identification. 783 clear illustrations of flowers, fruit, leaves. An unmatched permanent reference work for all nature lovers. Second enlarged (1926) edition. Synopsis of families. Analytical key to genera. Glossary of technical terms. Index. 783 illustrations, 1 map. Two volumes. Total of 982pp. 5⅜ x 8. T277 Vol. I Paperbound **$2.25**
T278 Vol. II Paperbound **$2.25**
The set **$4.50**

TREES OF THE EASTERN AND CENTRAL UNITED STATES AND CANADA, W. M. Harlow. A revised edition of a standard middle-level guide to native trees and important escapes. More than 140 trees are described in detail, and illustrated with more than 600 drawings and photographs. Supplementary keys will enable the careful reader to identify almost any tree he might encounter. xiii + 288pp. 5⅜ x 8. T395 Paperbound **$1.35**

GUIDE TO SOUTHERN TREES, Ellwood S. Harrar and J. George Harrar. All the essential information about trees indigenous to the South, in an extremely handy format. Introductory essay on methods of tree classification and study, nomenclature, chief divisions of Southern trees, etc. Approximately 100 keys and synopses allow for swift, accurate identification of trees. Numerous excellent illustrations, non-technical text make this a useful book for teachers of biology or natural science, nature lovers, amateur naturalists. Revised 1962 edition. Index. Bibliography. Glossary of technical terms. 920 illustrations; 201 full-page plates. ix + 709pp. 4⅝ x 6⅜. T945 Paperbound **$2.25**

FRUIT KEY AND TWIG KEY TO TREES AND SHRUBS, W. M. Harlow. Bound together in one volume for the first time, these handy and accurate keys to fruit and twig identification are the only guides of their sort with photographs (up to 3 times natural size). "Fruit Key": Key to over 120 different deciduous and evergreen fruits. 139 photographs and 11 line drawings. Synoptic summary of fruit types. Bibliography. 2 Indexes (common and scientific names). "Twig Key": Key to over 160 different twigs and buds. 173 photographs. Glossary of technical terms. Bibliography. 2 Indexes (common and scientific names). Two volumes bound as one. Total of xvii + 126pp. 5⅝ x 8⅜. T511 Paperbound **$1.25**

INSECT LIFE AND INSECT NATURAL HISTORY, S. W. Frost. A work emphasizing habits, social life, and ecological relations of insects, rather than more academic aspects of classification and morphology. Prof. Frost's enthusiasm and knowledge are everywhere evident as he discusses insect associations and specialized habits like leaf-rolling, leaf-mining, and case-making, the gall insects, the boring insects, aquatic insects, etc. He examines all sorts of matters not usually covered in general works, such as: insects as human food, insect music and musicians, insect response to electric and radio waves, use of insects in art and literature. The admirably executed purpose of this book, which covers the middle ground between elementary treatment and scholarly monographs, is to excite the reader to observe for himself. Over 700 illustrations. Extensive bibliography. x + 524pp. 5⅜ x 8. T517 Paperbound **$2.45**

COMMON SPIDERS OF THE UNITED STATES, J. H. Emerton. Here is a nature hobby you can pursue right in your own cellar! Only non-technical, but thorough, reliable guide to spiders for the layman. Over 200 spiders from all parts of the country, arranged by scientific classification, are identified by shape and color, number of eyes, habitat and range, habits, etc. Full text, 501 line drawings and photographs, and valuable introduction explain webs, poisons, threads, capturing and preserving spiders, etc. Index. New synoptic key by S. W. Frost. xxiv + 225pp. 5⅜ x 8. **T223 Paperbound $1.45**

THE LIFE STORY OF THE FISH: HIS MANNERS AND MORALS, Brian Curtis. A comprehensive, non-technical survey of just about everything worth knowing about fish. Written for the aquarist, the angler, and the layman with an inquisitive mind, the text covers such topics as evolution, external covering and protective coloration, physics and physiology of vision, maintenance of equilibrium, function of the lateral line canal for auditory and temperature senses, nervous system, function of the air bladder, reproductive system and methods— courtship, mating, spawning, care of young—and many more. Also sections on game fish, the problems of conservation and a fascinating chapter on fish curiosities. "Clear, simple language . . . excellent judgment in choice of subjects . . . delightful sense of humor," New York Times. Revised (1949) edition. Index. Bibliography of 72 items. 6 full-page photographic plates. xii + 284pp. 5⅜ x 8. **T929 Paperbound $1.50**

BATS, Glover Morrill Allen. The most comprehensive study of bats as a life-form by the world's foremost authority. A thorough summary of just about everything known about this fascinating and mysterious flying mammal, including its unique location sense, hibernation and cycles, its habitats and distribution, its wing structure and flying habits, and its relationship to man in the long history of folklore and superstition. Written on a middle-level, the book can be profitably studied by a trained zoologist and thoroughly enjoyed by the layman. "An absorbing text with excellent illustrations. Bats should have more friends and fewer thoughtless detractors as a result of the publication of this volume," William Beebe, Books. Extensive bibliography. 57 photographs and illustrations. x + 368pp. 5⅜ x 8½. **T984 Paperbound $2.00**

BIRDS AND THEIR ATTRIBUTES, Glover Morrill Allen. A fine general introduction to birds as living organisms, especially valuable because of emphasis on structure, physiology, habits, behavior. Discusses relationship of bird to man, early attempts at scientific ornithology, feathers and coloration, skeletal structure including bills, legs and feet, wings. Also food habits, evolution and present distribution, feeding and nest-building, still unsolved questions of migrations and location sense, many more similar topics. Final chapter on classification, nomenclature. A good popular-level summary for the biologist; a first-rate introduction for the layman. Reprint of 1925 edition. References and index. 51 illustrations. viii + 338pp. 5⅜ x 8½. **T957 Paperbound $1.85**

LIFE HISTORIES OF NORTH AMERICAN BIRDS, Arthur Cleveland Bent. Bent's monumental series of books on North American birds, prepared and published under auspices of Smithsonian Institute, is the definitive coverage of the subject, the most-used single source of information. Now the entire set is to be made available by Dover in inexpensive editions. This encyclopedic collection of detailed, specific observations utilizes reports of hundreds of contemporary observers, writings of such naturalists as Audubon, Burroughs, William Brewster, as well as author's own extensive investigations. Contains literally everything known about life history of each bird considered: nesting, eggs, plumage, distribution and migration, voice, enemies, courtship, etc. These not over-technical works are musts for ornithologists, conservationists, amateur naturalists, anyone seriously interested in American birds.

BIRDS OF PREY. More than 100 subspecies of hawks, falcons, eagles, buzzards, condors and owls, from the common barn owl to the extinct caracara of Guadaloupe Island. 400 photographs. Two volume set. Index for each volume. Bibliographies of 403, 520 items. 197 full-page plates. Total of 907pp. 5⅜ x 8½.
Vol. I **T931 Paperbound $2.50**
Vol. II **T932 Paperbound $2.50**

WILD FOWL. Ducks, geese, swans, and tree ducks—73 different subspecies. Two volume set. Index for each volume. Bibliographies of 124, 144 items. 106 full-page plates. Total of 685pp. 5⅜ x 8½.
Vol. I **T285 Paperbound $2.50**
Vol. II **T286 Paperbound $2.50**

SHORE BIRDS. 81 varieties (sandpipers, woodcocks, plovers, snipes, phalaropes, curlews, oyster catchers, etc.). More than 200 photographs of eggs, nesting sites, adult and young of important species. Two volume set. Index for each volume. Bibliographies of 261, 188 items. 121 full-page plates. Total of 860pp. 5⅜ x 8½.
Vol. I **T933 Paperbound $2.35**
Vol. II **T934 Paperbound $2.35**

THE LIFE OF PASTEUR, R. Vallery-Radot. 13th edition of this definitive biography, cited in Encyclopaedia Britannica. Authoritative, scholarly, well-documented with contemporary quotes, observations; gives complete picture of Pasteur's personal life; especially thorough presentation of scientific activities with silkworms, fermentation, hydrophobia, inoculation, etc. Introduction by Sir William Osler. Index. 505pp. 5⅜ x 8. **T632 Paperbound $2.00**

Puzzles, Mathematical Recreations

SYMBOLIC LOGIC and THE GAME OF LOGIC, Lewis Carroll. "Symbolic Logic" is not concerned with modern symbolic logic, but is instead a collection of over 380 problems posed with charm and imagination, using the syllogism, and a fascinating diagrammatic method of drawing conclusions. In "The Game of Logic" Carroll's whimsical imagination devises a logical game played with 2 diagrams and counters (included) to manipulate hundreds of tricky syllogisms. The final section, "Hit or Miss" is a lagniappe of 101 additional puzzles in the delightful Carroll manner. Until this reprint edition, both of these books were rarities costing up to $15 each. Symbolic Logic: Index. xxxi + 199pp. The Game of Logic: 96pp. 2 vols. bound as one. 5⅜ x 8.　　　　　　　　　　　　　　　　　T492 Paperbound **$1.50**

PILLOW PROBLEMS and A TANGLED TALE, Lewis Carroll. One of the rarest of all Carroll's works, "Pillow Problems" contains 72 original math puzzles, all typically ingenious. Particularly fascinating are Carroll's answers which remain exactly as he thought them out, reflecting his actual mental process. The problems in "A Tangled Tale" are in story form, originally appearing as a monthly magazine serial. Carroll not only gives the solutions, but uses answers sent in by readers to discuss wrong approaches and misleading paths, and grades them for insight. Both of these books were rarities until this edition. "Pillow Problems" costing up to $25, and "A Tangled Tale" $15. Pillow Problems: Preface and Introduction by Lewis Carroll. xx + 109pp. A Tangled Tale: 6 illustrations. 152pp. Two vols. bound as one. 5⅜ x 8.　　　　　　　　　　　　　　　　　T493 Paperbound **$1.50**

AMUSEMENTS IN MATHEMATICS, Henry Ernest Dudeney. The foremost British originator of mathematical puzzles is always intriguing, witty, and paradoxical in this classic, one of the largest collections of mathematical amusements. More than 430 puzzles, problems, and paradoxes. Mazes and games, problems on number manipulation, unicursal and other route problems, puzzles on measuring, weighing, packing, age, kinship, chessboards, joiners', crossing river, plane figure dissection, and many others. Solutions. More than 450 illustrations. vii + 258pp. 5⅜ x 8.　　　　　　　　　　　　　　　　　T473 Paperbound **$1.25**

THE CANTERBURY PUZZLES, Henry Dudeney. Chaucer's pilgrims set one another problems in story form. Also Adventures of the Puzzle Club, the Strange Escape of the King's Jester, the Monks of Riddlewell, the Squire's Christmas Puzzle Party, and others. All puzzles are original, based on dissecting plane figures, arithmetic, algebra, elementary calculus and other branches of mathematics, and purely logical ingenuity. "The limit of ingenuity and intricacy," The Observer. Over 110 puzzles. Full Solutions. 150 illustrations. vii + 225pp. 5⅜ x 8. T474 Paperbound **$1.25**

MATHEMATICAL EXCURSIONS, H. A. Merrill. Even if you hardly remember your high school math, you'll enjoy the 90 stimulating problems contained in this book and you will come to understand a great many mathematical principles with surprisingly little effort. Many useful shortcuts and diversions not generally known are included: division by inspection, Russian peasant multiplication, memory systems for pi, building odd and even magic squares, square roots by geometry, dyadic systems, and many more. Solutions to difficult problems. 50 illustrations. 145pp. 5⅜ x 8.　　　　　　　　　　　　T350 Paperbound **$1.00**

MAGIC SQUARES AND CUBES, W. S. Andrews. Only book-length treatment in English, a thorough non-technical description and analysis. Here are nasik, overlapping, pandiagonal, serrated squares; magic circles, cubes, spheres, rhombuses. Try your hand at 4-dimensional magical figures! Much unusual folklore and tradition included. High school algebra is sufficient. 754 diagrams and illustrations. viii + 419pp. 5⅜ x 8.　　　　　　　　T658 Paperbound **$1.85**

CALIBAN'S PROBLEM BOOK: MATHEMATICAL, INFERENTIAL AND CRYPTOGRAPHIC PUZZLES, H. Phillips (Caliban), S. T. Shovelton, G. S. Marshall. 105 ingenious problems by the greatest living creator of puzzles based on logic and inference. Rigorous, modern, piquant; reflecting their author's unusual personality, these intermediate and advanced puzzles all involve the ability to reason clearly through complex situations; some call for mathematical knowledge, ranging from algebra to number theory. Solutions. xi + 180pp. 5⅜ x 8.
T736 Paperbound **$1.25**

MATHEMATICAL PUZZLES FOR BEGINNERS AND ENTHUSIASTS, G. Mott-Smith. 188 mathematical puzzles based on algebra, dissection of plane figures, permutations, and probability, that will test and improve your powers of inference and interpretation. The Odic Force, The Spider's Cousin, Ellipse Drawing, theory and strategy of card and board games like tit-tat-toe, go moku, salvo, and many others. 100 pages of detailed mathematical explanations. Appendix of primes, square roots, etc. 135 illustrations. 2nd revised edition. 248pp. 5⅜ x 8.
T198 Paperbound **$1.00**

MATHEMAGIC, MAGIC PUZZLES, AND GAMES WITH NUMBERS, R. V. Heath. More than 60 new puzzles and stunts based on the properties of numbers. Easy techniques for multiplying large numbers mentally, revealing hidden numbers magically, finding the date of any day in any year, and dozens more. Over 30 pages devoted to magic squares, triangles, cubes, circles, etc. Edited by J. S. Meyer. 76 illustrations. 128pp. 5⅜ x 8.　　　　　T110 Paperbound **$1.00**

THE BOOK OF MODERN PUZZLES, G. L. Kaufman. A completely new series of puzzles as fascinating as crossword and deduction puzzles but based upon different principles and techniques. Simple 2-minute teasers, word labyrinths, design and pattern puzzles, logic and observation puzzles — over 150 braincrackers. Answers to all problems. 116 illustrations. 192pp. 5⅜ x 8.
T143 Paperbound **$1.00**

NEW WORD PUZZLES, G. L. Kaufman. 100 ENTIRELY NEW puzzles based on words and their combinations that will delight crossword puzzle, Scrabble and Jotto fans. Chess words, based on the moves of the chess king; design-onyms, symmetrical designs made of synonyms; rhymed double-crostics; syllable sentences; addle letter anagrams; alphagrams; linkograms; and many others all brand new. Full solutions. Space to work problems. 196 figures. vi + 122pp. 5⅜ x 8.
T344 Paperbound **$1.00**

MAZES AND LABYRINTHS: A BOOK OF PUZZLES, W. Shepherd. Mazes, formerly associated with mystery and ritual, are still among the most intriguing of intellectual puzzles. This is a novel and different collection of 50 amusements that embody the principle of the maze: mazes in the classical tradition; 3-dimensional, ribbon, and Möbius-strip mazes; hidden messages; spatial arrangements; etc.—almost all built on amusing story situations. 84 illustrations. Essay on maze psychology. Solutions. xv + 122pp. 5⅜ x 8.
T731 Paperbound **$1.00**

MAGIC TRICKS & CARD TRICKS, W. Jonson. Two books bound as one. 52 tricks with cards, 37 tricks with coins, bills, eggs, smoke, ribbons, slates, etc. Details on presentation, misdirection, and routining will help you master such famous tricks as the Changing Card, Card in the Pocket, Four Aces, Coin Through the Hand, Bill in the Egg, Afghan Bands, and over 75 others. If you follow the lucid exposition and key diagrams carefully, you will finish these two books with an astonishing mastery of magic. 106 figures. 224pp. 5⅜ x 8. T909 Paperbound **$1.00**

PANORAMA OF MAGIC, Milbourne Christopher. A profusely illustrated history of stage magic, a unique selection of prints and engravings from the author's private collection of magic memorabilia, the largest of its kind. Apparatus, stage settings and costumes; ingenious ads distributed by the performers and satiric broadsides passed around in the streets ridiculing pompous showmen; programs; decorative souvenirs. The lively text, by one of America's foremost professional magicians, is full of anecdotes about almost legendary wizards: Dede, the Egyptian; Philadelphia, the wonder-worker; Robert-Houdin, "the father of modern magic;" Harry Houdini; scores more. Altogether a pleasure package for anyone interested in magic, stage setting and design, ethnology, psychology, or simply in unusual people. A Dover original. 295 illustrations; 8 in full color. Index. viii + 216pp. 8⅜ x 11¼.
T774 Paperbound **$2.25**

HOUDINI ON MAGIC, Harry Houdini. One of the greatest magicians of modern times explains his most prized secrets. How locks are picked, with illustrated picks and skeleton keys; how a girl is sawed into twins; how to walk through a brick wall — Houdini's explanations of 44 stage tricks with many diagrams. Also included is a fascinating discussion of great magicians of the past and the story of his fight against fraudulent mediums and spiritualists. Edited by W.B. Gibson and M.N. Young. Bibliography. 155 figures, photos. xv + 280pp. 5⅜ x 8.
T384 Paperbound **$1.35**

MATHEMATICS, MAGIC AND MYSTERY, Martin Gardner. Why do card tricks work? How do magicians perform astonishing mathematical feats? How is stage mind-reading possible? This is the first book length study explaining the application of probability, set theory, theory of numbers, topology, etc., to achieve many startling tricks. Non-technical, accurate, detailed! 115 sections discuss tricks with cards, dice, coins, knots, geometrical vanishing illusions, how a Curry square "demonstrates" that the sum of the parts may be greater than the whole, and dozens of others. No sleight of hand necessary! 135 illustrations. xii + 174pp. 5⅜ x 8.
T335 Paperbound **$1.00**

EASY-TO-DO ENTERTAINMENTS AND DIVERSIONS WITH COINS, CARDS, STRING, PAPER AND MATCHES, R. M. Abraham. Over 300 tricks, games and puzzles will provide young readers with absorbing fun. Sections on card games; paper-folding; tricks with coins, matches and pieces of string; games for the agile; toy-making from common household objects; mathematical recreations; and 50 miscellaneous pastimes. Anyone in charge of groups of youngsters, including hard-pressed parents, and in need of suggestions on how to keep children sensibly amused and quietly content will find this book indispensable. Clear, simple text, copious number of delightful line drawings and illustrative diagrams. Originally titled "Winter Nights Entertainments." Introduction by Lord Baden Powell. 329 illustrations. v + 186pp. 5⅜ x 8½.
T921 Paperbound **$1.00**

STRING FIGURES AND HOW TO MAKE THEM, Caroline Furness Jayne. 107 string figures plus variations selected from the best primitive and modern examples developed by Navajo, Apache, pygmies of Africa, Eskimo, in Europe, Australia, China, etc. The most readily understandable, easy-to-follow book in English on perennially popular recreation. Crystal-clear exposition; step-by-step diagrams. Everyone from kindergarten children to adults looking for unusual diversion will be endlessly amused. Index. Bibliography. Introduction by A. C. Haddon. 17 full-page plates. 960 illustrations. xxiii + 401pp. 5⅜ x 8½.
T152 Paperbound **$2.00**

Entertainments, Humor

ODDITIES AND CURIOSITIES OF WORDS AND LITERATURE, C. Bombaugh, edited by M. Gardner. The largest collection of idiosyncratic prose and poetry techniques in English, a legendary work in the curious and amusing bypaths of literary recreations and the play technique in literature—so important in modern works. Contains alphabetic poetry, acrostics, palindromes, scissors verse, centos, emblematic poetry, famous literary puns, hoaxes, notorious slips of the press, hilarious mistranslations, and much more. Revised and enlarged with modern material by Martin Gardner. 368pp. 5⅜ x 8.   T759 Paperbound **$1.50**

A NONSENSE ANTHOLOGY, collected by Carolyn Wells. 245 of the best nonsense verses ever written, including nonsense puns, absurd arguments, mock epics and sagas, nonsense ballads, odes, "sick" verses, dog-Latin verses, French nonsense verses, songs. By Edward Lear, Lewis Carroll, Gelett Burgess, W. S. Gilbert, Hilaire Belloc, Peter Newell, Oliver Herford, etc., 83 writers in all plus over four score anonymous nonsense verses. A special section of limericks, plus famous nonsense such as Carroll's "Jabberwocky" and Lear's "The Jumblies" and much excellent verse virtually impossible to locate elsewhere. For 50 years considered the best anthology available. Index of first lines specially prepared for this edition. Introduction by Carolyn Wells. 3 indexes: Title, Author, First lines. xxxiii + 279pp.
T499 Paperbound **$1.35**

THE BAD CHILD'S BOOK OF BEASTS, MORE BEASTS FOR WORSE CHILDREN, and A MORAL ALPHA-BET, H. Belloc. Hardly an anthology of humorous verse has appeared in the last 50 years without at least a couple of these famous nonsense verses. But one must see the entire volumes—with all the delightful original illustrations by Sir Basil Blackwood—to appreciate fully Belloc's charming and witty verses that play so subacidly on the platitudes of life and morals that beset his day—and ours. A great humor classic. Three books in one. Total of 157pp. 5⅜ x 8.   T749 Paperbound **$1.00**

THE DEVIL'S DICTIONARY, Ambrose Bierce. Sardonic and irreverent barbs puncturing the pomposities and absurdities of American politics, business, religion, literature, and arts, by the country's greatest satirist in the classic tradition. Epigrammatic as Shaw, piercing as Swift, American as Mark Twain, Will Rogers, and Fred Allen, Bierce will always remain the favorite of a small coterie of enthusiasts, and of writers and speakers whom he supplies with "some of the most gorgeous witticisms of the English language" (H. L. Mencken). Over 1000 entries in alphabetical order. 144pp. 5⅜ x 8.   T487 Paperbound **$1.00**

THE PURPLE COW AND OTHER NONSENSE, Gelett Burgess. The best of Burgess's early nonsense, selected from the first edition of the "Burgess Nonsense Book." Contains many of his most unusual and truly awe-inspiring pieces: 36 nonsense quatrains, the Poems of Patagonia, Alphabet of Famous Goops, and the other hilarious (and rare) adult nonsense that place him in the forefront of American humorists. All pieces are accompanied by the original Burgess illustrations. 123 illustrations. xiii + 113pp. 5⅜ x 8.   T772 Paperbound **$1.00**

MY PIOUS FRIENDS AND DRUNKEN COMPANIONS and MORE PIOUS FRIENDS AND DRUNKEN COMPANIONS, Frank Shay. Folksingers, amateur and professional, and everyone who loves singing: here, available for the first time in 30 years, is this valued collection of 132 ballads, blues, vaudeville numbers, drinking songs, sea chanties, comedy songs. Songs of pre-Beatnik Bohemia; songs from all over America, England, France, Australia; the great songs of the Naughty Nineties and early twentieth-century America. Over a third with music. Woodcuts by John Held, Jr. convey perfectly the brash insouciance of an era of rollicking unabashed song. 12 illustrations by John Held, Jr. Two indexes (Titles and First lines and Choruses). Introductions by the author. Two volumes bound as one. Total of xvi + 235pp. 5⅜ x 8½.
T946 Paperbound **$1.25**

HOW TO TELL THE BIRDS FROM THE FLOWERS, R. W. Wood. How not to confuse a carrot with a parrot, a grape with an ape, a puffin with nuffin. Delightful drawings, clever puns, absurd little poems point out far-fetched resemblances in nature. The author was a leading physicist. Introduction by Margaret Wood White. 106 illus. 60pp. 5⅜ x 8.
T523 Paperbound **75¢**

PECK'S BAD BOY AND HIS PA, George W. Peck. The complete edition, containing both volumes, of one of the most widely read American humor books. The endless ingenious pranks played by bad boy "Hennery" on his pa and the grocery man, the outraged pomposity of Pa, the perpetual ridiculing of middle class institutions, are as entertaining today as they were in 1883. No pale sophistications or subtleties, but rather humor vigorous, raw, earthy, imaginative, and, as folk humor often is, sadistic. This peculiarly fascinating book is also valuable to historians and students of American culture as a portrait of an age. 100 original illustrations by True Williams. Introduction by E. F. Bleiler. 347pp. 5⅜ x 8.
T497 Paperbound **$1.35**

THE HUMOROUS VERSE OF LEWIS CARROLL. Almost every poem Carroll ever wrote, the largest collection ever published, including much never published elsewhere: 150 parodies, burlesques, riddles, ballads, acrostics, etc., with 130 original illustrations by Tenniel, Carroll, and others. "Addicts will be grateful . . . there is nothing for the faithful to do but sit down and fall to the banquet," N. Y. Times. Index to first lines. xiv + 446pp. 5⅜ x 8.
T654 Paperbound **$2.00**

DIVERSIONS AND DIGRESSIONS OF LEWIS CARROLL. A major new treasure for Carroll fans! Rare privately published humor, fantasy, puzzles, and games by Carroll at his whimsical best, with a new vein of frank satire. Includes many new mathematical amusements and recreations, among them the fragmentary Part III of "Curiosa Mathematica." Contains "The Rectory Umbrella," "The New Belfry," "The Vision of the Three T's," and much more. New 32-page supplement of rare photographs taken by Carroll. x + 375pp. 5⅜ x 8.
T732 Paperbound **$1.65**

THE COMPLETE NONSENSE OF EDWARD LEAR. This is the only complete edition of this master of gentle madness available at a popular price. A BOOK OF NONSENSE, NONSENSE SONGS, MORE NONSENSE SONGS AND STORIES in their entirety with all the old favorites that have delighted children and adults for years. The Dong With A Luminous Nose, The Jumblies, The Owl and the Pussycat, and hundreds of other bits of wonderful nonsense. 214 limericks, 3 sets of Nonsense Botany, 5 Nonsense Alphabets, 546 drawings by Lear himself, and much more. 320pp. 5⅜ x 8.
T167 Paperbound **$1.00**

THE MELANCHOLY LUTE, The Humorous Verse of Franklin P. Adams ("FPA"). The author's own selection of light verse, drawn from thirty years of FPA's column, "The Conning Tower," syndicated all over the English-speaking world. Witty, perceptive, literate, these ninety-six poems range from parodies of other poets, Millay, Longfellow, Edgar Guest, Kipling, Masefield, etc., and free and hilarious translations of Horace and other Latin poets, to satiric comments on fabled American institutions—the New York Subways, preposterous ads, suburbanites, sensational journalism, etc. They reveal with vigor and clarity the humor, integrity and restraint of a wise and gentle American satirist. Introduction by Robert Hutchinson. vi + 122pp. 5⅜ x 8½.
T108 Paperbound **$1.00**

SINGULAR TRAVELS, CAMPAIGNS, AND ADVENTURES OF BARON MUNCHAUSEN, R. E. Raspe, with 90 illustrations by Gustave Doré. The first edition in over 150 years to reestablish the deeds of the Prince of Liars exactly as Raspe first recorded them in 1785—the genuine Baron Munchausen, one of the most popular personalities in English literature. Included also are the best of the many sequels, written by other hands. Introduction on Raspe by J. Carswell. Bibliography of early editions. xliv + 192pp. 5⅜ x 8.
T698 Paperbound **$1.00**

THE WIT AND HUMOR OF OSCAR WILDE, ed. by Alvin Redman. Wilde at his most brilliant, in 1000 epigrams exposing weaknesses and hypocrisies of "civilized" society. Divided into 49 categories—sin, wealth, women, America, etc.—to aid writers, speakers. Includes excerpts from his trials, books, plays, criticism. Formerly "The Epigrams of Oscar Wilde." Introduction by Vyvyan Holland, Wilde's only living son. Introductory essay by editor. 260pp. 5⅜ x 8.
T602 Paperbound **$1.00**

MAX AND MORITZ, Wilhelm Busch. Busch is one of the great humorists of all time, as well as the father of the modern comic strip. This volume, translated by H. A. Klein and other hands, contains the perennial favorite "Max and Moritz" (translated by C. T. Brooks), Plisch and Plum, Das Rabennest, Eispeter, and seven other whimsical, sardonic, jovial, diabolical cartoon and verse stories. Lively English translations parallel the original German. This work has delighted millions, since it first appeared in the 19th century, and is guaranteed to please almost anyone. Edited by H. A. Klein, with an afterword. x + 205pp. 5⅝ x 8½.
T181 Paperbound **$1.00**

HYPOCRITICAL HELENA, Wilhelm Busch. A companion volume to "Max and Moritz," with the title piece (Die Fromme Helena) and 10 other highly amusing cartoon and verse stories, all newly translated by H. A. Klein and M. C. Klein: Adventure on New Year's Eve (Abenteuer in der Neujahrsnacht), Hangover on the Morning after New Year's Eve (Der Katzenjammer am Neujahrsmorgen), etc. English and German in parallel columns. Hours of pleasure, also a fine language aid. x + 205pp. 5⅝ x 8½.
T184 Paperbound **$1.00**

THE BEAR THAT WASN'T, Frank Tashlin. What does it mean? Is it simply delightful wry humor, or a charming story of a bear who wakes up in the midst of a factory, or a satire on Big Business, or an existential cartoon-story of the human condition, or a symbolization of the struggle between conformity and the individual? New York Herald Tribune said of the first edition: ". . . a fable for grownups that will be fun for children. Sit down with the book and get your own bearings." Long an underground favorite with readers of all ages and opinions. v + 51pp. Illustrated. 5⅜ x 8½.
T939 Paperbound **75¢**

RUTHLESS RHYMES FOR HEARTLESS HOMES and MORE RUTHLESS RHYMES FOR HEARTLESS HOMES, Harry Graham ("Col. D. Streamer"). Two volumes of Little Willy and 48 other poetic disasters. A bright, new reprint of oft-quoted, never forgotten, devastating humor by a precursor of today's "sick" joke school. For connoisseurs of wicked, wacky humor and all who delight in the comedy of manners. Original drawings are a perfect complement. 61 illustrations. Index. vi + 69pp. Two vols. bound as one. 5⅜ x 8½.
T930 Paperbound **75¢**

Say It language phrase books

These handy phrase books (128 to 196 pages each) make grammatical drills unnecessary for an elementary knowledge of a spoken foreign language. Covering most matters of travel and everyday life each volume contains:

Over 1000 phrases and sentences in immediately useful forms — foreign language plus English.

Modern usage designed for Americans. Specific phrases like, "Give me small change," and "Please call a taxi."

Simplified phonetic transcription you will be able to read at sight.

The only completely indexed phrase books on the market.

Covers scores of important situations: — Greetings, restaurants, sightseeing, useful expressions, etc.

These books are prepared by native linguists who are professors at Columbia, N.Y.U., Fordham and other great universities. Use them independently or with any other book or record course. They provide a supplementary living element that most other courses lack. Individual volumes in:

Russian 75¢	Italian 75¢	Spanish 75¢	German 75¢
Hebrew 75¢	Danish 75¢	Japanese 75¢	Swedish 75¢
Dutch 75¢	Esperanto 75¢	Modern Greek 75¢	Portuguese 75¢
Norwegian 75¢	Polish 75¢	French 75¢	Yiddish 75¢
Turkish 75¢		English for German-speaking people 75¢	
English for Italian-speaking people 75¢		English for Spanish-speaking people 75¢	

Large clear type. 128-196 pages each. 3½ x 5¼. Sturdy paper binding.

Listen and Learn language records

LISTEN & LEARN is the only language record course designed especially to meet your travel and everyday needs. It is available in separate sets for FRENCH, SPANISH, GERMAN, JAP-ANESE, RUSSIAN, MODERN GREEK, PORTUGUESE, ITALIAN and HEBREW, and each set contains three 33⅓ rpm long-playing records—1½ hours of recorded speech by eminent native speakers who are professors at Columbia, New York University, Queens College.

Check the following special features found only in LISTEN & LEARN:

- **Dual-language recording. 812 selected phrases and sentences, over 3200 words,** spoken first in English, then in their foreign language equivalents. A suitable pause follows each foreign phrase, allowing you time to repeat the expression. You learn by unconscious assimilation.

- **128 to 206-page manual** contains everything on the records, plus a simple phonetic pronunciation guide.

- **Indexed for convenience. The only set on the market** that is completely indexed. No more puzzling over where to find the phrase you need. Just look in the rear of the manual.

- **Practical.** No time wasted on material you can find in any grammar. LISTEN & LEARN covers central core material with phrase approach. Ideal for the person with limited learning time.

- **Living, modern expressions,** not found in other courses. Hygienic products, modern equipment, shopping—expressions used every day, like "nylon" and "air-conditioned."

- **Limited objective.** Everything you learn, no matter where you stop, is immediately useful. You have to finish other courses, wade through grammar and vocabulary drill, before they help you.

- **High-fidelity recording.** LISTEN & LEARN records equal in clarity and surface-silence any record on the market costing up to $6.

"Excellent . . . the spoken records . . . impress me as being among the very best on the market," **Prof. Mario Pei,** Dept. of Romance Languages, Columbia University. "Inexpensive and well-done . . . it would make an ideal present," CHICAGO SUNDAY TRIBUNE. "More genuinely helpful than anything of its kind which I have previously encountered," **Sidney Clark,** well-known author of "ALL THE BEST" travel books.

UNCONDITIONAL GUARANTEE. Try LISTEN & LEARN, then return it within 10 days for full refund if you are not satisfied.

Each set contains three twelve-inch 33⅓ records, manual, and album.

SPANISH	the set **$5.95**	GERMAN	the set **$5.95**
FRENCH	the set **$5.95**	ITALIAN	the set **$5.95**
RUSSIAN	the set **$5.95**	JAPANESE	the set **$5.95**
PORTUGUESE	the set **$5.95**	MODERN GREEK	the set **$5.95**
MODERN HEBREW	the set **$5.95**		

Americana

THE EYES OF DISCOVERY, J. Bakeless. A vivid reconstruction of how unspoiled America appeared to the first white men. Authentic and enlightening accounts of Hudson's landing in New York, Coronado's trek through the Southwest; scores of explorers, settlers, trappers, soldiers. America's pristine flora, fauna, and Indians in every region and state in fresh and unusual new aspects. "A fascinating view of what the land was like before the first highway went through," Time. 68 contemporary illustrations, 39 newly added in this edition. Index. Bibliography. x + 500pp. 5⅜ x 8.   T761 Paperbound **$2.00**

AUDUBON AND HIS JOURNALS, J. J. Audubon. A collection of fascinating accounts of Europe and America in the early 1800's through Audubon's own eyes. Includes the Missouri River Journals —an eventful trip through America's untouched heartland, the Labrador Journals, the European Journals, the famous "Episodes", and other rare Audubon material, including the descriptive chapters from the original letterpress edition of the "Ornithological Studies", omitted in all later editions. Indispensable for ornithologists, naturalists, and all lovers of Americana and adventure. 70-page biography by Audubon's granddaughter. 38 illustrations. Index. Total of 1106pp. 5⅜ x 8.

T675 Vol I Paperbound **$2.25**
T676 Vol II Paperbound **$2.25**
The set **$4.50**

TRAVELS OF WILLIAM BARTRAM, edited by Mark Van Doren. The first inexpensive illustrated edition of one of the 18th century's most delightful books is an excellent source of first-hand material on American geography, anthropology, and natural history. Many descriptions of early Indian tribes are our only source of information on them prior to the infiltration of the white man. "The mind of a scientist with the soul of a poet," John Livingston Lowes. 13 original illustrations and maps. Edited with an introduction by Mark Van Doren. 448pp. 5⅜ x 8.

T13 Paperbound **$2.00**

GARRETS AND PRETENDERS: A HISTORY OF BOHEMIANISM IN AMERICA, A. Parry. The colorful and fantastic history of American Bohemianism from Poe to Kerouac. This is the only complete record of hoboes, cranks, starving poets, and suicides. Here are Pfaff, Whitman, Crane, Bierce, Pound, and many others. New chapters by the author and by H. T. Moore bring this thorough and well-documented history down to the Beatniks. "An excellent account," N. Y. Times. Scores of cartoons, drawings, and caricatures. Bibliography. Index. xxviii + 421pp. 5⅝ x 8⅜.   T708 Paperbound **$1.95**

THE EXPLORATION OF THE COLORADO RIVER AND ITS CANYONS, J. W. Powell. The thrilling first-hand account of the expedition that filled in the last white space on the map of the United States. Rapids, famine, hostile Indians, and mutiny are among the perils encountered as the unknown Colorado Valley reveals its secrets. This is the only uncut version of Major Powell's classic of exploration that has been printed in the last 60 years. Includes later reflections and subsequent expedition. 250 illustrations, new map. 400pp. 5⅝ x 8⅜.

T94 Paperbound **$2.00**

THE JOURNAL OF HENRY D. THOREAU, Edited by Bradford Torrey and Francis H. Allen. Henry Thoreau is not only one of the most important figures in American literature and social thought; his voluminous journals (from which his books emerged as selections and crystallizations) constitute both the longest, most sensitive record of personal internal development and a most penetrating description of a historical moment in American culture. This present set, which was first issued in fourteen volumes, contains Thoreau's entire journals from 1837 to 1862, with the exception of the lost years which were found only recently. We are reissuing it, complete and unabridged, with a new introduction by Walter Harding, Secretary of the Thoreau Society. Fourteen volumes reissued in two volumes. Foreword by Henry Seidel Canby. Total of 1888pp. 8⅜ x 12¼.   T312-3 Two volume set, Clothbound **$20.00**

GAMES AND SONGS OF AMERICAN CHILDREN, collected by William Wells Newell. A remarkable collection of 190 games with songs that accompany many of them; cross references to show similarities, differences among them; variations; musical notation for 38 songs. Textual discussions show relations with folk-drama and other aspects of folk tradition. Grouped into categories for ready comparative study: Love-games, histories, playing at work, human life, bird and beast, mythology, guessing-games, etc. New introduction covers relations of songs and dances to timeless heritage of folklore, biographical sketch of Newell, other pertinent data. A good source of inspiration for those in charge of groups of children and a valuable reference for anthropologists, sociologists, psychiatrists. Introduction by Carl Withers. New indexes of first lines, games. 5⅜ x 8½. xii + 242pp.   T354 Paperbound **$1.75**

Art, History of Art, Antiques, Graphic Arts, Handcrafts

ART STUDENTS' ANATOMY, E. J. Farris. Outstanding art anatomy that uses chiefly living objects for its illustrations. 71 photos of undraped men, women, children are accompanied by carefully labeled matching sketches to illustrate the skeletal system, articulations and movements, bony landmarks, the muscular system, skin, fasciae, fat, etc. 9 x-ray photos show movement of joints. Undraped models are shown in such actions as serving in tennis, drawing a bow in archery, playing football, dancing, preparing to spring and to dive. Also discussed and illustrated are proportions, age and sex differences, the anatomy of the smile, etc. 8 plates by the great early 18th century anatomic illustrator Siegfried Albinus are also included. Glossary. 158 figures, 7 in color. x + 159pp. 5⅝ x 8⅜.   T744 Paperbound **$1.50**

AN ATLAS OF ANATOMY FOR ARTISTS, F Schider. A new 3rd edition of this standard text enlarged by 52 new illustrations of hands, anatomical studies by Cloquet, and expressive life studies of the body by Barcsay. 189 clear, detailed plates offer you precise information of impeccable accuracy. 29 plates show all aspects of the skeleton, with closeups of special areas, while 54 full-page plates, mostly in two colors, give human musculature as seen from four different points of view, with cutaways for important portions of the body. 14 full-page plates provide photographs of hand forms, eyelids, female breasts, and indicate the location of muscles upon models. 59 additional plates show how great artists of the past utilized human anatomy. They reproduce sketches and finished work by such artists as Michelangelo, Leonardo da Vinci, Goya, and 15 others. This is a lifetime reference work which will be one of the most important books in any artist's library. "The standard reference tool," AMERICAN LIBRARY ASSOCIATION. "Excellent," AMERICAN ARTIST. Third enlarged edition. 189 plates, 647 illustrations. xxvi + 192pp. 7⅞ x 10⅝.   T241 Clothbound **$6.00**

AN ATLAS OF ANIMAL ANATOMY FOR ARTISTS, W. Ellenberger, H. Baum, H. Dittrich. The largest, richest animal anatomy for artists available in English. 99 detailed anatomical plates of such animals as the horse, dog, cat, lion, deer, seal, kangaroo, flying squirrel, cow, bull, goat, monkey, hare, and bat. Surface features are clearly indicated, while progressive beneath-the-skin pictures show musculature, tendons, and bone structure. Rest and action are exhibited in terms of musculature and skeletal structure and detailed cross-sections are given for heads and important features. The animals chosen are representative of specific families so that a study of these anatomies will provide knowledge of hundreds of related species. "Highly recommended as one of the very few books on the subject worthy of being used as an authoritative guide," DESIGN. "Gives a fundamental knowledge," AMERICAN ARTIST. Second revised, enlarged edition with new plates from Cuvier, Stubbs, etc. 288 illustrations. 153pp. 11⅜ x 9.   T82 Clothbound **$6.00**

THE HUMAN FIGURE IN MOTION, Eadweard Muybridge. The largest selection in print of Muybridge's famous high-speed action photos of the human figure in motion. 4789 photographs illustrate 162 different actions: men, women, children—mostly undraped—are shown walking, running, carrying various objects, sitting, lying down, climbing, throwing, arising, and performing over 150 other actions. Some actions are shown in as many as 150 photographs each. All in all there are more than 500 action strips in this enormous volume, series shots taken at shutter speeds of as high as 1/6000th of a second! These are not posed shots, but true stopped motion. They show bone and muscle in situations that the human eye is not fast enough to capture. Earlier, smaller editions of these prints have brought $40 and more on the out-of-print market. "A must for artists," ART IN FOCUS. "An unparalleled dictionary of action for all artists," AMERICAN ARTIST. 390 full-page plates, with 4789 photographs. Printed on heavy glossy stock. Reinforced binding with headbands. xxi + 390pp. 7⅞ x 10⅝.   T204 Clothbound **$10.00**

ANIMALS IN MOTION, Eadweard Muybridge. This is the largest collection of animal action photos in print. 34 different animals (horses, mules, oxen, goats, camels, pigs, cats, guanacos, lions, gnus, deer, monkeys, eagles—and 21 others) in 132 characteristic actions. The horse alone is shown in more than 40 different actions. All 3919 photographs are taken in series at speeds up to 1/6000th of a second. The secrets of leg motion, spinal patterns, head movements, strains and contortions shown nowhere else are captured. You will see exactly how a lion sets his foot down; how an elephant's knees are like a human's—and how they differ; the position of a kangaroo's legs in mid-leap; how an ostrich's head bobs; details of the flight of birds—and thousands of facets of motion only the fastest cameras can catch. Photographed from domestic animals and animals in the Philadelphia zoo, it contains neither semiposed artificial shots nor distorted telephoto shots taken under adverse conditions. Artists, biologists, decorators, cartoonists, will find this book indispensable for understanding animals in motion. "A really marvelous series of plates," NATURE (London). "The dry plate's most spectacular early use was by Eadweard Muybridge," LIFE. 3919 photographs; 380 full pages of plates. 440pp. Printed on heavy glossy paper. Deluxe binding with headbands. 7⅞ x 10⅝.   T203 Clothbound **$10.00**

THE AUTOBIOGRAPHY OF AN IDEA, Louis Sullivan. The pioneer architect whom Frank Lloyd Wright called "the master" reveals an acute sensitivity to social forces and values in this passionately honest account. He records the crystallization of his opinions and theories, the growth of his organic theory of architecture that still influences American designers and architects, contemporary ideas, etc. This volume contains the first appearance of 34 full-page plates of his finest architecture. Unabridged reissue of 1924 edition. New introduction by R. M. Line. Index. xiv + 335pp. 5⅜ x 8.　　　　　　　　　　　　T281 Paperbound **$2.00**

THE DRAWINGS OF HEINRICH KLEY. The first uncut republication of both of Kley's devastating sketchbooks, which first appeared in pre-World War I Germany. One of the greatest cartoonists and social satirists of modern times, his exuberant and iconoclastic fantasy and his extraordinary technique place him in the great tradition of Bosch, Breughel, and Goya, while his subject matter has all the immediacy and tension of our century. 200 drawings. viii + 128pp. 7¾ x 10¾.　　　　　　　　　　　　T24 Paperbound **$1.85**

MORE DRAWINGS BY HEINRICH KLEY. All the sketches from Leut' Und Viecher (1912) and Sammel-Album (1923) not included in the previous Dover edition of Drawings. More of the bizarre, mercilessly iconoclastic sketches that shocked and amused on their original publication. Nothing was too sacred, no one too eminent for satirization by this imaginative, individual and accomplished master cartoonist. A total of 158 illustrations. Iv + 104pp. 7¾ x 10¾.　　　　　　　　　　　　T41 Paperbound **$1.85**

PINE FURNITURE OF EARLY NEW ENGLAND, R. H. Kettell. A rich understanding of one of America's most original folk arts that collectors of antiques, interior decorators, craftsmen, woodworkers, and everyone interested in American history and art will find fascinating and immensely useful. 413 illustrations of more than 300 chairs, benches, racks, beds, cupboards, mirrors, shelves, tables, and other furniture will show all the simple beauty and character of early New England furniture. 55 detailed drawings carefully analyze outstanding pieces. "With its rich store of illustrations, this book emphasizes the individuality and varied design of early American pine furniture. It should be welcomed," ANTIQUES. 413 illustrations and 55 working drawings. 475. 8 x 10¾.　　　　　　　　　　　　T145 Clothbound **$10.00**

THE HUMAN FIGURE, J. H. Vanderpoel. Every important artistic element of the human figure is pointed out in minutely detailed word descriptions in this classic text and illustrated as well in 430 pencil and charcoal drawings. Thus the text of this book directs your attention to all the characteristic features and subtle differences of the male and female (adults, children, and aged persons), as though a master artist were telling you what to look for at each stage. 2nd edition, revised and enlarged by George Bridgman. Foreword. 430 illustrations. 143pp. 6⅛ x 9¼.　　　　　　　　　　　　T432 Paperbound **$1.50**

LETTERING AND ALPHABETS, J. A. Cavanagh. This unabridged reissue of LETTERING offers a full discussion, analysis, illustration of 89 basic hand lettering styles — styles derived from Caslons, Bodonis, Garamonds, Gothic, Black Letter, Oriental, and many others. Upper and lower cases, numerals and common signs pictured. Hundreds of technical hints on make-up, construction, artistic validity, strokes, pens, brushes, white areas, etc. May be reproduced without permission! 89 complete alphabets; 72 lettered specimens. 121pp. 9¾ x 8. T53 Paperbound **$1.35**

STICKS AND STONES, Lewis Mumford. A survey of the forces that have conditioned American architecture and altered its forms. The author discusses the medieval tradition in early New England villages; the Renaissance influence which developed with the rise of the merchant class; the classical influence of Jefferson's time; the "Mechanicsvilles" of Poe's generation; the Brown Decades; the philosophy of the Imperial facade; and finally the modern machine age. "A truly remarkable book," SAT. REV. OF LITERATURE. 2nd revised edition. 21 illustrations. xvii + 228pp. 5⅜ x 8.　　　　　　　　　　　　T202 Paperbound **$1.65**

THE STANDARD BOOK OF QUILT MAKING AND COLLECTING, Marguerite Ickis. A complete easy-to-follow guide with all the information you need to make beautiful, useful quilts. How to plan, design, cut, sew, appliqué, avoid sewing problems, use rag bag, make borders, tuft, every other aspect. Over 100 traditional quilts shown, including over 40 full-size patterns. At-home hobby for fun, profit. Index. 483 illus. 1 color plate. 287pp. 6¾ x 9½.　　　　　T582 Paperbound **$2.00**

THE BOOK OF SIGNS, Rudolf Koch. Formerly $20 to $25 on the out-of-print market, now only $1.00 in this unabridged new edition! 493 symbols from ancient manuscripts, medieval cathedrals, coins, catacombs, pottery, etc. Crosses, monograms of Roman emperors, astrological, chemical, botanical, runes, housemarks, and 7 other categories. Invaluable for handicraft workers, illustrators, scholars, etc., this material may be reproduced without permission. 493 illustrations by Fritz Kredel. 104pp. 6½ x 9¼.　　　　　　　　　　　　T162 Paperbound **$1.00**

PRIMITIVE ART, Franz Boas. This authoritative and exhaustive work by a great American anthropologist covers the entire gamut of primitive art. Pottery, leatherwork, metal work, stone work, wood, basketry, are treated in detail. Theories of primitive art, historical depth in art history, technical virtuosity, unconscious levels of patterning, symbolism, styles, literature, music, dance, etc. A must book for the interested layman, the anthropologist, artist, handicrafter (hundreds of unusual motifs), and the historian. Over 900 illustrations (50 ceramic vessels, 12 totem poles, etc.). 376pp. 5⅜ x 8.　　　　　　　　　　　　T25 Paperbound **$2.00**

Fiction

FLATLAND, E. A. Abbott. A science-fiction classic of life in a 2-dimensional world that is also a first-rate introduction to such aspects of modern science as relativity and hyperspace. Political, moral, satirical, and humorous overtones have made FLATLAND fascinating reading for thousands. 7th edition. New introduction by Banesh Hoffmann. 16 illustrations. 128pp. 5⅜ x 8.
                                                                                    T1 Paperbound **$1.00**

THE WONDERFUL WIZARD OF OZ, L. F. Baum. Only edition in print with all the original W. W. Denslow illustrations in full color—as much a part of "The Wizard" as Tenniel's drawings are of "Alice in Wonderland." "The Wizard" is still America's best-loved fairy tale, in which, as the author expresses it, "The wonderment and joy are retained and the heartaches and nightmares left out." Now today's young readers can enjoy every word and wonderful picture of the original book. New introduction by Martin Gardner. A Baum bibliography. 23 full-page color plates. viii + 268pp. 5⅜ x 8.
                                                                                    T691 Paperbound **$1.50**

THE MARVELOUS LAND OF OZ, L. F. Baum. This is the equally enchanting sequel to the "Wizard," continuing the adventures of the Scarecrow and the Tin Woodman. The hero this time is a little boy named Tip, and all the delightful Oz magic is still present. This is the Oz book with the Animated Saw-Horse, the Woggle-Bug, and Jack Pumpkinhead. All the original John R. Neill illustrations, 10 in full color. 287 pp. 5⅜ x 8.
                                                                                    T692 Paperbound **$1.50**

FIVE GREAT DOG NOVELS, edited by Blanche Cirker. The complete original texts of five classic dog novels that have delighted and thrilled millions of children and adults throughout the world with their stories of loyalty, adventure, and courage. Full texts of Jack London's "The Call of the Wild"; John Brown's "Rab and His Friends"; Alfred Ollivant's "Bob, Son of Battle"; Marshall Saunders's "Beautiful Joe"; and Ouida's "A Dog of Flanders." 21 Illustrations from the original editions. 495pp. 5⅜ x 8.
                                                                                    T777 Paperbound **$1.75**

TO THE SUN? and OFF ON A COMET!, Jules Verne. Complete texts of two of the most imaginative flights into fancy in world literature display the high adventure that have kept Verne's novels read for nearly a century. Only unabridged edition of the best translation, by Edward Roth. Large, easily readable type. 50 illustrations selected from first editions. 462pp. 5⅜ x 8.
                                                                                    T634 Paperbound **$1.75**

FROM THE EARTH TO THE MOON and ALL AROUND THE MOON, Jules Verne. Complete editions of 2 of Verne's most successful novels, in finest Edward Roth translations, now available after many years out of print. Verne's visions of submarines, airplanes, television, rockets, interplanetary travel; of scientific and not-so-scientific beliefs; of peculiarities of Americans; all delight and engross us today as much as when they first appeared. Large, easily readable type. 42 illus. from first French edition. 476pp. 5⅜ x 8.
                                                                                    T633 Paperbound **$1.75**

THE CRUISE OF THE CACHALOT, Frank T. Bullen. Out of the experiences of many years on the high-seas, First Mate Bullen created this novel of adventure aboard an American whaler, shipping out of New Bedford, Mass., when American whaling was at the height of its splendor. Originally published in 1899, the story of the round-the-world cruise of the "Cachalot" in pursuit of the sperm whale has thrilled generations of readers. A maritime classic that will fascinate anyone interested in reading about the sea or looking for a solid old-fashioned yarn, while the vivid recreation of a brief but important chapter of Americana and the British author's often biting commentary on nineteenth-century Yankee mores offer insights into the colorful era of America's coming of age. 8 plates. xiii + 271pp. 5⅜ x 8½.
                                                                                    T774 Paperbound **$1.00**

28 SCIENCE FICTION STORIES OF H. G. WELLS. Two full unabridged novels, MEN LIKE GODS and STAR BEGOTTEN, plus 26 short stories by the master science-fiction writer of all time! Stories of space, time, invention, exploration, future adventure—an indispensable part of the library of everyone interested in science and adventure. PARTIAL CONTENTS: Men Like Gods, The Country of the Blind, In the Abyss, The Crystal Egg, The Man Who Could Work Miracles, A Story of the Days to Come, The Valley of Spiders, and 21 more! 928pp. 5⅜ x 8.
                                                                                    T265 Clothbound **$4.50**

DAVID HARUM, E. N. Westcott. This novel of one of the most lovable, humorous characters in American literature is a prime example of regional humor. It continues to delight people who like their humor dry, their characters quaint, and their plots ingenuous. First book edition to contain complete novel plus chapter found after author's death. Illustrations from first illustrated edition. 192pp. 5⅜ x 8.
                                                                                    T580 Paperbound **$1.15**

GESTA ROMANORUM, trans. by Charles Swan, ed. by Wynnard Hooper. 181 tales of Greeks, Romans, Britons, Biblical characters, comprise one of greatest medieval story collections, source of plots for writers including Shakespeare, Chaucer, Gower, etc. Imaginative tales of wars, incest, thwarted love, magic, fantasy, allegory, humor, tell about kings, prostitutes, philosophers, fair damsels, knights, Noah, pirates, all walks, stations of life. Introduction. Notes. 500pp. 5⅜ x 8.
                                                                                    T535 Paperbound **$1.85**

Music

A GENERAL HISTORY OF MUSIC, Charles Burney. A detailed coverage of music from the Greeks up to 1789, with full information on all types of music: sacred and secular, vocal and instrumental, operatic and symphonic. Theory, notation, forms, instruments, innovators, composers, performers, typical and important works, and much more in an easy, entertaining style. Burney covered much of Europe and spoke with hundreds of authorities and composers so that this work is more than a compilation of records . . . it is a living work of careful and first-hand scholarship. Its account of thoroughbass (18th century) Italian music is probably still the best introduction on the subject. A recent NEW YORK TIMES review said, "Surprisingly few of Burney's statements have been invalidated by modern research . . . still of great value." Edited and corrected by Frank Mercer. 35 figures. Indices. 1915pp. 5⅜ x 8. 2 volumes. **T36 The Set, Clothbound $12.50**

A DICTIONARY OF HYMNOLOGY, John Julian. This exhaustive and scholarly work has become known as an invaluable source of hundreds of thousands of important and often difficult to obtain facts on the history and use of hymns in the western world. Everyone interested in hymns will be fascinated by the accounts of famous hymns and hymn writers and amazed by the amount of practical information he will find. More than 30,000 entries on individual hymns, giving authorship, date and circumstances of composition, publication, textual variations, translations, denominational and ritual usage, etc. Biographies of more than 9,000 hymn writers, and essays on important topics such as Christmas carols and children's hymns, and much other unusual and valuable information. A 200 page double-columned index of first lines — the largest in print. Total of 1786 pages in two reinforced clothbound volumes. 6¼ x 9¼. **The set, T333 Clothbound $17.50**

MUSIC IN MEDIEVAL BRITAIN, F. Ll. Harrison. The most thorough, up-to-date, and accurate treatment of the subject ever published, beautifully illustrated. Complete account of institutions and choirs; carols, masses, and motets; liturgy and plainsong; and polyphonic music from the Norman Conquest to the Reformation. Discusses the various schools of music and their reciprocal influences; the origin and development of new ritual forms; development and use of instruments; and new evidence on many problems of the period. Reproductions of scores, over 200 excerpts from medieval melodies. Rules of harmony and dissonance; influence of Continental styles; great composers (Dunstable, Cornysh, Fairfax, etc.); and much more. Register and index of more than 400 musicians. Index of titles. General Index. 225-item bibliography. 6 Appendices. xix + 491pp. 5⅝ x 8¾. **T705 Clothbound $10.00**

THE MUSIC OF SPAIN, Gilbert Chase. Only book in English to give concise, comprehensive account of Iberian music; new Chapter covers music since 1941. Victoria, Albéniz, Cabezón, Pedrell, Turina, hundreds of other composers; popular and folk music; the Gypsies; the guitar; dance, theatre, opera, with only extensive discussion in English of the Zarzuela; virtuosi such as Casals; much more. "Distinguished . . . readable," Saturday Review. 400-item bibliography. Index. 27 photos. 383pp. 5⅜ x 8. **T549 Paperbound $2.00**

ON STUDYING SINGING, Sergius Kagen. An intelligent method of voice-training, which leads you around pitfalls that waste your time, money, and effort. Exposes rigid, mechanical systems, baseless theories, deleterious exercises. "Logical, clear, convincing . . . dead right," Virgil Thomson, N.Y. Herald Tribune. "I recommend this volume highly," Maggie Teyte, Saturday Review. 119pp. 5⅜ x 8. **T622 Paperbound $1.25**

Prices subject to change without notice.

Dover publishes books on art, music, philosophy, literature, languages, history, social sciences, psychology, handcrafts, orientalia, puzzles and entertainments, chess, pets and gardens, books explaining science, intermediate and higher mathematics, mathematical physics, engineering, biological sciences, earth sciences, classics of science, etc. Write to:

Dept. catrr.
Dover Publications, Inc.
180 Varick Street, N.Y. 14, N.Y.